Judgement Day
Seekers: Book Two

Josie Jaffrey

CONTENT WARNINGS & SERIES RECAPS

There is a full list of content warnings at the back of this book, and also available at Josie's website at the link on the left below.

Recaps of the Silverse books are available on Josie's website at the link on the right below.

By Josie Jaffrey

Stories from the Silverse: the World of the Silver

The Seekers Series
Killian's Dead (short story prequel, free to Josie's subscribers)
May Day
Judgement Day
Winta's Day
Valentine's Day
Dark Days
End of Days

The QuickSilver Trilogy
Kill Me Quick
A Quick Study
Quick and the Dead
QuickSilver Omnibus Edition

The Solis Invicti Series
A Bargain in Silver
The Price of Silver
Bound in Silver
The Silver Bullet

The Sovereign Trilogy
The Gilded King
The Silver Queen
The Blood Prince

Silverse Serialised Stories
Dead Box
Dead Road

Silverse Short Stories
Encounters: Silverse Short Stories

Other Fiction

The Deluge Series
The Wolf and the Water

Short Stories
Broken Wings (collection)
Ring The Bell

1

'JACK VALENTINE. PLEASE stand.'

I do as I'm told, for once in my life. This isn't quite a trial and Killian Drake's office isn't quite a courtroom, but it's as close to it as the Silver get. Four of Drake's goons are lined up in front of the door in case things get out of hand, and a single representative for each of the defence and the prosecution has been invited: Captain Langford – my boss – for me and Sir Percival Windsor – a rich, entitled wanker – for the supposed victim. I don't want either of them here.

'Matthew Felton. Please stand.'

It gratifies me that he struggles to comply. He's the reason that four months have passed between the incident and this kangaroo court. It's taken that long for him to put himself back together. I wish I'd made the fire burn hotter, because he is surprisingly well-recovered.

Matthew Felton is not an attractive man. He should look like the rat he is, but actually he's more like a mouse: soft face, chubby body and hair of such a light brown that it's practically grey. He vibrates with a prissy kind of anger. I'm expecting him to start cleaning his whiskers at any moment.

But if Matthew Felton is a mouse, then Killian Drake is a

1

snake. He sits behind his gargantuan desk like a cobra spreading its hood. His hair is dark, but his eyes are pure black. He is arrogance and poise, with the kind of slick, irritating good looks that I might find irresistible if he were anyone else. Unfortunately, he's the Baron of Oxford, my archnemesis and a terminal pain in the backside.

I haven't seen him since the incident he's put me on trial for today. It's not that I haven't been busy catching scabs – that's what we call the Silver whose activities endanger the secrecy of our existence – it's just that once I've caught them, I've left the other Seekers to bring them to Drake for his version of justice.

In other words, I've been avoiding him.

'Ms Valentine,' he says. 'You know the charges. Do you have anything to say in your defence?'

I'm guilty as sin. I know it, he knows it and Felton knows it. My personal defence – the reason I haven't lost any sleep over this – is that Matthew Felton is a cockroach. If anyone deserved to be burned alive, it was him. It's not hard to convince myself that I was performing a public service, but it's probably a bad idea to say that out loud.

I look straight into Drake's bottomless eyes. He's already made his decision. I can tell from the slight twitch of his eyebrow, from the way that he's trying not to smile. He knows what my sentence is going to be, and he knows I'm not going to like it.

'I deny all the charges,' I say.

Felton starts huffing and puffing immediately, his little mousy face going an interesting shade of pink.

'But,' I continue, 'if I *had* done it, then the bastard would have brought it on himself. He was reckless with those girls, not to mention the morality of–'

'You want to talk about morality?' Felton interrupts. 'You

burned me alive, you psycho bitch!'

'I did not,' I lie primly, 'and I resent the implication.'

'I'm not *implying* anything. I'm saying you're a fucking lunatic.'

He might have a point there, but it doesn't seem healthy to dwell on that right now.

'Oh, come on. You had an attic full of chemicals and you smoke in bed. It was bound to happen sooner or later. Why would I bother interfering with natural selection?'

Felton is so agitated that he can't muster a response beyond a splutter of anger. His nose is twitching.

'What makes you think Ms Valentine was involved?' Drake asks him.

'She had a grudge against me from day one. The first time she interviewed me, she kicked my face in. It took me a day to recover.'

'Actually, that was Naia, not me,' I say.

'Whatever. The both of you had it in for me.'

'Because you were kidnapping and drugging humans, posing them like creepy puppets, then stealing their blood. It's sick.'

'And they never found out! It was well within the rules. Totally under the radar and totally above board.'

This is the problem with being a Seeker: justice doesn't come into what we do. Our objective is to make sure that the existence of the Silver isn't revealed to humanity. We stop anyone who threatens that objective. Felton might be a creep who kidnaps girls and strings them up like marionettes for his own weird gratification, but as long as they're returned to their beds afterwards none the wiser, he hasn't actually done anything wrong. Not by Seeker standards, anyway.

My own standards are a little different.

'Let's hear your evidence, Mr Felton,' says Drake.

I don't even try to hide my smirk. He doesn't have the tiniest shred of evidence and we both know it. That's why he tries to shift focus onto Drake, which is a very bad idea, since the man is both judge and jury here.

'Baron,' he says, 'with all due respect, I don't think you're in a position to be impartial.'

A cold silence falls over the room. I hear the goons behind me take in a sharp breath that means *Oh, shit*. In the chair next to Felton, Windsor is laughing quietly into his hand.

'Oh, really?' Drake replies, his unblinking eyes fixed on Felton, who swallows.

'It's just that…' he tries, then decides on a new approach. 'You were in a relationship with her.'

'Well, that's a load of bollocks,' I say.

Felton doesn't look my way, but his little nose is twitching again.

'You have to admit, Baron,' he goes on, 'that you and she. At Percy's party. You, well, you know.'

'I'm afraid that I don't know, Mr Felton,' Drake says. 'You will have to enlighten me.'

The bastard is enjoying this, but I'm not. I don't want to rehash the shame of my brief dalliance with Killian Drake. It wasn't real, anyway. We were just pretending we were a couple because I needed Drake's reputation to get me inside Sir Percival Wanker's house. Sure, we kissed a few times, but it was nothing serious. I've been doing a very good job of repressing the entire incident.

Until now.

'You kissed,' Felton says finally. 'A lot. I mean, *a lot*. In front of everyone. I can only imagine–'

'I'd rather you didn't,' I say.

'My point is that you were involved.' Felton is red-faced, but determined to see this through. He's not flinching from

Drake's gaze. 'You're biased. You have feelings for her.'

I laugh out loud, because the idea of Drake giving a shit about me is frankly hilarious. Once upon a time he might have wanted to have sex with me, but that was short-lived and had nothing to do with emotion.

'Mr Felton,' Drake says, steepling his fingers, 'we're all men of the world here. You know as well as I do that these things happen. There were no feelings – nor, regrettably, was there any thought – involved. A few days of madness four months ago aren't going to prejudice me in Ms Valentine's favour. We all make mistakes.'

My mouth drops open. I have no words.

How dare he?

Felton seems satisfied by my public humiliation, if nothing else.

But I shouldn't be humiliated. I'm not humiliated. Drake's right. It's ancient history. It was all swept under the carpet months ago. We've been avoiding each other ever since, but not because there's anything romantic – ick – between us. I've been staying out of Drake's way because he shared a secret with me that I didn't want to know, a secret about the captain and the Invicti. I haven't found a way to deal with his revelation yet, so I've kept his number blocked on my phone and kept out of his way. I don't trust him.

Turns out I was right to be cautious.

'All right, then,' Drake says. 'If you've both said everything you want to say, then I think I've heard all I need to hear. I'm ready to deliver my verdict.'

The next words he says take my breath away.

He's kidding. He has to be kidding.

'I object!' Felton and I both yell at the same time.

But Drake won't budge.

* * *

'The bastard,' I say as I stomp back into my rooms. 'The scheming, slimy, unbelievable bastard.'

'You're here,' Tabitha says, jumping up from my sofa. They wouldn't let her come to the trial, so she's been waiting here for me. 'I was so worried, hen. I thought they were going to take you away.' She barrels into my arms.

Tabitha is a short, soft confection of Scottish extraction. She dresses like a librarian and wears her reddish-brown curls piled on top of her head, secured with whatever stick-like objects she has to hand. Today it's a fork and a toothbrush.

Tabitha is my girlfriend. My actual girlfriend. I still get a kick from the thought. She's beautiful and generous and she calls me *hen* and sometimes, if I'm very good, she wears her lab coat home from work so I can take it off her. Home is mostly here, in my rooms at Solomon College in central Oxford, but occasionally I stay at her cottage in Nash Lee, a little village near Aylesbury. She has a lab in her back garden where she does lots of things involving "samples" that I'd rather not think about. Tabitha is a doctor, but one of those multi-disciplined types that are so common amongst the long-lived Silver. She has several specialties. She's a pathologist, but also a haematologist and a surgeon, amongst other things.

She's far too clever for me, so clever that I'd ask her what she sees in me if I weren't so scared of losing her. If she wants to slum it, that's her decision. This is the first decent relationship I've had in my entire life and I don't want to mess it up. In fact, I've spent the past three weeks trying to find a way to tell her that I love her.

But now is not the time.

'He's put me on probation,' I say.

She lifts her cheek away from my shoulder. 'Probation?'

'I have to check in every week, to keep me on the straight and narrow, he says. I start tomorrow.'

'But that's good, right? I was worried they were going to box you, hen. Probation is great news. Why aren't you happy?'

Boxing is awful. It's the most common punishment for serious Silver transgressions and it is exactly what it sounds like: you're drained of blood, then boxed up and sealed away in Drake's basement. The prisoner is stuck in a half-conscious state, in agonising pain, weak as a kitten, for the duration of their sentence. More than a year in the box would send most Silver mad.

'Box me?' I scoff. 'There was no evidence. No evidence at all.' I was careful. I burned that bastard Felton and his lab to a crisp.

'It doesn't sound too bad, is all I'm saying. Who's your probation officer?'

I look at her, letting my frustration show. 'Who do you think?'

'No.'

'Yes. Killian Fucking Drake.'

'The bastard.'

'I told you.'

Tabitha sits down on the edge of my bed. She looks shellshocked.

Things have been good between us these past few months, but there's still a thread of tension between us, and Drake is the problem. I'm keeping his secrets from her. Worse, I'm keeping my own secrets from her. Distasteful as it is, Drake and I have been in this together since we went undercover at Windsor's party, when we discovered that the third-in-command of the Solis Invicti was involved in some seriously shady shit. Tabitha is officially employed by the Solis Invicti

– they're the ones who pay her bills and assign her caseload – so I can't tell her my and Drake's suspicions about their scab activities, not when the individuals implicated are the very same people who control her and have her loyalty. Secret-keeping isn't a great way to foster a new relationship, I grant you, but the alternative is too risky. Until I have proof that the Invicti are killing humans for cash, she just can't know, so I keep my mouth shut, leaving her to guess at the source of my anxiety. Unfortunately, she keeps guessing wrong, which is why dropping Drake's name is like dropping a stink bomb.

Tabitha looks up at me with big, round eyes.

'What do we do, hen?'

'What do you mean?' I'm confused because there isn't anything to debate. I'll suffer through my probation like a good girl; I don't have any other option.

'I don't trust him,' she says.

'You mean you don't trust me.'

'That's not what I said.'

But it's clearly what she meant. I can't blame her for it. When Tabitha and I were first getting together, I fucked up royally with Drake. Things got out of hand after we kissed. I should have stayed away from him, but somehow I kept getting dragged back in. I don't know how to explain that, and I can't excuse it. He was magnetic. Dark. Dangerous. I can't stress that last one enough.

'Tabs,' I say, dropping to my knees at her feet. I take her chin gently in my hand and tilt her face down to mine. 'You know I'd get out of this if I could. You know I think he's the worst person in the world.'

'I know. I'm sorry, hen. I thought I was over this.'

'It's not your fault.'

We're interrupted by a knock at the door. After a

millisecond's pause, it opens to reveal Naia on the other side. She generally likes to wear short sleeves to show off her arms, which are muscular and wrapped with tattoos, but today she's got her coat on. That's how I know she's about to drag me away.

I glare at her. She glares back, but not with any malice. She's like a sister to me; we're grumpy with each other because we're close, not because we don't like each other.

'What do you want?' I ask.

'Get your things,' she says. 'We've got a case.'

2

THE RADCLIFFE CAMERA – the Rad Cam to the locals – sits squatly in the centre of Oxford, rising from the cobblestones in the middle of Radcliffe Square like a giant boob poking out of the ground. Despite the misleading name, it's actually a library. The University of Oxford's History Faculty library, to be precise. It's called the Camera because it's round and ornamental and… I'm buggered if I know the real reason, but it's something to do with Latin. Who cares? It's a library.

When Naia and I push our way through the doors, we find a bunch of people gathered by a bookcase at the far side of the room. There are bookshelves all around the circular walls, tucked under the overhang of the gallery on the mezzanine floor above. Rows of desks stretch from the edges of the room to the centre, like spokes. Two of them have been moved out of the way to reveal a body underneath. It's been here for a few hours at least, long enough that it's swarming with flies, releasing not only the classic eau de corpse but also the maggoty, ammonia sharpness that I associate with carrion. I'm glad I haven't had time to eat lunch.

'Hey, Jack,' Cam says.

Cam is my best friend in the Seekers – my best friend anywhere, in fact – loveable and cuddly despite the fact that he's all gangly limbs and elbows. He's basically what the puppy from the Andrex adverts would look like if it grew to six foot two and put on people clothes. That's why Cam's so incongruous at a crime scene, standing over the body taking pictures.

'How did the hearing go?' he asks me.

'I don't want to talk about it,' I reply. 'Suffice it to say that Killian Drake is a dead man.'

Cam rolls his eyes and mutters, 'Not this again.'

'What?'

'This vendetta of yours. I don't know how you have the energy for it.'

'He's forcing me into probation, with him as my probation officer. Don't you think I have good reason to be pissed off?'

'I think Tabby probably does.'

I put my hands on my hips. 'What are you implying?'

'Just that weekly probation meetings are a really good excuse for the baron to get you alone in his office.'

'It's not like that. You know I love Tabs.'

'And have you told her that yet?'

I squirm, because Cam has been bullying me about this for weeks. I know I love her. Cam knows I love her. But, as Cam has so eloquently pointed out to me on several occasions, there's no way for Tabitha to be sure I love her if I don't actually tell her.

The words are simple: *I love you*. But somehow, when the right moment comes around, I can never bring myself to say them.

'You're a mess,' Cam says to me, shaking his head. 'Speaking of which, meet District Judge Nora Mitchell.'

He stands aside to let me get a good view of the corpse. She was probably attractive in life – late fifties, steel-grey hair in a pixie cut with delicate features to match – but she isn't anymore. Blood has trickled its way along every line and valley on her face, highlighting otherwise invisible wrinkles in reddish brown. It looks like her face has been crazy-paved with rusty grouting.

'Oh my god,' I say, leaning in for a closer look. 'How the hell did that happen?'

'Fascinating, isn't it?' Ed says.

Ed's our lab guy. He's crouched at the foot of the body, peering through his unnecessary glasses. They're entirely cosmetic – the Silver have twenty-twenty vision – but he thinks they make him look clever, as though he needs any help with that. The man's already a genius.

Ed and Cam used to be a couple, but that seems to be over now. Cam's taken it remarkably well, on the outside at least.

'Have you got any ideas?' he asks Ed.

'It looks deliberate, doesn't it? I'll need to sample it when you're done with your photos. Naia, can you give me a hand?'

She grabs some sample kits from her coat and gets to work, scouring the body for evidence.

'Why are you the one doing this?' I ask Ed. 'Where are the SOCOs?'

Scenes Of Crime Officers should be swarming all over this place, cataloguing evidence in concert with the police. Instead, there's just Naia, Ed and a couple of assistants. The only people in the room are Silver. It's almost eerie.

'Turns out the judge is the captain's several-times-great-granddaughter,' Cam whispers to me. 'We're thinking it's personal.'

'Shit,' I say.

An attack directed at one of the Seekers is bad news for all of us, so it makes sense that my team has taken over. At any other crime scene we'd be working quickly, trying to gather all the information we could before the police arrived, but this time that's not necessary; the Seekers are in charge. I should have realised something was up when I walked in, because Boyd is perched on the gallery above us, vulture-like in his possessiveness. He's tall with dark skin and darker eyes, and close-cropped hair that he trims so regularly that it borders on the obsessive. Never a hair out of place, that's our deputy. But today he looks sharp. He's on show, so we must be expecting company.

'Where's the captain, then?' I ask Cam.

He shrugs and returns to taking photos. This leaves me in something of a bind, because usually it's my job to be the camera. I have a decent memory for pictures, so normally I'm tasked with memorising every detail of the body in the few seconds we have until the police step in. Today, I've been replaced. It doesn't feel great.

I bounce on the balls of my feet, hands in my pockets, wondering what I should be doing.

Deciding that the best place to start is with my normal job, I stare past Cam to the body, but there's not much more to see. The blood spiderwebbing over her face is the highlight. The scent of Silver violence is so strong I could smell it from the front door, so she was definitely killed by one of the Silver, but I knew that already. If she'd been killed by a human then we wouldn't be here. Other than that, she looks unremarkable in her navy skirt suit, dark tights and sensible leather heels.

'Did you find a handbag?' I ask Ed.

'Not yet.'

'Has the building been searched?'

'Yep. Nothing turned up. Give it another sweep, if you like.'

'Yeah, go on,' Cam says. 'It's weird having you looking over my shoulder.'

I do as he asks and go to find someone else to annoy.

'Hello, Deputy.'

I've snuck up on Boyd so quietly that the words make him jump.

'Not funny, Jacqueline,' he says. He's the only person who calls me that. I hate it. 'What are you doing?'

'Checking out the scene,' I say, 'looking for her handbag. What are *you* doing? Waiting for someone?'

His jaw clenches, which tells me two things: firstly, he's definitely waiting for someone, and secondly, it's not just about the case. He's embarrassed that I've called him out on it, so it must be someone he wants to impress, for a reason he doesn't want to disclose.

Interesting.

'Who found the body?' I ask him.

'The librarian. Came in to open up this morning and… Well. You've seen it. She called the police, who came to check out the body. Faizan smelled the violence mark and called the captain.' Faizan is our Silver mole inside the police. 'The captain identified her. I think she put in a call of her own, because the police cleared out pretty quickly after that.'

That's surprising.

'I didn't know the captain had those kinds of contacts.'

'Make the most of it,' Boyd says. 'I'm not sure how long it'll last.'

So I do. I look under every desk, in every bookshelf, and in every corner. Her handbag isn't here. I check out all the windows on each floor while I'm at it, but they're all locked or don't even open.

'Do we know why she was here?' I ask Boyd, returning to his spot on the gallery. He hasn't moved an inch since I saw him last.

'No. The librarian had never seen her before. We're just checking whether she had a university library card, but if she did then it would have made more sense for her to be in the law library rather than here.'

'How did she get in?'

'No idea. Everything's locked up tight. Maybe someone carried her in through an open window.'

'And locked it after themselves on the way out?'

Boyd shrugs.

'We'll know more when we have a time of death,' he says. 'Tabitha's waiting for Ed at the lab. As soon as we're done here—'

The front door to the library opens, one floor down and directly opposite us, and a woman walks in. She looks about thirty, tall, with East Asian features in a shockingly symmetrical face. She looks up at us and smiles.

Boyd straightens his back and sucks in his stomach. There's a twinkle in his eye.

'Oh my god,' I say under my breath. 'That's why you're standing here, looking like a general commanding his underlings. You've got a crush.'

'Shhhh!'

'You have!' I say, so delighted that I'm struggling to keep quiet. 'I can't believe it. Bachelor Boyd bites the dust.'

For the entire time I've known the deputy, he's been determinedly single. I thought for a while that he might be gay and closeted, or that he just had no interest in romance, but it turns out I was wrong. I'm so distracted by this revelation that I don't notice the woman's most important feature until she's already joined us on the mezzanine.

She's human.

Boyd is head over heels for a human. It's not completely unheard of for Silver to have romantic relationships with humans, but for obvious reasons they don't usually last. There's a power imbalance, not just physically but also because of the inevitable age gap, which makes the whole thing a bit taboo. If I'd had to guess which one of my team would go that way, not in a million years would I ever have picked Boyd.

'Ms Chen.'

He moves forward to shake her hand, but then changes his mind and ends up doing a little half bow instead. It is intensely adorable and completely unlike the deputy, but he recovers well.

'This is my colleague,' he says, 'Jacqueline Valentine.'

Ugh. Can you see why I don't like it when people use my full name?

'Jacqueline,' Boyd goes on, 'Ms Chen is the head librarian.'

'Nice to meet you, Ms Valentine,' she says, with a shy smile. She's trying to be polite, but finding a dead body has clearly shaken her more than she wants to let on.

'It's Jack, please,' I say. 'Any news on that library card?'

'Yes,' she says, handing a Boyd a single sheet of paper.

It's a printout from the database, which is probably as old as the deputy. There's a fuzzy black and white photo of the judge, followed by the card details and a list of the various times the card was used to access a library. It doesn't look like she was a regular patron.

'All of the check ins were at the law library or the Bodleian,' she says. 'None at the Rad Cam. But there is the

Gladstone Link.' She leans over the banister and points to a spot on the ground floor where a staircase disappears downwards.

'What's that?' I ask.

'The rest of the History Faculty library. It's a set of underground stacks that joins the Bodleian to the Rad Cam. Technically, she could have come here through the Link without using our front door.'

'Is that what she did last night?' Boyd asks, but Ms Chen shakes her head.

'She hasn't used her card for a month.'

That's one lead thoroughly squashed. We don't have much else to ask Ms Chen – she didn't know the judge and she's already given us all the information held by the university libraries – but she's hanging around as though she has something else to offer. Boyd looks like he's desperately searching for a topic of conversation.

'I love this building,' he says to her after an awkward few seconds. 'I'm not usually a fan of the neo-classical style, but I make the odd exception. It's a Gibbs, isn't it?'

'That's right.' Ms Chen smiles back. 'You know your architecture.'

'One can hardly live in Oxford and ignore it. What a waste that would be.'

'I couldn't agree more.'

I stifle a yawn. One Boyd was bad enough, but now it seems there are two of them.

They start dissecting the building, using words I vaguely recognise but that all sound vaguely sexual – cupola, balustrade, rotunda – because they're using them as a strange form of flirtation. I never expected to witness Boyd's mating ritual, but it might be one of the weirdest I've ever seen.

When Ms Chen finally waves her goodbyes, leaving Boyd

with her number "just in case you have any follow-up questions", he's grinning like a schoolboy.

'Picking up women at a crime scene, Deputy?' I tease. 'Isn't that a sackable offence?'

'Nonsense,' he says. 'She's just friendly, that's all.' But I notice that the piece of paper with her number on it goes into Boyd's wallet, not into his notebook with the rest of the case notes.

'Sure.' I smile, letting it drop. The way the nerdy sparks were flying, I'm sure I'll have plenty of opportunities to tease him about it later, when we're not in the middle of an investigation.

'Where next, then?' I say. 'The victim's home? Her work?'

'Work,' Boyd replies, all business. 'Take Naia and Faizan; they won't let you in without a police representative.'

'Will do.' I make to leave, but he calls me back.

'One more thing to think about,' he says. 'According to the court list, she was on family cases yesterday, sitting in chambers. Do you know what the term for that is in Latin, Jacqueline?'

I sigh. 'You know I don't.'

He smiles grimly and says, 'It's "in camera", actually.'

I look around the building, noting that we're also in the Camera. Boyd nods once he sees that I've got the reference.

I groan.

Someone's trying to be clever, and they're not very good at it.

3

THE OXFORD COMBINED Court Centre is gorgeous limestone on the outside and pure misery on the inside. I'm sure Boyd would be able to tell you all sorts of fascinating things about the architecture, but all I can tell you is that there are pillars above the front doors and the doors themselves are glass, which seems like a stupid choice for a building that hears criminal cases. I wonder how often they have to reglaze them. On the inside, the building looks like a struggling state school, with metal detectors at the doors.

My top tip for any day trip to the court: take tissues, because even if you don't need them, someone else will. Every visit makes me glad that, unlike our human counterparts, we rarely have a reason to come here.

Faiz walks over to meet us on the pavement outside. The police station is close, directly across the road from the court, ostensibly to smooth the course of justice. I think the real reason is so it's easier to pick up the usual suspects coming in and out of the court doors, but who am I to judge? I'm on probation for setting a suspect on fire.

'Jack Valentine,' Faiz says with a grin. 'What have you done this time? Burned down another house? Murdered an ex-lover? Kicked a puppy?'

'I would never kick a puppy,' I say, with mock affront, then grin back at him.

DCI Faizan Malik is young for a detective chief inspector. At least, his colleagues think he's young. He looks like he's in his mid-thirties, but really he's one of us: Silver. Fuck knows how long he's really been kicking around for. He's got thick black hair, deep brown skin and the longest, prettiest lashes I've ever seen. He's also extremely married, which drives Naia crazy. I can practically hear her libido spinning up behind me.

'How are you, Faiz?' I ask.

'Good, thanks. Eating well.' He laughs and pats his flat stomach. 'Meera's been on a cookery course.'

'About time.'

'I'll tell her you said that. You all right, Naia?'

'Yes,' she replies, abruptly and without smiling.

Faiz must think she's a grumpy cow, but the real problem is that she doesn't know how to talk to people she finds attractive without flirting with them. My team is just a hotbed of hormones today.

'Well,' he says to us both. 'Shall we go in, then?'

The queue for security isn't long; we've missed the rush. All the lawyers get here early so they can bagsy one of the private waiting rooms before they're taken.

Once we're inside, bags searched and pockets emptied for inspection, Faiz goes to find the court clerk. We wait for him in the entrance hall, giving him the space he needs to work his magic. Five minutes later he's back, ushering us upstairs, past the clerk's desk and down the hallway where the judges have their private audience chambers. District Judge Mitchell's is the one at the very end of the corridor, earning her two windows instead of the usual one. It's a nice office as far as the public sector goes – books on the walls, lots of wood, carpet without too many stains – but there's no getting away from the fact that this is not really a private space. There are no personal photos, no pictures on the walls, and no knickknacks. With half the world traipsing through their chambers, you can understand why judges need to be cautious with their personal effects.

Which is why I'm surprised to see the contents of Nora Mitchell's handbag strewn across her desk: lipstick, tissues, pens, phone, wallet, keys. Everything is here, including a small blue gift box and a piece of purple ribbon that must have been wrapped around it.

Faiz sees the box before I do. He's already pulled on his gloves and now he's skirting around the edge of the desk, hand outstretched to take it.

'Wait,' I say as his fingers touch the top. 'Let's just be careful here, shall we?'

Faiz looks at me as though I've grown a second head. 'Jack Valentine advising caution? Are you unwell?'

'Yes, ha ha, but this is a courthouse, and she was a judge. Who knows what she could have been sent?'

'It's not going to be an explosive,' Naia says. 'Anything like that would have been caught by the detectors on the way in, and if it came in the post then that's all scanned.'

'Then why are you hanging out by the door?' I ask her.

'Because I'm not an idiot. There are worse things than explosives. Anthrax. Ricin. Poisonous spiders.'

'But you're Silver. None of that would kill you.'

'Maybe not, but it would hurt like hell. Plus, I hate spiders.'

'I'll open it then, shall I?' Faiz offers.

He reaches for the box and I nod at him, taking a step closer just to wind Naia up. We both brace ourselves as he lifts off the lid.

Nothing happens.

'What is it?' Naia calls from the doorway.

Faiz lifts out a small digital camera, flipping it over with a puzzled look on his face.

'I didn't know they even made those anymore,' Naia says, walking back into the room now she knows it's safe. 'Doesn't everyone just use their phones to take photos?'

'She was in her fifties,' I say. 'Maybe she preferred to have a separate device.'

'But why send her a camera?'

Faiz puts it back in the box. 'Maybe it was her birthday,' he suggests.

'It wasn't,' Naia says. 'She was born in January.'

'All I'm saying is that it doesn't have to be sinister,' says Faiz. 'Let's not jump to conclusions and go off down the wrong road.'

'Except it's here,' I say, 'along with her handbag, and she's not. Can you get into her phone? See if she was called away?'

Faiz pulls it out of the jumbled mess on top of her desk and tries.

'Access code,' he says. 'We'll need to get the computer guys on it.'

'Bag it up and we'll take it to Frank the Hacker,' I say. Frank is our resident computer expert back at Solomon College. He's the only thing that stands between the ageing Silver population and total obsolescence. Without him, some of us wouldn't even know how to use the internet. 'He'll get it working for us.'

Faiz puts the phone in an evidence bag and tosses it to Naia, who stows it in her rucksack. She likes to be the one who collects and carries the evidence. She might look tough, but secretly she's a packrat, never secure unless she's surrounded by carefully-catalogued stuff, all of it within her control.

'Do you want the camera too?' Faiz asks, getting another evidence bag ready.

'Wait,' I say, because something's itching at me. We've missed a step. When I realise what it is, I groan.

'Have you tried looking *in* the camera?' I ask.

Faiz presses the power button and the thing comes to life with an ascending tinkle of music. Naia and I crowd around the desk behind him, looking over his shoulders.

'Shit,' Naia says as Faiz scrolls through the photos.

They start out relatively inoffensive – pictures of crowds on the High Street, in Radcliffe Square, outside the courthouse on St Aldate's – then they change. Now they're candid close-ups of District Judge Mitchell in those crowds, her face in the middle of each shot. They follow her around the centre of Oxford as she eats her lunch, does a bit of shopping, goes out for a drink. The second-to-last photo is a message, written in black marker across a sheet of lined paper.

You know what I want, it reads. *Meet me at 8, in camera.*

'In camera?' Naia asks.

'It's like the worst word game ever,' I say, explaining what Boyd told me about the Latin. 'So the judge is sitting *in camera*, gets this message in a camera, and ends up dead in the Camera.'

Naia's brow furrows. 'But why? What does it mean?'

'Don't ask me,' I reply. 'This is Boyd's deal, not mine.'

There's one more photo. It almost makes Faiz drop the camera.

'Oh, no,' he says, looking away. 'I did not need to see that.'

Naia takes the camera from him and squints at it, tilting it from side to side as though she can extract some deeper meaning from the image if she finds the right angle. If anyone can, then it's Naia. After all, this is her area of expertise.

It's a dick pic.

'I don't recognise it,' Naia says.

'Did you expect to?' I ask, incredulous. I know she likes to get around, but a mental dick Rolodex feels like a stretch, even for her.

She shrugs. 'You never know.'

'What do you think this was about?' Faiz asks. He's scratching the back of his neck, awkward. 'A booty call?'

'I don't know,' I reply. 'It's a bit creepy for that. Whoever sent her this has basically been stalking her. It feels like a threat to me.'

'Possibly,' Naia says. 'But some people like creepy. Practically everything you can think of is a kink to someone. Maybe she wanted it like this.'

'A fifty-eight year old judge?' Faiz says. 'The captain's great-granddaughter?'

'Old people do have sex, you know,' Naia says to him.

'Case in point: the two of you,' I say. 'You're both older than the judge, and I bet–'

'Yes, thanks, Jack,' Faiz interrupts. 'Let's just get the rest of this room searched, shall we?'

He's looking flustered, so I give him a break from the teasing and get back to work.

It takes us the rest of the afternoon to go through every piece of paper in the judge's chambers. Other than the contents of her handbag, there's nothing that doesn't relate to her job. She keeps handwritten notes on each of the cases she's hearing – it looks like they start out on a pad then end up in individual files – but most of it seems to be digital. She has the files she's working on right now, but the other paper records aren't here. Faiz tells us the court holds them centrally, so off we go back to the court clerk. He promises to get Faiz a list of all the judge's recent cases, but not until tomorrow. Maybe the next day. Definitely by the end of the week. The courts are very busy, and they're chronically underfunded, you know.

We say goodbye to Faiz and slope back home to Solomon College with our prizes. Faiz has taken the handbag and most of its contents back to the police station, but we've got the phone and the camera, plus the library card we found in her wallet. Naia takes them to Frank the Hacker while I go to my rooms to take a shower. The stench of courtroom misery is thick on my skin and I'm desperate to be rid of it.

I open my door to find Tabitha working on my sofa. My place is tiny – just a bedroom with a single bed, a box-like ensuite bathroom, and a kitchen-slash-sitting room that's barely large enough to be functional – but Tabitha says she likes it. There are original wood floors, which is a bonus, but there's also the original paint, which is not. Tabitha calls it "cosy". I call it damp, mouldy and cramped, but each to their own.

'How was it?' she asks, looking up from her laptop.

'Weird,' I say. I kiss her forehead by way of hello, then sit down beside her on the sofa. 'Have you seen the body yet?'

'No. We had some trouble with the Mortuary Service. There was a bit of a tussle and they ended up taking it, but the captain got involved and we won in the end. They're bringing it back first thing tomorrow.'

'Then you've got a treat coming. It might be the weirdest one yet,' I say, thinking about the blood spiderwebbed over the judge's face.

'Why?'

'Not telling. I don't want to spoil the surprise. I'm going to grab a shower. I stink of public sector disinfectant.'

'You're such a snob.'

'Says the woman who won't eat own-brand ketchup. Back in a bit.'

I'm half hoping that Tabitha will join me in the shower, but tonight she's got something on her mind. She's brooding when I come out of the ensuite, wrapped in a towel. The little crease between her eyebrows is working overtime. It's cute, but concerning. I know what she's thinking, because it's the same thing I've been thinking since I walked in the door: probation is looming. It was bad enough seeing Drake at the hearing this morning, but tomorrow it'll be just the two of us in his office.

It doesn't bear thinking about, but Tabitha is thinking hard. She never stops thinking, that beautiful brain of hers calculating and speculating, but I don't want her distracted by this. I wish I could set her mind at ease.

I need to address it head-on.

'Are you worried about him?' I ask.

'Should I be worried, hen?' she replies. The vulnerability in her eyes breaks my heart.

'No. God, Tabs, no.' I crouch beside her and take her hands in mine. 'You have nothing to worry about. I'd stay away from him if I could. I've been keeping my distance, you know that.'

'I know,' she says, looking down and away from me, avoiding my eyes. 'That's the problem, that you feel you can't be near him. Are you worried about what you'll do if you get too close?'

I shake my head emphatically. 'It's not like that. This isn't like the thing in May.' We don't talk about the thing in May. 'There's nothing tying me to him except this stupid probation,' I say, even though it's not strictly true. There are the secrets we share, the ones I can't tell Tabitha. But my next words are nothing but the truth. 'I'm yours, Tabby. Just yours.'

Her gaze meets mine. 'Does he know that?'

'Yes. And if he doesn't, I'll make sure he does.' I smile. 'You know the best way to do that, right?'

She smiles back at me reluctantly, her lips twitching as she tries to resist. I lean in and press the smallest of kisses to the edge of her mouth, once, twice. The third time, she turns her head, opening her lips against mine.

She's going to mark me.

It's that simple for us now. This used to be difficult, but now the moment we give in to it I can feel the mark rising around us like a burst of sunshine. I feel it before I smell it: Tabitha's scent, nectarines and honey. It sinks into my skin, where it'll stay for the next twenty-four hours, however hard I scrub, in the same way that my mark is now sinking into hers. This is how the Silver claim each other. All the other Silver will be able to smell her mark on me, and mine on her, and know that we belong to one another.

But this isn't targeted at all the Silver. It's targeted at one in particular, one neither of us can seem to put out of our minds.

'Come on,' I say. 'Let's take this to the bedroom.'

She lets me lay her down on the bed to remove her clothes and worries in one fell swoop. I let go of my own at the same time. There is nothing but Tabitha and me, me and Tabitha, wrapped in each other's arms and scents. For once, my bed doesn't seem too small. Like this, there is no space between us.

Afterwards, it's difficult to remember what I was worried about. When Tabitha is next to me, held tight to my side so she doesn't topple onto the floor, there's no one else in the world. My consciousness narrows to these three rooms, these two bodies, this one mingled scent of our two marks. It's difficult for me to define my own, because it's always there, but I can recognise the sharp spice it adds to Tabitha's sweetness. I like that; the combination of the two of us is richer than we are individually. We augment each other. We are a good match.

I'm floating happily through these thoughts, eyelids heavy, when Tabitha pushes herself up onto her elbow and puts on her serious face. It drags my eyes open and shunts my sluggish body into awareness.

'What is it?' I ask.

She licks her lips, taking a deep breath as though she's preparing to deliver bad news.

'I need to tell you something,' she says.

'That sounds ominous.'

'Nothing's settled yet, and if you don't want me to then I won't, but… I'd like to do some research on Silver blood-drinking.'

I shuffle up the bed so I'm sitting with my back against the wall and turn to look at her, feeling like I've just been doused with a bucket of water. So much for a postcoital glow.

'Why?' I ask.

'Because no one ever has before. And because I need to know. I think you need to know, too.'

'I'd rather forget about the whole thing,' I say, even though I know she's right. That thing that happened in May, that thing we don't talk about, has been following us around for the last four months like a shadow.

Drake kissed me. Felton wasn't lying about that. I guess I kissed him back, too, and we ended up marking each other. But there was a very good reason for it: I was undercover and I needed to make our fake relationship look convincing. It honestly made perfect sense at the time.

Then came the few days of madness. The problem is that the scent mark wants to replicate itself, so it makes you crave the person whose mark you're wearing. Somehow things got a little out of hand. Drake went from kissing me to biting me, hard enough to make me bleed, and it felt so good that I still can't let myself remember it in polite company.

That's bad enough on its own, but it gets worse: something goes wrong when a Silver drinks the blood of the person who's marked them. Drake lost his shit. He went full-on stalker. I tried to get away from him, we fought, and he hit me. Hard. At the time, Tabitha told me it was an aftereffect of him drinking my blood, that his possessive rage was a kind of psychosis that he couldn't be blamed for, but I've wondered. We've both wondered.

I'm pretty sure Tabitha wants to prove he was in control. I don't know what I want, but I know that life would be easier if he really was the monster I imagine him to be.

'I think we both need to know,' she says. 'No one's ever looked into it properly. I think it's time.'

I breathe out, trying to get my ragged emotions under control.

'Okay,' I say eventually, but I'm feeling claustrophobic. I crawl out of bed and into my clothes. I have to get out of here, out of this conversation, and go somewhere I can forget all about it.

'What are you doing?' Tabitha asks.

'Going out.'

'It's late,' she says, but she's resigned. She knows when I

need to be alone and she won't try to make me stay.

'I'll be back before dawn,' I say on my way out. 'I need to do some research of my own.'

I don't want to think about tomorrow's probation. I don't want to think about anything, so I go to the college bar.

Normal alcohol isn't going to cut it tonight, so I order a bottle of gin, a bottle of blood and a glass, then take them to my table and mix up a Valentine's Massacre. You might have heard of my eponymous beverage: a blend of alcohol, human blood and Silver blood. I donate the latter myself, slashing my wrist over the glass with my penknife. It's a little pervy to drink your own blood, almost masturbatory, but these are desperate times.

I lied when I said this was research. I've already done extensive testing of the Valentine's Massacre and I am one hundred percent certain that, as long as there's no scent mark involved, drinking Silver blood in this form is entirely safe.

Well, I suppose "safe" is a relative term. It's safe in that it's not going to turn anyone into a hyper-possessive stalker, but if you have too many Massacres then you will definitely be extremely unwell. In this context, "too many" is one.

I've had three by the time Cam interrupts me.

'Drinking alone, Jack? That's a little unhealthy.'

'Judgy pants,' I say, draining my glass.

'Okay, drunky.' He pries the glass out of my hand and takes it away. The gin and blood bottles are empty now anyway, and the wound at my wrist has healed up nicely. Unfortunately, it bled a lot while it was healing and now my blood is all over the table. Cam grabs some paper towels from the bar to clean it up – apologising on my behalf to the bartender – then sits down and puts a pint of water in front of me.

'Right,' he says. 'What's up?'

'Probation tomorrow.'

'Ah.'

Apparently I don't need another excuse, but there's more.

'Tabs is sad,' I say. Somehow I'm crying, the tears sploshing onto the tabletop in big, wet drops.

'Which makes you sad,' Cam says.

I nod, because if I open my mouth to reply then I'm just going to start bawling. Christ, what happened to me? I'm Jack Valentine, not some lovesick puppy.

Cam drags my barstool towards him, then pulls me into his arms. I bury my face in his shoulder.

'I. Just. Love. Her. So. Much,' I say through gasping sobs.

'I know you do.' He rubs my back. 'I know you do, Jack. But you've got to tell her that. That's the problem. You're shit at showing your emotions.'

'No,' I snuffle, wiping my nose on his shoulder. 'The problem is Killian Drake and his stupid probation and his stupid bite and his stupid bloody everything else.'

'I know.'

'He's a bastard.'

'I know.'

'And Tabs is soooo pretty. And cute. And clever.'

Everything's going sideways and fuzzy.

'Oh, sweetie,' Cam murmurs, stroking my hair as I fall asleep in his lap. 'You are so fucked for tomorrow.'

<h1 style="text-align:center">4</h1>

MY FIRST PROBATION meeting isn't going well. I've been in Drake's office for ten minutes now, but neither of us has said a word. We sit in silence.

I hate this room. It's obnoxiously masculine, filled with wood, stone and leather. I clawed holes into the back of one of the armchairs earlier this year when Drake was really pissing me off, and I see with some satisfaction that although he's had it reupholstered, he couldn't get a perfect colour match to the leather of the other chairs in the set. I bet that drives him bonkers.

Right now, he doesn't seem the least bit perturbed. In fact, he's annoyingly calm.

'So, is this like therapy?' I say eventually. 'You think if you give me enough quiet time then I'll spill my guts and give you a way to fix me?'

Drake's sitting at his desk, the sun streaming through the sash window behind him. He looks up from his papers and blinks, as though surprised to see me.

'I'm sorry, Ms Valentine. I forgot you were there.'

I am going to hit him.

'You're the one who told me to come,' I say. 'You're the

one who wanted to do this stupid probation thing. The least you could do is acknowledge my existence.'

'And you burned down a house full of Silver chemicals, endangering one of your own and bringing human attention to his operations.'

'Matthew Felton is not *one of my own*.'

'My point is,' he says, 'that you broke the rules. I could have boxed you. I should have boxed you. But instead, I've been lenient. In return for that leniency, the least you could do is arrive for your probation meeting on time, rather than three hours late, reeking of blood and alcohol and sex.'

He caps his fountain pen with a click and lines it up neatly beside his blotter, as calm as though he's just told me the weather forecast. He gives every impression that this is a clinical bollocking. He's not invested in it, or me. I have no reason to expect him to feel otherwise, but his apathy pinches. So does the way that he's started calling me "Ms Valentine". It used to be "Jack" or, in particularly heated situations, "Valentine". Not that I want to be in a heated situation with him ever again. But *Ms Valentine* just feels cold.

I try to brush it off.

'I'm behind on my laundry,' I say, as though that's an excuse. 'Not all of us live in a mansion with hundreds of slaves to do our bidding. It's very colonial of you.'

'Employees, Ms Valentine, not slaves. There is a difference. I look after the people who look after me. If you want to find out what I do to the people who oppose me, then keep pushing.'

'Ooo, am I supposed to be scared?'

He sighs. 'You're supposed to be even a tiny bit penitent, but apparently that's too much to ask. It's like trying to reason with a child,' he mutters.

'You're one to talk. What kind of game are you playing here, Drake? Why the probation? Why does it have to be you? Why not literally anyone else?'

'Because there is literally no one else I trust right now. Or did you want me to put you under the charge of your captain?'

I've been trying to stay out of Captain Langford's way for the past few months. Ever since seeing the photos, I find it hard to look at her without scowling. The betrayal runs deep.

'But you don't trust me, either,' he says, sighing.

'You've given me no reason to.'

'Haven't I?' He looks me dead in the eye.

He's the one who sent me the photos in question. I've looked at them a million times. He told me to burn them, but how could I? They're the only concrete evidence I have that something is wrong.

This is the secret Drake shared with me.

The photos show Captain Langford, the captain of the Seekers, meeting with Benedict, the Tertius of the Solis Invicti. In one, she's passing him a vial-carrying dart. It once contained a new sedative, one that's effective in a matter of seconds, even against the Silver. I've seen it in action; it knocked Drake out back in May. It was meant to hit me, but he walked right in front of it. That might have been heroic, him taking a bullet for me, if he hadn't been beating me up at the time.

The dart was supposed to deter me from investigating Benedict. I saw him at Sir Percival Wanker's party earlier this year, offering humans the opportunity to turn Silver in exchange for vast sums of money. But it was a scam; Benedict was taking the money and killing the humans. At least, that was my theory. According to the Primus and the captain, it was a sting operation. I don't believe that – their denials just made it more obvious to me that something fishy was going on – but I'm still not any closer to finding out what Benedict's planning. The unofficial Silver-turning parties have come to an end. No more middle-aged rich guys have gone missing along with their money. Every one of my leads has dried up.

But I haven't told a soul about the photos. Not even Tabitha. Drake is the only other person who knows.

His nostrils flare.

'You finally decided to keep her, then,' he says. He's talking about Tabitha. He can smell her scent mark on my skin.

'I'm hers for as long as she wants me,' I say. 'Exclusively.'

'And how long do you think that will be?'

I laugh. 'Why? Are you clock-watching?'

Despite myself, I get a little thrill at the idea that he might be waiting. But his pulse is steady, calm, disinterested. It tells me: nothing to get excited about here.

'It's a conflict,' he says. 'You know it's a risk. The Solis Invicti–'

'Everything is a risk. There's no one we can trust.'

'So you haven't told her?'

As he speaks, he leans forward over his desk. The movement sends a waft of air from him to me, carrying his scent: spice, copper and something darker. My body remembers it, even though I'm desperate to forget.

'I'm not going to talk to you about her,' I say, pushing away the memory of all the terrible things I've done with him in this office. On that desk. 'It's not relevant.'

'It's very relevant. She's theirs.'

'No,' I say, feeling fire flash through my veins. 'She's mine, Drake. *Mine*. You don't talk about her and you don't go near her. Don't bring her up again.'

'You're the one who brought her into the room with you.'

Which was deliberate, granted, but I'm not sure why he's surprised that I'm wearing my girlfriend's mark.

'How does this stupid probation work?' I ask, just to change the subject.

'Well, to start with, you arrive on time.'

I flick my hand dismissively.

'Then we talk about your week,' he says, 'to make sure you're staying within the terms of your probation.'

'Which are?'

'Don't set anyone else on fire, and stay away from Matthew Felton.'

'We're good, then. I haven't set anyone at all on fire this week, and yesterday was the first time I've seen Felton in months. So, are we done here?' I slap the arms of my chair, making to leave.

'Sit down, Ms Valentine. We are not done. We will also use these sessions to talk about your behaviour and how you manage situations of conflict.'

'Oh god,' I groan. 'It *is* like therapy.'

'For instance,' he continues, 'there's the conflict between you and me. That might be a good place to start.'

'There's nothing between you and me, Drake. No conflict. Just a big heap of nothing.'

He takes the lid off his fountain pen, looks me in the eye for a second, then writes something down in the notebook on his desk.

'What?' I ask, craning my neck to see what he's written.

'Denial,' he says, clicking the cap back onto his pen. 'A big heap of denial. You're angry, Ms Valentine.'

'Well, that's a fucking revelation. Thanks very much, Dr Freud. It had never occurred to me that I might be *angry*.

Now all my problems are solved.'

'You're angry with *me*.'

'Well, in my defence, you're very annoying.'

He uncaps his pen again, tilting the notebook away from me so I can't see what he's writing.

'What I'm struggling to understand,' he says, 'is why you're *still* angry, despite the fact that I've just saved you from a boxing. Why are you still fighting when you've already got what you wanted?'

'You think I wanted *this*?'

'More than the box, yes.'

'I'm not going to thank you for messing with me. You're always playing a game. Or you think you are, anyway. The truth is, you're just a dick.'

He scribbles some more.

I sigh audibly.

'This isn't the first time you've been angry with me,' he says.

He's fishing. I know he's fishing, but it irritates me into retaliation, so I say something I shouldn't.

'These things happen.' I deliberately echo his words from yesterday. 'We all make mistakes.'

He sits back in his chair, satisfied, and I know I've fucked up.

'So that's it,' he says. 'Are you insulted because I said I felt nothing for you?'

'I'm not angry about that,' I say, determined to brazen this out. 'And I'm not insulted. You were right.'

'Words I never thought I'd hear from your lips, Ms Valentine. Tell me, how was I right?'

I'm certain that he was a torturer at some point in his past, because he is determined to make this as painful as possible.

'We were involved in a covert operation,' I say, pouring

ice into my voice. 'I made the terms of that operation clear. Everything was going fine, then you crossed a line. That was your mistake. My mistake was letting you get away with it.'

'And when you came back here for more, that was a mistake too, was it?'

It's such an offhand comment – so dismissive, so clinical, so mocking – that it seems calculated to annoy. I can feel the heat building in my cheeks. He's throwing my vulnerability back in my face. I can't even blame him for that; I'd do the same to him in a heartbeat.

'That was just the mark,' I reply, trying to show how little I care. 'Like you said, there were no feelings involved. It was a reaction to a chemical imbalance. Fascinating stuff, actually. Tabitha's looking into it. How the mark works, and how it interacts with blood-drinking. That night in the alley, when you…' My voice gets stuck in the back of my throat. I'm sitting here trying to be the ice queen, trying to rub his nose in it, and my body is betraying me.

My only consolation is that Drake's not happy either. He looks down at his blotter and fiddles with his pen, off-balance for the first time since I walked in.

'That was the biggest mistake I ever made,' he says quietly.

This small triumph over him should make me gleeful, but it doesn't come without its price. I don't want to think about what happened that night. The anger in his eyes, the need to break free, the impotence in my body as I realised the galling truth: he is strong enough to overpower me.

He only had a fraction of my trust in the first place, but he's not going to earn it back any time soon.

I can't let him see me vulnerable, so I buckle down my feelings, slamming shut the doors in my mind that lead to dangerous places. It leaves me feeling empty, like I'm deliberately ignoring something important, but at least the searing sensation in my chest has gone. I can breathe again, but the longer we sit in this silence, the bigger the past looms between us. I search desperately for a way out of the conversational dead-end into which I've steered us. Looking around the room, I say the first thing that comes to mind.

'Actually, I think the biggest mistake you ever made was choosing those velvet curtains to go with this stone flooring. Tacky, Drake. Very eighties.'

'It's been a while since I redecorated,' he concedes.

He doesn't fight me for the win, so it's a hollow victory. He's letting me have it. He's being *kind*.

It's the last thing I want from him. I want him to be vile, because kindness from Killian Drake is like a consolation prize: he only offers it when he knows you've already lost, and I can't lose to him. I just can't.

'You know, I'm not sure I like this psychiatrist thing you've got going on,' I say, gesturing at him. 'It's not a good look on you.'

'Oh?' His eyebrow twitches. 'And what *is* a good look on me?'

Thankfully, my phone buzzes in my pocket, saving me from having to answer him. I take the call.

'Hello, Deputy,' I say. 'What's that? You need me to come immediately on urgent Seekers business? A matter of life or death, you say?'

'No,' Boyd says from the phone. 'I was asking what kind of pizza you want. We're settling in for an afternoon with the court papers.'

'Right away, Sir,' I reply.

'Jacqueline—'

'I'll be there as fast as I can,' I say loudly, then hang up on Boyd before turning back to Drake. 'Got to go. Emergency, you know.'

'So I heard. Quick, or they might get you pepperoni. You hate pepperoni.'

Shit. I forgot that he has Silver hearing too.

'Don't pretend you know me,' I say.

He leans forward, elbows on his desk.

'But I do know you, Valentine. And you really hate that, don't you?'

I glare at him for a moment, trying to come up with a retort, but I've got nothing. I'm feeling too raw, and he's right. I hate how well he knows me. I hate that he knows exactly how to push my buttons. And I hate the way he calls me *Valentine*, putting that whisper into my name that speaks of shared intimacy I want to deny, but can't.

In lieu of a witty response, I say, 'Fuck you, Drake,' then make my exit.

'See you next week,' he calls after me.

I have to clamp my jaw shut to hold in the scream.

Although I'm avoiding the captain for the reasons previously stated – conspiring with Benedict, covering up his part in the Windsor scam, possibly planning something worse – I can't ignore her summons when she calls the whole team into her office at the end of the day.

'Don't look so glum,' she says, pushing her chair back from her desk. 'You all look like you're here for a funeral.'

Captain Langford is a petite woman, but fierce with it. She wears her short blonde hair in a bob brushed back from her face. I'm convinced that the main reason for this style choice is to leave her forehead unencumbered so that her raised eyebrow – universally feared within the walls of Solomon College and beyond – will have the biggest impact. She deploys it now.

Naia cringes.

'What's going on?' the captain asks. 'Out with it.'

'We were sorry to hear about your great-granddaughter,' Cam says. As the only one amongst us who can do feelings, he's been nominated to give our condolences. 'Are you okay?'

She waves her hand.

'That's very sweet of you, Cameron, but actually I never met her. Her death means no more to me than any other human's.'

This might sound cold, but it isn't that surprising. Captain Langford has a Silver family of her own – a husband, a daughter, a dog, although obviously the dog isn't Silver – so why would she worry about her human descendants? Not everyone cares about their genetic legacy, particularly when it was created in less than perfect circumstances. The captain's been around long enough that I'm sure her human life was far from rosy, and probably not filled with decisions she got to have a say in. Maybe she'd rather forget that her descendants even exist.

'So you don't think her murder was targeted at you?' Boyd asks.

'It might be. Perhaps someone assumes I care more than I do. But actually, I didn't call you here about the case.'

My stomach drops.

Uh-oh.

I've never liked surprises, and I particularly don't like them when they come from the captain. She's surprised me enough lately, and never in a good way.

'I called you all here because we've been asked to provide security at an event.'

Boyd's stern face crinkles in confusion. 'With all due respect, Captain, we're the Seekers. We don't do private security.'

'We do when it gives us access to the first open blood bar outside London.'

Boyd's mouth drops open.

I'm not sure what I was expecting, but it definitely wasn't this. I'm not even sure it's a bad surprise, for once.

There are a couple of blood bars in Oxford – the Solomon College bar and the private club on Holywell Street – which basically do what they say on the tin: they're bars that serve blood. Generally, they're secretive places that only let the Silver in.

An open blood bar is different. Instead of being hush-hush, they open to all comers, generally offering fancy cocktails and upmarket liquor, with a substantial cover charge. That way, they keep human customers to a minimum – only the wealthiest and best-connected people can drink there – but maintain a veneer of respectable desirability that makes them more attractive to the Silver. Of course, there are still exclusive Silver-only areas within open blood bars, like VIP areas, but the humans are never aware of the admittance criteria. They're right next to the Silver patrons, watching the VIPs behind the rope, elbow-to-elbow at the bar with people ordering blood-laced drinks that are off the menu to all but select clientele. I guess it's a thrill.

That edge of danger, the flirtation with secrecy, is the reason the Silver love going to the open bars. But they're also insanely expensive to run and a nightmare to police, which is why they've only been established in London so far, where the Solis Invicti keep an eye on them. The news that one is coming to Oxford cuts both ways: it'll be fun, but potentially dangerous, and hard work for us.

'When did this happen?' Naia asks.

'A while ago, apparently. Unbeknownst to me.' The

captain doesn't sound happy to have been kept out of the loop. 'A couple of the Invicti are coming over to keep an eye on things for the opening, but they want four of us on the doors. I thought it would be a good fit for your team, Deputy.'

'Which Invicti?' I ask.

I'm praying, *not Benedict*.

'They didn't say. You'll meet them outside the club at eight o'clock and they'll assign your posts.'

'Eight o'clock *tonight*?' Naia asks.

'Yes. Is that a problem?'

'No, Captain. No problem.'

'Good. You'll each bring a plus one, because it's important that you don't look like bouncers. Try not to bring anyone too embarrassing.' She looks at Naia as she says this, which I think is a bit harsh. Fair, but harsh. 'Remember that not all of the attendees will be Silver. Your job is to monitor people coming in and out, while keeping an eye on the bar to make sure none of the Silver get carried away and try to drink directly from the tap, as it were.'

'And the case, Captain?' Boyd asks.

'It can wait until tomorrow. Dr Ross will be giving us the post mortem results first thing, so I'll expect you all in the conference room at nine.'

No rest for the wicked.

Boyd salutes, then we're all dismissed.

'Oh, and wear something nice,' the captain says as we're leaving, eyeing each of us in turn. I try not to be offended that her eyes linger on me the longest.

$$5$$

CRIMSON.

It's not a very subtle name for a blood bar. I feel like a cliché coming here with my high heels and a bodycon cocktail dress that seems determined to bunch itself up around my bust. Cam assured me that it makes my bum look great, but I'm starting to think it only achieves that effect because it's so tight that it's physically holding my arse up, a full inch above its normal cruising altitude.

'You look gorgeous,' I say to Tabitha, partly to distract myself from my own discomfort and partly because it's true. She's wearing a little emerald number with an A-line skirt and a sweetheart neckline. I'm hoping there'll be dancing later so I can spin her around and watch her skirt twirl.

If I'm ever allowed away from my post, that is. That seems increasingly unlikely, because I've just spotted the Invicti delegate by the club's entrance on Park End Street. He's standing with Boyd, and it's exactly who I hoped it wouldn't be.

'Oh, good,' Benedict says as Tabitha and I approach. 'My favourite Seeker.'

'Tertius,' I say, using his formal title, because I promised

Tabitha I'd be good tonight. After all, she works for this dickhead.

'Set anyone on fire lately?' he asks.

'Shoot anyone with a poison dart lately?' I reply. I couldn't resist.

'Jacqueline,' Boyd says quietly, warning me off.

I simmer down, trying to ignore the fact that my nemesis – well, one of them – is going to be telling me what to do this evening. It's galling, to say the least.

Benedict just smiles at me and says, 'Careful, Jack.'

I hate his smile. It's creepy. The guy is huge, layered with so many muscles that it's a miracle he can fit into his clothes. His face is handsome, I guess, but made for scowling. When he smiles, it looks like he has to break his mouth to do it.

Naia and Cam arrive shortly after Tabitha and me. Cam has brought Carrie – Ed's girlfriend – and Naia's brought Ed. It's sweet of them to step in at such short notice, and nice to see Cam and Carrie on such friendly terms. It's not a surprise, though; Cam makes it his mission to get along with everyone.

Benedict looks at them for a moment then says quietly, 'Seekers, over here.'

He leads the four of us a little way from the door and hands out assignments.

'Boyd and Jack, I want you inside the entrance at the front. Naia and Cam, at the back of the room by the bar. I'll be walking around, keeping an eye out for trouble. Thomas is on the side door already.'

I met Thomas Meyer earlier this year. He's decent enough, for one of the Invicti.

'Are you expecting trouble?' Boyd asks.

'No, but we need to be prepared for it. You never know who's going to walk in.'

This seems like a ridiculous statement to me, because this is the one night when we know exactly who's going to walk in. The opening is invitation-only. The only way to explain the extra security is as a show of strength to the owners of the new bar, to intimidate or support. I'm not sure which it is yet.

'Get to your posts,' Benedict says, dismissing us, 'but keep it natural.'

Cam and Naia go first, heading straight to the bar with Ed and Carrie. When they're settled, I offer Tabitha my arm and we follow Boyd inside.

The inside is pretty much how I expected it to be: crimson, silver and glass, with wipe-clean surfaces that give the bar the same sterile edge as a hospital. It's an odd juxtaposition, but one that seems to be winning over its audience. It's exactly the kind of pretentious bollocks the more style-conscious Silver prefer.

Tabitha and I chat with Boyd for a few minutes, making it seem as though we're just three friends who are catching up, then Tabitha goes off to fetch us some drinks.

'So,' I say to Boyd. 'Couldn't get a date?'

'I have a date.' He's gruff, defensive.

'Who is she? The invisible woman?'

'She's running late.' He glances over his shoulder, through the bar's front window to the street.

'Is she,' I say. It's not a question. I'm thinking he's been stood up, if he ever had a date in the first place.

'Yes, she *is*,' he insists.

He looks out to the street again and the tension in his face disappears, eyes lighting up for a second before his expression settles into concern.

'Please be nice,' he begs me. 'Please don't ruin this for me.'

I follow his gaze to see Ms Chen walking across the road towards us.

'No,' I say. 'You didn't.'

'I know it's a bit unprofessional to date a witness–'

'Boyd. Please tell me you didn't invite a human as your date to the opening of a blood bar.'

'Why shouldn't I?' he says.

'Do you not like her or something?' I reply, exasperated. 'Are you actively trying to scare her off, or trying to get someone else to sink his teeth into her? What were you thinking? We're here to do a job, but you're going to have to spend your whole night watching her like a hawk so no one else swoops in. For fuck's sake.'

'I hadn't thought about it like that,' he admits.

'Because it wasn't your brain doing the thinking, it was another part of your anatomy entirely. A part I wasn't sure you even possessed.'

Ms Chen is at the door now, smiling at the greeter outside as she gives him her name. She's on the bloody list as Boyd's plus one, irrevocably linked with him and the Seekers. If anything goes wrong, then we are in the shit. Boyd has obviously just realised this, because now he's panicking.

'Help me,' he whispers, his eyes wide and pleading. The idiot.

'I'll ask Tabs to look after her. But you owe me, Deputy.'

'Fine, fine,' he says under his breath as Ms Chen walks in. 'Whatever you need. Just… please.'

I was expecting any number of things to go wrong tonight, but I never would have guessed that Boyd would be the cause of them. The man has lost his mind over this librarian.

Not that she looks much like a librarian tonight. She's wearing a ruby-red sheath dress with black lace detailing on the bodice, paired with strappy black heels. It's almost as though she knew she was coming to a vampire party.

'Hi, Jack.' She turns to Boyd with a smile. 'Hi, Ronald.'

Ronald? No wonder Boyd uses his last name.

Boyd smiles back and says, 'Good evening, Mildred.'

Ronald and Mildred. A match made in heaven. At least, it would be if they weren't a vampire and a human.

'Why don't you go to the bar?' I suggest to him. 'You can introduce Mildred to Tabby. My girlfriend,' I explain to her. 'Then come back here. Quickly.'

He does as I suggest, which might be a first, while I try to work out how we're going to get Mildred through the night alive.

Half an hour in, I'm already regretting these shoes. What was I thinking? I knew we were on security detail all night, so why in the name of all that is holy did I think a four-inch heel was reasonable? I hate myself.

I hate Boyd more.

He's been making awkward architectural small talk with Mildred ever since they got back from the bar, and it's starting to grate. Even the object of his affections is losing interest. Meanwhile, Tabitha's on her third drink and I'm trying to keep an eye on Boyd's section of the bar as well as my own. With so many people pouring through the door, this is not an easy task.

We're interrupted by a screech of feedback from the side of the room as the music cuts out. There's a small stage there, presumably intended for live music, but tonight it has just a single occupant.

'Good evening, ladies and gentlemen and everyone in between,' the woman says.

She's one of the most imposing people I've ever seen. It's

not that she's particularly beautiful, although her paleness and platinum hair are striking in the dimly-lit room, it's more that she takes command of the space like a ringmaster. Her demeanour says: *This is my gig. I'm in control every step of the way, but if you're good, I'll let you come along for the ride.* Within seconds, the audience is eating out of the palm of her hand.

'Thank you for coming to our little celebration,' she says. 'I hope this will be the first of many visits you make to Crimson, where you are always assured of an unforgettable experience. Our mixologists are waiting to take your orders free of charge and, if you ask very nicely, they might make something extra special, just for you. Enjoy!'

When the music floods back in, it's louder and more abrasive than it was before. It grates. I might not look older than twenty, but in real time I'm nearly forty, which means it's too loud in here, the men are wearing too much aftershave and the women too much makeup. Any day now, I'll be telling them all to get off my lawn.

'Shall we have a dance?' Tabitha suggests to Mildred.

I'm more than a little jealous when she leads Mildred through the crowds to the dance floor next to the stage. Even in her heels, Tabitha is short enough to get lost – I can only track their progress by watching Mildred's back – but when she starts twirling around, her face bright with alcohol-fuelled joy, she's impossible to miss. People make space for her.

I wish we had come here because we wanted to dance together, not because I'm here for work. It's been too long since I took her dancing.

'Sorry, Jacqueline,' Boyd says.

'You're an idiot.'

'I know. I didn't think.'

'I hate to admit it, but that's not like you. What's wrong?'

'I don't know. I like her.'

'And it's making you stupid?'

'Apparently.'

I laugh, because Boyd does not admit his faults, ever. The fact that he's doing so now is frankly astounding.

'Where's the stick gone?' I ask him.

He looks puzzled.

'What stick?'

'The one you usually keep up your arse.'

'Oh, very funny.'

'No, seriously, it's a good thing. But next time, maybe think it through first. And for tonight, you're going to have to fake a headache or something to get her out of here before things get too rowdy.'

He nods solemnly, because we both know that things are definitely going to get rowdy. I can feel it in the air, in the manic edge to the smiles around me, in the strange mix of pheromones that fills the club: excitement, arousal, fear. Until the tension breaks, none of us can relax.

I've got my eye on a few likely disruptors.

The first is a Silver woman with brown skin and skyscraper heels, sitting on a tall stool at the end of the bar. She's petite, with straight black hair so long that it falls in a sheet down her back and past the seat of her stool, draping halfway to the ground. She's beautiful, but that's not why she catches my attention. I'm watching her because she's a manipulator. In the space of ten minutes, she's wangled four drinks out of turn and countless smiles from various patrons, by the application of charm alone. And she looks bored. If anyone here would orchestrate a fight simply to make things more entertaining, it would be her.

A little further down the bar, my second potential agitator

has been waiting to be served for twenty minutes now, and he's getting itchy. He's human, a big guy with muscles that have been perfectly sculpted in the gym to make him feel superhuman. From the way he's acting, he doesn't realise he's surrounded by actual superhumans. If he kicks off, it'll be a bloodbath in here.

The third is the worst of the bunch, because I can't keep him in sight. He's a shadow at the edge of my vision, in the crowds, behind the bar. I say "he", but I have no idea what gender the shadow is because I never get a clear look at it. All I have is a scent in the air, a lingering odour of old paper that catches in the back of my throat every time the shadow hides from me.

In the end, I'm not sure where the tension breaks, because something distracts me before it happens.

'Oh, shit,' I say to Boyd. 'Look who it is.'

A lackey unhooks the red rope that seals off the VIP area from the rest of the club, and out walks Sir Percival Wanker, the elitist bastard in chief.

I scowl as he approaches us.

'Ms Valentine,' he says. 'How lovely to see you.'

Windsor hasn't made a secret of the fact that he hates the Seekers in general, and me in particular, so this friendly greeting rings alarm bells. I squint at his face, looking for sarcasm, but find none. Its absence just makes me more suspicious.

'What are you doing here?' I ask.

His fat, hairless face creases into a smile that might be called amiable by someone who hadn't met the man before. The expression sits strangely on him. He's looking smart this evening, smarter than I've ever seen him. There's even some kind of product in his hair, doing its best to tame the platinum bird's nest and failing miserably. He's trying to make an impression.

'Where else would I be on the opening night of my club?' he asks.

'*Your* club?'

'Silent partner,' he says, stretching his smile wider.

Inevitably, this is the moment when all hell breaks loose. Windsor ducks as glass shatters behind him. Over his shoulder, I see the glass sheet behind the bar dissolving into a shower of tiny shards. It brings several bottles down with it, each of which detonates on the bar top. One or two land next to the tea lights that sit along the length of the bar, shattering the glass cups that hold them and releasing the flames to rush along the starbursts of spilled spirits. Within a second, the whole bar area is on fire.

I lock eyes with Boyd. His face has paled, his eyes wide and terrified.

'Go,' I say. 'Find her.'

He doesn't need to be told twice.

The screams are loud enough to drown out the music.

Windsor runs like the coward he is, despite the fact that he's old enough to weather the fire without suffering for more than an hour or two afterwards. He could be in the thick of it with the rest of us, pulling the humans out of harm's way, but of course he isn't. He doesn't think their lives are worth his discomfort.

'Extinguisher!' I yell to Cam. He and Naia are on the other side of the bar, evacuating people through the side door. It's a fire exit, so that's where the fire-fighting gear is.

He lifts the red canister and throws it across the room – a clear fifty feet – to where I'm standing at the bar. There are a couple of bartenders trapped back there between the flaming surface and the taproom: a girl and a boy, both about twenty, both entirely human. When I activate the extinguisher, strafing the hose across the fire, they get drenched in foam.

The flames go out.

The music stops.

For a moment, an unnatural quiet descends over the bar. Almost everyone is out on the street now, having escaped through the alley at the side. The only people left behind are my team and the few humans who weren't able to move under their own power: the bartenders, a couple of men on the floor who look like they've been bottled, and a girl who got trampled in the panic.

'Is everyone okay?' Cam asks.

The trampled girl gets to her feet, the bartenders wipe themselves down, and the guys by the bar are helped up by Tabitha.

'It's not bad,' she says, examining them. 'Just a bit of shrapnel from the bottles. They won't even need stitches.'

Mildred is standing at her side, looking dazed. A small trickle of blood snakes down her cheek from her hairline.

'Are you all right?' Boyd asks her.

She nods, but she doesn't look all right. She looks as though she's just had a baptism by fire. Her red dress is now mostly black, partly with soot and partly because she's fallen over at some point. There's now a lake of dark-coloured drink soaking into her back. It has some blood in it, but it's not her own.

'Come on,' he says quickly, leading her away. 'Let's get you home.'

By the time he returns, it's as though nothing happened. The bar top is stainless steel and the front is glass, so the whole thing has been wiped clean with little trace of the fire. The glass has been swept up, the floor mopped, and the bottles replaced, so except for the lingering scent of smoke and the back panel missing from behind the bar, it's almost as good as new. We're ready to open up again.

Benedict insists on it.

He made sure the emergency services weren't summoned. Within seconds of Boyd leaving with the remaining humans, he had the shutters drawn so we could work at Silver speed to clear away the evidence. Now he reopens them and spreads the doors wide to admit Windsor and the woman who spoke on stage earlier, our hostess.

She makes her way back to the stage, picking up the microphone with a smile as people shuffle back inside.

'Apologies, ladies and gentlemen. It seems that one of our patrons dropped a bottle or two.' She smiles indulgently, suggesting this was just a tiny mishap instead of a major incident. Given that there's no trace of the fire and no trace of glass, the humans present might be convinced that they imagined the whole thing.

The crowd draws closer, taken in.

She smiles again.

'Let's get on with the celebration!'

The music cranks back up. People flood to the dance floor. The VIP area is once again populated and admired.

Boyd comes to stand at my elbow.

'Any damage?' I ask.

'A small cut on her head. Nothing serious. She was standing close to the bar when it happened.'

'You got her home okay?'

'I put her in a cab,' he replies. 'She didn't want an escort.'

'She's not the damsel in distress type.'

'No.'

His face is blank, his eyes fixed on the bar. I can see that he's replaying the whole thing in his mind: the bar back shattering, the glass flying, with Mildred in the firing line.

'She'll be okay, Boyd.'

'Yeah.'
'On balance,' I say, 'I think you got away lightly.'
He nods and looks at his feet.
We both know it could have been so much worse.

6

NOW THAT THE worst has happened and Mildred – the important human – has been shuffled off practically unharmed, we all start to relax. Tabitha's next to me, while Boyd stands alone on the opposite side of the front door.

The club has emptied out a little, partly because a good portion of the humans have been scared off and partly because the Invicti have ejected the Silver troublemakers. This ice-breaker was obviously anticipated because it's only now, approaching midnight, that the big guns start showing up: Windsor's cronies. They arrive in limos, wearing evening dress that looks effortless, with partners that are far too beautiful to make a pair with them. That in itself is a sign of wealth and status for dinosaurs like these.

With them come the local Silver elite: Lydia Gainsborough, half-naked and dripping with jewels; Captain Langford, out of uniform but still as fierce as ever; and Sir Percival Windsor, who has apparently nipped out the back of the club and run around the block to make a proper entrance. There are others too, making such a spectacle that I'm half expecting cameras and a red carpet to materialise around them. I see a few phones lifted to snap photos, but that's all.

No one's invited the national press, let alone the locals.

This event is the epitome of discreet chic.

'Holy shit,' I say to Tabitha. 'Is that Carlotta Arden?'

Argentinian-born, French-raised and now an international model and actress, Carlotta Arden is a Silver goddess. She's wearing tailored trousers, a red blouse and red-soled Louboutin heels, as though she's just walked straight out of a magazine. Her skin is golden brown, her hair a chestnut waterfall pulled over one shoulder. As she walks into the room, I can't drag my eyes away from the sensuous roll of her hips. I've had a photo of her on my wall since I first turned Silver. I only finally took it down when I got together with Tabitha earlier this year.

And she's walking towards me. Carlotta Arden is through the door and walking towards me.

'You're Jacquéline?' she says. I normally hate being addressed by my full name – Boyd is the only one who gets away with it – but in her sultry French accent I find myself falling in love with it.

'Hi,' I say, then I run out of words.

Carlotta Arden knows my name. I feel like I'm having a heart attack.

While I gawp like a fish, Tabitha introduces herself and shakes Carlotta's hand.

'I'm such a huge fan of yours,' I say, pulling myself together. I'm not normally one to gush, but suddenly I'm going full-on fangirl. 'I loved you in *Every Night*, and that scene at the end of *Blood Bound* where you and Sam Hayworth had to take down the traffickers in the warehouse and there was blood *everywhere–*'

She laughs. 'I know. It was a lot of fun.'

'I'm sorry. I can't believe I'm meeting you. When I think of all the amazing things you've done–'

'But you do it for a living, Jacquéline. You're the real action hero. I've heard all about you.'

'You–' I have to swallow because my throat is so dry. 'You have?'

Carlotta turns to the man beside her. I've been so focussed on her that I didn't even realise there was someone standing with her.

'Hello, Ms Valentine.'

Killian Drake. Of course. Carlotta Arden is here on the arm of Killian Fucking Drake.

'Oh,' I say. 'You.'

'Yes.' He smiles. 'Me.'

Drake's smile is somewhere between a leer and a threat. Usually he smiles only because he knows something I don't, and he's going to use it to win whatever game we're playing. Tonight, it's extra smug.

'I should have guessed you'd be here,' I say.

'Nice to see you too,' he replies. 'Well, we'd better make the rounds.'

'*Absolument*,' Carlotta says, then she turns to me. 'Perhaps we can catch up later?'

'Um, sure?'

Carlotta Arden wants to chat with *me*? I'm so nervous that my palms are sweating, and I'm hyper-aware of this stupid dress, which is trying to bunch itself up into my armpits.

Carlotta smiles at me and Tabitha, then follows Drake. They don't stop at the bar, but go straight past the red rope to the raised area at the back of the club. The booths are mostly full already, but one is quickly emptied for them. Baron Drake is in his element, the elite of the elite.

'Holy shit,' I whisper again. 'Carlotta Arden.'

'A little starstruck are you, hen?' Tabitha asks, but her playful tone doesn't match her expression. She looks worried, even angry.

'Are you okay?' I ask.

She slaps on a smile that looks fake.

'Of course,' she says. 'I think I'll go to the bar. Do you want a drink?'

'No, thanks. I'd better not. On duty, you know.'

'So dutiful,' she teases. 'I'm going to find Ed and Carrie. I'll loop back later, okay?'

'Okay.'

I smile back, but I'm uneasy.

She's not happy. I'm not sure what's wrong, but I can't help but feel that it's my fault.

The night passes slowly now the excitement is over. The fire has burned the tension out of the air, leaving a relaxed atmosphere that lends itself to dancing and laughter.

Unfortunately, I'm stuck by the door watching the room. On my own. For *hours*. My feet are numb, which is a small mercy, and I've stopped trying to tug my dress back down to its proper place. If it wants to show the entire bar my knickers, then good luck to it. I'm past caring.

It's not that I didn't expect this. Security detail always sucks. I've done it often enough to know that I'll feel like a spectator, watching and working while the people around me enjoy themselves. The whole point is that I'm here to keep them safe so they can have a good time, so if they weren't having fun it would almost be worse.

But I expected to have some company. When Tabitha said she'd "loop back later", I thought she meant fifteen minutes later, not three hours later. I've watched her dance with Ed and Carrie, chat with Ed and Carrie, get introduced to a couple of their friends, dance with them, then introduce *herself* to the striking hostess. She's been chatting her up at the bar for half an hour now.

She must know that I'm watching, so why is she doing this? Is she trying to punish me for something? When I see them heading towards the dance floor, I'm ready to lose my cool.

'Jack?'

I was so focussed on Tabitha that, for the second time tonight, I didn't notice Drake approaching. Sneaky bastard.

'What's wrong?' he asks me.

'There's nothing wrong.' I almost stop there, but I'm riled up enough to get petty. 'And even if there were something wrong, you'd be the last person I'd tell.'

He sighs. 'It doesn't have to be like this.'

'I'm trying to work here, Drake. I have to keep an eye on the bar.'

'Really? Because it looks to me like there's only one person you're watching.'

I follow his pointed stare and see the hostess twirling on the dance floor with Tabitha. Jealousy stabs me in the stomach. My head empties out until all I can think is: *That should have been me*.

'Jacquéline!'

Carlotta has joined us. I'm having a jealous breakdown in front of Killian Drake and the most beautiful woman I've ever seen in real life, or anywhere for that matter. I wish I were somewhere else, but if I move from this spot then I'll have Benedict to deal with too. When I look over Drake's shoulder, I can see the big man slinking through the bar like a tiger, his eyes watchful, his body poised. The moment I step out of line, he'll pounce.

'She's working,' Drake says to Carlotta.

Her mouth purses into a moue of distaste. As a gesture, it is very French.

'All night?' she asks.

'Until the opening is over, I assume,' Drake replies, raising an eyebrow at me.

'That's right,' I reply.

'Well, that's disappointing,' says Carlotta. 'I was hoping we would have some time together.'

She puts a purr into her voice that finally drags my attention away from the dance floor. Then I notice the scent in the air: pheromones. It takes me a while to reach the obvious conclusion, longer than it should given that Carlotta is looking me up and down appraisingly.

Oh my god.

Is Carlotta Arden coming onto me?

I feel like the world has just flipped on its head.

She turns to Drake and whispers in his ear, keeping one eye on me as she does so.

He smiles at her as she smoulders back.

'I don't think her girlfriend would like that,' he says, then he looks at me with mischief in his eyes. It's impossible to miss his meaning.

'Girlfriend?' Carlotta turns to me in surprise, just as Tabitha comes to join us. She's standing right next to me now, glaring.

'Er, right,' I say, stumbling over my words. 'Yes. My girlfriend. Tabitha. You met her earlier.'

'Oh,' Carlotta says. 'I'm sorry, it's just–' She looks between the two of us, but she doesn't have to say it. I know: there's no scent mark on either of us.

'It doesn't mean we're not together,' I say quickly. 'I've been working.'

'Of course.'

This is the problem with the scent mark: miss one day and everyone starts reading into it. Cam took me back to his place last night – rightly assuming that Tabitha wouldn't be pleased to see me paralytic again – which means I didn't see her this morning, then she had to go back to her place after work to change into her pretty dress and meet me here, all of which means the scent mark she put on me last night has now disappeared without being replaced. Basically, it's been a while since we had a proper snog.

'I'm sorry,' Carlotta says. 'I didn't realise you were together.' Then she seems to have another bright idea, looking at the two of us speculatively. 'Perhaps–'

'Excuse me,' Tabitha says, smiling sweetly. 'I'm going to go and get another drink.'

I watch her as she disappears into the crowd. Tabitha is definitely not the swinging type.

Shit.

'Erm,' I say to Carlotta, 'I have to–'

'Go, go,' she says with a wave of her hand.

I abandon my post without a second thought. It doesn't take me long to reach Tabitha.

'Tabs, that wasn't what it looked like. I don't know what–'

'You can probably catch them if you hurry,' she says over her shoulder as she pushes her way towards the bar.

'What are you talking about?'

'The three of you were dripping in pheromones.'

'That doesn't mean–' Someone grabs me by the arm and I whirl around to face them, yelling, 'What?'

It's Benedict, and he is not happy. For a moment I think he's going to lash out – he clenches his fist at his side – but then he drops my arm and points towards the door.

'Back to the door, Jack.'

'But I just–'

'Now.'

I do as he says, because there's no point arguing with him.

It's too late, anyway. Tabitha has already disappeared.

When the club finally empties out, Benedict releases us from duty, debriefing my team before leaving us at the bar. I groan and thunk my head down onto its fireproof surface.

'Bad night?' he asks.

'I mean, what are the odds? Carlotta Arden and Killian Drake.'

Cam looks at me, surprised. 'Didn't you know?'

'Huh?'

'They've been dating for a few months. One of the world's most eligible Silver bachelors and the world's most eligible bachelorette. How have you not heard about this? They're a power couple.'

'Since when?'

He shrugs. 'The end of May, I think?'

'May?' I can hear my teeth grinding together. 'You mean all the time that he was tormenting me, he had Carlotta Arden waiting in the wings? Are you kidding me?'

'Calm down, Jack. Have a drink. You're approaching decibel ranges only dogs can hear.' He shoves me down onto a bar stool. 'It was after all that was over, I think.'

'You think? Oh my god.' I bury my head in my hands. When I look up again, there's a bottle of gin by my elbow. I take a long slug.

'Look, you can't have it both ways. Either you're jealous because you like him, or you hate him and couldn't care less. Pick one and commit.'

'It's not that. It really isn't.'

'Then what is it?'

I'm not going to tell him that Carlotta Arden just propositioned me. It's too strange, and he'd be weird about it. Especially the threesome part.

I might tell Naia later, though.

'I love Tabitha,' I say. 'So it's all irrelevant.'

'All right, then. Why don't you go and tell her that?'

But Tabitha is nowhere. I scan every inch of floorspace, plus the loos, but I still can't see her. Finally, I go out into the street. Her car is gone.

She's left without me.

'Don't worry, darling,' says a voice from behind me. 'She'll come around.'

I turn to see Carlotta leaning against the front of the club, smoking a cigarette. It's not a popular habit amongst the Silver, because our enhanced senses of smell and taste make the whole experience a bit repugnant, but if people smoked in their human lives then the habit often follows them after they turn.

'Did you want one?' she asks, shaking the packet at me.

'No, thanks.' I gave up shortly before my own transition and I've never looked back. It's the only addiction I've ever managed to kick.

'So,' I say, leaning against the wall beside her. 'You and Drake.'

She laughs delicately. 'It's so funny that you call him that. So disrespectful. No wonder he finds you attractive.'

I worry that she might feel like I'm stepping on her toes, but she just seems amused.

'The offer is still open, you know,' she says, her eyes twinkling.

I can imagine it. I'll doubtless be imagining it for the rest of my life, kicking myself for turning her down. But, no. Tabitha.

In the end, I just shake my head.

She shrugs back.

'It's nothing personal,' I say. 'I think you're fucking

amazing. It's just, you know. Girlfriend. Plus, there's Drake.' I shudder.

'You don't like the baron?' Carlotta asks, raising a delicate eyebrow.

'I know him too well. It's complicated.'

'Oh.' She laughs again. 'I can see that. He's not a man to be free with his emotions. His body, however…' She twinkles at me again. She's very good at it.

'Well, you don't have to worry about that. Not with me, anyway.'

'It's not you I'm worried about, *chérie*. Perhaps you don't know him as well as you think. Still waters run deep, I believe they say.'

'I'm not sure they say it about Drake.'

Carlotta takes a final puff of her cigarette, then lifts her foot and crushes the filter out on the pretty red sole of her shoe, immediately reducing the value of the pair by about five hundred pounds.

'Do you love him?' I ask. I'm not sure where the question came from, but it's out there now. I can't take it back.

'Does that worry you?' Her tone is one of interest rather than reproach, so I give her an honest answer.

'I don't know.'

She smiles. 'That's my answer too.'

The door beside us opens and out comes Drake, holding Carlotta's jacket. She takes it and shrugs it on gracefully over her shoulders, smiling up at him all the while. She definitely looks like she's in love.

'Ms Valentine,' Drake says to me. 'I'll see you on Wednesday. Ten o'clock sharp, if you can manage to be on time for once.'

I roll my eyes at him. 'Yes, fine.'

Carlotta gathers me into her arms and kisses me on both

cheeks. I'm overwhelmed by the scent of her – exotic perfume and champagne – far too rich for my blood. It's a good thing I met Tabitha when I did, because I would be miles out of my depth with Carlotta.

'Goodbye, Jacquéline,' she says. 'I'm sure we'll meet again.'

As I watch them cross the road into their waiting limo, I catch myself thinking, *I hope not.*

The last person out of the club is the hostess. She gives me a wave as she climbs into a taxi, wiggling her diamond-encrusted fingers. Familiarity creeps across my skin. Even here in the street, she has the same overwhelming presence that she had on stage: commanding and striking. I have the strange sensation that I'm missing something, that I know her, that we've met somewhere before.

As the car door closes behind her, the breeze brings her scent with it, leaving me with a breath of sugary sweetness and old paper.

Then I'm certain: she was the shadow in the crowd.

I have no idea what that means.

'Right,' I say, storming back into the bar. 'Who's drinking?'

It's just the staff and the Seekers left now. The Invicti are long gone.

'We're closing up for the night,' says the girl behind the bar. She's human, and she can't be much more than eighteen.

'You guys stay for a drink after the bar shuts, though, right?' I ask. 'Have a little lock in, to celebrate the opening?'

'Well, it's really just for–'

'They can stay,' Windsor says to her, passing us on his way out. 'But no homemade cocktails.' He points his finger at me, so I guess he remembers the drinks I made at his party earlier this year. He doesn't want me mixing Massacres in front of the humans, as if I would. 'If you want something like that,' he says, 'Owen will make it for you.'

He nods to the other person behind the bar, a man with olive skin and dark hair who looks to be in his mid-twenties, but he's Silver, so who knows how old he really is.

'That's very gracious of you, Sir Percy,' I say, full of mock obsequiousness.

He ignores me and shakes Boyd's hand.

'Thank you, Deputy,' Windsor says, then he heads for the door.

'What the hell?' I ask Boyd when he's gone. 'Is that the same guy we interviewed in May? The same guy who was an utter arse, who sneered when we told him we were Seekers?'

Boyd shrugs, as confused as I am.

If I'd met Windsor for the first time tonight, I might have assumed he was a genial old duffer, tolerant and indulgent, but I know that's not who he is. I know he's the kind of person who'll serve up unconscious humans as unwilling blood donors at his parties, and who'll scam the conscious ones out of millions of pounds, then have them killed. So why the sudden affability?

'Fuck,' Naia says, hauling herself up onto a barstool. 'That was a complete shit show, wasn't it?'

'I don't know,' Cam says. 'I thought it was fun.'

'Right,' I say. 'Fun. You didn't have to deal with Benedict, and Drake, and every other fucking thing that happened tonight.'

'Plus, the bar was on fire,' Naia adds. 'How was that fun?'

'We put it out pretty quickly,' Cam says. 'No one got hurt. Not seriously, at least.'

'But one of the not-seriously-injured was the deputy's new *human* girlfriend,' Naia says.

Boyd groans.

'She's never going to go out with me again.'

'*That's* what you're worried about?' says Naia. 'If one of us had brought a human you would have told the captain on us. What's happened to you?'

'Give him a break,' I say. 'He's obviously new to the whole girlfriend thing. You can't expect him to get it right first time.'

That winds Boyd up, just as I intended. He's so easily provoked.

'I'll have you know,' he says, 'that I have had several girlfriends.'

Which makes us all laugh, because he says it as though dating *several* women over a centuries-long lifespan is an impressive accomplishment. Don't feel too sorry for him; it's our job to keep him humble.

'Anyway,' he says defensively, 'I wasn't the one being chatted up by a film star. Why don't we talk about that?'

'Why don't we not?' I suggest pointedly.

But there's no escaping it. I can see Naia's eyes lighting up and know I'm about to be grilled for sordid details. Which I'll probably tell her, because it's been a shit night and I need to tell *someone*.

I turn to the barman.

'Line them up, Owen,' I say. 'Things are about to get messy.'

7

I WAKE UP the next morning with a heavy head and bloodshot eyes. That's a first for me. Not the hangover – even as a Silver I've had enough of those, yesterday being a prime example – but the red eyes are new. And this hangover is bad enough that my eyes stay red even when I stand in front of the mirror and stop hiding my silver, the one physical sign of my inhumanity.

All of the Silver have it: the silver threads following the veins in the whites of our eyes. But we suppress it when we're in public. It's a technique that every new Silver learns as soon as possible, though it can take some decades to master. I was lucky in that respect. After only a few weeks, I could make myself appear completely normal. If I'd known that I could hide my silver simply by getting rat-arsed on Owen's cocktails and letting the redeye take over, then my early days as a vampire might have been easier.

Today, however, is going to be extremely hard. I drag myself out of bed, through the shower and down to the conference room for the results of the autopsy on District Judge Mitchell.

Tabitha didn't come home last night. I guess she must

have gone back to Nash Lee, but when I messaged and called to check she'd got there safely, she didn't reply. I've been pissed off about that because it seemed unnecessarily petty, but when she walks into the conference room this morning I'm so happy to see her alive and well that I can't sustain my anger.

I smile at her. Although she doesn't smile back, she looks me in the eye and twists her mouth in a way that means *I'm sorry*.

My heart is full. We're going to be okay.

I'm not sure I can say the same for the rest of my team, though. The captain isn't here today, so it's just the four of us. Everyone who was drinking last night looks about as good as I feel, bloodshot eyes all round. Owen mixes a fierce cocktail.

'I have good news, and I have bad news,' Tabitha says to us.

'My brain is trying to escape from my skull right now,' Naia says, rubbing at her temples. 'I can't handle any more bad news.'

'It looks like I had a lucky escape last night.' Tabitha laughs and Naia grimaces at the sound. 'I guess I'll start with the good news, then. The cause of death was easy to pin down once I ran toxicology. She died from cardiac arrest, likely preceded by seizure and apnoea, and caused by an oral solution containing several poisons, including cyanide. It attacks the mitochondrial electron transport chain. She was probably dead in seconds. I suspect the discolouration we saw on her skin – the spider-webbing – might have been a side effect caused by increased venous haemoglobin oxygen saturation.'

God, I love it when she uses science words.

'The bad news,' she goes on, 'is that there's no way to tell for sure, because the Mortuary Service got hold of the body first, and by the time they finally released it to me the discolouration had disappeared.'

'What?' Cam asks. 'How?'

'Who knows? If it was caused by blood under the skin, as I suspect, then it could have dissipated over time. If it was something applied to the skin, then I have no idea. Maybe they wiped it off and didn't want to own up.'

'Didn't Ed get some samples from her face?' I ask Cam. 'I thought he took them at the crime scene.'

'I'll give him a call.'

Cam gets to his feet, pulling his phone from his pocket. While he steps outside, Tabitha finishes running through the autopsy. There's not much else to note, except for the stomach contents: porridge, fruit and coffee.

'Ed should have the results by the end of the day,' Cam says as he joins us again. 'You were saying something about porridge?'

'That's the thing,' Tabitha says. 'Time of death was Tuesday morning, not the previous night. The food in her stomach was her breakfast.'

'But no one at the court saw her leave on Monday night,' Naia says. 'No one saw her at all after her last hearing.'

'Just because no one saw her,' I say, 'that doesn't mean she didn't leave.'

'So you're suggesting that she crept out of the court on Monday night,' says Naia, 'then crept back in again to leave her handbag there?'

'Maybe she just wasn't noticed,' Boyd suggests. 'If you see the same people coming and going every day, how easy is it to overlook them? Either way, we know she was in the office early on Tuesday.'

'Because of the note in the camera,' I say. 'You think it

was telling the judge to meet whoever wrote it at eight in the morning, not eight in the evening?'

'Could be,' Boyd says. 'The library opens at nine.'

'Did your girlfriend tell you that?' Naia teases.

'Yes. She did actually.'

Boyd's reaction is not what I expected. He should be getting riled up at Naia's tone, but instead he looks slumped and defeated.

Naia's brow crinkles. It's no fun when Boyd doesn't play along.

The mood in the room shifts.

'How is she?' Cam asks.

'She's fine,' Boyd says. 'I think.'

'Have you spoken to her?'

'She won't pick up the phone,' Boyd admits. 'I went by her place last night to check on her–'

'Slightly stalker-ish, maybe?' I say.

'I didn't knock on the door or anything. I just waited outside and listened to her heartbeat and breathing until I could be sure she was all right. She didn't even know I was there.'

'*Very* stalker-ish,' I amend.

'Not now, Jack,' Cam says.

I shut up and let him deal with it. He's better at this stuff anyway.

While Cam does his counsellor routine, Tabitha moves around the table and leans in to whisper in my ear.

'Have you got a minute?'

Judging that it's going to take more than a few minutes for Cam to put Boyd back together again, I follow Tabitha outside into the corridor.

'So,' she says.

'So.'

There's an awkward pause. It goes on for long enough that I start to wonder if she's ever going to break it. Eventually, she takes my hand.

'I'm sorry,' she says with a regretful smile.

I hadn't realised how tightly wound I was until that moment. As she speaks those magic words, all the tension runs out of my neck and shoulders.

'I'm sorry, too,' I say, bringing her hand to my lips so I can kiss her fingers.

'It's just that I worry, hen. I worry about him.'

'You think I don't? He's a bastard.'

'I think he's worse than that, and I see the way he looks at you. With the pheromones last night–'

'He was with *Carlotta Arden*. I'm sorry. I didn't mean to upset you, and I hope you know that I would *never* do anything about it, but she's *Carlotta Arden*. I've had a crush on her forever. Whatever pheromones were swirling around, Drake had nothing to do with them.'

'I know you think that.'

'No, I *know* that.'

Tabitha shakes her head, frustrated.

'I just wish you could see him the way I do.'

'As a self-important prick?'

'No, hen.' She squeezes my hand. 'As a threat.'

She gives me a look that begs me not to dismiss this, but I am so sick of rehashing the same argument. We've been over this so many times that I'm not sure how many of Tabitha's concerns are real and how many are fuelled by paranoia. It's all getting blurred into a mess that hangs between the two of us and there's nothing I can say to make it go away. Every time I think I'm finally rid of it, it comes rushing back like flotsam returning on the tide.

'Is this why you spent all of last night dancing with

another woman?' I say.

'You mean Yolande?'

'Whatever her name was. The hostess with the blonde hair,' I say, trying and failing to keep the grumpiness from my voice.

Tabitha smiles like the cat who got the cream.

'Why?' She leans in. 'Were you jealous, hen?'

'Of course I was jealous.' I put my hands on her hips and pull her closer. 'I was supposed to be the one dancing with you.'

'But you wouldn't.'

'I *couldn't*.'

'Because you were too busy flirting with *Carlotta Arden*.'

'No, because I was working. I tried to go after you, but Benedict shouted me back to my post. I would have danced with you if I could have. And you know that, which is why you decided to torment me, you minx.'

She puts her cheek against my shoulder and wraps her arms around my waist.

'I'm sorry,' she says. 'It was childish. Can you forgive me?'

'I forgive you.' I press a kiss into her hair. 'Tabby?'

'Yeah?'

'Do you think we'll ever be able to put him behind us?'

She pauses for too long before she answers.

'I don't know,' she whispers.

It hurts. I don't want to lose her over this. I'm about to say as much, but then Cam sticks his head out of the conference room and calls me back in.

'Assignments,' he says. 'We need you.'

'Okay,' I say. 'Be there in a minute.'

Tabitha has already pulled away, fumbling in her bag for her car keys.

'Will I see you tonight?' I ask.

'Sure, hen.' She kisses me lightly on the lips. 'See you later.'

I watch her walk away with a curdling sensation in my stomach. Everything is going wrong, and once again it's all Drake's fault.

Nora Mitchell's house makes me sad. It's clearly worth an awful lot of money because it's a detached building only ten minutes' walk from the centre of Oxford – someone must have levelled three terraced buildings to put up this monstrosity – yet the inside is underwhelming. The furniture is old and looks hand-me-down, but in the "no one else wants this" way rather than the "prized family heirloom" way. There's a ratty brown sofa in the sitting room, a plastic-topped table in the dining room that's covered with coffee-cup rings and cigarette burns, and the bathroom is an avocado nightmare. On top of all that, the place is dirty. Really dirty.

'Wow,' Cam says as we let ourselves in with the judge's spare key, 'you'd think she could afford a cleaner.'

'You'd think she could afford some standards.'

'That's rich, coming from you.'

It's true that I'm not the best housekeeper in the world, but at least there aren't rodent droppings scattered amongst the clothes on my floor.

'It doesn't look like she spent much time here,' I say, picking my way up the stairs around the obstacle course of books, clothing, mouldy cups and abandoned post that Nora Mitchell has left in her wake. 'Didn't she have a family?'

'Not according to the captain,' Cam shouts up from the kitchen. 'Never married, never had kids, never seemed interested in either. Oh my god. Do *not* come in here.'

'Ugh. Don't come up here, either.' I've just found the bedroom. The sheets are dirty, the whole room stinks of stale sex and latex, and there are used condoms stuck to the carpet. 'She might not have settled down, but it looks like she had one hell of an active sex life.'

Which isn't a criticism – I'm sex-positive – I just don't want to have to wade through the aftermath.

In the end, we work through each of the rooms together, because the horror of facing the judge's rubbish dump alone is too much to handle. We open all the windows, then hold our breath as we dig in, starting in the bedroom.

'The detritus of human sex is revolting,' I say.

I'm wearing gloves, but the cesspit on the judge's carpet is so disgusting that I'm still holding each piece of evidence at arm's length.

'Makes you glad we don't have to bother with this anymore, right?' Cam says, putting yet another condom in a plastic bag. The DNA testing on this lot is going to keep Ed busy for a while.

'Tell me about it.'

I'm not prissy about old people having sex. Hell, most of my friends are older than the judge was when she died, but there are limits. You clean up after yourself, at least. With her bedroom in this state, I'm surprised she managed to convince anyone to sleep with her in it.

'You don't think this was just one bout, do you?' I ask.

'No.' Cam looks thoughtful for a moment, then counts the specimen bags we've collected so far. 'No. No way. A weekend, maybe, at a push.'

'They would have needed a lot of lube.'

Cam picks up a couple of empty tubes and flourishes them at me.

'They had a lot,' he says.

I whistle, impressed. The judge must have had the sex drive of a porn star. A Silver porn star.

'Good on her,' I say. 'Naia is going to be so pissed off that she missed this scene.'

'I would gladly swap with her.' Cam peels the last condom off the carpet. 'In fact, I'd pay good money to have her here right now instead of me.'

I sympathise. We spend the rest of the day picking through drifts of paper and clothing, finding such treasures as moth-infested coats, mouldy knickers and a furry husk that used to be a mouse, but nothing that ties the judge to the Silver. The only evidence that seems relevant to the case is, typically, in the very last place we look.

At the very top of the house, in a room that looks like a study, there's a stack of photographs hidden at the back of a drawer.

'Oh, god,' I say, cringing away as I get my first look at them.

'What have you found?' Cam abandons the boxes at the other end of the room and comes to look over my shoulder. 'Oh. Right. More penises.'

They are not the most attractive specimens I've ever seen.

'We should show them to Naia,' I say.

I only meant it as a joke, but it's the first thing Cam does when we get back to the college.

Naia grabs the stack and flicks through them with prurient interest.

'I recognise that one,' she says, stopping at a photo that's so graphic it makes me wince. 'I think his name was Magnus Dick.'

'Oh my god.' I gape at her. 'You really do have a mental dick Rolodex.'

'Why would you call it a "mental dick Rolodex",' she

says, 'when *Rolodicks* is right there?'

It takes a while for Cam to get himself back under control.

'Anyway,' Naia says when the laughter has died down, 'I'm just messing with you. I don't actually have a built-in penis recognition system. But these do all look like they're the same guy.'

'Really?' I ask. 'How can you tell?'

'He's got a mole, see? Right here.'

She points to an area I'd rather not look too closely at, which is exactly why I missed it. She's right: there's a mole.

'Have you got the print-out from the camera we found on her desk?' I ask Cam.

He riffles through the stack of photos and comes up with the one I'm after. All three of us crowd around it, looking for the telltale mole. Naia spots it first, because of course she does. When she points at it triumphantly, the accurate scaling of the photo makes it look as though she's really touching *it*.

Rather her than me.

'A boyfriend, then?' I ask. 'If they're all the same guy?'

'Looks like it,' says Naia. 'Well, I'm off to dinner. My work here is done.'

'No, it's not,' Boyd calls from their office across the corridor. 'You've still got your share of the judge's case files to go through.'

'Fuck,' Naia mutters. 'I hate paperwork.'

One of the best things about being a Seeker is that there's usually not much of it. No reports, no files, no nothing. All we have are a couple of hard drives with information on the people we're keeping an eye on, and the people we've put away. But we still have to look through other people's files when they become the subjects of our investigations. This case has been an education in all the tedious shit we don't have to bother writing down. There's so much pointless bureaucracy in the judge's files that I'm surprised she ever had time for a social life. No wonder her house is such a tip.

'Let's go take this lot to Ed,' Cam suggests, hefting our evidence bags. 'We need to pay him a visit anyway. He can run the DNA results, and maybe then he'll be able to put a name to the mole.'

'And a face to the—'

'Yes.' Cam interrupts. 'Thanks.'

A day spent sifting through used condoms hasn't made him any less of a prude.

<h1 style="text-align:center">8</h1>

ED'S TESTS ARE still running when we get to the lab, so Cam and I leave our evidence bags with him and call it a night. The next morning, it's our turn to sift through the paperwork while Boyd and Naia go out in the field.

'I take it back,' I groan. 'I didn't want to swap places with Naia yesterday. I'd happily dredge through all the used condoms in the world to avoid another minute of this torture.'

'You're such a drama queen,' Cam says. 'Drink your coffee. Make it to eleven, and I'll get you a pastry and some blood.'

'I'll need it to heal all the paper cuts. These files are vicious.'

'Just get on with it, will you?'

I sigh and turn back to the court papers, but it's like wading through treacle. Thankfully, my eyes are better today – silver-threaded as usual, and no longer throbbing with yesterday's hangover – but I'm still struggling. This isn't what I'm built for. There's a reason I never made it to university, besides the whole getting-turned-into-a-vampire thing. I hate sitting behind a desk.

When Boyd and Naia come back at lunchtime, I'm ready to throw myself on their mercy, but before I can start pleading Boyd beckons us into their office. Naia checks the corridor before slipping inside and closing the door behind us.

'News?' Cam asks.

'News,' Boyd replies.

'Good news, I think,' Naia says.

'We went back to the Rad Cam.'

'That's my nickname,' Cam says with an impish grin.

'Sure it is,' I snort-laugh. 'Maybe back in the seventies, doofus.'

'What would you know? You weren't even born then, young 'un.'

For someone who's hundreds of years old, Cam is far more of a kid than he should be. It's like he never grew up. I love it.

'As I was saying,' Boyd goes on, glaring at us both, 'we went back to the Rad Cam and asked around. Quietly, while the head librarian was out.'

'You went behind Mildred's back?' I ask.

'Of course not.' Boyd seems affronted by the suggestion. 'I told her what we were doing and asked her to make up a reason to leave the library for a bit.'

Cam and I exchange a look. This isn't the Boyd we know. Normally, he wouldn't think twice about lying to a witness. This sudden change in attitude can only mean one thing: he's got it bad.

'So everything's okay with you and Mildred now?' I ask.

'Everything's fine. We met up last night.' He's trying – and failing – to hide his smile.

I'm not sure how to feel about this. I'm pleased for the deputy, because it's nice to see him happy for once in his life, but I'd be lying if I said I wasn't concerned. Human and Silver just don't mix. I'm living proof of that.

Boyd is lost in his own little world, staring off into the middle distance with a misty look on his face. Naia rolls her eyes. Apparently we're on the same page.

'If we can get back to the point,' she says. 'We found a witness.'

'To what?' I ask. 'The murder?'

'No, we didn't get that lucky. But apparently one of the assistant librarians lost his keys a few weeks ago. He didn't want to report it, because he thought he'd get fined, so he's been using the spare set ever since.'

'That's not really a witness,' I say. 'Sure, it explains how someone could have got into the library out of hours, but how does it help us to find them?'

'There's more. On the day he lost his keys, the assistant librarian left his bike outside the library. As he was locking it to the railings, another guy came and chained up his own bike alongside it. Somehow, they got tangled together, and they spent some time sorting that out. The whole encounter was friendly and jokey, he said, so he didn't think anything of it until we asked him.'

'Sounds like a genius,' I say.

'Properly naive,' Naia agrees. 'It never occurred to him that he'd been pickpocketed, but he still remembered enough to give us a brief description of the guy. He was lightly built, with soft features and a punky hairstyle, wearing a retro coat.'

'That's all we've got?' Cam asks.

'That's all.'

'No other witnesses? No CCTV footage?'

'No. The cameras don't cover that part of the square.'

'Then why the whole cloak and dagger routine?' I ask. 'If

all we have is a crappy description, then why were you being so shifty when you brought us in here?'

They're both being far too serious for what seems like an unexciting piece of evidence.

'We suspect the pickpocket is the murderer,' Boyd says, spelling it out for us, 'so we know they're Silver. Can you think of anyone we know who matches that description?'

Cam gets there first.

'No,' he says. 'He wouldn't.'

'Who?' I ask.

'Quentin,' says Naia.

I hadn't even considered him, because who would? He's a Seeker, in Ellie's team. Sure, he has a punk hairstyle – a pink mohawk earlier this year, now a blue undercut – and an inclination towards vintage couture, but he's also completely harmless. A little feckless too, truth be told. Earlier this year, he was investigating a disappearance that I suspect is linked to Windsor's clandestine parties. Unfortunately, Quentin botched the case by mishandling the blood samples, so we'll never know what really happened. That was down to incompetence, though, not duplicity.

Despite his intimidating appearance, Quentin wouldn't hurt a fly. He wouldn't have the balls.

'No,' I say. 'It must be a mistake.'

'I hope so,' Boyd says, 'but for now, we need to keep this between us. The assistant librarian's coming in tonight – to give an official statement, he thinks – and we'll make sure he gets a good look at Quentin. Until then, you stay on the paperwork while we go back to the court. We'll talk to the judge's colleagues and see if we can track down any friends or relatives.'

'Other than the captain,' Naia says.

'Other than the captain.'

'Can't you just look up the judge's contacts in her phone?' I ask.

'No,' Naia says. 'It's weird. The call log's been wiped, there's not a single text message, and there are no numbers saved in her contacts.'

'She's not on social media, either,' Boyd chips in. 'It's like she's trying to live as far under the radar as possible.'

'Makes sense,' I say, thinking about all the damning evidence I saw in the court files I read this morning: print outs of text messages, call logs, tweets. 'When you spend every day watching people get caught out by conversations recorded on their phones, I guess you learn to be cautious.'

'Still, it seems a bit excessive,' Boyd says.

'Unless she had something to hide,' Cam suggests.

'Maybe.'

It feels like there's something we're missing, but if the judge had a reason to play it safe, then we haven't found it yet.

I'm falling asleep at my desk looking through the eleventy-billionth court file when my phone rings.

'Thank Christ,' I mutter, grateful for the interruption. 'Hello?'

It's Ed.

'I've got your results,' he says.

'We're on our way.' I hang up and say to Cam, 'How'd you like to check out some sperm?'

'You're revolting.'

'No, I just know what you like. Are you coming, or what?'

Thankfully, by the time we get to the lab there's no sperm in sight. Instead, Ed is flicking through a file that he's placed precariously close to the Bunsen burner. A corner of paper catches as we walk in, which he douses absentmindedly with his sleeve.

'Blood or semen?' he asks, his attention still on the file.

'What?' I say.

He looks up. 'Do you want to start with the report from the blood on her face, or the semen in the condoms?'

'Oh, I don't know. Surprise me.'

'Blood it is, then.'

In stark contrast to Tabitha's lab, Ed doesn't keep the high-tech kit out front. Instead, he packs all the machines into a back room and leaves the crucibles and distillation columns on display. It's all very mad-scientist aesthetic, but it's not very practical. When he wants to show us results, there's no screen on which to display them. Instead, he has to nip out into the room of beeping technology and collect print-outs to show us. The man suffers for his vanity.

'If you remember,' he says, spreading the crime scene photos on the bench in front of us, 'a blood-like substance had settled into the wrinkles and fine lines of District Judge Mitchell's face.'

'Is that what it was?' I ask. 'Blood?'

'Yes. Here.' He points to a close-up showing the crazy-paved pattern of blood lines. 'I've tested the substance, and it is indeed blood.' He hands over a sheet of data that I can't decipher. 'To be specific, it's her blood. Nothing special, nothing noteworthy. It's just… blood.'

'What?' Cam takes the report and scans it. He's spent enough time with Ed over the years that, unlike me, he understands a little of the science. 'That doesn't make sense. You're not seriously suggesting that someone sat next to her body and spent hours painting blood into the creases of her skin?'

'It wouldn't have taken hours if it was a Silver,' I say. 'Maybe minutes for a Silver. And we know a Silver killed her, or we wouldn't be here.'

'No, we know a Silver *attacked* her, to leave the violence mark,' Cam points out, being uncharacteristically pedantic. He's only ever like this around Ed. 'Anyone could have given her the poison that killed her.'

He's technically correct. I don't think it's likely that the poisoner and the attacker are different people, but I can't argue with his logic.

'Poisoning committed by a Silver would still leave a violence mark, you know,' Ed says, looking between the two of us. 'It's a violent act. But anyway, I'm not suggesting that the blood was painted on. If it had been, I'd expect to see brush strokes, or errors. If you look closely at this photo–' He pushes it forward. '–you'll see it looks more like the blood settled there on its own.'

'But how?' I ask.

'Well, I gave Dr Ross a call, and our best guess is haematidrosis.' I don't pay enough attention to memorise the new word. 'It's a condition that ruptures the capillaries feeding the sweat glands, essentially making you sweat blood. If the judge suffered from the condition, then the diluted blood could have settled into the lines of her face after her death, resulting in the patterning you saw. It's the best explanation we have for you right now, but the condition is incredibly rare, and we haven't been able to prove the judge had it. It would also be strange for the reaction to be concentrated on her face, but not impossible.'

'What causes it?' Cam asks.

Ed refers to his notes.

'It's triggered by extreme physical or mental stress, which causes an overreaction in the nervous system, resulting in the haemorrhaging.'

Hearing Ed talk like this just makes me miss Tabitha. She

got called away last night before we could eat dinner; the Invicti had a body they needed her to look at. I kissed her goodbye and tried to be cheery about it because fine, it's her job, but I don't have to like it. I don't trust the Invicti, and I don't want Tabitha away from me right now, not when things are so precarious between us.

Why hasn't she called?

I wish she were here, telling us all this instead of Ed. I'm willing to bet that the explanation he just gave was hers, word for word, written down to relay to us.

'And that's all I have on the blood,' he says. 'It's a bit of a mystery, I'm afraid. Do you want to hear about the semen?'

'Cam is *dying* to hear about the semen,' I say.

He glares at me, and I ignore him. It's payback for his pedantry.

'Okay,' Ed says, 'well, you'll be pleased to hear that the semen results are much more conclusive. Here's the big news: there's more than one DNA profile.'

'More than one partner, then?' I ask.

'I'm guessing not. Every sample contained the same mix of DNA, which means…'

Ed loves science so much that he wants us to get as excited by it as he does. He has his encouraging face on right now, urging us towards the conclusion he's already drawn. He knows the answer, but he doesn't want to tell us. He wants us to guess it.

All of my guesses are more than a little NSFW. I'm not completely naive; I've heard stories about the biscuit game. But thankfully, Cam has put the pieces together to make a more palatable picture.

'Her partner was Silver,' he says. 'The different DNA profiles are a mix of his most recent meals.'

'Correct,' Ed says with a grin.

This is the problem with investigating scab cases: DNA is basically useless to us. The Silver don't have their own DNA profile. After we're turned, we become a chimaera of all the DNA we consume through the blood we drink. If you take a sample of Silver blood – or any other bodily fluid, apparently – you'll find the most recent donors. If you take a tissue sample, you could find DNA profiles from blood we've consumed years previously, depending on when that part of our body was last regrown. Our bodies use the blood we consume to patch us up.

'I can be more specific, too,' Ed goes on. 'I'd speculate that all of the samples you found were produced in a single, um, session, because the mix is the same in each. Even if this Silver has a set of regular donors, he'd have to consume their blood in exactly the same ratio to make samples from different times match. Just a single bottle of the kind of blood we get in the canteen would skew the profile, and give a different mix.'

'So,' I say, 'a marathon bonkfest?'

'I'm not sure I'd use those exact words, but yes. Someone had a very dirty weekend.'

'But,' Cam says, 'why would a Silver use condoms? That doesn't make sense.'

'It does if the judge thought he was human,' I say. 'That makes perfect sense. This is the connection, Cam. This is why she was killed. She was fucking a Silver guy, and she didn't know what he was. Who knows what she could have walked into? Judging by the state of her bedroom, I'd say he was a guy with weird sexual appetites. Maybe he was into snuff. Or maybe it was a sexy accident.'

'An accidental poisoning? During sex?'

'People have weird kinks. Ask Naia.'

'Not that weird,' Cam says. 'Plus, if it was an accident

then there'd be no violence mark. All we know is that she was in some kind of a relationship with a Silver man.'

'But who?'

'I'm afraid I can't help you there,' Ed says. 'You're going to have to find him yourselves.'

Just when I thought we were getting somewhere.

One step forwards, two steps back.

The assistant librarian comes to the college that evening. Cam and I meet him in the lodge and escort him to the meeting room we use for interviews, making sure that we bump into Boyd and Quentin in the corridor before we leave him inside with Naia.

Boyd watches the librarian's eyes.

'Not even a flicker of recognition,' he says to us when Quentin has left. 'Quentin's in the clear.'

'Phew,' says Cam. 'Well, that's a relief. Finally, something in this case has gone right. Since it's Friday night, how about a drink to celebrate?'

'I'm not sure it's good news,' Boyd says. 'We still can't identify the pickpocket.'

'But at least it wasn't one of our own, right? That would have been awful.'

I nod, but my mind is elsewhere. I'm thinking about the photos of Captain Langford and Benedict together. I'm thinking that maybe the captain needs allies within the Seekers as well as outside them. Then I'm thinking how convenient it was that Quentin mishandled blood evidence on that one case, of all cases.

It feels uncomfortably like conspiracy.

As I follow the others to the bar, I'm questioning everything. Am I overreacting? Probably, but it's like the song says: just because I'm paranoid, doesn't mean they're not after me.

9

WE DON'T NORMALLY get time off when we're in the middle of a case. In this job, we might have weeks on end when nothing happens at all, so when an investigation is open we're expected to work solidly until it's closed.

But, just occasionally, the planets align in such a way that we're mid-case with nothing to do. This is one of those times. The reality is that we've hit a dead end. We can't identify the man the assistant librarian saw at the Rad Cam, and anyway he might be completely irrelevant. The only thing that ties the judge to the Silver is the condoms, but the DNA in them is useless to us. We've been through all the case files the court gave us. We've talked to everyone we could find who knew the judge, and until we get her call logs, we won't be able to track down anyone new.

We're stuck until something shakes loose.

Ed spends the weekend in the lab going over the samples again in the vain hope of finding something he missed. The rest of us are waiting for the phone company to release the judge's call records, and for the court to send over some of her older files, but neither of those things is going to happen until Monday. That leaves us in limbo, half-heartedly picking over the information we already have in an attempt to see the case in a different light.

It's a bloody boring way to spend Saturday and Sunday, particularly since my evenings are empty; Tabitha's still out of town working for the Invicti.

I don't like that. I don't like it one bit.

I can't wait for the weekend to be over.

Boyd's waiting for us when we get into the office on Monday morning.

'Cam, Jaqueline,' he says. 'In here, please.'

He opens the door to the conference room and ushers us inside. He and Naia are both grim-faced and tense.

'What's up?' I ask. 'Is everything okay?'

Naia hands me a file.

'One of the older cases from the court?' I ask, flicking it open.

'They came over first thing this morning,' Boyd says.

'But Nora Mitchell isn't listed as the judge on this case,' I say, confused. 'Why did they send us this?'

'Read the name of the applicant.'

'Enid Carlisle Langford.' *Captain Langford.* 'Shit.'

I skim through the details on the application form, then hand the file to Cam.

He flicks through the first few pages, then looks up and says, '*Shit.*' His face is pale.

'Have you spoken to her yet?' I ask.

'We were waiting for you,' says Boyd. 'I thought we should do this together. Come on.'

He leads us out of the room to the end of the corridor, then knocks on the captain's door, but he doesn't wait for her reply before opening it.

'What's this?' she asks as we troop inside.

Boyd drops the file onto her desk.

'Why did you lie to us, Captain?' he asks. 'You must have known we'd find out.'

She opens the folder, takes a cursory glance to confirm its contents, then lets it fall shut again with a sigh.

'Because I knew it wasn't relevant,' she says. 'I had nothing to do with Nora's death and I didn't want you to waste time investigating me when you should be out there tracking down the real killer.'

'You didn't think it was relevant?' Boyd asks, his tone verging on insubordinate. 'You applied for contact with your descendants' children. You said you didn't care about your human family. You said you'd never met Nora Mitchell. But she opposed your application.'

'I know what I said. Look, perhaps you'd better sit down,' the captain says to us all. 'This might take a while to explain.'

We do as she suggests – Boyd reluctantly – dragging chairs out from around the small table in her office. She waits until we're settled before she begins, as though we're small children gathering around the campfire for a ghost story.

'Nora was the children's aunt and guardian,' the captain says. 'So yes, I met her. I knew her quite well, actually.'

'Did she know what you are?' Boyd asks.

'Of course not. It would have been irresponsible to tell her.' Her tone is snippy and sharp. It makes me wonder whether she feels the judge's death more keenly than she's letting on. 'In any case, we hadn't been acquainted long enough for that to become necessary.'

'How did you meet?'

The captain places her palms flat on the desk in front of her, as though she's drawing strength from the wood. It's an incongruous gesture from someone who's usually so unflappable.

'I've always kept track of my family,' she says. 'First it was because I wanted to know where they were so I could avoid them, particularly my former husband, but over the centuries I just… wanted to make sure they were all right. I never truly intended it, and I was never intrusive, never part of their lives, but I was there. Sometimes, on a Friday night, I'd find myself unexpectedly in the same tavern as one of my children. Twenty years after my grandchildren were born, I was travelling north when I was overcome with tiredness and decided to rest early for the night. It turned out that I had stopped in the town to which my eldest grandchild had moved. He was the innkeeper who rented me a room.

'After that, I was no longer surprised when I came into the orbit of my descendants without consciously deciding to do so. They have my blood, so I'm aware of them. I suppose that phenomenon must have been documented once upon a time, but there are so few of us with direct blood descendants. There was always a fashion for turning people Silver in their youth, before they had children, and that persisted. Perhaps the interconnectivity of our races has suffered for that.'

'And Nora Mitchell?' I ask, keen to avoid wandering off into the past. I don't like the captain's nostalgic tone.

'I never approached her,' she says, 'but I watched from a distance. That sounds voyeuristic, I know, but I suppose it had become a compulsion by then. I just wanted to know that she was safe and well. Her and her sister.'

'The children's mother?' Cam asks.

'That's right. Andrea Mitchell. She never married, but she had twin girls: Sydney and Melbourne.'

I wince, because those are two of the most burdensome

names I've ever heard. The English are not forgiving to children whose parents get creative on their birth certificates.

'I know,' the captain says, with a long-suffering sigh. 'Apparently they're the two places they might have been conceived. Maybe. Andrea was not particularly responsible. She didn't know who the girls' father was, either – or if she did, she never said – so when she died in a car crash when they were only twelve, Nora became their guardian. Then everything went downhill. You've been to Nora's house by now, I assume?'

Cam grimaces. 'Yes.'

'Then you know why I was anxious about the girls living with her. How she chose to live was her own business, but it wasn't right to raise two small girls in that environment. I tried to stay out of it. I didn't want to interfere, especially since Nora had made some effort to clear up the house before the girls arrived. She seemed to be balancing her work as a barrister with parenting the girls. The social worker was satisfied, so who was I to object? None of them even knew who I was. It wouldn't have helped if I'd turned up out of the blue and started demanding that Nora changed the way she was raising them. So for six months I kept an eye on them, constantly on the edge of intervening, but things didn't ever seem bad enough. Then Nora's work dried up and she had to switch specialisms. Suddenly she was working around the clock, and Sydney and Melbourne were turning up late for school in dirty uniforms. Nora could afford cleaners, she could afford babysitters, but she was so neurotic about having strangers in her house that she wouldn't hire help, and everything went to shit.'

The captain is spitting the words now. She's usually nothing less than professional, so when she starts swearing we know she's *really* angry.

'I couldn't just sit by,' she goes on. 'My own daughter was just two years old at the time, my Silver daughter, but we had space. We could have taken care of Melbourne and Sydney, and I knew we'd look after them a hell of a lot better than Nora would. The problem was that I couldn't exactly tell the court I was their mother's several-times-great grandmother. The only option was to pretend a relationship with the girls' father – I said I was his sister – then fabricate the DNA evidence to support my case. It meant breaking every single rule I put in place for myself about interacting with my family, but those girls needed me. What choice did I have?'

'But it didn't work,' Naia says. I guess she and Boyd had time to read the entire case file while they waited for us.

'It didn't,' the captain replies. She slumps forward, her head propped up in her hands. 'I didn't want to go to court. I thought it would be difficult for the girls, and I was there to make their lives better, not worse. So I introduced myself to Nora, showed her the evidence I'd prepared, and asked if there was anything I could do to help. Maybe I could see the girls one day a week, or help with the school run, or look after them over the holidays? But she was instantly defensive. She didn't want anything from me. I tried for a year, through letters and emails and knocking on her door, but she wouldn't budge. She was stubborn like that.'

'So you went to court,' said Boyd.

'It was the only option left. I think it would have worked, too, but Nora knew the judiciary. She knew the law. She knew exactly how much she had to do to keep custody of the girls, and she made sure she did it. Maybe I would have managed to get visitation rights at least, or shared custody, but she played the system, spinning the case on with delay after delay. By the time we were ready to go to the final hearing, the girls were sixteen and more than able to shift for themselves. By then they were keeping Nora's house clean, getting themselves to school, doing the laundry, handling everything while Nora worked. They looked after their aunt as though she were their responsibility, and not the other way around. And they were protective, too, because over the years she'd poisoned them against me. They told the court they didn't want to see me or have anything to do with me, and the court decided they were old enough to make that decision if they wanted to. I never met them. And I never spoke to Nora again after that final day in court.'

'And the girls?' Boyd asks.

'They're in their twenties now. Sydney stayed in Oxford, but never made much of herself. She's living in shared housing, working at pubs and doing too many drugs. She only visited Nora when she needed money. Melbourne lives in Nottingham with her husband. They run a tech company together. She had an argument with Nora about five years ago and, as far as I know, they hadn't spoken since.'

'Do you know what they argued about?'

'The past. Apparently, some memories came back in therapy, and Melbourne finally realised what a neglectful parent Nora had been.'

'And you know this because...?' Naia asks.

'Because I happened to be in the area when they met to discuss it.'

Naia looks at her skeptically, turning the captain's signature eyebrow back on her.

The captain sighs pointedly.

'I am the captain of the Seekers,' she says. 'If I weren't curious and nosy, this is hardly the profession I would have chosen for myself. Of course I followed them closely after the trial. Of course I wanted to see Nora get her comeuppance. That doesn't mean I delivered it to her, or that I wanted her dead. When you first spoke to me about Nora's murder, I said I didn't care. That was a lie. I cared deeply, but I pretended otherwise because I didn't want anyone to go digging around and find out about Melbourne and Sydney. I'm trying to protect them. I've kept my family safe for centuries, and now Nora's murder has drawn the Silver's attention to them, which was the last thing I wanted. That's why I would never have done anything to harm Nora, whatever personal disagreements we had. Whatever else she did, however selfish she was, she was family too.'

We're all quiet for a moment, processing the captain's story.

Personally, I think she's been a high-handed idiot. In her centuries of existence, she must have seen her family in far worse situations than Melbourne and Sydney's. They had a roof over their heads, an aunt who loved them and money to feed themselves. The less-than-sanitary conditions of Nora Mitchell's house hardly seem to warrant an intervention like the one the captain launched against the judge. If the kids were happy, why disrupt their lives with a protracted court case? It seems like a vanity project to me. I'm guessing the captain saw the opportunity to overstep her bounds, and jumped at it.

She's always been a control freak.

'I believe there's a fact you overlooked, Captain,' says Boyd. He seems even less moved by this sob story than I am.

'And what is that, Deputy?'

'This is a record of your relationship with them,' he says, leaning over to tap the case file. 'It's in the system. If someone wanted to get to you, all they'd have to do is look at the court record.'

'Don't be ridiculous. They don't make the details of

family cases public.'

'No, but how hard would it be for a Silver to find them? I bet you had court correspondence by post. If someone was intercepting your mail, or trawling through your recycling, they'd have all the evidence they needed to link you to Nora Mitchell and her nieces.'

'I don't think that's likely,' says the captain. She's smiling, but it's obvious her patience is wearing thin. 'Do you really think I would have kept my position this long if I were stupid enough to leave my papers unsecured?'

'And what about Nora Mitchell?' he persists. 'You spent enough time visiting and writing to her that someone might have realised you were connected. You know what her house was like. Do you think she was as careful with her paperwork?'

We all know that a grenade could have exploded in the judge's house and she wouldn't have noticed the debris.

'It was years ago,' the captain says. 'If they knew that Nora was one of my descendants, why would they wait all this time to make a move? It doesn't make sense.'

'The Silver have long memories,' Boyd says.

The captain eyes him for a moment before making her decision.

'All right, Deputy,' she says, handing him the file. 'Do what you have to do. You'll have my full cooperation.'

'What now?' I ask when we're back in the corridor.

'We sift through the captain's life,' Boyd says. 'Every detail, every piece of correspondence, and we keep going until we find out who had a reason to go after her and, by extension, the judge.'

Cam's phone rings.

'Yeah?' he answers.

There's a moment of silence. He has the volume turned down too low for me to eavesdrop, even with my Silver hearing. It reminds me of my gaffe with Drake on Wednesday. I should probably adjust the volume on my phone.

'Now?' Cam is saying. 'Okay, sure. We're on our way. See you there.'

He hangs up and turns to me.

'Ed's got something,' he says. 'Something big.'

'Big how?'

'I don't know, but whatever it is, it's big enough that he didn't want to say over the phone. Come on, he's waiting at the lab.'

Ed is pacing when we arrive, fiddling with the pocket of his lab coat as he does so. For once, he doesn't seem excited by the science he's about to impart to us like a generous benefactor. Instead, he's tightly-wound and nervous.

'What is it?' Cam asks him.

Ed licks his lips.

'I don't know how you're going to feel about this,' he says. 'I found a fingerprint.'

'What? Where?' Cam asks.

'On one of the condoms.'

'Oh. Ew.'

Ed grabs a sheaf of papers from the nearest lab bench and worries them as he talks.

'I went back to check over the DNA samples to make sure I hadn't missed anything,' he says. 'One of the, um, receptacles had a smear on the outside where part of the, er, sample had dried.'

'Oh god.' I groan as the memory of the reek of the judge's bedroom comes rushing back. 'I am so glad I don't have your job.'

'I took the print,' Ed says, ignoring me. 'And I got a hit.'

That gets our attention.

Fingerprints have been a thing for a very long time now. Every idiot criminal knows that if you want to hide your identity while indulging in some crime, then you wear gloves on your hands, or socks if you're clever and don't want the police asking why you're carrying gloves in warm weather. Widespread knowledge of fingerprinting techniques has pretty much wiped them out as effective forensic tools, so the Seekers don't often look for them, and rarely find them. Ed keeps a database, but it's almost never useful.

Hence our surprise. This is the first time we've had a useful fingerprint on a case in years. So, of course, Ed is drawing out the moment.

'Well?' I say impatiently. 'Spill it.'

He grimaces. 'I have a feeling this is going to get messy.'

'Messier than the bagful of used condoms you've spent the past few days wading through? Just get on with it.'

'Windsor,' he says, holding out the papers. My mouth drops open as I take them. 'Sir Percival Windsor.'

10

EARLY THE NEXT morning, Boyd drives me out to Aston, the sleepy Cotswolds village where Windsor has his family pile. Given how long he's been alive, I wouldn't be surprised to learn that he'd had the house built himself. Any wealth he inherited would have passed to him centuries ago.

'This place again,' I say as we pull up.

The mansion is enormous: an edifice of pale stone sitting in a lake of gravel that makes up the drive. It's big enough to hold about fifty cars, which is necessary given the number of attendees Windsor's parties pull.

Last time I was here, Drake and I were tumbling into the back of his car together in the darkness, more drunk than we should have been, covered in the scent of each other's marks.

A lot's changed in the past four months.

'Before we go in,' Boyd says, 'there's something I need to talk to you about.'

'Oh?'

My stomach drops, because I think he's going to ask for advice about Mildred. That's a conversation I don't want to have, because I know he won't like hearing what I think: he should stop seeing her.

But it turns out that he's not thinking about Mildred at all.

'I was clearing out my office, getting rid of the old financial papers on the Grant case,' he says.

David Grant was murdered back in May. Initially, we thought his death was something to do with Windsor's parties because there was a fortune missing from Grant's accounts. As it turned out, his death had nothing to do with Windsor or the money.

'You remember them?' Boyd asked.

'You mean the accounts of the shell companies Grant used to embezzle money from his company?'

'That's right.'

I had a theory that Grant was using that money to pay off Benedict and buy his way into turning Silver. I still think that's what the money was destined for, but it's not where our investigation led. Instead, Grant was killed by Gabriella De Palma, the Silver friend of an opera singer he'd raped. She took the money and gave it to his victim, which was fine by me, but not by Seeker law. Drake boxed Gabriella for a year as punishment for endangering the secrecy of the Silver. We never got to the bottom of the shell company accounts.

'I thought I'd just check on them,' Boyd goes on, 'tie up the loose ends, you know.'

'And?' I say.

'They've been cleaned out and shut down. All but one: Silver Services Ltd. It looks like it bought the others out, consolidating everything into one company.'

'Okay. What does that mean?'

Boyd shrugs. 'Maybe whoever's behind it is getting ready for something. I thought you should know, particularly since the Tertius is due at the office today.'

'He is?'

'A follow-up from the opening night at Crimson. He's

meeting with the captain.'

'I bet he is.'

Boyd doesn't know what to say to that. I haven't shown him the photos Drake sent me of Benedict and the captain together. None of my team gave serious weight to my suspicions about Benedict and the con he was running at Windsor's parties. Unlike me, they didn't see it with their own eyes. They accepted there was something fishy going on, but wouldn't go so far as to denounce the Tertius, and didn't want me to rock the boat. I understand that, even if I can't sympathise.

'Anyway,' Boyd says as we get out of the car, 'I thought you'd want to know.'

'Thank you. I appreciate that.' I make sure he knows I mean it.

Boyd rings the doorbell. A minute later, a man opens the door, human. From the way he's dressed, he's obviously the butler, but not the same one who was working for Windsor in May.

'Mr Boyd and Ms Valentine, to see Sir Percival,' Boyd says.

'Do you have an appointment?' The butler's supercilious tone tells me he knows we don't.

'He'll see us,' Boyd replies, with more confidence than I feel.

Two minutes later, Boyd is proved right when the butler returns to lead us into a large sitting room with a wide mantelpiece and leather chairs. I know it's not a public part of the house, because it wasn't open during the party I attended. Windsor's not just inviting us in, he's allowing us access to the inner sanctum.

It smells of wet dog.

'Mr Boyd, Ms Valentine,' Windsor says, getting to his

feet. He's wearing a tweed suit, of all things. I heard they treat the wool with urine to soften it, which – if true – would be satisfying because I hate him, and appropriate because Windsor's messy hair is the exact colour of weak piss.

'Sir Percival,' Boyd says, shaking Windsor's hand. I clasp mine behind my back to make it clear I won't be doing the same; I know where Windsor's hands have been.

'Well,' he says. 'Won't you take a seat? Thank you both for your assistance at the grand opening last week, without which I am certain it would not have run smoothly.'

'Several humans were injured,' I say, remaining standing while Boyd sits, 'and the bar was set on fire.'

'A little bit of drama, but nothing too serious. What is any social event without a little drama? It's only to be expected. Can I offer either of you a drink?' He clicks his fingers for the butler, then waves him away when we both decline.

I am bewildered. If I thought Windsor was being uncharacteristically friendly at the opening of Crimson, then this is on another level entirely. Last time Boyd and I rocked up here wanting to ask questions, he wouldn't even let us in the house. He called us "new blood", sneering like we were no higher up the evolutionary ladder than earthworms. On the drive over here, I assumed we'd have to tell the butler about the judge's death, then have him shuttle messages back and forth between us and Windsor before the honking posho would admit us to his hallowed premises.

His friendliness makes me suspicious. I don't believe centuries-ingrained elitism can vanish overnight. If he's suddenly treating us like people rather than maggots, there must be a reason for that.

'Tell me,' he says, 'how can I help you?'

He smiles, showing off teeth that are too white. I'd swear they didn't look like that last time we met.

'We're investigating a scab murder,' Boyd says. 'We've come across evidence that ties you to the victim, District Judge Nora Mitchell.'

The blood drains from Windsor's already-pale face.

'Nora?' he says, his voice croaky and raw.

Either he's the best actor I've ever met, so good that he can pantomime his body's stress responses, or he genuinely didn't know. That's an unwelcome surprise.

'She was found in the Radcliffe Camera early last Tuesday morning,' Boyd continues.

'A week ago?' Windsor blinks rapidly, incredulously. 'You found her a *week* ago?'

'You didn't know?' I ask.

'No.' He rubs a hand over his face, dragging his sallow skin tight. 'I wasn't expecting to see her until next weekend. With the launch of Crimson, she knew I was going to be busy.'

'No one told you what happened?' Boyd asks.

'No one knew we were seeing each other. I was worried for her. I thought if people knew that she was important to me, then it would put her in danger. I didn't want anything to happen to–'

His words are choked off by a sob. It seems to catch him unaware, taking his breath in a hiccuping gulp of sorrow that's so ugly it's hard to doubt. He seems entirely sincere.

'You didn't arrange to see her at eight in the morning last Tuesday?' I ask once he's got his breath back.

'No. No, I didn't.'

'How long had you been seeing each other?'

'Three months.' Windsor's voice is cracking with emotion. 'I've never been interested in anyone for more than a week, then Nora comes along and…'

He wipes a tear from his cheek. At this point, I would

swear by any deity in the world that his grief is genuine. Boyd looks at me, a cue for me to produce the camera and ask Windsor the last thing I have ever wanted to ask anyone.

'Sir Percival,' I say, clicking the camera on and turning the screen to face him. 'Is this your penis?'

His face flushes red.

'Yes,' he says. 'She… Nora is – was – remarkably liberal. Sexually, I mean. She enjoyed receiving photographs.'

'And you took this one for her?' I ask, pushing him to be explicit.

His eyes flick back to the camera screen for a moment before coming to rest on the floor. He's much more prudish about this than I expected. For someone so unapologetically brash and rude, he's surprisingly English about sex.

'Yes,' he says. 'I took that photograph for Nora. She took it, actually. That's her camera.'

'And did you take this one too?'

I click back to the previous photo, the one of the handwritten message saying "meet at 8".

'No,' he says, his brow creasing into a field's worth of furrows as he squints at the camera's tiny screen. 'That's not my handwriting. Is that what happened?' He looks at me. 'Did someone lure her to her death with this message and a photo of my… my–'

'It's a theory,' I say, cutting him off. I don't want to know what pet name he's given to his penis.

'And what about these?' I ask him, flicking back through the candid shots of the judge walking around Oxford city centre.

'No. I didn't take those, either. But…'

'But?'

He shakes his head and mutters, 'It's a game we played. Sometimes. Only here or at her house, not out on the street.

She liked it when I followed her with the camera. She enjoyed being stalked as a prelude to… Well, you can use your imagination.'

I'd really rather not, but apparently Naia's now living in my head because my brain is throwing up all sorts of images I don't want to see. Thankfully, Boyd takes over the questioning and gets us back on track.

'And the Radcliffe Camera,' he says. 'Was that somewhere you'd been together before?'

'She liked the books.'

'Out of hours?'

'It was a game, Deputy,' he says, blushing even redder. 'Sexy librarian, you know.'

I guess that strikes a chord with Boyd, because he has to clear his throat before he can carry on.

'Yes,' he says. 'I see. How did you access the library?'

'We hid in the stacks while they were closing up. It was part of the game. We'd wait until the librarians had finished their circuit of the Gladstone Link, then nip down there to hide while they cleared the rest of the library. Then we had the Camera to ourselves.'

'And how exactly did you get out afterwards?' I ask.

'We'd make our way back through the Link to the Bodleian Library and leave with the last of the staff. One of them is a friend.'

'But you never met there in the morning?' Boyd asks.

'No. Never. We talked about it, but Nora liked the night.'

Windsor smiles at the memory, then looks down at the carpet, the smile sliding off his face like butter off a hot plate.

'Did she ever talk about her family?' Boyd asks.

Windsor looks up, blinking. 'She didn't have one. She was single. Until I came along, that is. I mean, no one else would live in that house. I call it her hoard. Called it. She could be a bit of a dragon when she didn't get her way.'

'Did that happen often?'

'Not around me. Believe it or not, I liked to make her happy. She was a remarkable woman.'

His bottom lip starts wobbling, so I know our time is running out.

'Her mobile phone had been wiped,' I say.

'Yes,' he sniffs. 'That was because of me. She did it regularly. I wanted her to be careful. We kept things very hush-hush. We never went out in public, and I never let the Silver see us together. This won't surprise you, but I've made some enemies amongst our number.'

'You astound me.'

'Yes, well, those of us agitating for change are never very popular.'

'You don't strike me as an innovator, Windsor. From what I saw at that little party of yours, it looked to me like you and your friends were holding onto the past with everything you've got, trying to bring back the glory days of elitism, sexism, racism, and all the other isms.'

'My friends don't speak for me, Ms Valentine.'

His mask is slipping. For a fraction of a second, I see a flash of the Windsor I know behind the courteous front he's presenting. He's more than a little pissed off. Or is he just upset? Now that I'm seeing a softer side to him, I'm struggling to parse his emotions.

'If you have any more questions,' he says, 'perhaps you could ask them another day. I've just found out that my lover has died and I'd like a little time to myself.'

'Of course,' Boyd says.

'Good. Thank you. You can see yourselves out, can't you?'

We watch him bumble out of the room, cowed in his tweed and looking for all the world like a man who just lost the only person he's ever loved.

We're both a little shaken as we crunch across the gravel to the car.

'That was surprising,' Boyd says.

'I suppose even bastards like Windsor have feelings. Who knew?'

'Everyone has feelings, Jacqueline. It's just that some people think theirs are the only ones that matter.'

'You're very philosophical today, Deputy,' I say.

'No more than usual.'

'Well, he didn't seem to know about the judge's history with the captain. Or the girls.'

'He didn't seem to know anything helpful at all.'

We get into the car and strap in. I don't even try to argue for the driver's seat, because I know Boyd won't let me have it. He says I'm reckless and irresponsible and generally acts like the geriatric he is when I'm behind the wheel.

Killjoy.

'What next?' I ask him as he turns the car around.

'We'll need to talk to Sir Percival again. In the meantime, we'll dig into the captain's life and hope that throws something up. We should have the phone records–'

'Wait!'

The butler comes running out of the front door, waving his arms to attract our attention. Boyd stops the car.

'What's this about?' he asks me.

I shrug and roll down my window.

'So glad I caught you,' the butler says, out of breath. He hands me a large brown envelope through the car window. 'This arrived this morning. Sir Percival only just opened it.

He asked me to bring it straight to you, and he also asked me to give you this.' He passes me a piece of paper with a telephone number on it. 'He apologised for his abruptness earlier. He's had a shock. He's retired for the day, but he wanted me to assure you that he will make himself available from tomorrow for any and all further questions you might have. Just call this number and he'll present himself at your convenience.'

'Thank you,' I say, a little overwhelmed with the properness of it all.

'My pleasure.'

The butler bows and walks back to the house.

'Did he just bow at us?' I ask.

'He did.' Boyd looks as shocked as I feel.

I open the envelope as we drive away.

'Well,' I say, 'I can understand why he came running out here.'

'What is it?'

Despite the tantalising clue in my hands, Boyd's eyes stay resolutely glued to the road. It's a point of pride with him that his driving is never less than perfect.

I wave the page in front of his face just to piss him off. He bats it away.

'There's a photograph of the judge's body printed on A4 paper,' I say. 'And there's a note scribbled underneath it that says "this was your fault". It's written in red ink.' I sniff the page. 'No, scratch that. It's blood.'

'Interesting,' he says, but evidently it's not interesting enough for him to pull over and take a look.

'If this is genuine, then I think Windsor might be the better lead here, Deputy.'

'Convenient that he's being so accommodating, then.'

'It is, isn't it? What do you think the charm offensive was

about?'

'I don't know, but it was costing Sir Percival to maintain it while we were in there. He really doesn't like you, Jacqueline.'

'I know.' I grin, feeling smug that I managed to rile Windsor out of his performance.

'Just be careful,' Boyd cautions. 'He's a bad enemy to have.'

'Pfft, whatever. People say that about all my enemies.'

'We need his help. You could be less provocative.'

'Could I, though?' I ask.

I know I'm winding Boyd up now, because his fists are tightening around the steering wheel. Probably time to dial it down a bit.

'Did you believe him?' I ask.

'Yes.'

'Me too. Much as I hate him, I don't think he killed the judge. He's not that good an actor.'

'He seemed very upset.'

'Hmm.'

Boyd isn't wrong, but I don't want to admit the possibility that Windsor might be grieving. If he truly cared for Nora Mitchell – a human – then I'll have to reassess all my assumptions about him, which is inconvenient and, frankly, annoying. I'd like to keep him in the box where I've put him.

'People are too complicated,' I say aloud.

'Tell me about it,' Boyd says. He speaks quietly, muttering to himself, so I know he's thinking about Mildred.

'There is one thing we could all learn from this,' I say.

'What's that?'

'Relationships between humans and Silver don't often end well.'

'We've just agreed that Sir Percival had nothing to do

with Nora Mitchell's death,' Boyd says. His tone is shirty, because he knows this isn't about the case. It's about Mildred.

'No, we haven't. All we agreed was that he wasn't the one who killed her. I'm not trying to piss on your bonfire, Boyd. I'm just worried about you. Dragging humans into our world puts them in danger. Look at what happened to me. And look at what happened to the judge. Windsor may not have killed her, but given how many people want to screw him over, I think it's a good bet she was killed because of him. Don't you?'

I can see the muscle in his jaw moving as he clenches his teeth together.

Eventually, he says, 'Perhaps.'

He's quiet for the rest of the drive. That's fine with me; I've said my piece. It's up to him now.

11

'NEWS?' CAM ASKS when I walk back into our office.

He's spent the day digging into the captain's court case. There are five lever-arch files filled with papers, and someone has to read them all. Cam drew the short straw.

'The good news,' I say, dropping gracelessly into my chair, 'is that we have positive identification on the penis.'

'Oh.' He screws up his face. 'Well, I guess that is good.'

'But the bad news is that we've both touched Sir Percival Wanker's sperm.'

'Wearing gloves,' Cam says, horrified. 'Not with our actual hands, Jack.'

'Still. I'm going to be having nightmares for weeks. Also, I pissed Boyd off about the Mildred thing. I told him it wouldn't end well.'

'It probably won't, but if he wants to find that out for himself then it's his decision.'

'Is it, though?' I say, shrugging off my leather jacket. 'He's putting her life in danger, just like Winta endangered mine twenty years ago. He's a little less deliberate than she was – I mean, I don't think he has any firm plans to go biting her anytime soon – but you can't expect me not to draw parallels between him and Mildred, and Windsor and the judge. She has no idea what he is, so can she really consent to this relationship?'

'And if he wanted to tell her? What would you say then?'

'That it's a fucking bad idea. We'd have to take him into custody and drag him up in front of Drake for breaking the secrecy pact.'

'So he can't win either way, is what you're saying. If he's finally found someone he cares about, and he's careful, then I don't see the problem. Live and let live, I say. He can't control the way he feels.'

'That doesn't make it right.'

'It doesn't make it wrong, either.'

'Yeah, yeah,' I say. 'Be Mr Reasonable if you want, but we're never going to agree on this. Any news on the files?'

'Nothing you want to hear. Everything the captain said adds up, but there were a few details she missed out.'

'Like?'

'Like the fact that she collected the kids from school without permission on more than one occasion, each of which was reported as an abduction.'

'But she said she'd never met them.'

'She lied.'

'Oh, god.'

I wonder if this is the time to tell him about the photos of the captain with Benedict, but before I can come to a decision, he passes me a file.

'It gets worse,' he says. 'The judge applied for a restraining order against her.'

'Excuse me?'

'You heard.'

'Jesus Christ.' I slump in my chair. 'What a fucking mess. Speaking of which, I should have shown you this the moment I walked in.' I send the photo from my phone to his. 'Sorry, got distracted by the sperm and the fact that our captain's a criminal, apparently.'

Cam stares at his phone screen.

'What am I looking at?' he asks.

'Someone sent it to Windsor. Boyd's taking it to the lab now. The writing is blood.'

'The judge's blood?'

'Maybe. I guess Ed will be able to tell us.'

Cam stares at the photo on his phone a little longer, then he squints and brings it closer to his face.

'There's something in the background. Did you see that?'

'The picture is crappy resolution,' I say, coming around the desk to peer over his shoulder. 'What are you seeing that I'm not?'

'There,' he points to his phone screen. 'It looks like her handbag, but you found that in her chambers at the court, didn't you? This photo was obviously taken in the Rad Cam. Look, you can see the bookshelves behind her.'

None of these details were obvious on the paper copy. Maybe it's something to do with the light, but somehow the picture is easier to decipher now it's been condensed to a smaller size. The minimised image resolves the details into clarity. The A4 print out was so pixelated that I didn't look beyond the body, but on the small screen I can see not only the judge's handbag behind her, but also its contents.

'That's her digital camera,' I say, pointing to the screen. 'You can just make out the edge of the lens.'

'She brought it to the library,' Cam says, voicing the inevitable conclusion. 'She brought her handbag and the camera.'

'Then after she was dead, someone delivered them back to the judge's chambers, leaving them in plain view to be found,' I say. 'Which makes no sense. If the killer had been trying to mislead the police, to make it seem as though she'd disappeared from work, then wouldn't he have made some attempt to dispose of her body? And if he wasn't trying to conceal the body, why not just leave the bag with it?'

'Maybe the killer was interrupted before he had a chance to hide the body,' Cam suggests. 'Maybe he just grabbed the handbag and ran.'

'But we're assuming that the killer and the person who moved the bag were the same person,' I say. 'We don't know that for certain.'

'Okay, but whoever moved it must have had a reason. Maybe the bag had something important in it, something valuable.'

'Like what?'

'I don't know. A key? Maybe it unlocked something in the judge's chambers. That would explain why the bag was taken back there.'

'But we searched her chambers,' I say.

'How well?'

I sigh.

'You want me to go back to the courthouse, don't you?' I say.

'Yes, please.'

'But this is all just conjecture, Cam. I'm telling you, we searched that room.'

'Before you knew what you were looking for. You could have missed a hidden lock somewhere.'

I have to concede that, but then something else occurs to me.

'Did Ed check them for prints?' I ask. 'The bag and the camera?'

'After what happened with the condoms, he checked

everything. There were none.'

'But there should have been at least a few prints on them from the judge.'

'Someone wiped them down,' Cam says. 'Someone wiped everything down, then posed the bag and its contents on her desk, arranging the digital camera in the gift box like a present.'

'But it wasn't,' I say. 'Windsor said the camera was hers. It wasn't new. It wasn't a gift.'

'Then why do it?'

Neither of us can answer that question. That leaves us with only one option: we have to check the room again. I pull out my phone and call Faiz. After a few minutes of chit-chat, he promises to make the arrangements for a second visit to the judge's chambers.

'Okay,' I say after I've hung up. 'What next?'

'More questions for Windsor, I guess,' says Cam.

'Boyd and Naia are going back tomorrow morning for another interview. Apparently I'm a disruptive influence.'

'No!' Cam says in mock affront. 'Surely not.'

'I know!' I say, joining in. 'But for some reason, the deputy thinks Windsor will be more forthcoming without me there.'

'Probably fair. And of course, you'll be busy tomorrow morning anyway.'

'What? Why?'

I run through my mental list of things to do on the case.

Visit the courthouse – Faiz is going to call me back once he's arranged everything. There's nothing more I can do for now.

Look at phone records – We're still waiting for the phone company to send them through. I chased them up this morning.

Go through the judge's case files – Cam's on it.

Talk to Windsor again – Naia and Boyd are doing that.

And that's it. There's nothing I've missed.

'It's Wednesday tomorrow,' Cam prompts me. 'You've got probation with the baron?'

I groan.

'Don't tell me you'd forgotten,' he says.

'I was clearly repressing it. My psyche is protecting me from having to be in the same room as him. It's for everyone's benefit, really.'

'Except if you don't show up, he'll box you.'

'He wouldn't dare.'

Cam's lips twist into a wry smile.

'Are you absolutely, one hundred percent sure?' he asks.

The problem is that I'm not. I don't *think* he'd box me, but I'm not sure enough to risk it. If I want to skip probation tomorrow, I'm going to have to come up with a good excuse.

'I'll tell him I'm sick,' I say.

'The Silver don't get sick.'

'Then I'll tell him I'm hungover.'

'Even you can't get *that* hungover.'

'Then I'll tell him I'm dead.'

Cam laughed. 'Yeah, I'm sure that if you rang him up and told him that, he'd be totally fooled.'

'I meant *you* should ring him.'

'Nope.'

'Oh, come on, Cam. You can be my best friend.'

'I already am, and I don't see anyone else queueing up for that dubious honour.' He looks over his shoulder to demonstrate his point.

'Well,' I grump, 'then you're a crappy best friend.'

'Sucks to be you.' He grins. 'Because I'm the only one you've got.'

'Fuck,' I say, reclaiming my chair and thunking my forehead onto my desk. 'I'm going to have to go, aren't I?'

'Yup.'

Bugger.

'Cam,' I say, looking up at him. 'Before this thing with the captain goes much further, there's something I should tell you.'

'That doesn't sound good.'

'It isn't. Will you come with me?'

'Oh-kay.'

He pushes back from his desk, suspicious but intrigued, then follows me to my room. For once, I'm glad that Tabitha is out of town, because I know we'll have the place to ourselves.

'Sit,' I say to him, pointing at the sofa.

He makes himself comfortable while I go into my bedroom to retrieve the photos from the back of my underwear drawer. It's not a very original hiding place, but it works for me.

'Here,' I say, perching on the edge of the coffee table as I hand them over.

He doesn't rush through the photos like I did the first time I saw them. Instead, he looks carefully at the first, then turns to the second, and so on until he's exhausted the stack.

'That's the dart, isn't it?' he asks, flipping back to the most incriminating one: the captain handing Benedict the vial.

'Yes.'

'So the captain and Benedict are working together. Do you think the judge's death has something to do with it? That it's related to Windsor's parties and the unofficial turnings?'

'I don't know,' I say. 'Maybe, but I can't see a way to make it all hang together yet. It's messy as fuck.'

'You're telling me.' Cam looks at the photo as though he can unravel this whole case if he just stares at it hard enough.

'Maybe killing the judge was a way of threatening the captain,' I speculate. 'A way to make sure she kept her mouth shut. Or,' I say, considering it from the opposite perspective, 'maybe it was a favour to repay services rendered. Maybe the captain wanted the judge out of the way to clear her access to the children.'

'Either of those things could be true,' Cam says. 'Or neither of them. I thought we agreed that all signs were pointing to Sir Percival?'

'Who says they can't both be involved?'

'Shit.' Cam flicks through the photos one last time before handing them back to me. 'Where did these come from?'

I bite the inside of my cheek.

'What?' he asks.

'They came from Drake.'

'The baron?'

'Who else?'

Cam pushes a hand through his hair, making the dark blond strands stick up in unruly clumps.

'You know how you were just on your high horse about Boyd and Mildred, and how destructive their relationship could be?' he says.

'Ye-es.' I don't like where this is going.

'I don't want to sound judgemental or anything, but are you sure you can trust him as a source? You and the baron have a history of your own.'

'That has nothing to do with this.'

'Doesn't it? He has a habit of putting himself in your way.'

'You sound just like Tabby.'

Cam looks around my rooms, doubtless noting the

absence of Tabitha's stuff. 'Where is she, anyway?'

'She's working a case for the Invicti.'

'Uh-huh. How long has she been gone?'

'Not long.'

Cam sits up straighter, his ears pricking up at my dismissive tone.

'How long, Jack?'

'Coming up to a week.'

'Shit.'

'I know,' I groan.

I flop down on the sofa next to him.

'She says the same as you,' I say. 'She's worried about Drake. She thinks he's a threat to our relationship. You know she's looking into Silver blood drinking?'

'No.'

'Well, she is. Now that I'm stuck in probation with him every week, I think she wants to prove to me that he's a bad guy, and she's trying to use science to do it.'

'Using that time he attacked you?'

'Yeah.'

'Wow. What happens if she does?'

'What do you mean?'

'If she can prove to you that he wasn't acting under the influence when he hit you, what happens?'

I haven't even considered that possibility.

'I don't know.'

I accepted Tabitha's initial theory in May: that drinking my blood might have made Drake go off the deep end. It fit the circumstances too well for me to doubt it and, as much as remembering that night still makes me feel small and powerless, I don't believe that it was entirely Drake's fault. We were careless with the mark, and we got carried away. I should never have let him bite me in the first place, so it feels right that I am somehow to blame for what happened in that dark alley.

I'm more comfortable with the idea that I brought this on myself than I am with the idea that nothing I did made a difference either way, because at least that gives me some agency in the situation.

I want it to be my fault. I don't know what I'll do if it turns out to be his.

12

WEDNESDAY MORNING. TIME for my next sparring session with Drake. I think I've come prepared, but I'm wrong.

The first thing he says when I walk in is, 'Trouble in paradise?'

I'm immediately furious.

'Last week you objected that I brought Tabitha's scent into your office,' I say, stomping angrily to one of his leather armchairs. 'Now you're complaining that I'm not wearing her mark. Are you ever satisfied?'

'I wasn't complaining,' he replies.

'I don't know what you've got against her.'

'Don't you?'

That question is a trap. Whatever way I answer it, I'll be wrong and he'll laugh. I can see his intent playing around the edges of his mouth. Well, if he thinks I'm falling for it then he's going to be disappointed.

Lesson number one: give Killian Drake an inch and he'll take the whole damn ruler.

Time to change tactics. I sit up properly in my chair, knees together, ankles elegantly crossed and hands resting in my lap.

'Well, Baron, it's been a good week.'

I've never called him by his proper title. Not once. He is visibly shaken by this new development.

Lesson number two: give Killian Drake exactly what he asks for and he'll be so busy wondering what you're playing at that he'll never get to enact his own diabolical plans.

'I've not seen Mr Felton,' I say, counting my virtues on my fingers, 'I haven't set anyone on fire, nor have I threatened to disembowel anyone. I am also addressing my anger management issues.'

'Oh?' he asks, blinking as he adjusts uncomfortably to Compliant Jack. 'How?'

'Whenever I feel like murdering someone, I just smile sweetly at them instead. That way, when I do murder them, they'll never see it coming.'

'I see.'

He clears his throat.

'The flaw in your plan,' he continues, 'is that if you tell your targets about it in advance, you'll ruin the surprise.'

'But…' I gasp, flattening my hand against my chest in alarm like a Southern Belle. 'Surely, Baron, you don't think that you would ever be a target?' I try my best to sound horrified.

Then slowly, deliberately, I smile at him sweetly.

He laughs.

He actually laughs. He doesn't do that often, certainly not around me. He smiles a lot, sure, but not from genuine pleasure. His smile is normally filled with malice. This is different.

I can feel my advantage slipping through my fingers.

'Oh my god,' I say. 'It has emotions, just like a real boy.'

He leans forward with a smile.

'I have plenty of emotions, Valentine. Sometimes so many that I let myself get carried away by them.' His voice becomes low and intimate. 'But you already knew that.'

He looks pointedly at the desk. Four months ago, I was lying across it with his teeth in my neck. That might sound violent and invasive, but – to my eternal shame – it was one of the most mind-blowingly erotic experiences of my life. I can't linger on the memory for more than a split-second, because if I do then the pheromones are going to start pouring off me, and he'll have won. Again.

'Lust isn't an emotion, Drake.'

'Why not? You feel it, don't you?'

It sounds like an innocent question, but it's loaded with subtext. His gaze is dancing over my face, flitting down to my mouth. This is how he's trying to win today: he wants me to admit that I wanted him. I can only imagine his glee if he ever discovered that, even after all the shit he's pulled, I still find it difficult to sit opposite him like this and not think about his bite, about how it felt to be completely possessed by him. There's been more than one night where I've woken up moaning with the weight of that memory pressing between my legs. Even though it ended with him back-handing my face in an alley – the effect of the blood-drinking, maybe – I can't say I truly regret it.

But I can't let myself fall for this again. Once was enough.

'How are things going with Carlotta?' I say.

'About as well as they are with you and Dr Ross, from the sound of it.'

'There is *nothing* wrong with me and Tabby.'

'So you say.'

It's a seamless transition into pseudo-psychologist Drake. He sits back in his chair and picks up his fountain pen, turning it between his fingers like it's the world's tiniest twirling baton.

I hate that stupid pen.

'Your response is interesting, though,' he says.

'Why?' I grit the question out between clenched teeth.

'If you take a moment to think back over our conversation, you'll note that I never actually said things between me and Carlotta were going badly. I simply said our relationship was going as well as yours. You assumed that meant *bad*.'

I replay our conversation in my head.

Dammit.

How can I salvage this?

'I only *assumed* that you and Carlotta were on the rocks because fiddling with phallic objects is a sign of sexual frustration,' I reply, watching his hands. 'And you are fiddling with that pen *a lot*.'

He puts it away in the top drawer of his megalithic desk.

'Happy now?'

I shrug. 'Not really. I'm still stuck here with you.'

One of Drake's goons knocks on the door then pokes his head into the room.

'Sorry to interrupt, but could we borrow you for a moment, Sir?'

Drake stands from the desk. 'Excuse me, Ms Valentine.'

'Oh good. A reprieve.' I smile, starting to rise from my chair. 'See you next week.'

He points at my chair and says, 'Sit.'

'I'm not a dog.'

'I'm well aware of that. Even the stupidest of dogs responds to basic obedience training.'

I'm still wondering whether or not that's an insult when he walks out of the room, shutting the door behind him. I've never been alone in Drake's office before. Mostly I'm with the other Seekers: escorting a scab, or being reprimanded for some minor misdemeanour. Less commonly, it's just Drake and me: for these probation meetings, or when I've come to shout at him for all of *his* misdemeanours, in various stages of undress that I'd rather not dwell on just now. But being here alone is a real novelty.

I don't know how much time I have, but I'm not going to waste a second.

I jump out of my chair and nip around to the other side of his desk. There's nothing exciting in plain view, but there are three drawers on each side. They're in keeping with the size of the desk, which is to say that you could put a baby to sleep in any one of them and still have enough space for stationery and a pack of Hobnobs.

I have a cursory rootle through the top two on each side. There's not a chocolate biscuit in sight, but there are plenty of treasury tags. What kind of man prioritises treasury tags over snacks?

Things start to get interesting when I open the bottom drawers. Or, at least, the one that's not locked. It holds a rack of hanging files that slide back on their runners as I pull it open. They're full of innocuous nonsense – visitation permissions, financial records, building plans – but right at the back of the drawer, tucked away behind the files, is a bottle of very good whisky. I don't know much about scotch because I think it tastes like mud, but given that there's a well-stocked bar in the corner of the room I can only assume this bottle contains the sacred stuff Drake's not prepared to share.

Apparently he's the jealous type.

I'm guessing that the bottom drawer on the other side of the desk contains more hanging files, probably the juicier ones, but I can't get it open. I go looking through the top drawers for something to pick the lock with, or to jimmy it open, but all I find is more treasury tags. Who even uses treasury tags? They're the most boring paper-fastening tools known to man. Even a paperclip would be more exciting – and more useful for lock-picking, if I actually knew how to do that – but no, it's all treasury tags with Drake.

Finally, I locate a letter opener buried under a pile of post-it notes and wedge it into the gap between the top of the drawer and the desk frame. The lock is pitifully weak; all I have to do is slide the letter-opener sideways to unhook the latch. I can feel it starting to tumble at the same time as I hear footsteps coming up the corridor outside.

Drake is on his way back. Being caught breaking into his desk during a probation meeting doesn't seem like a great career move.

I scramble to my feet and stow the letter opener back where I found it in the top drawer, wishing I'd had just two more seconds, just enough time to force the lock and take a peek. The curiosity is killing me, but he can't be more than ten feet away from the door now. I'm out of time. I'm about to go back to my seat when something catches my eye, nestled in amongst the treasury tags.

Drake's fountain pen.

I don't even hesitate.

I'd like to say I had a purpose in snatching it, but it was pure petulance. It's already stowed safely in my bra while I silently close the drawers. When Drake opens the door, I'm sitting in my chair examining my fingernails as though I haven't moved an inch since he left. He raises an eyebrow at me as he returns to his desk; he's not buying it.

'Sorry to keep you waiting, Ms Valentine.' He looks at his blotter suspiciously, but everything is exactly as he left it.

'No problem. I hope nothing's wrong?' I ask sweetly.

'On the contrary.' He smiles at me with his shark's eyes. 'I've just received some good news.'

'Oh? What's that?'

The smile grows, splitting his lips apart to show his teeth.

'You'll find out soon enough,' he says.

'Fine. Be cryptic.' I feign nonchalance. 'Shall we get on with this meeting?'

'Of course,' he says. 'I am at your service.'

But the smile doesn't go away. This isn't like the laugh; I'm not sharing the joke. Whatever he just discovered, he's holding it over me for a reason.

I'm not sure I want to know what that reason is.

'How was Sir Percival Wanker?' I ask Naia on my return to the college.

'A fucking delight,' she replies.

She's sitting in the common room with a novel, her legs crossed over one arm of the loveseat she's hogging. She doesn't look up from the book. She has ridiculous powers of concentration, so she tends to get stuck in the zone like this.

'Did he say anything helpful?' I ask.

'We've got a list of people to check out. Nothing promising.' She turns a page and adds, 'I'm on my tea break.'

'Oh. Okay.'

I lean against the back of the chair, looking over her shoulder to see what she's reading.

'Romance?' I ask.

'Spy thriller.'

'Then why's everyone naked in this scene?'

'Sometimes spy thrillers have sex in them.'

'Oh. Like James Bond?'

Naia sighs heavily then says, 'What do you want, Jack?'

I'm not sure how to phrase my question. I've thought about it for the whole angry, half-hour march back here. The problem is that I'm not sure how to ask Naia for the information I need without inviting her to take the piss. In the end, I just dive straight in.

'I'm thinking of getting a tattoo,' I say.

'Oh?' she replies absently. 'What of?'

'A tabby cat.'

She puts her novel facedown on her lap, looking up at me with an expression that says, *Seriously?*

'I think it's a nice gesture,' I say, defensively.

'I think it's a collar around your neck,' she snorts. 'Is wearing her scent mark not enough for you?'

'I just think it gives the wrong message. What happens if she's away on a case? What happens if we're apart for more than twenty-four hours? She shouldn't have to be physically intimate with me to mark me, you know? It's not about that. It's about how I *feel*.'

Naia swings her legs down from the arm of the chair and stands up.

'I'm out,' she says. 'If you want to talk about your feelings, go and find Cam.'

'No, I'm sorry, I don't,' I say, urging her to sit back down. 'What I want to talk about is good tattoo artists. Do you know any? Who did yours?'

She gives me a long look, clearly judging me for my choices, but in the end I get the recommendation I need.

'I still think you should talk to Cam,' she says.

'Why?'

'Because it's pretty obvious that this decision of yours has more to do with the baron than it does with Tabitha.'

'That's ridiculous,' I say. 'Just because I want to do something to show my girlfriend that I love her–'

'Jack. Feelings. Stop.' She picks up her book and finds her place again. 'Go find Cam, I'm begging you, and leave me in peace.'

He's in our office, pretending to look through the court files while actually flicking through social media apps on his phone.

'Faiz called,' he says as I walk in.

'What? Why did he call you?' I'm a little put out. 'I was the one who put in the request.'

'Because I actually answer my phone.'

'Since when don't I?'

'Have you checked yours recently?'

I pull it out of my pocket and see that I have ten missed calls, all of them from Faiz. I had the stupid thing set on *do not disturb* for my stupid probation meeting. It's one of Drake's stupid rules, ever since the pizza incident.

'Oh,' I say. 'Right. What did he say?'

'He's ready when we are. We can go back to the court whenever. Like now,' he says, shoving away the court papers. 'Preferably now. Please.'

Cam is about as fond of paperwork as I am.

The cleaners have been busy in the judge's chambers. Every wooden surface is polished, every inch of window is shining and every book is stacked neatly on the shelves. The room wasn't particularly untidy before, but those small changes have rendered it not just empty, but obviously unoccupied.

'Here you go,' Faiz says, ushering Cam and me inside. 'Take your time.'

He sets the judge's handbag and all its original contents on her desk. Everything is still in evidence bags: her wallet, her keys, and her pile of revolting handbag detritus. We're hoping something in it might give us a clue.

'Sparse,' Cam says, looking around the room.

'I told you,' I reply. 'There's not much to search.'

'What exactly is it that you're looking for?' Faiz asks.

'He doesn't know,' I say.

'Yes, I do,' Cam replies. 'We're looking for a reason why someone would have brought her bag back here. I'm guessing there's a lock somewhere and the key is in her handbag, or maybe there's a password in her wallet for a file on her computer. Something like that.'

Faiz looks at Cam dubiously.

'There were no passwords in her purse. At least, none that I saw. And her computer login was "password1", so anything computer-related is probably out.'

'Then a key,' Cam says, no less determined.

I pick up the evidence bag holding the judge's keys.

'There's a lot of them in here,' I say.

In fact, there are more than twenty. That's not a surprise. We already knew the judge was disorganised, and disorganised people never bother to take old keys off their key rings. The bundle in my hand likely represents every item she's had to unlock over the past fifty years.

'Any small ones, like for a safe?' Cam asks.

'Lots,' I say, squeezing the bag to fan them out. 'I really don't want to know how many of these are handcuff keys.'

'Oh yeah,' Faiz says with a smirk. 'Naia told me about the judge's house.'

'Ugh,' says Cam. 'Don't remind me. Let's get the pictures off the walls and the books off the shelves. See if we can find a lock that fits.'

Half an hour later, the room looks like a rubbish dump and we're seeing nothing but bare walls.

'I hate to say it,' Faiz says, surveying the room with his hands on his hips, 'but this is starting to feel like a wild goose chase.'

'There has to be something here,' Cam says. He's feeling along the walls with his fingertips, desperately looking for a crack in the plaster. 'It's the only thing that makes sense. Why else would someone bring her handbag back here?'

'I'm sorry, Cam, but I wasn't convinced about the key theory in the first place,' I say. 'If someone wanted one of her keys, why bring the whole handbag back here? Why not just bring her key ring?'

'Because of this,' Faiz says.

He's been pawing through the handbag's contents, looking for another clue. Now he's holding up a small bag that's filled to the brim with gold chain.

'A necklace?' Cam asks.

'A keychain,' says Faiz. 'It was attached to her keys at one end and her handbag at the other. The lab unhooked the ends so they could fingerprint everything.'

'It still doesn't make sense,' I insist. 'No one would bring the whole bag if they could just unhook the keys from the chain.'

'But it's not that simple. Look,' Faiz says, showing us the ends of the chain. Each one is formed from a split ring. 'These things are tricky. If someone was in a rush, or had shaky hands, then it would have been easier to grab the whole bag rather than waste time unthreading the key.'

'But the key to what?' I ask.

We look around the room again, still seeing nothing.

'It has to be here,' Cam says, starting to tug up the carpet in one corner.

'Whoa,' says Faiz, rushing over to tread it back in place. 'I don't think I'll be very popular with the clerks if we just trash the place.'

'Come on, Cam,' I say. 'This is a council building.

They're not going to have a floor safe. Or a wall safe, for that matter. In fact…'

I look around the room one last time, trying to put myself in Nora Mitchell's shoes. If I were in my chambers and I wanted to hide something where no one would find it, what would I do?

I reject the filing cabinet; the clerks would be in and out of that all day. For the same reason, I reject the desk. There's only one place she could have been absolutely certain that no one else would ever bother to look.

'The books,' I say, going down on my knees to scrabble through the pile that we've emptied out from the bookshelves onto the floor. 'If I were Nora Mitchell and I wanted to hide something personal in here, I'd put it inside the most boring law book I could find.'

Faiz and Cam exchange a look, then join me on the floor. We aren't methodical. We should be, but hope makes us frantic, digging through the pile and tossing books aside at random. On the first pass, we find nothing. I'm ready to give up, but Faiz suggests we try again, this time re-shelving each book as we eliminate it.

I know I've found the right one the moment I pick it up, because it's far too light for its size.

'Guys,' I say.

They stop, our gazes locking over the book in my hands.

I flip open the cover, which is made from ancient blue fabric stretched over cardboard. It couldn't be more inconspicuous on the outside, but inside the pages have been hollowed out to make room for a small metal lockbox. I lift it out and place it gently on the judge's desk.

'Keys,' I say, holding out my open palm to Faiz. He pours them from the evidence bag straight into my hand.

The anticipation makes me breathless. The keys are cold

and heavy in my hands, and suddenly I understand the clumsiness that might have affected the person who brought the handbag here after the judge's death. Right now, I don't think I could slide a key off a split ring either.

Mercifully, by the operation of some kind of magic I can't explain, the very first key I select slides perfectly into the lock. It turns. Faiz and Cam crowd over my shoulders from either side, craning to get a peek at the contents as I lift up the lid.

We stare into the lockbox.

For a moment, no one moves.

Then Cam says, 'Oh.'

It's empty.

13

THE PHONE RINGS early the next morning. At least, it feels early, but my phone says nine o'clock.

'Yeah?' I croak into it.

It's Cam.

He says, 'Rise and shine, Jack.'

'What are you talking about?' I say, trying to pretend he hasn't just woken me. 'I've been up for hours.'

I don't want him to know that I did the clichéd detective thing again last night, drowning my sorrows in a bottle of gin mixed into a three-litre Massacre that I drank alone in the dark. It was not my finest hour, but I needed a bit of quiet self-indulgence.

I wish I could say I was disappointed by the lack of progress on the investigation and that it's my dedication to the job that's causing my blue mood, but the truth is that I have bigger problems than a dead judge right now. Tabitha still isn't home. She's sent me a couple of messages to let me know she's fine, that she's just caught up in this big case for the Invicti, but that feels like an excuse. It's been a week since I last saw her and I'm starting to wonder if this is her way of letting me down easy.

'Just get out of bed,' Cam says. 'We've had a call.'

'Did Ed get the blood results from the letter?'

'Yes, and the blood belongs to the judge, but that's not why I woke you up.'

'You didn't–' I start to protest, but he cuts me off.

'I mean we've had a *call*, Jack.'

Uh-oh.

'Apparently it's an accident,' he says.

I groan.

I hate calls like this. They make up about a quarter of our workload, but they're never comfortable. Some poor idiot gets carried away while drinking from a human, or their covert blood-drinking scheme goes wrong, and they call us. At least, they're supposed to. The other three-quarters of our workload is the ones who don't.

I prefer that work. The accidents are just depressing. At least with our usual work, we get the thrill of tracking down the perpetrator and bringing them to justice. There's some satisfaction in that. The accidents are nothing but death and regret. They remind me how inhuman we are, while at the same time how much of our humanity we retain. We are all so fallible.

'Meet me in the lodge in ten minutes,' Cam says. 'I suppose I'd better drive.'

The journey is torture. I regret last night's drinking each and every time he hits a pothole. By the time we arrive, I'm starting to believe he's aiming for them on purpose. Finally, he parallel-parks outside a small terrace of Victorian houses off the Cowley Road. Our destination is a cheery little house, if run-down, with a purple door and green window-frames. Unfortunately, it's also a house I know quite well.

'This is the place?' I ask Cam. 'You're sure?'

'Number twenty-three. That's what the deputy said.'

Shit.

I've been here tons of times, always drunkenly. It's one of those houses you end up at when the pubs have closed, but you're not quite ready to go to bed. It's better than most because firstly it's owned by a Silver, so you can drink blood openly here, and secondly any after-hours drinking is likely to continue beyond dawn. When we've finished a case and I need to wind down without the judgement of my peers, I'll trawl every pub on Cowley Road looking for the guy who owns this place, because I know he'll welcome me with open arms.

Not today, though.

We don't have to knock on the door, because it's already ajar.

'Hello?' I call as we walk in. 'Anyone here?'

'Sitting room,' Raul calls, his voice breaking. It might be the cigarettes or the booze, but I'm betting it's because he's in bits over what he's done. 'She's in the bedroom,' he adds.

We go there first. It's at the top of the stairs, a large master bedroom with an ensuite. The woman is on the bed, the sheet pulled up over her head. It's stained with blood. Cam reaches over and flicks the top corner down, revealing a gaping hole where her throat should be. It's not hard to work out what happened here. She stinks of Silver violence, but there's another mark here too: Raul's possessive scent mark. He kissed her before this happened, and it meant something to him.

'Fuck,' I murmur.

I go back downstairs to the sitting room while Cam calls the clean-up crew.

'Jack,' Raul says when I walk in. 'I was hoping it would be someone else.'

'Me too, mate,' I say, taking a seat next to him on the sofa.

'Me too.'

I've known Raul for years. He's one of those Oxford people you see around all the time, particularly if – like me – you tend to frequent places that serve a lot of alcohol. He's always skint because he doesn't just buy drinks for himself, he buys them for the whole bar. I like him. I like him a lot. We're close enough that seeing him like this is a real wrench.

'What happened?' I ask him.

'I don't know.' He has his face in his hands, so his words are muffled. 'We were having a drink. You know.'

'I know.'

We've sat together on this sofa more times than I can count, trying to prolong our drinking sessions because neither of us wanted to be alone. They say misery loves company, and that's what we gave each other. We both understand how it feels to be on your own in a crowd.

'Then this morning, I woke up and...' He gestures helplessly towards the bedroom.

'You mean you didn't do this?'

'No.' He rubs his face. 'I know I did. I remember parts of it, in flashes. I remember the hunger, the emptiness. It was me, but it wasn't *me*.'

I believe him. Raul's a big guy, but he's a total teddy bear. Everything about him is gentle, from the soft curls of his hair to his calming voice, to the shuffling way he walks. He moves through the world as though he's permanently stoned, worried that if he doesn't step smoothly then he might startle someone, or himself. He's just not the violent type.

'Tell me everything that happened,' I say. 'From the very beginning of the night.'

'I went to the Cape.' He means the Cape of Good Hope, a pub on the way into town. It's where he always starts the night. 'Then I ended up at the King's Arms. She–' He drops his head into his hands again. I think he's crying.

'Who is she?' I ask when he's settled down a bit.

'Rachael,' he mumbles into his hands. 'I only met her a few weeks ago. She's one of Dim's friends. You know Dim. Comes into the King's Arms sometimes.'

I have no idea who Dim is, but I nod anyway so as not to break Raul's flow.

'Anyway,' he says, 'she hangs out with us if we bump into her, and it always turns into a night. You know how it goes.'

I do, better than I'd like to admit. Before Tabitha, I had that kind of night far too frequently. The memories aren't all good. On that kind of night, when it's just you and the darkness with no inhibitions to temper you, it's easy to cross a line you shouldn't.

'Dim said Rachael liked me,' he goes on, 'and I kind of liked her too, but nothing was ever supposed to happen. I mean, she's human. Was human.'

I can see he's about to go over the edge, emotionally speaking, so I interrupt him there.

'You met up with her in the King's Arms,' I prompt. 'What next?'

'Then we decided to check out Crimson.'

'Wait,' I say, 'you mean the new blood bar on Park End Street?'

'Yeah. It's not my usual scene – they make you wear shoes, you know, no trainers – but I thought I'd check it out. That was a mistake. It's all flashy lights and glass and the vibe in there is *not* relaxing. We only stayed for one drink.'

'What did you have?'

'I asked for a beer, but the order got messed up so I had a blood drink instead. It was actually all right.'

'It just had blood in it?' I ask.

'Yeah, nothing but blood. Nothing else.' He fiddles with

his sleeve. 'Not then.'

Which means this story is about to get worse. I brace myself for it.

'Tell me what happened next.'

'We hit up a few pubs on the way home. The Half Moon, the Jamaican, you know. The late-openers. Then we came back here, and after that everything gets a bit fuzzy. I know we had some more drinks, because…' He gestures around at the sitting room.

It doesn't usually look like this. Raul's not a fastidious guy, but this morning the place is off-the-charts messy. There are beer cans strewn across the floor, full ashtrays on every surface and empty bottles of spirits lined up along the coffee table. It looks as though they didn't just come back here for a drink, they came back for a whole crate.

'How many of you were there?' I ask.

'I'm not sure. Just the usual crowd. Maybe eight?'

I look around the room again. This is a hell of a lot of booze for eight people to consume, even if they're Silver.

'How messy did things get, exactly?' I ask, my voice low.

He knows what I'm asking, and I know his answer before he says a word because his cheeks have pinked through his light-brown skin.

'Pretty messy,' he admits.

'You were drinking Valentine's Massacres?'

'Not in front of her, but yes.' He swallows, as though part of him is trying to drag the confession back. 'I had a few.'

His eyes lock with mine. They are bottomless. He's falling backwards into despair and I'm not sure I can catch him.

Here's the problem: blood and alcohol don't mix. When you drink them together, they make the Silver go a little loopy, which is why my namesake beverage is so much fun. It's also why you shouldn't drink it in an unsafe environment where humans are present. He knows that and I know that, but for some reason he didn't stop himself, and nor did anyone else.

Maybe if I'd drowned my sorrows in his company last night instead of at home on my own, none of this would have happened. I count the bottles again. More likely, I would have been too wasted to get in his way.

'You know you marked her?' I ask.

He rubs his eyes with the heels of his hands and says, 'Yeah. I don't remember doing that.'

'You remember going upstairs?'

'Not really. Fuck. I can't believe I…'

His voice breaks and I decide he's had enough for now. I need to get him out of here.

'Okay,' I say, reaching out to squeeze his arm. 'You hang tight. I'll be right back.'

I find Cam on the landing upstairs, taking photos of the bedroom from the doorway.

'Never seen an accident with a marked human before,' Cam whispers. 'That's new. Weird.'

I shake my head. 'This whole thing is weird.'

'Well, it isn't looking good,' he says. 'How well do you know this guy?'

'Well enough. This isn't him, Cam. He's not denying that he did it, and he was definitely a bit battered last night, but I've seen him when he's wasted and this isn't it. He's a happy drunk, not a violent one. And he's gentle. I'd be less surprised if someone told me you'd done this.'

'But he did do it?'

'That's what he says.'

Cam gives me a long look, then says, 'I'm sorry, Jack.'

It doesn't matter what I think of Raul, or how well I know him. He killed a human. These things happen in our blended society, however well-meaning the individuals involved might be, but that doesn't mean they can just be forgiven. It's Raul's fault for getting drunk, for mixing alcohol with blood when a human was present, and for losing control. All we can do now is collect the evidence and deliver him for sentencing.

That obligation weighs me down.

'I'll take him to see Ed,' I say. 'Can I leave the scene to you?'

Cam nods. 'I'll call Naia and the deputy. We'll finish up here and meet you back at the college. You take the car.'

He hands me his keys.

Raul is silent as I steer him out of the house and into the front seat. When he remains silent on the drive, I start to worry that he's gone catatonic.

'Are you okay there, Raul?'

He breathes out, long and hard, then says, 'Not really. I liked her, Jack. I never meant to—'

'I know you didn't, mate. I know.'

After that, there's nothing much to say.

Ed is brusque when we arrive at his lab, but I take him aside and give him a talking to until he gets the message. He's careful from that point onwards, moving Raul's hands gently as he takes samples from under his fingernails and between the creases on his palms. He takes blood and saliva too, because that's the protocol, though there's little purpose to it since Raul has already admitted his guilt.

There'll be no trial for him.

Normally, we take suspects straight up to Summertown after Ed's done, but instead I put Raul up in one of the college rooms and arrange to collect him first thing tomorrow morning. His sentencing can wait until then. In the meantime, he could really use some sleep, though it looks like he may never get a moment's rest again.

I'm over the moon when Tabitha finally comes home that afternoon. She drops her bag at the door and barrels into my arms like a plump, ballistic kitten, wrapping her claws into my back. I can't keep myself from laughing at her enthusiasm. Our reacquaintance kisses are long and deliberate, telling me I've been worrying about our relationship for no reason at all.

But the funk from the day isn't lifting. I can't stop seeing Raul curled up on his sofa with his head in his hands, weeping like a child. It's burned into my brain.

'Bad day?' Tabitha asks me, gauging my mood. She's good like that.

'I had to take in a friend,' I say. 'There was an accident. Drake'll probably box him tomorrow.'

'Oh, god. I'm sorry, hen,' she says, folding me back into her arms. 'Is there anything I can do?'

'You could try distracting me. How was your day?'

'Interesting, actually,' she says. 'I had some time after I got back from London so I did some work on that project of mine. I need samples for my study. Blood samples from Silver who are marked, so I can compare them to the samples of unmarked Silver. I thought maybe you could be one of my donors. What do you think?'

She leans in to bump her hip against mine, teasing.

'Why, Dr Ross,' I say, forcing a smile into my voice. 'What are you suggesting?'

'What I'm suggesting, Ms Valentine, is that perhaps I could get you pissed and take advantage of you. Maybe, if you're drunk enough, you might even let me kiss you. And mark you.'

'And then what?'

She kisses my neck.

'Then I take all your clothes off.'

'No,' I say, laughing as I push her away. 'I mean, are you going to ruin the mood by poking me with needles? S&M isn't really my scene.'

'Nah, we'll go and see Ed tomorrow. He's taking some other samples for me anyway.'

'Him and Carrie?' I grimace.

'Amongst others. Now why would that make you pull a face, hen?'

'I don't know. Residual sympathy for Cam? And there's something a bit weird about asking volunteers to suck face then donate their blood, isn't there? It's awkward.'

'Edmund is a scientist, like me,' Tabitha says sternly. 'He's a professional. We're only interested in the results. He'll be as detached as I am.'

'You're fucking one of your donors,' I point out.

'All right, yes, but only because you're so cute.' She presses her fingertip to the end of my nose.

'Did you just boop me?' I ask, incredulous.

'I'll be doing a lot more than that later. Let's go get drunk, shall we?'

No one has ever had to ask me that question twice. In fewer than five minutes, we're out of my rooms, across the quad and into the Solomon College bar. Cam and Naia are already there.

'Welcome,' Cam says. 'Shitter of a day, am I right?'

'You could say that,' I reply. 'But there's interesting news, too. Tabs was just telling me about her new project. She's investigating the effects of the mark on blood-drinking, and how it changes Silver behaviour.'

Cam raises his eyebrows at me. He knows why this is significant. It's not just about Drake anymore, it's about Raul too.

'I'm calling it haematopsychosis,' Tabitha says. 'It takes too many words to explain what it is. It needed a name.'

'So you've replaced several short, easy to understand words with an incomprehensibly long one?' I say, teasing. 'You're such a doctor.'

'Shush.' She pushes me playfully. 'Let me have my big words and I'll get you a big drink.'

I grin. 'Done.'

14

DESPITE THE BIG drinks, I'm up with the birds the next morning and so, for the first time ever, I'm early for probation. About five days early.

Drake doesn't hide his surprise.

'Ms Valentine,' he says, standing from his desk as I enter his office. He pulls up short when he sees that I have company. 'And who is this?'

I found Raul asleep on the sofa of his college suite this morning. It took me a while to get him up and out. At first I thought he was red-eyed because of whatever substances he'd used to chase away the memories, but there were no empty cans or bottles, no suspiciously empty packages. His hangover this morning is purely emotional.

'This is Raul Ortiz,' I say quietly, leading him to a seat like I would a small child. 'There was an accident yesterday.'

'Yesterday?' Drake asks. He's wondering why it's taken so long for me to bring Raul in.

'He's a friend.'

Drake raises his eyebrows and says, 'You'd better start at the beginning.'

Raul's face creases up in tears the second I mention

Rachael's name. I give Drake the bare details: she was marked, she was bitten, she's dead. Before I can get much further in the timeline than their return to the house, Raul interrupts.

'I did it.' The tears are flowing down his face now. 'It was me.'

Drake examines Raul carefully. 'Are you sure that your investigation is complete?'

I don't expect compassion from him, but he's giving it to me anyway. He's offering me a delay. The question is: do I want it? Raul's obviously ready to walk into the box right now, but I don't think I'm ready to let him go. I can't let the hammer fall without understanding why this happened.

'We're still gathering evidence,' I say, even though I know this case is open and shut. 'The lab's running tests.'

'All right, then.' He picks up his desk phone and dials.

'Yes,' he says into the handset. 'To the holding cell for now.'

Seconds after he puts it down, a goon walks in and takes Raul's arm. Raul doesn't look at her; he just stands from his seat and lets her lead him to the door.

'I'll come back tomorrow,' I say to Raul's retreating back. I might as well be talking to the furniture for all the reaction I get.

The goon closes the door behind them, shutting Drake and me in together. This morning I'm too exhausted to worry about that. I drop down into the chair Raul has just vacated, feeling more than a little defeated.

'You care about him?' Drake asks, taking his own seat.

I shrug, trying to make light of it. 'He's been good to me. He's a good guy.'

'Then I'm sorry.' He gentles his voice. 'This isn't going to end well, Valentine. You know that as well as I do.'

I nod glumly, looking down at my hands.

'And you're sure you don't want to just… get it over with?' he asks.

'There's still a chance.'

'There's always a chance.' His words are soft, but the meaning is granite-hard.

'It's different this time. Tabby's been doing some research that might help.'

'Dr Ross is home, then?' he asks, his nostrils twitching. Doubtless he can smell her mark on me again.

'She is.'

I expect him to make some kind of crack about that, but he just lets it slide. Still, he looks concerned. No, not concerned: preoccupied.

'What is it?' I ask him.

'Nothing,' he says, shaking his head as though to clear it. 'There are a lot of moving parts. I'm just trying to understand how they all fit together.'

'Welcome to the club.'

A muscle moves in his jaw. He says, 'Are we never going to talk about the photos? About Nora Mitchell's death?'

I don't know what he's getting at. Does he feel left out because I'm not talking about our current investigation with him? Usually, he's content to deliver his verdict when we've wrapped it up and presented it to him for rubber-stamping. He doesn't often want to be involved.

I just shrug in response, because I'm confused.

'This concerns me, too, you know,' he says. 'First the Invicti get themselves involved in a scam at Sir Percival's parties. I might have been willing to overlook that as a get-rich-quick scheme, but then I get shot with a poison dart, and the captain of the Seekers is photographed handing the evidence over to the Tertius of the Invicti, after which it promptly disappears. And now Sir Percival's human girlfriend – the captain's descendant – has turned up dead. Don't try to pretend there's no connection.'

He is surprisingly up-to-date with our case. I guess bad news like Sir Percival Wanker travels fast in the Silver community.

'We'll deal with it,' I say.

'No, you won't.' His tone is clipped and angry. 'Not alone. I was the one who sent you the pictures in the first place. This is my city. My jurisdiction. You might not like me very much, but I am the Baron of Oxford and you are a Seeker. Believe it or not, we are on the same side.'

I say nothing. I don't believe it.

He leans back in his chair, watching me from under his brows.

'What if I could help with your friend, Mr Ortiz?' he asks. 'Would that convince you to trust me?'

I've been jiggling my knee since the moment I sat down, but now I still.

'What are you suggesting?' I say, suspicious.

'Nothing untoward,' he replies quickly. 'If your friend truly is guilty then he belongs in a box, but I wonder whether you've considered all the possibilities.'

His eyes flick pointedly towards the door, then to the phone on his desk, then up to the ceiling. He's worried about us being overheard. He pulls a small pad of paper across the desk towards him, then opens the top drawer and starts rifling through it, searching for something, before stopping abruptly with a sigh.

'Carlotta gave me that pen,' he says.

I blink at him, pasting on my innocent face. 'What pen?'

'You know very well what pen.'

'I don't have the faintest idea what you're talking about.

But supposing for just one second that I do, she gave you a *pen*? The sexiest woman in the world gave you a *fountain pen*? What was it, a consolation prize?'

His gaze darts up to meet mine. 'I never said it was a fountain pen.'

Oops.

'But as it happens,' he goes on, 'it was. And it has sentimental value.'

'I have a hard time believing that you'd get sentimental over anything, let alone a pen.'

'Even the worst of us has feelings, Valentine. We might try to hide it, but we still care, and sometimes we even want to help.'

I'm left to contemplate that in silence as he pulls out a crappy biro from the drawer. He has nicer pens – I know because I saw them in there – but he's making a point. He writes something on the pad, then rips off the top sheet.

'Maybe there are more connections here than we're seeing,' he says, sliding the paper across the desk towards me. 'Maybe you just have to know where to look.'

There are five words scrawled on it in his elegant hand. I don't know what he's trying to communicate by them, but before I can ask him to clarify he holds his finger to his lips and nods to the door.

'Goodbye, Ms Valentine.'

Apparently, I've been dismissed.

I stuff the paper into my pocket as I leave. I'll have to decipher it later. Maybe it'll be the key to saving Raul, or maybe it's designed to lead me off course.

With Drake, either is a possibility.

When I get back to the college, the deputy calls us together in the conference room for an update on the Nora Mitchell case. I'm grateful for the opportunity to refocus. This thing with Raul has spun me out.

'Okay,' Boyd says, grabbing a whiteboard pen. 'Let's pull the pieces together.'

Normally, the captain would be sitting in on this meeting. For obvious reasons, she hasn't been invited to participate today. I know that's weighing on the deputy's mind, because he starts with her.

'There was some animosity between the judge and the captain.' He writes Captain Langford's name on the board. 'She admits that. I'm not going to ignore the possibility that Nora Mitchell was killed as a threat to the captain, but at the moment it's looking unlikely. We have a much stronger line of enquiry in Sir Percival Windsor, so I suggest we concentrate our efforts there for the time being.'

Cam and I exchange a glance, because we know the judge isn't the only connection between the captain and Windsor. There's another of which Boyd is unaware: Benedict. Cam's eyes widen and he tips his head towards the deputy, urging me to tell him, but I just give my head a small shake in response. Boyd knows I think the Tertius was mixed up in the Grant case and, by extension, with Windsor. That's enough. If I tell him the captain might be involved too, it won't progress the case any further, but it would be a risk. I'm not sure who he might tell. After all, he is the deputy.

Cam settles back in his chair, relenting, but his expression says we'll be talking about this later.

In the meantime, Boyd has added Windsor's name to the board.

He says, 'We know Sir Percival was in a relationship with the judge. He thinks it wasn't public knowledge, but someone knew about it, because Sir Percival didn't write the note in the camera that invited Mitchell to the library the morning she was murdered. Then there's the second note.' Boyd passes out copies. 'When Jacqueline and I were leaving Aston, the butler handed us this. The lab confirmed the blood used to write it belongs to Nora Mitchell, so we can be fairly certain the note came from the murderer. The handwriting isn't a match to the note that was photographed by the judge's camera, but both are so messy that we can't read into that. Naia and I spoke to Windsor again on Wednesday.' Boyd nods at Naia to pass the conversational baton.

'He wasn't much help,' she says. 'I checked out every name on his list of possible enemies, and none of them seems likely. They either didn't have the skills or the access, or they're alibied out. Windsor didn't know anything about the note, or why this is supposed to be his fault.'

'Okay. Jacqueline,' Boyd says. 'The handbag.'

'Cam noticed the judge's handbag in the background of the photo,' I say, 'which means she had it with her when she was killed. Whoever took it back to the courthouse, it wasn't Nora Mitchell. We searched her chambers again on Wednesday afternoon to try to work out why someone would bother, and the answer is: keys. There was a lockbox hidden in one of her books.' I push a photo across the table so Naia and Boyd can see it for themselves. 'It was empty, so whoever stole the judge's keys got what they were looking for.'

'And we have no idea what it was?' Boyd asks.

'Well, obviously it was something small,' I say. 'It took us ages to find that lockbox, but the books were all in order the first time we saw the judge's chambers, so I'm guessing that whoever stole her keys knew exactly which book to look for. Other than that…'

I shrug.

'So we have a possible motive, but no tangible evidence,' Boyd says.

'It also throws our timeline off,' says Cam.

'Right,' I agree. 'We know the judge ate breakfast that morning because Tabby found porridge in her stomach, and that lines up with time of death. We'd assumed that she ate at home, then went to work at the courthouse before leaving unexpectedly to meet someone in the Radcliffe Camera at eight am. We thought she left her handbag on her desk, but now we know that someone else put it there, staging the camera inside the gift box. Long story short, we have no idea what happened to her after she left work on the Monday night.'

'You think it was the killer who staged the handbag?' Naia says. 'That they were trying to point the finger at Windsor?'

'Maybe. It certainly distracted us from looking for the lockbox, which was likely the real reason the handbag was left in her chambers. Either way, the judge wasn't the last person to touch that camera. We don't know if she even saw the photos. She might have been snatched on the Monday night, giving the murderer the opportunity to load the photos onto the camera before he killed her and dumped her in the library.'

'So the killer gave her breakfast?' Naia says. 'Why bother?'

'She was poisoned,' I say. 'Her breakfast was probably the murder weapon.'

'Do we know when those photos were taken?' Boyd asks.

'The camera's with Frank,' Cam says. 'He's working on the metadata now.'

'What about the phone records?' I ask. 'Did they finally come through?'

'Yes,' Naia says. 'And there's nothing except calls to

Windsor, cab companies and colleagues. Dead end.'

'The court files?' Boyd asks.

'Nothing we didn't know already,' Cam says. 'I've gone back a decade. I'm happy to keep going if you want…'

From his grimace, it's obvious that he is anything but happy at the prospect.

'Let's leave it for now. Then there's still the matter of the missing library key,' Boyd says, adding it to the list on the board. 'Someone stole the assistant librarian's key to the Radcliffe Camera, a skinny man with a punky hairstyle. So that's probably who we're looking for.'

'Or it's a random coincidence,' Naia says.

'Or that.'

There's a long silence.

'Are we stalled?' Cam asks. 'Again?'

'Not yet,' Boyd insists. 'We need to look again at who might have had a grudge against Windsor.'

Naia groans, not looking forward to repeating her work.

'And we're still waiting on the camera metadata,' Boyd adds.

'Which is probably nothing,' says Naia.

'So to sum up: we know someone's trying to get at Windsor,' I say, 'but we don't know why. All we've got is a poisoned judge, a missing library key and an empty lockbox, which the killer knew exactly where to find. No suspects. No motive. Is that about right?'

I look around the room, seeing nothing but downcast faces.

Cam called it. Our investigation is dead in the water.

15

TABITHA'S DOING RACHAEL'S post mortem this afternoon. She knows about my friendship with Raul – we talked about it over drinks last night – and she thought I'd want to be here. Cam offered to come too, but someone has to pretend to keep working on the Mitchell case, even if we're stuck.

'Ready?' Tabitha asks once I'm suited up in protective gear.

'Ready,' I say, though I'm not sure I am.

She pushes open the mortuary doors and leads me inside. Rachael's body is already on the slab, waiting for us. She looks small and frail, even though she would have stood taller than me in life. In death, she looks short. The blood is all over her, caked across her shoulders and neck. It's so thick that I can see the patterns that have been left in it by the crumpled bedsheets. We don't need to cut her open to know how she died, but it's procedure in scab cases, because you never *really* know. Surprises happen.

But not today.

The post mortem is aggressively gruesome and time-consuming. This is far from my first time in the mortuary, but I'll never get over the amount of force required to take a body apart. The Silver are used to thinking of humans as fragile creatures, but Tabitha still strains to crack the bones.

When it's all over, we take the samples to Ed in his lab.

'This is the Ortiz victim?' he says as Tabitha hands them to him. There's no preamble with Ed.

'Just finished the post,' she says. 'There's probably nothing here, but…'

'I'll let you know,' he promises.

'Did you find anything from the samples you took from Raul yesterday?' I ask Ed. 'Anything in his blood?'

'Nothing other than alcohol. If he did take something, then it didn't leave a trace. Not one I know how to look for, anyway.'

'Are you thinking some kind of new drug?'

He shifts his weight uneasily, not meeting my eye.

'What?' I ask.

'Thing is, Jack, there's another explanation. He's not a young Silver, and from what you've said he doesn't look after himself properly, and, well…'

'What are you trying to say?'

'It might not be physical.' He sighs. 'You have to consider that possibility.'

'No, I don't,' I snap.

'Or,' Tabitha interrupts, 'it could be something like haematopsychosis.' She turns to Ed. 'You remember I was telling you about the research I've been conducting?'

'Right,' Ed says, his eyes lighting up at the opportunity to talk science with someone who will actually understand it. 'You wanted those blood samples.' He bustles off into the back room. There's the sound of a fridge opening and closing, then he returns with two vials. 'Here they are. I've spun and separated them for you. You wanted me to take a sample from Jack too, I think?'

He looks a little intimidated by the prospect.

'Play nice,' Tabitha says, stroking my hair. 'Please. For me.'

'Fine.'

I hold out my arm, baring the vein on the inside of my elbow for Ed. He gathers his kit quickly. To his credit, it takes less than a minute for him to slide in the needle, take the sample and clear everything away again. He can be very efficient when he puts his mind to it.

'You want me to stick this in the centrifuge too?' he asks Tabitha, holding up my blood sample.

'Please.'

'Thought so. Between your research and all the blood samples I'm getting from this case Jack's on, the old centrifuge is getting a lot of use. It's a new model, you know. Top of the line. I had to fight the captain to get it approved, but it's paying for itself now.'

'Which model?'

He and Tabitha talk about machine specs for a bit, then Ed takes her and the vial into the back room where he keeps his beeping equipment. There's some cooing over the shiny toys, but it all goes over my head.

'One question,' he says when they return to the main lab. 'How could haematopsychosis be at play here? The victim was human. Isn't haematopsychosis only activated when a Silver drinks the blood of another Silver? I mean, we drink human blood all the time.'

'We know very little,' says Tabitha. 'There's a desperate need for thorough testing. At this stage, I'm not prepared to confirm or deny anything.'

Ed laughs. 'You should have been a politician.'

'I'm just a careful scientist. It's empirical evidence or

nothing, Dr Castell.'

'Just as you say, Dr Ross.'

I am surrounded by brainiacs.

Ed bundles his and Carrie's blood samples into what looks like an insulated sandwich bag, then hands them to Tabitha.

'Is that all you need?' he asks.

'For now, yes. Thanks. I'll pick up Jack's sample on Sunday. There's plenty for me to be working with in the meantime. With any luck, we'll start seeing results by then, so I can give you a sneak peek.'

'I'm looking forward to it. It's all very exciting, isn't it?'

He puts his hands in his lab coat pockets and leans back on his heels, smiling. He's not being sarcastic; he *really* loves science.

Tabitha is just as sincere, humming happily all the way back to my rooms, where she stows the samples in the fridge.

'Please tell me those won't be in there long,' I say.

'Why, hen?' she asks. 'You can't be squeamish about blood. You drink it almost every day.'

'Medical blood is different. Separated blood. Ick.'

Tabitha wrinkles her forehead at me like she thinks I'm being ridiculous. It makes her nose twitch, which is utterly adorable.

'Look,' I say, 'it's just weird. It's like steak is amazing, but I wouldn't want to eat meat from a cow that had been used as a lab animal. You don't know what's in it.'

'But I haven't even done anything to those blood samples yet.'

'It doesn't matter.' I shudder. 'It's creepy.'

She shakes her head at me. 'You are the most illogical person I have ever met.'

'Thank you.'

'It wasn't actually a compliment.'

'And yet I am choosing to take it as one.'

I grin at her as I pull a bottle of non-medical blood out of the fridge and pop the cap. 'You want one?'

'Nah,' she says as I glug down my drink. 'I had a few vials with Ed earlier.'

I freeze, then put my half-drunk bottle down on the side.

'You're revolting,' I say.

'And you are *so* gullible!' She laughs. 'As if I'd drink blood from Ed's lab.'

I pick up my bottle again, partly placated.

'Why would I bother,' she goes on nonchalantly, 'when I can get it straight from the mortuary?'

I know she's joking because she can't keep the smirk off her face, but I've still lost my appetite.

'Ugh,' I say, passing her the rest of the bottle. 'You drink it.'

'What? With your backwash?' she teases. 'Ew.'

'How can you complain about my backwash when you spend so much time with your tongue in my mouth?' I ask, leaning forward to catch her hands. I wrap my arms around her and pull her close. It's difficult to plant a kiss on her mouth because she's giggling nonstop. I have to pick my moment. 'You're so *illogical*,' I say against her lips.

We get distracted by each other for a while, kissing up against the wall, but I'm too preoccupied to ease into it.

'You all right, hen?' she asks when I press one final kiss to her lips, then pull away.

'I'm fine,' I say, but I'm not.

'Worried about your friend?' she asks.

'A bit.' I can't get the image of it out of my head: Raul sobbing into his hands, surrounded by the detritus of the night before. 'These blood samples you're testing, how soon will you know?'

'A while,' Tabitha says, sitting down on the sofa. 'Well, not long for these samples, but for the study as a whole? These things take time, hen.'

'Could they take a little less time on this occasion?'

She gives me a look, which I should have expected. Like Ed, she takes her science seriously.

'Well,' I say, 'just let me know when the results are in.'

'Of course.'

I flop down onto the sofa next to her, putting my feet up on the coffee table.

'Long day?' she asks.

'The longest.'

There's a pause before she speaks again. I might have thought it was a comfortable silence of the sort we often share, except she's nibbling at her lip as though she's worrying at something in her head.

'When you took Raul in, how was the baron?' she asks eventually. She tries to make her tone light, but it's obvious that she's more interested in my reaction to the question than she is in my answer.

'Tabs,' I say.

'I know.' She takes a deep breath. 'I'm sorry. I just don't trust him.'

'You don't have to, but you can trust me.'

She picks at the hem of her skirt, looking at it so she doesn't have to look at me. This sucks. A few minutes ago we were laughing and kissing and Killian Drake didn't even exist, but somehow he's here again, getting between us.

'This isn't about him,' I say. 'It's about Raul. You know that, don't you?'

'You'll be going back to Summertown tomorrow, then?' she says.

'To see Raul.'

'Not the baron?'

'Not if I can help it. Tabby, please. We can't keep having this same argument over and over. You have nothing to worry about.'

She nods to herself, but she doesn't look convinced.

Although she stays with me that night, curled up in my arms in my tiny bed, I can't help feeling that she'd rather be alone in Nash Lee.

There's a room at the back of Drake's mansion. It's technically underground, but a tiny window at ceiling height leaks murky light inside. I guess it was once a cellar, because a flight of concrete steps leads down here from the kitchen. The floor is concrete too, the walls are bare plaster, and there's a line of iron bars that cuts the space in half.

I don't like this room. The last time I spent any time here was twenty years ago, and I was human. To start with, at least. This is where the woman I thought I loved turned me Silver. She was in the cell back then, but now its only occupant is Raul.

He's sitting on the floor, crumpled in on himself like a used tissue. He's slouching so hard that, even though he's not a short guy, I sit taller than him when I join him on the floor. I reach through the bars to pat his shoulder, which is about as comforting as it sounds.

I have to get him out of here.

'We tested your blood,' I say.

'And?' he asks, but he already sounds resigned.

I want to hear some hope in his voice. I want him to be hanging on my words, as desperate for me to find a way out of this as I am, but he's given up. We might as well have boxed him already.

'There was nothing unusual about it,' I admit.

He nods, as though this is exactly what he expected to hear. I need to give him something to hold on to.

'Tabitha's working on a theory that might explain all this,' I say.

'Tabitha, the new girlfriend?' He wipes his nose with his sleeve.

'That's right. It's called haematopsychosis.' I've been practising until I can say it correctly, because Tabitha cares about that kind of thing. 'At least, that's what she's calling it. You marked Rachael, right?

'I didn't mean to. I didn't mean for anything to happen. I'm not into that kind of line-walking. You know that.'

It's true. He's never been a thrill-seeker. He likes his life quiet and pleasant, with no unnecessary drama, but a Silver in any kind of relationship with a human is the very definition of "unnecessary drama". I can't imagine him falling into bed with Rachael on a whim.

'How did it happen?' I ask.

'I don't know.' He clenches his fists and his jaw as he replies, letting his frustration show. 'I've been going over it in my head and I just don't know. One minute everything was normal and the next I just… *wanted* her. No, that's not right. I've always wanted her. We had chemistry, I guess. Then we kissed, which was a mistake, but not one I haven't made with a human before. Everyone was still at the house then, as well. It was normal; just a kiss at a party, you know?'

'So what changed?'

'It got more intense.' He's blushing, dipping his head as though he can hide it from me. We both know that's pointless with my Silver senses, but social convention is sometimes too ingrained to shake. 'I marked her. I don't remember doing it, but it was there when I came around, so I must have. The biting…' He drops his face into his hands, muffling his words with his fingers. 'I don't know.'

'What do you remember?'

He looks up at me, blinking away tears.

'The *need*. The instant, unstoppable *need*. Like a hunger I couldn't control. It was…' His head drops once more, so his next words are muffled. 'I never want to feel that way again.'

'We'll get to the bottom of this, Raul. I promise you.'

I check he has everything he needs before I leave him, then head back to the college, dodging out of the back door to avoid any chance of running into Drake.

There's a sick feeling in my stomach, because I can't help but make comparisons. The hunger Raul described, the fact that he marked Rachael, and the violence of it all has me recalling that night in the alley with Drake. He lost control in the same way. If I had been human instead of Silver, I might have ended up the same way as Rachael.

It's starting to look a lot like haematopsychosis.

16

BY THE TIME I get back from Summertown, the camera's metadata report is in. Cam is already combing through it when I walk into our office.

'We were right,' he says, not looking up from the papers. 'The photos in the camera were taken on another device and uploaded to it in the early hours of the morning the judge died.'

'All of them?' I ask. 'Even the dick pic?'

'No,' Cam grimaces. 'That was already on there, but the timestamp was altered. Badly.'

I take a seat. Our desks are back to back, so now we're face to face.

'What time were they uploaded?' I ask.

'Just after three AM.'

'So you think she was taken from her house?'

'That's what the deputy thinks. He and Naia have gone to have another poke around, see if they can find anything we missed.'

I snort. 'In that bomb site? Good luck to them.'

'Yeah,' he agrees. 'Unlikely, I know. Where have you been?' He looks up at our wall clock. It's past eleven. 'This is a late start, even for you.'

'I went to see Raul.'

Cam breathes in through his teeth. 'Any news?'

'Nothing good. I'm rolling with Tabby's theory at the moment.'

'You mean haematopsychosis?' He pronounces it perfectly.

'Have you been practising that?' I ask, but he pretends he doesn't understand the question. 'Yes, *haematopsychosis*,' I say, tripping over the syllables a little. I still haven't got the hang of it. 'There was nothing in his blood, so it's basically his only shot at staying out of the box. But to be honest, he doesn't seem to care much either way.'

Cam nods sympathetically.

'I've seen people go that way before,' he says. 'Difficult to bring them back from the edge once they've decided they've had enough.'

'And I am absolutely not the right person for the job.'

'Don't say that.'

'I mean it, Cam. Raul's a drinking buddy. Whenever we hang out, we get lashed and depressed. The point was never to cheer each other up, just to be miserable together. I'm not a good cheerleader.'

'Good thing you've got me, then. We'll go together next time. How about that?'

'Well…' It isn't an awful idea.

'Just give me a time and place,' Cam insists. 'I'll be there.'

'Tomorrow morning, here, nine o'clock?'

'Done.'

This is why Cam is the best friend I could ever ask for. He smiles and I feel like a weight has been lifted from my shoulders. Between Tabitha looking into the science and

Cam helping with the moral support, responsibility for Raul is no longer mine alone.

'Thanks, Cam.'

'No worries. Here,' he says, shoving a pile of papers onto my desk, 'you can show your appreciation by going over this list from Sir Percival again.'

'Hasn't Naia already been through it twice?'

'Yup, but someone needs to go over it again now that we've thrown the timeline out of the window, and Naia was not keen. How do you think I convinced her to go to Nora Mitchell's house instead of me? Seemed like a fair trade.'

I think of the rodent droppings, mouldy crockery and inch-thick dust embedded into the judge's carpet, and can't help but agree. In any case, I'm interested to see who's on Windsor's list of enemies.

And surprised.

At the very top of the list, it says: *Baron Killian Drake*.

'Holy shit,' I say, 'have you looked at this?'

'Not really,' Cam murmurs, still concentrating on the metadata report.

'Did you know Drake is Windsor's number one suspect?'

'Oh, yeah. I did know that.'

'And you didn't tell me? Why wouldn't you tell me?'

Cam puts down his papers with a sigh.

'You know exactly why I didn't tell you,' he said. 'Remember David Grant? Remember how we had absolutely zero evidence against the baron, and yet you were so set on your vendetta against him that you wouldn't consider any other suspects?'

I shift in my seat. 'That's not quite how I remember it.'

'Well, it's how it happened. If you look at those papers a bit more closely, you'll see that the baron has already alibied out, because he was with Carlotta Arden from dusk til past dawn on the night of the judge's death. Even with the amended timeline, he's covered.'

'But she's his girlfriend,' I protest. 'You can't take her word for it.'

'What about his staff? What about the forty Silver who were partying at his mansion that night and swear he never left the building?'

'He threw a party?' I ask.

Cam gives me a frank look.

'Are you sad you didn't get an invitation?' he asks.

'No, that's not–' I can feel my cheeks burning. 'No.'

'Jack,' he says, 'that man is your Achilles heel. The moment his name comes up in an investigation, you get weird and irrational about the evidence, twisting it however you can to make it point to him. You need to drop it. Please, I'm begging you, take my word for it: Baron Drake was not involved in Nora Mitchell's death.'

I slump back in my chair, feeling thoroughly called out.

'Fine,' I say. 'I'll just get back to work then, shall I?'

Cam smirks at me and says, 'Good idea.'

I love having Cam as my best friend for all of the reasons I've stated previously, but sometimes I wish he didn't know me so well. Just once, it would be nice if I knew how I felt before he did.

After a fruitless day spent on the phone checking the alibis of some of the most odious Silver I've ever had the misfortune to come across, I'm glad to get back to my rooms and shut the door on the world. It's much nicer in here. Not only is Tabitha staying over, but she's also brought dinner. We eat sitting side by side on the sofa, which is the best we can manage in my tiny flat.

'I've finished some preliminary work on the blood

samples I've taken,' she says.

'Oh?'

I'm only half-listening. My mind's still on the case, trying to work out what we've missed. Someone's alibi has to have a hole in it somewhere, or maybe Windsor has an enemy he's missed. My money's on the latter; Naia and I have been more than thorough with his list. What this means, of course, is that Drake's in the clear. I knew that anyway, but it's still a disappointment. I'd really like to see him boxed. Then he'd be out of the way and I wouldn't have to think about him anymore.

Tabitha can obviously tell that she doesn't have my full attention, because she puts her hand on my knee and taps it gently until I look up.

'You need to listen to this, hen.'

'What?' I say. 'What's wrong?'

'Nothing's wrong. That's what I'm telling you. I've looked at all the blood samples. I've even run a few limited studies to see what happens when people who are marked drink each other's blood, and there's nothing.'

I stare at her for a moment.

'But you've only just started testing. You haven't even picked up my sample from Ed yet.'

She nibbles at her lip, which is how I know she's about to say something I won't like.

'I've been working on this for a while,' she says.

'Since when?'

'Since May.'

My stomach plummets. She's been lying to me.

'I didn't want to upset you,' she says in a rush. 'I didn't want to tell you about it at all until I knew the results, because why bring it up if it's not even a thing, you know? But then you started seeing more of the baron–'

'Not by choice.'

'I know, but I felt I had to warn you. And now I have enough results to be certain. There's nothing. No negative effects. No anger. No psychosis.'

'What are you saying?'

'It's just anecdotal, hen.' She pulls a pencil from her hair before reinserting it, securing her bun. A nervous habit. 'The whole thing. There's no hard evidence to suggest that drinking the blood of someone you've marked will cause psychosis.'

'Oh.'

I don't know what else to say.

I put my food on the coffee table; I've lost my appetite.

Haematopsychosis isn't real.

I was so sure that Tabitha's research would support what I've told Raul, that it would be the evidence we needed to get him out. His behaviour that night was a perfect match for the symptoms Tabitha first described. All the evidence fits. And yet.

It isn't real.

But I've seen the effects of haematopsychosis with my own eyes. I've seen the jealous rage, the uncontrollable destruction. I've seen Drake's eyes blazing at me with violence, just a second before he stepped in front of a bullet to save me. I've seen that possessiveness in action.

Haven't I?

When Tabitha clears her throat, I realise I've been silent for too long.

'Are you upset?' she asks, her voice very small.

I know what she's really asking: *Do you care that Killian Drake is exactly the kind of fickle, violent bastard you feared he might be?*

It shouldn't make any difference. I should be thinking

about Raul. Of course Drake's dangerous. I've always known that. Yet part of me hoped that he wouldn't turn that side of himself on me, that I'd be the one person who was always safe from the monster. I allowed myself to believe he was driven by some chemical reaction that night in May, instead of by his nature. The truth is that no one is safe from Killian Drake.

I shouldn't be surprised, and I definitely shouldn't be hurt, but I am both of those things and Tabitha can see it.

'I'm sorry,' she says.

'You're sure?' I ask. 'There's no mistake?'

'No mistake. I checked it. I'll keep studying it, because I'm planning to write a paper and I'll need a lot of data for that, but I have enough to satisfy myself of the basic principle. I'm certain.'

And so it's settled: Drake had no excuse for what he did to me.

'Well,' I say. 'That's the end of that. I'm going to shower.'

She lets me go.

I stand under the spray for long enough that my skin turns pruny. One of the advantages of college accommodation is that the water pressure is great and it never runs cold. Right now that's not a good thing, because it means I have no motivation to move. The longer I stand here, the faster the memories spool in my head, showing me that night again and again. The echo of his voice purrs at me.

You don't just move on without finishing what you've started.

Stop fighting, Valentine.

His hand clamped around my wrists, his fingers in my hair, trailing down my neck. I don't remember the pain of the blow that followed, but I remember the shock, the way it made my heart race with panic when I realised he could do whatever he wanted to me and I would never break free. But the worst thing, the very worst thing, was that it didn't make me angry at him. Instead, I was angry with myself for my impotence. The memory alone is enough to make me blush with shame.

But he stepped back. He realised that there was something wrong and he stopped. He was not himself. I would swear that he was not himself.

But.

Haematopsychosis isn't real.

I turn off the water and step out of the shower, towelling off quickly before throwing on some relatively clean clothes.

'Tabby?' I call.

'Yes, hen?'

When I walk out of the bedroom she's still on the sofa, nibbling on an apple. She's the only person I know who eats fruit for pudding out of choice rather than because she feels she should.

'I'm going to need to see the report,' I say.

I don't have to specify what report; there's only one thing on both of our minds right now. She isn't surprised that I'm asking for it.

'I'll have the initial results ready tomorrow,' she says. 'I'll send them over.'

'Thank you.'

She pats the sofa, inviting me to join her, but I hesitate in the doorway. The way her face falls is almost unbearable.

'Do you want me to go back to Nash Lee?' she asks.

'No,' I say, sitting down quickly. 'Christ, no. I just…' I look down at my hands, unsure how to explain what I'm feeling.

'I know,' she says, putting her hand over mine. 'I know it's a lot. I won't pretend that I ever liked the baron, but I am sorry.'

'I'm just worried about Raul,' I say, trying to shift focus. 'If it wasn't haemato-wotsit, then could it have been a drug? How likely do you think that is?'

She crosses her legs, her top foot swinging as she considers the question. She's wearing a short skirt and teal tights today, showing off every curve of her legs. If I weren't so wound up right now, we'd be spending the rest of the evening in bed.

'It's possible,' she says. 'It's much easier to detect an active drug than the traces of a drug that the Silver body has already burned through. We can't find those until we know exactly how the drug functions and what traces it leaves behind. The problem is that people are making new drugs all the time. You know that well enough, hen. There's a reason you burned Matthew Felton's lab to the ground.'

With her words, something clicks in my brain. For a moment, I just freeze, scared that if I move I might shake the pieces of the thought loose, but when it coalesces fully I know I'm right.

I shove my hand into my pocket and pull out the piece of paper Drake gave me yesterday. I haven't worn these jeans since then and, with all the Raul drama, I'd entirely forgotten about it, but now, finally, his words make sense.

'You brilliant woman,' I say, kissing her forehead, her cheeks, her lips. 'You utter genius.'

'Okay,' she says, kissing me back. 'I'm not sure what I said, but I'll take it.'

'Gotta go.'

I wriggle free from her arms and grab my jacket.

'What?' she says. 'You can't go now. Things were just getting interesting.'

'Sorry,' I say, meaning it. 'You're wonderful and gorgeous

and you've just given me an idea I have to follow up on right now. Tell you all about it later, I promise.'

'So my reward for being wonderful and gorgeous is that you run away?'

'I know, I'm sorry. But you can watch my bum while I go.'

I wink at her and turn to hurry out of the door.

'I guess it could be worse,' she says with a sigh. 'At least it's a nice bum.'

After ten minutes of frantic searching, I find Cam in the canteen, his head bent over a sad-looking pile of spaghetti; too much pasta, not enough sauce.

'Cam,' I say. 'I need a drink. You coming?'

He swallows. 'I'm eating dinner.'

'I'll buy you kebab-van chips later. But right now, I need a drink. Urgently.'

He pushes his plate away, apparently as unimpressed with his meal as I am.

'Okay,' he says. 'At the bar?'

'Into town.'

We're not going to the college bar tonight. We're going *out* out.

Cam gives me a quizzical look, but he follows me through the college, out of the lodge and through the city to Park End Street.

'You should have told the deputy about the photos,' he says as we walk.

'It wouldn't be fair to him,' I reply. 'He's the deputy. And they're hardly evidence. For all we know, the captain and Benedict were both ordered by the Primus to cover up Drake's shooting. Maybe they were just doing what they were asked. Maybe there's a good reason for it.'

'Is that what you think?'

I don't bother replying to that.

'I didn't think so,' he says.

'Look, it's a bad idea to spread conspiracy theories around right now. I'm just trying to be careful.'

'And what inspired this? You're not the cautious type.'

'Drake,' I concede reluctantly. 'It's possible he put the idea in my head.'

'Oh?'

'He thinks everything is connected. The turning scam at Windsor's parties, the poisoned dart, the judge's death.'

'Then he agrees with you.'

'Apparently,' I grumble. 'Anyway, he's worried.'

'And that worried you.'

I don't like what Cam's implying, particularly now that I know the truth about haematopsychosis.

'I'm not worried because I give a shit about Drake, okay? Let's be clear about that. But when was the last time you saw him break a sweat over anything? Whatever's happening here has him shaken up. That should be enough to worry anyone.'

'If you say so. Then why are we going to Crimson?' Cam asks as we walk past the Castle. 'Because that's where we're heading, right?'

'For Raul. Here.'

I pass him the piece of paper Drake handed me yesterday.

'*There's bad blood at Crimson,*' Cam reads. 'What's that supposed to mean?'

'It means we've overlooked a player.'

'Who?'

'You'll see,' I say as we approach the door.

Just occasionally – very occasionally indeed – things work out more perfectly than I could ever have planned. This is one of those times, because when we walk in, Matthew Felton is behind the bar.

Suspicion confirmed.

'Oh, no,' he says, backing up against the optics. 'Fuck, no. You're not allowed within fifty feet of me.'

'Don't be ridiculous,' I scoff. 'It's not a restraining order. I just have to leave you alone. It's not my fault that you happen to be here, in a public bar, where I've come for a drink. I'm not doing anything wrong.'

'I'll call the Seekers,' he threatens.

I laugh. 'We *are* the Seekers.'

'Then I'll call the Invicti.'

'Sure, go ahead,' I say, calling his bluff. 'I'm sure they'll come running.'

We glare at each other.

'Tell you what,' Cam suggests, stepping between us. 'How about I get the drinks, and Jack goes and sits by the window. No one calls anyone, and everyone's happy. Deal?'

He's such a peacemaker.

I slope off to a table at the front of the bar, eavesdropping while Cam puts our order in. Felton makes Cam's drink, then turns to start on mine.

'I'm not drinking anything he's touched!' I yell across the room.

There's a lot of huffing and puffing, then Felton switches places with a woman who's serving at the other end of the bar.

Peace is restored.

Cam brings the drinks.

We clink our glasses together. I have straight gin, but Cam has a weird froufrou concoction in a martini glass. It looks like pure blood.

'House speciality, apparently,' he says.

'Felton made it himself?'

'From a special bottle marked with his name, kept in a locked fridge that I'm guessing only he has the keys to.'

'Interesting.'

'Isn't it?' Cam checks over his shoulder, making sure Felton is focussing his attention elsewhere. 'Okay. We're good.'

I pull a zip-lock bag out of my jacket and hold it open while Cam pours his cocktail inside. There's no way in hell that either of us is drinking it. It's going straight to the lab. In the space of a moment, I have it stowed away safely and I'm sipping at my gin like nothing happened. I finish my drink at a leisurely pace, then give Felton the finger as we leave.

'I'm reporting this to your captain!' he yells after us.

I just laugh.

If the pieces fall into place like I think they will, it won't be long before I'm coming back for him.

The last time I went after Matthew Felton, I did it outside official channels. This time, we're doing it the right way. When we take Felton down for poisoning Raul Ortiz, it won't just get him out of circulation for a few months. This time, I'm going to put him away for good.

17

I DIDN'T THINK it was possible, but Raul looks even worse today than he did last time I visited. It's only been twenty-four hours, but his clothes are hanging off him and his cheeks look hollowed out.

'Jesus, Raul,' I say, rushing down the steps towards him. 'Have they not been feeding you?'

He wipes his mouth with the back of his hand. 'Can't keep it down. Can't keep anything down.'

'Are you sick?'

He shakes his head. 'I just can't stop thinking about it.'

'You need to talk to someone.'

He looks around the cell. I take his point: who's he going to talk to in here?

'Talk to us, then,' I suggest. 'You remember my friend Cam?'

'Hey, Raul,' Cam says. 'How are you doing?'

Raul just laughs, which is when I know he's really losing it. There's a reason he's always hanging out in pubs or throwing impromptu house parties: Raul doesn't do well on his own. He's the kind of guy who spends all his time with his friends, enjoying their company without giving much thought to romance, then looks around one day to find that they've paired up and married off, leaving him alone. But when you're Silver, your friends don't just get married off, they die off too.

Raul's been alone so long that a relationship with Rachael might even have been good for him, which makes the situation all that much harder to bear.

'I have some good news,' I say, forcing a smile. 'We've got another lead.'

'Wait,' Raul says. 'What happened to the last one? I thought you said it was psycho something or other?'

'Haematopsychosis.'

'Right.'

'Yeah, we're not sure about that yet,' I say. I can't bear to tell him the truth. 'Tabby's still looking into it. But I think there's something in the drinks they're serving at Crimson. You said you had a blood cocktail?'

'Yeah?'

'I think they're spiking them. Cam and I went down there yesterday and this dodgy guy was behind the bar. You know Matthew Felton?'

Raul swallows. It sounds as though his throat is desert-dry.

'The guy you set on fire?' he asks when he can get the words out.

'Yeah, that one.'

'You should stay away from him, Jack. He's a dangerous guy.'

'Felton?' I laugh. 'Maybe he thinks so. Anyway, he's mixing the blood drinks and he's got a reputation for pharmaceutical experiments. There's a sample of one of his concoctions at the lab, and I'd bet my entire salary that he's behind this.'

Raul squints at me, as though the tiny amount of light

leaching into the basement hurts his eyes.

'I think you should just drop it,' he says. 'I'm done. It's over.'

'No way. I'm not giving up on you. Can you think of any reason someone might want to hurt you? A grudge, or a secret, anything at all?'

He looks at his hands. 'I'm just some guy, Jack. Why would anyone care about me?'

'I care,' I say. 'Felton did something to you, and I'm going to prove it so we can get you out of here. We're going to beat this thing. I'll let you know as soon as we have the results back from the lab, just don't give up. All right?'

He doesn't reply, doesn't move, doesn't give any indication that he's heard what I've said.

'Raul?'

'What if there's nothing?' he says, all in a rush. 'What if there is no explanation for this? What if it's just me? Maybe I deserve to be boxed. Maybe I'm the kind of person who just… snaps.'

Cam and I exchange a look.

This was Ed's theory, but I can't believe it of Raul. He's a teddy bear. Teddy bears don't snap; they're too soft.

'Look at me, Raul,' I say.

He does, reluctantly. I can see how much it's hurting him.

'I know you,' I say. 'You are not that kind of person. You'd never do this, not on your own. I'm going to get you out of this. You're not going in the ground. I'm going to find whatever did this to you, and whoever's responsible for it, and we're going to box them instead.' And if it turns out that Felton's the one responsible, that'll be the icing on the cake.

'Thanks, Jack,' Raul says, but only to keep me happy. I can tell he isn't convinced. 'Hey, Cam?'

'Yeah?' Cam's been hanging back, but now he steps

forward and crouches down by the bars.

'Can we have a word?' He glances towards me for a split-second, then looks away. 'Just the two of us?'

'Sure,' Cam says. 'If Jack–'

'Of course.' I smile, trying to show Raul that I don't mind. If he's more comfortable talking to Cam than he is talking to me, that's just fine. As long as he's talking to someone.

'I'll be back soon, okay?' I say, reaching through the bars to squeeze his hand. 'You hang in there.'

It's at times like this that I wish I still smoked. If Cam and I had driven up here then I could have waited for him in the car and listened to the radio, but we walked so I'm stuck hanging around the back of Drake's mansion like a stalker. At least if I were smoking, I'd have something to do with my hands. Instead, I lean against the wall and watch the garden's falling leaves, which sounds autumnal and romantic, but is actually just bloody boring.

I haven't been waiting long before I have another reason to wish myself elsewhere. What I failed to realise is that the doors to Drake's conservatory are just around the corner. He must have seen me through the glass.

'How is he?' Drake asks, stepping out into the garden.

'How do you think?' I keep looking at the trees, dreaming of nicotine. 'He's broken.'

'And your investigation?'

This is why he's the last person I want to see. It's not just that Tabitha's proof against haematopsychosis makes him a certifiable monster, it's that without the possibility of pleading temporary psychosis, Raul is left swinging in the wind. Yes, we'll probably find something in the blood from Crimson, but we haven't yet. Until we do, all I have is a clean blood sample from Raul and no other theory.

That's why, much as I want to confront Drake about that night in the alley, I keep my mouth shut. For as long as I keep quiet about Tabitha's research, Raul's sentencing is on hold. I'll have to tell Drake soon, I know, but not now. It doesn't have to be now.

'We're pursuing a few leads,' I say.

'And how long do you think it'll be before you have anything concrete?'

I shrug, keeping my gaze fixed straight ahead. Still, I can feel him coming closer. I can hear the soft crunch of his feet on the gravel, feel the disruptions in the air that his movement creates, and – irritatingly – I can smell his scent, even here in the great outdoors. I wish I could stop responding to it.

Stop fighting, Valentine.

I shudder at the memory.

'Cold?' he asks.

'No.'

'You've worn that jacket thin,' he says, fingering the cuff.

I snatch my arm away, finally looking at him.

'Jack...' he says.

There's more softness in his eyes than I expected to see. I don't want it. I reject it. I reject every kind word, every insinuating smile, and every hand he held out to me in the pretence of friendship. I reject the memory of his kisses and caresses and dark eyes, because I know their blackness is truly bottomless. There's no soul behind them, just an abyss that yawns with sharp teeth.

I know what he is now, and I won't forget.

'What do you want?' I ask.

My tone is sharp enough to cut. He's not stupid enough to ignore it. If there's one thing I'll say for Killian Drake, it's that he's a clever bastard. He takes a step back, then leans against the brick beside me, leaving enough room between us to make it clear he's giving me space.

'Are you ready to call it yet?' he asks quietly.

'What?'

'With Ortiz. Are you ready to let it go?'

'No!' I say. 'Of course not.'

Drake looks down at the gravel and says, 'He wants me to box him. He's been asking every hour since you left yesterday.'

I want to be angry about that, but it hollows me out instead. Raul is a lonely man, but he's never let that defeat him before. Despite his solitary life, he had joy enough to spread around to other people. His smile always touched his eyes. Whoever the zombie caged up beneath my feet is, welcoming the escape of death, it's not Raul. I'm determined to bring him back.

'This wasn't his fault,' I say. 'You know that. If you thought I should just give up, then why did you even give me that note?'

'I was trying to help, but now I'm not sure that's the help Ortiz needs. The box might be kinder, in the long run.'

'How did you know about the house speciality?' I ask.

'Call it an informed guess,' he says. 'Jack, I can't hold off forever. I have people to answer to.'

'You mean the Primus.'

'He's keeping a close eye on Oxford. You need to tread carefully. This is bigger than Ortiz, bigger than the judge's murder or a dart in my neck.'

'You think it's *all* connected?' I ask. 'Even Raul?'

'Even Raul,' he says. 'Something's coming, and it's not going to be good. Lines are being drawn, sides chosen. People are talking about succession.'

I cross my arms over my chest and turn to face him, one

shoulder resting against the wall.

'I'm sick of riddles, Drake. If you know what's going on, then why not just tell me?'

'Because I don't, not entirely.' It looks as though this bothers him. 'I'm seeing patterns. It's what I do. If I couldn't feel the way the wind was blowing, then I wouldn't have lasted as Baron of Oxford for this long. We're heading for a bad patch.'

'What do you mean?'

'Just think about it,' he says, 'and be careful.' Then he pushes off from the wall and goes back inside the house. Cryptic bastard.

When Cam comes up from the basement, he finds me standing alone, staring at the conservatory doors.

'Peeping Tom,' he says.

'Layabout,' I reply. 'You took your time.'

'Raul was feeling chatty.'

That sounds like an improvement to me, but Cam looks troubled.

'So?' I ask as we walk towards the road.

'So what?'

'So what did he want to talk to you about?'

Cam shakes his head. 'That's between me and Raul.'

'Cam.'

'He did something stupid. He didn't want me to tell you.'

'Okay,' I say, trying not to sound put out. 'But he's all right?'

'Did he look all right?'

'Christ,' I say, clenching my fists, 'you are so infuriating.'

He smiles.

'Don't worry, I won't take it personally. I know you're not really pissed off with me, you're just annoyed that the baron found your hiding place.'

'How did you–'

'I can smell his scent on your jacket.'

'Right.'

Not for the first time, I wish Drake would keep his hands to himself.

18

THE NORA MITCHELL case is in desperate need of resuscitation.

We gather together in the conference room that afternoon and try once again to make sense of the evidence, but none of us has our mind on the job. Boyd is distracted by his librarian – date number four tonight – Naia and Cam are bored to death with case files, and I'm busy worrying about what Drake said this morning.

Which is just as well, really, because I think I've figured it out.

I need to be sure, so I examine the idea carefully as I check the reports spread out on the table, then look something up on my phone. This can't be just a hunch; I don't want anyone crying "vendetta" at me and I'm not going to trust Drake's suspicions. I need to make sure I can support this theory with solid reasoning.

But I'm pretty sure. I just hope I can convince the others to come along for the ride.

'I might have a new motive,' I say.

They all turn to me. We've been so hopelessly lost on this case that this is a big deal.

'You know about my friend Raul?' I say.

'The one responsible for the accident?' asks Boyd.

'*Alleged* accident. He was drinking at Crimson before it happened. Cam and I went there to pick up a sample of what Raul drank, and Matthew Felton was behind the bar. We know he likes messing around with drugs, and I think he's poisoning patrons of the club. I don't think what happened to Raul was an accident at all.'

'Okay,' says Naia. 'But what possible motive could someone have for going after a loser like Ortiz? No offence, Jack.'

'Maybe he knows something he shouldn't,' I suggest. 'Maybe he was poisoned to get him out of the way.'

I look at Cam. He looks back pleadingly, his expression an agony of indecision. I knew it: this has something to do with what Raul said to him.

'Go on,' I say.

'But I promised not to tell.'

'And if it's the key to getting him out, Raul will understand.'

'I'm just not comfortable–'

'Okay, hang on a second,' Naia interrupts. 'What has any of this got to do with Nora Mitchell's murder?'

'Windsor,' Boyd says. 'He said he was a silent partner in Crimson.'

'Right,' I say. 'He was also at my hearing with Felton, which means Felton owes him a favour or two. If Windsor wanted someone out of the way, he'd rope Felton in to do it for him.'

'And the judge?' Boyd says. 'You think her death was connected with Crimson too?'

'The timeline fits. She died just before it opened.'

'That's a bit tenuous, Jacqueline.'

'Only because we don't have enough information yet.' I look pointedly at Cam. 'But everything's leading back to Windsor. The note he received said the judge's death was his fault. We assumed that meant someone had something personal against Windsor, but maybe their grudge was professional. Have we looked into the owners of the open blood bars in London? If anyone would be pissed off about a new place opening here in Oxford, it would be them. Why would Oxford Silver bother going to the capital if they could get what they wanted locally?'

'Come on, Jack,' Naia says irritably. 'This is all just speculation.'

Which takes me to the crux of it all.

'Okay,' I say. 'Here it is. I've thought through this over and over, and there's only one possibility that makes sense to me: I think the Silver are fighting over whatever was in the box.'

'Which was?' Boyd asks.

But I'm watching Cam. Throughout this, he's been getting paler and paler, as though the tan is leaching out of his skin.

'Will you tell us now?' I ask him.

'Shit,' he says, rubbing the back of his neck. 'I didn't make the connection.'

All eyes are on him now. He knows he'll have to break Raul's confidence, but that doesn't mean he's happy about it.

'Shit,' he says again.

'Out with it,' says Boyd.

Cam sighs heavily, then starts talking.

'Raul didn't tell you everything that happened that night,' he says to me. 'He didn't want you to think he was the kind of person that… Well, he liked Starblood.'

'Jesus, Raul,' I mutter.

'Yeah,' Cam says. 'He thought that would be your

reaction.'

Starblood is basically cocaine for vampires. If you think Valentine's Massacres are dangerous when imbibed around humans, you should see what a Silver who's snorted a line of Starblood can do to a crowd. There's a reason it's outlawed by the Primus, but some of the more disreputable dealers still manufacture it.

'He was buying off Felton,' I say, my heart breaking a little as I put the pieces together. 'I didn't think Raul was that much of an idiot.'

'That's why he didn't want to tell you.'

'Then that's the end of the investigation, isn't it?' says Naia. 'No wonder he killed that girl if he was on Starblood.'

'But he wasn't,' says Cam. 'He went to Crimson to buy some from Felton, but he couldn't find him. He wasn't behind the bar. So Raul told the others he was going to the bathroom and snuck out of the side door, thinking Felton was on a cigarette break. He was right, but Felton wasn't alone. Someone else was out there with him.'

'Who?' I ask.

'He didn't see.'

Naia rolls her eyes. 'We have got to find ourselves some better witnesses.'

'But he heard them talking,' Cam went on. 'Something about missing files. They called them a "game-changer".'

'And then?' I ask.

'Then that's it. Raul went back inside. He didn't think the conversation was important, but if you're saying Windsor had him poisoned because of it, then it must have been. I didn't think it was important either, until you mentioned the box.'

'Cam,' I say, chastising him.

'I thought they were talking about drugs!' he says. 'Like, a

USB drive with supplier data on it or something.'

'A USB drive would fit in the judge's lockbox,' says Naia.

'Yes,' I say, 'but there could be anything in those files.'

'I realise that now,' says Cam, 'but it was a drug dealer talking to someone in an alley. What was I supposed to think? Anyway, how did you know?'

It was mostly gut instinct, but I'm not going to admit that. In retrospect, there were clues.

'Raul tried to warn me off Felton,' I say. 'There's a reason he's given up fighting this, Cam: he'd rather be in a box than face whatever's waiting for him out there. He's hiding because he's scared, but Felton is one of the least intimidating drug dealers I've ever met. It doesn't make sense for Raul to be hiding from him. It's whoever's standing behind him that's the problem.'

'Windsor?'

'That old duffer? I don't think he's much of a threat.'

'And his butler's reporting back to us,' Naia chips in. 'He hasn't left the house since he got the news about the judge. He's taking telephone calls only. He couldn't have been the one in the alley.'

'So Felton's been acting as Windsor's go-between?' says Boyd.

'That's my guess,' I say, 'Felton could have talked to Windsor inside the club without it seeming suspicious. He'd only meet someone outside if they were trying to keep their identity secret. It has to be something clandestine, involving high-ranking Silver.'

'Oh no,' Cam groans. 'You're going to say this is about the Tertius, aren't you?'

'Yes,' I say. 'At the risk of being called a conspiracy theorist again, I have a conspiracy theory. I think it was Benedict at the club that night, talking to Felton. I think Raul saw them together, and I think that's why Felton poisoned Raul.'

'He told me he didn't see anything,' Cam insists.

'Because you're a Seeker. He's not going to tell you he saw the Tertius having some secret conversation with Felton, is he? Technically, Benedict's our superior. Raul doesn't want to be in any more trouble than he already is.'

'Then why tell me about the conversation at all?'

I shrug. 'He's scared, and he sometimes acts stupid, but he's a good guy. I guess he was trying to do the right thing, the only way he knew how.'

That would be just like Raul. He likes to fade into the crowd, never the type to court controversy or danger, but he's a decent person. He'll want to see this work out the right way, even if he isn't brave enough to lead the charge himself.

'But why would the Tertius be meeting with Felton?' Naia asks.

'Have you got your laptop, Deputy?' I ask Boyd.

Of course he has. Technophile that he is, he always keeps it close. He pulls it out of its pristine leather case and flips it open.

'Can you log in to the Land Registry and check the lease for Crimson?' I ask.

I drag my chair around the table so I can sit next to Boyd as he types. He elbows me away because I'm crowding him, but I can't help it. I know where this is leading. I know what the document's going to say before he brings it up on screen, because I've already looked.

He clicks the mouse one last time and there it is.

Tenant: Silver Services Ltd.

This is what it was all about. This is why Benedict and Windsor ran their little scam, pretending they would turn people Silver in return for vast sums of cash. They needed the money for this: to set up the first open blood bar outside of London. I wonder how many palms they had to grease to make this happen. I wonder how much blood they had to spill to gather the means to do it.

No wonder someone wanted revenge on Windsor.

I swivel the laptop around so the others can see the screen.

'Windsor and Benedict are all over this,' I say. 'Crimson is their little project. They're setting themselves up in opposition to the London blood bars.'

'There's a problem with that theory,' Cam says. 'Whoever's got their name on the lease for the London open blood bars, there's only one person who controls them: the Primus. The Tertius wouldn't challenge him.'

'Wouldn't he?' I say, following Drake's hunch. 'He's the *Tertius*. Not the Primus, not the Secundus, but the Tertius. He has no hope of ever rising any higher, unless he knocks someone down a peg.'

Boyd and Naia take this in their stride, but Cam goes wide-eyed, looking around at us as though the concept of insubordination had never occurred to him. For someone so old, he can be terribly naive.

'You think this is a coup?' Naia asks.

'It feels more like a gang war between the Secundus and the Tertius,' I say. 'That would explain everything that's happened this year: David Grant, Nora Mitchell, the dart that shot Drake. I think two factions of the Silver are fighting for dominance, and a lot of humans are getting caught in the crossfire. People are choosing sides, willingly or otherwise.'

'The Primus wouldn't let that happen,' says Cam, horrified.

'It wouldn't be the first time,' says Boyd. 'It's been a hundred years or so there's been this kind of infighting, but he won't intervene. He'll let the Invicti sort it out amongst themselves, and whoever wins will be his Secundus. That's the way it works. They don't care about morality, they care about power.'

'Why didn't I know about this?' Cam says, looking around at each of us.

Naia reaches out and strokes his hair like she would stroke a puppy's ears. 'Sweetie, sometimes you're too soft for this job.'

'The real question is,' I say, 'how did we not find out about this sooner? It's not just the Invicti who are at war here. Silver civilians are involved too.'

Boyd's brow wrinkles. 'Someone's been hiding it from us.'

He doesn't have to say who, because his anger does it for him. Captain Langford has been keeping us in the dark. Drake tried to tell me. All this time, he's been trying to tell me, and I've been too stubborn to hear it.

Naia and Boyd have come far enough down the conspiracy road with me that I owe it to them to tell them the truth, so I show them the photos of the captain passing Benedict the dart vial. I'm expecting Boyd to take it hard, but it's almost as though he's been expecting it. This case has shaken the whole team's faith in our captain.

'She's been working with Benedict and keeping it from us,' he says.

'But now things have escalated,' says Naia. 'It won't be long before everyone knows.'

'Maybe that's the whole point,' I say. 'They want people to know. Nora Mitchell didn't have to die. If someone wanted her keys so badly, they could have just stolen her bag and got into the lockbox. But they wanted to send a message. They wanted Windsor to suffer.'

'And they wanted whatever was in the box,' says Naia.

'Both sides are fighting over the information in those files. The game-changer.'

'Which is a little scary when you put it in context,' Cam says. 'What kind of game-changer can end a war between two factions of Invicti?'

We all think about that for a moment, coming up with our own worst-case scenarios.

'Look, it fits,' Boyd says. 'This is a theory, but that's all it is right now. Until we have proof, let's just concentrate on our murder investigation,' he suggests. 'We know the killer stole the key from the judge to get the files from the lockbox, assuming that files are what was in there. The killer then set up the body in the library and the camera in the judge's chambers to point to Windsor.'

'Which was clumsy,' says Naia. 'We were obviously going to check the camera's metadata, so either the murderer is being incredibly clever by double-bluffing us, or someone stupid thinks they've set a clever decoy.'

'We need to talk to Windsor again,' I say. 'We haven't spoken to him about the lockbox. He's in the middle of all of this, and he's acting suspiciously.'

'How?' asks Naia.

'He was polite to me.'

She nods, accepting this as incontrovertible proof that Windsor is up to something. I might be insulted if he was less of a wanker.

'All right,' says Boyd. 'But this theory of Jack's doesn't leave this room. We'll ask Windsor about Matthew Felton and the empty lockbox, but we say nothing about Mr Ortiz or the missing files, and we stonewall the captain. We can't have this information leaking out through her. Agreed?'

We all agree.

'I'd like to do the interview with Windsor,' I volunteer.

'Not alone,' Boyd says. 'I'll go with you. Tomorrow. Cameron, make the call.'

Cam looks hesitant, but he doesn't contradict Boyd. After so long working on this case without direction, it's just a relief to have a plan. I can feel the mood lifting even before Naia pushes back from the table.

'Okay, then,' she says. 'Let's call it a night. This is depressing and I'm starving.'

'Me too,' says Cam. 'Shall we go out for pizza?'

My stomach grumbles in response.

We all look at Boyd, waiting for him to give us our freedom. He doesn't look inclined to do so.

'Oh, come on,' I say. 'You've got a date, and we need food. It's Sunday night, and if I'm right about this coup, then it's already been going on for months. It's not going away overnight. There's nothing else we can do right now.'

'Fine,' he grumbles.

Naia jumps up with a 'Whoop!'

I sympathise. After all this drama, I really need a drink.

'Quick,' Cam says, grabbing his wallet and keys, 'before he changes his mind.'

'Give me a sec,' I say, starting back towards my rooms. 'I'll get my things and meet you in the lodge.'

'Hurry!' Naia yells after me.

'Two minutes!'

I go as fast as I can. I know from bitter experience that it is a very bad idea to come between Naia and her grub.

19

PROBLEM: I CAN'T find my leather jacket.

I was wearing it this morning when we went to visit Raul, and I remember taking it off when I went back to my rooms after lunch, which means it should be here. I look in all the usual places I keep it – the wardrobe, the bathroom, the floor – then turn the place upside down looking again, but there's no mistake.

And it gets worse: I can scent him on the air. Killian Drake has been in my rooms, and he's stolen the only personal possession I give a damn about.

I check my front door, but the lock isn't broken or scratched. The windows are shut tight too, the catches sealed from the inside. I have no idea how he got inside. He probably had one of his goons pick the lock on the door. If anyone would have a man for that, it would be him.

I get out my phone and call Cam.

'Hey,' he says.

'Hey. You guys go to dinner without me. There's something else I need to do.'

'Um, all right. Is everything okay?'

'No.'

197

'Is it the case?'

'No.'

'Tabby?'

'No.'

'Ah. Then are you sure you want to piss him off when you're already on probation?'

'If he didn't want me to piss him off, then he shouldn't have stolen my leather jacket.'

'He stole your jacket?' There's a pause on the other end of the line. 'Well, I guess you did steal his pen first.'

I wish I'd never told him about the damn pen.

'Cam, this is not the time for reasonableness. Whose side are you on, anyway?'

'Fine.' He sighs. 'I'll bring you back some takeaway.'

'You are a prince among men.'

'I know.'

We say our goodbyes and twenty minutes later I'm hammering on the door to Drake's mansion. One of his goons opens it and peeks out, a tall woman with mid-brown skin and muscles bigger than Naia's. I've seen her here a couple of times before. From the way her jaw clenches, I'm pretty sure she remembers me, too.

'Yes?' she says.

'Where is he?'

'It's not Wednesday. You don't have an appointment.'

'I don't need an appointment. The bastard stole from me. Where is he?'

'Otherwise engaged.'

'Doing what?'

'Me, actually.' The voice comes from behind the goon. She swings the door wide open to reveal Carlotta Arden walking down the corridor towards us, on her way out. She's wearing a deceptively casual outfit, but I can see the tailoring in her trousers, and her shirt is definitely silk. I can smell the sex on her when she's still metres away from the door, along with the inimitable spice of Killian Drake's scent.

It's not his scent mark, though. It's too weak for that. This is nothing more than transference, and it'll be gone within the hour.

'Jacquéline,' she says as she exits the building. 'How lovely to see you. You should join us next time.'

My mouth drops open and it takes me a few seconds to pull myself together, by which time she's standing right in front of me, smiling to herself as she waits for my response. She has a post-coital glow that makes her practically irresistible. How could Drake let her go?

'Um, thanks,' I stammer. 'Yeah. No. You know. Girlfriend.'

'Still?'

'Still. I'm not planning for that to change anytime soon.'

'Shame.' She looks me up and down and I swear I can feel the heat of her gaze trailing over my skin. 'Well, *à bientôt, chérie*. Let me know if you change your mind.'

The gravel crunches under her heels, then she's slipping into the back seat of a waiting car with a wave. I wave back, struck dumb for possibly the first time in my life, and watch the car drive away.

'Fuck,' I mutter once it's out of sight.

'I know,' the goon sighs. 'Your girlfriend must really be something.'

'She is.'

We have a moment of wistful solidarity before I return to my assault on Drake's front door.

'You still can't come in,' the goon says.

'Why not? It looks like he's done.'

There's a distant buzzing that I realise is coming from her earpiece. It's sadly Silver-proof, so even with my heightened senses I can't hear what she's hearing. After a moment, she touches a device on her collar and says, 'Yes, Sir.'

She stands aside and says, 'You can go through. If you take my advice then you'll turn around right now, but if you're set on this…'

I don't wait to hear the rest of it.

Drake is waiting in his office.

'Ms Valentine,' he says. 'Just the nightcap I was hoping for.'

He's laying on the sarcasm, trying to sound as miserable as his doorstep goon was, but I'm not buying it. He's lounging against his desk with bare feet and a shirt that he hasn't buttoned up all the way. Together with the smell of sex on his skin and the satisfied look on his smug face, his attitude is positively louche. I've never seen him so disassembled, but it suits him.

The bastard.

'Where's my jacket?' I ask, stomping towards him.

'Your jacket?'

He tips his head to one side and adopts a quizzical expression, pretending he has no idea what I'm talking about.

'My leather jacket. My only jacket. The one I always wear and love like it's my own child.'

'Oh,' he says. 'That jacket.'

'Yes. If I had that jacket, then I wouldn't be wearing this enormous hoody I had to borrow from college lost property.'

'Well, I've got no idea where *that* jacket is,' he says. He's trying not to laugh.

'You utter bastard. I can't believe you'd break into my

rooms, rifle through my stuff and steal my most treasured possession.'

'Yes. Wouldn't that be awful, if I'd done something like that? I can't even begin to imagine how you feel. Why, it would be like someone going through my desk and stealing – oh, I don't know – the fountain pen Carlotta gave me.'

He holds my gaze, willing me to break.

'You are such a drama queen,' I say.

'Says the woman who stormed up here at–' He checks his watch. '–half nine at night, long after most people have settled into their *evening activities*, and forced her way into my house, all because she can't find a piece of clothing.'

'Don't you dare trivialise this.'

'Oh, trust me, I'm taking it very seriously.'

We glare at each other for several long seconds. If this goes on much longer, the rational part of my brain is going to catch up with my rage, and then I'm going to need some gin. Perhaps a bottle of it.

I just don't have the energy. I'm suddenly tired of this whole situation.

'Forget it,' I say, turning to leave. 'I'll buy another damn jacket.'

'What the hell?' he yells after me. 'You're leaving?'

'Sorry to interrupt your fuck-fest.'

He gets in front of me so quickly that I don't see him move before he slams the door shut in my face.

'What's wrong, Jack?'

'You mean besides Raul?'

'Yes. You've been upset about it since you brought him in, but not like this. What's changed since yesterday?'

I take a deep breath and a step back.

I always knew we'd be having this conversation sooner or later. I thought I wanted it to be later, or never, but apparently my subconscious has other ideas, because here I am again, back in his office, over a missing jacket. *Stupid, Jack.*

Best to get it over with.

I clear my throat.

'I told you that Tabitha was doing some work on blood-drinking. Do you remember?'

'I recall you mentioned something.'

'She's got results. It turns out that drinking the blood of someone you've marked is entirely harmless. There's no such thing as haematopsychosis.'

The silence that falls around us is loaded. I meet his eye, because although I need him to hear the subtext in my words – that I blame him entirely for what he did in May – I can't let him see how much it hurts me that he had no excuse for it. The helplessness he imposed on me was unforgivable. I've barely even admitted it to myself yet, so I'm not capable of saying it out loud, but if we hadn't been interrupted then things would have gone in a bad direction. Ironically, if Benedict hadn't tried to shoot me with a poison dart, I would have been the one in sick bay that night, not Drake.

He could have killed me.

He could have done worse.

'It's a mistake,' he says.

'Tabby doesn't make mistakes.'

'You're sure about that, are you?'

He takes his keys from his pocket and walks around his desk to unlock the bottom drawer, the one I couldn't get into last time I was in his office. He pulls out a file and opens it, revealing a handful of photos within.

'You need to see these,' he says, turning the pictures around and spreading them out on the desk.

I don't look. I keep my eyes fixed on Drake's, because I'm

pretty sure that whatever he's trying to show me, it's not something I want to see. The last photos he showed me were of the captain and Benedict. If these are something similar, but to do with Tabitha…

I don't believe that she's part of this coup. If she were, she would have told me. She loves me.

She loves me.

'Got your own private investigator on staff?' I ask, making light of it. 'Quite the little voyeur, aren't you?'

'When you have my kind of responsibilities, it's negligent not to look into your associates. And their associates.'

'Like my girlfriend.'

'I'm just asking you to consider that maybe she's wrong. Maybe she isn't the person you think she is.'

'You don't know her at all.'

'And you do? It's been four months, Jack. You think you know her inside and out after only that long, but after *twenty years* you still don't have the tiniest idea who I am, do you? Christ.'

He pushes a hand back through his hair, tousling his dark locks. They were already slightly disarrayed, but now they're so messy that it makes him look decadent.

'I know you well enough,' I say. 'Well enough to mistrust every word you say to me.'

He opens his mouth as though to protest, but then, all at once, I see the fight go out of him.

'Kulika,' he says, pressing down the intercom button on his desk phone. 'Please come and escort Ms Valentine out. I'm going to bed.'

'Sir,' the goon's tinny voice replies.

'You've got about sixty seconds,' he says to me, walking to the door without looking back. 'I'd make the most of them if I were you.'

I waste the first ten, looking out into the corridor as I wait for him to return and spring the trap, but he's really gone. As soon as I realise this isn't a trick, I step up to the desk and see what he's left for me.

Photos of Tabitha.

Tabitha in the college with the captain. Nothing strange about that.

Tabitha at Crimson on the opening night. Again, not a surprise.

Tabitha down the side of the club, her face lifted to a man who has his back to the camera. Another angle: he's whispering in her ear. In the final shot, I can see his face. It's Benedict.

I panic a bit, then.

But still, this is all completely explainable. Tabitha works for the Invicti. If it comes to it, on the opening night of Crimson I was working for the Invicti too. There's nothing here to suggest their conversation was anything but completely innocuous.

Drake's just stirring. Again.

I start off angry, but pretty soon I'm furious. It's not just that he has so obviously got it in for Tabitha, it's that he made me think there was a reason to doubt her. Hell, for a couple of seconds there, I did actually doubt her. I did exactly what he wanted me to do, and he's going to pay for that.

The manipulative bastard.

By my estimation, there's about twenty seconds left on my clock. I don't have time to pry open the mystery drawer, but I race around the desk and snatch the bottle of scotch from the other bottom drawer, hiding it under my big hoody as I stride from the room, seconds before Kulika arrives to drag me out.

If Drake's going to come for my girlfriend, then I'm coming for his whisky.

This. Is. War.

20

'YOU WERE RIGHT about Drake,' I say to Tabitha when I get back to my rooms. I go straight to the bedroom, stashing the stolen bottle, then join her in the sitting room-slash-kitchen.

'He's fucking with us,' I say. 'I can't believe I thought it was just the psychosis. The man is evil.'

'I tried to tell you, hen,' Tabitha says softly.

'I know, I know.' I bend down and kiss her.

She's sitting on the sofa, working on her laptop. Cam must have been by to deliver the takeaway, because there's a pizza box on the coffee table. Tabitha hasn't even cracked the seal. She looks tired out. There are dark circles beneath her eyes and her usually rosy cheeks are pale. Worse, the pencils in her hair are coming loose from her bun, but she hasn't adjusted them. That's not like her.

'Are you okay?' I ask.

'Fine,' she says, putting the laptop aside.

'You look tired.'

'I wasn't well this afternoon,' she admits grudgingly, 'but I'm feeling better now.'

'You weren't well?' I put my hand across her forehead to

feel her temperature. She leans into my touch. 'The Silver don't get unwell.'

'I was just a little sick,' she says. 'But really, I'm fine. I tired myself out. I've been working too hard on this project.'

'The haematopsychosis,' I say, taking care over each syllable.

'Aw, you got it right first time, hen.'

She smiles at me, proud of my pronunciation. From anyone else it would be condescending, but her approval just makes me grin.

'Well, I'm sorry it made you sick,' I say, 'but I'm glad we know.'

'Do you want to talk about what happened?' she asks me. 'I'm guessing you spoke to him.'

For a split-second, I consider telling her about the photos, but I discard the idea quickly. If I even mention them, she'll think I'm accusing her of things I don't believe she's done. Better to let it go.

'He was a dick,' I say. 'True to form. Let's leave it at that, shall we? The point is that you were right about him and I'll never doubt you again. It's just…'

'You wanted to believe he was acting under the influence?' she suggests.

'I guess.'

I sit down beside her and pull her into my arms.

'I can understand why,' she says, nestling her head against my shoulder. 'I know what the two of you had was… intense.'

'We didn't have anything, Tabs.'

'You had the biting. I can understand why that might have felt special.'

'But it wasn't. It was just, I don't know. It was a lot.'

A lot of anger. A lot of lust. A lot of pain.

'I can only imagine.' She pauses for a moment, and I have the feeling she's gearing up for something. That makes me tense, because anything that crosses the intersection of Tabitha and Drake makes me tense. 'Hen, look, I had an idea. We know biting is safe now. So I was thinking that maybe we could try it. If you want. For scientific purposes, I mean.'

I was not expecting that.

'Tabs…'

'It's safe. I promise you. I've tried every test I can think of, and it's safe. I was just thinking that if you liked it, I mean, maybe we could do it together. Maybe that would wipe away some bad memories. We might even make some new good ones. I don't know.'

I don't answer right away, because everything about this feels precarious. She's blushing so furiously that I can feel the heat of her cheek seeping through my T-shirt. We're having this discussion side by side, with her head tucked under my chin, as though she's too shy to have it face to face. That makes it worse, because if she's this embarrassed about it then the fact that she's brought it up at all means she really wants to do it.

I'm not sure I do.

It's awkward as hell. This is like raking through our exes together and making comparisons, except we're talking about Drake, who nearly destroyed our relationship before it had even begun. She knows how much he affected me. I've tried to hide it, but that day in his office, on his desk, with his teeth in my neck… I'm not going to forget it any time soon, just like I can't forget the shock of that night in the alley. I can't blame her for wanting to overwrite it. Maybe part of me wants to do the same, but it won't work. Me and Tabitha are not the same as me and Drake. I like that about

us. I don't want her to change, and I don't want the shadow of what I did with Drake to poison what we have now. Drake and I were, in his words, a few days of madness. What Tabitha and I have is an actual relationship.

For all of these reasons I want to say no, but I can't. If this is what she wants, if this is what she needs in order to put the whole Drake mess behind her, behind us, then for the sake of our relationship, I'll do it. I'll do anything for her.

I say, 'Okay.'

She gets up from the sofa and looks at me expectantly.

'You mean right now?' I ask, feeling like I've been caught on the back foot.

'Why not?' she asks, taking my hand and dragging me up.

'Are you sure you're feeling well enough?'

'I'm fine, hen.' She presses a kiss to my neck, which she can only reach on her tiptoes. 'Stop fussing.'

I let her lead me to the bedroom, suddenly feeling awkward. This isn't how sex usually starts for us. Usually, it's not planned. We'll just be sitting on the sofa together, then sitting will become kissing, and quickly degenerate into groping, after which we're lucky if we can make it to the bedroom before all our clothes are strewn across the coffee table. But this is different. There's ceremony to this, because it means something to her. The pressure of having to get it right makes my palms sweat.

'Hen?' she says. She's seen me rubbing my hands on my jeans.

'Yeah?'

'Don't you want to do this?'

Her eyes are blue and huge and round as she looks up at me. I can see the hurt hovering in her expression, ready to crash down if I deny her. This isn't just something she wants, it's something she needs.

'Of course I do,' I say, trying to hide the fact that I'm swallowing with a dry throat. 'Just a bit… nervous.'

She smiles and closes the door behind us, which makes it worse. We never close the door. Everything about this feels wrong.

I should stop it now. I should make my excuses – she's not well, it's been a long day, we're not in any rush – but it all feels weak, because the truth is that I just don't want to do it, and I can't tell her that.

Then she kisses me, and I forget. The fresh nectarine scent of her mark is surrounding me within a second and pouring into my lungs in the next. It spreads through my body like a sedative, settling all the anxious nerves that are telling me this is a terrible idea. It numbs me to the wrongness, calming and soothing and whispering through my veins like a prayer. Before I know it, I'm kissing her back. Our clothes are thudding on the floor like rain, a shower quickly becoming a downpour as she backs me towards the bed and pushes me down onto it.

Sitting on the edge of the mattress, I'm only a few inches shorter than she is standing up, but that disparity gives me easy access to her neck. She's manoeuvred me into this position for a reason. When I look up into her eyes, she's looking right back into mine, waiting. Her hair has come entirely loose in all the kissing, the pencils lost in the pile of clothes on the floor, so now it's cascading over her breasts in streams of shining chestnut. She reaches behind her head to catch one side of it, then draws it back like a curtain, gathering it over one shoulder so the other side of her neck is bared. She tilts it towards me as she steps between my legs: an invitation.

'You're sure?' I ask.

She smiles and leans down to kiss me, then pulls back and

looks at me expectantly. Her eyes are glinting, dilated, excited. I can smell the pheromones rolling off her. I guess that's a yes.

A few moments ago I was feeling distinctly hot and bothered from all the kissing, but suddenly I'm very aware that I'm naked in my draughty, single-glazed college bedroom. I'm on the verge of backing out, but Tabitha seems to mistake my chill-induced goose pimples for anticipation. Putting her hand on the back of my head, she pulls my mouth against her throat.

I bite. What else can I do?

Then things go a bit... weird.

I've read some of Tabitha's research notes, so I know a little of what to expect. Here's how it works: if you're going to indulge in Silver blood-drinking, you kiss your target first – properly – so they're wearing your scent mark. The mark acts as a sedative that anaesthetises the target so they don't feel the pain of the bite, just the pleasure that follows it. Nature's clever like that. Then both of you buckle in for some awesome sex.

That's what I was expecting, but it's not what I get.

Something's gone wrong.

I run through my mental checklist.

Is Tabitha wearing my mark? Yes.

Is Tabitha in any pain? Definitely not, though if anyone overhears the noises she's making right now, they might not be entirely sure.

So far, so good. So why is there a ball of tension in the middle of my chest? I expected arousal and adrenaline, but not this rage of... I don't know what. I just know that I didn't expect to feel like *this*.

When I pull away, I can see bruises on Tabitha's shoulders where I've gripped her during the bite. Big, dark bruises. If

I'd been holding her any tighter, I would have broken bones. I know they'll disappear quickly, but for the moment they're glaring at me from her ivory skin. That should horrify me. I know that I should be apologising for the marks I've left in my wake, but already my hands are clenching at my sides as though they want to latch onto her again, and all I can think is *I've left my mark*. This isn't me. I feel like I've stepped outside myself into a suit that doesn't quite fit.

A moment later, I realise there's nothing to worry about. This is right. It's all exactly as it should be.

When I grab Tabitha again and throw her onto the bed, I am not gentle and she doesn't ask me to be. I hold both of her wrists in one hand, pinning her down on the mattress while I take what I want from her with my hands, with my mouth, with my teeth. I only release her to readjust my grip, and only let her go for good when I have wrung everything I want from her.

When it's over, she kisses me and sighs.

'I like you like this,' she murmurs, pushing my hair back from my face. 'So domineering.'

The bite on her neck has already disappeared, leaving clear skin in its wake. I don't like that. I wanted the mark to linger. I want everyone who looks at her to know that she's mine, not just from the scent mark, but from the impression of my teeth in her neck. Its absence makes me almost angry.

Which is wrong. I don't think of myself as a possessive person. I don't like seeing my girlfriend flirt with other people any more than the next person would, but only because it makes me feel insecure, not because it makes me angry. Not like this. What's even more irrational is that she's in my arms right now, so why am I even bothered? Shouldn't I be enjoying this moment, instead of worrying about what will happen when she's out of my sight? The idea that something in me wants to control my girlfriend like that, to brand her with my teeth, is really fucking disturbing. I'd hate it if someone did that to me, and I'm sure I don't want to do that to her, not really.

Do I?

No. I don't. The impulse has passed. It felt like a dream, and like a dream it seems distant now that I'm outside of it, fading into memory. I remember bruising her, biting her, controlling her, but none of it feels quite real.

'You okay, hen?' she asks as I lie down beside her.

'Fine,' I say. 'A bit dizzy.'

'It's just the blood. Did you like it?'

She smiles wickedly, revelling in the deviance of it, so what can I do but smile back?

I can't tell her I enjoyed it any less than she did, not when her pleasure is so obvious; I can see the silver in her eyes. Hiding our silver is a voluntary act, so it doesn't work when we're unconscious, or really distracted. Apparently Tabitha found bitey sex pretty distracting, because she's still blinking the silver away now. Not that it matters. She doesn't have to hide it with me.

I love her. I really do love her.

'What?' she asks.

We're face-to-face, sharing a pillow as I gaze at her.

'Just wondering what your eyes would look like with a little more silver in them,' I say, cupping her cheek in my hand.

She smiles back. 'You know I love you, hen.'

'I know.'

It's the wrong thing to say. That line only ever worked for Han Solo, and even then, not very well.

'Are you really waiting for me to silver before you'll tell me how you feel?' she asks.

Silvering doesn't happen much these days. It's almost mythical, in fact, but apparently it does still happen occasionally. When one of the Silver is truly in love, the silver from the whites of our eyes floods into our irises, circling the pupils with what looks like liquid mercury. We can still hide it from humans like we hide the silver in the whites of our eyes, but for those to whom we're willing to show it, it's incontrovertible proof of our feelings.

For someone as emotionally fucked-up as me, that would be reassuring right now. Tabitha says she loves me. I know she loves me. But even though I know it's possible for her to love me and not silver for me – after all, I love her and my irises are still flat brown – I wish she would. Maybe part of me does want to see the evidence before I commit myself.

'I'm sorry,' I say. 'That wasn't how I meant it.'

'Yes, you did. But it's okay.' She presses a kiss to my forehead. 'I'll wait. I'm not going anywhere.'

And this is why I love her.

I would do anything for this woman. Weird though it was, if she wants me to bite her every night for the rest of our lives, I'll do it to make her happy. I'll fake it if I have to and I will never, ever let on that it feels any less mind-blowing than it did with Drake.

Ever.

I fetch the pizza box then curl up next to Tabitha as we demolish the contents. When we're done, I bury my face in her hair and breathe in our mingled scents: dark fruit, rich and sweet. It lulls me to sleep on a wave of pleasure, washing away all my anxiety.

She's my girlfriend, my heart, my world. Nothing can change any of that. Even if Drake is right about Tabitha, even if she's conspiring with Benedict, then I don't think I care. Whatever side she's on in this Silver war, I'll stand right next to her.

21

I WAKE UP grumpy. I often wake up on the wrong side of bed, but this is different. I'm not just irritated, I'm actively angry.

It doesn't help that I'm being dragged out of a really good dream – Tabitha features, extremely naked – by someone thumping on the door to my rooms. I check the clock: seven in the morning. Tabitha has already left for work, and it's too early for it to be one of my team, who would have called first anyway. They know I don't get out of bed before half eight unless they give me a really good reason.

The knocking won't stop.

'Fuck off!' I yell.

'Open this door, Jack.'

I freeze with the duvet pulled up over my head. That is not the voice I was expecting to hear.

'Fuck off and die!' I yell back.

For a moment I think he's actually gone away, but then I hear the ominous sound of a key thudding into the lock with force. The bastard has a bump key.

'Don't you *dare* come in here!' I yell, scrambling to pull the duvet up around me. I'm not a pyjama person, particularly not when my girlfriend is sleeping over, so I'm currently wearing the duvet and nothing else.

'Then come out here,' he says. He's past the front door now; I can hear it closing behind him.

'No!' I yell back. 'I'm not decent.'

'You haven't been decent for more than five minutes in a row since you were turned. You have precisely two seconds before I come in there and drag you out. One…'

I should move, but I'm stuck in my indecision: should I pull on some clothes, or barricade the door? I end up wasting the time thinking.

'Two,' Drake says as he opens my bedroom door.

He does not look happy. He's clearly come here in a hurry, because his hair is all over the place and he's missed one of the buttons on his shirt. It looks like he's been up all night.

'What part of "fuck off and die" did you misunderstand?' I ask, getting indignant with him because I feel vulnerable right now, swaddled in my duvet in the corner of my bed.

'What part of "personal property" did *you* misunderstand?' he replies. 'Where's my whisky?'

'I don't know, Drake. Where's my leather jacket?'

'Where's my fountain pen?'

'Where are your *manners*?'

'You surprise me,' he says, stalking into the room and slamming the door behind him. 'I wasn't aware that you knew what manners were. Now, where. Is. It?'

'Calm down,' I say, hitching the duvet up. 'It's just a bottle of booze.'

'That "bottle of booze",' he says, 'is a Macallan 1926. They only produced forty bottles, ageing it for sixty years before they sold the first one. It cost me one and a half million pounds at auction.'

Shit.

'You've crossed a line, Jack.'

'Oh, okay, because you've never done that before. Because you didn't cross a line when you hit me, or when you stole my leather jacket, or when you opened an investigation into my *girlfriend*!'

'I'm trying to protect you from your girlfriend, you idiot.'

I laugh.

'Right, because she's the one I need protecting from. Only she's never attacked me, has she? I think the only person I need protecting from is you.'

'And yet you're not the least bit afraid of me, are you?'

He's right. There's no hint of fear in my scent. Even after what happened in May, even after he's broken into my rooms while I'm dressed in only my duvet, I don't feel threatened by Drake. Despite what Tabitha has told me about the lie of haematopsychosis, I still don't believe that he would willingly hurt me.

'If you were,' he goes on, 'then you wouldn't be stealing my stuff like a fucking lunatic.'

'Hello, pot. Meet kettle. Do you know how crazy you look right now?'

He looks down at himself and then, seeing the state of his shirt, sits down on the end of the bed with a defeated sigh.

'It's been a long night,' he says.

'Carlotta keeping you up late?'

'No. You saw her leave.' He sniffs. 'But Dr Ross is obviously keeping you well-occupied.'

After last night's shenanigans, I am very definitely wearing Tabitha's scent mark.

I bunch the duvet up under my armpits, then settle back against the wall.

'Why are you here?' I ask. 'I mean really. You can't have stormed all the way over here just for a bottle of whisky.'

'It's great whisky,' he says, but he doesn't even try to make that sound convincing. 'I'm here because I'm worried. I know you don't believe me, but I'm trying to help with the Invicti.' I'm about to argue, to tell him that I know all about the coup, but he interrupts. 'Just hear me out for two minutes without complaining, if you're capable of it.'

'Fine,' I say grumpily.

'I've been looking into Benedict. Then last night, after you left, something happened.'

'Something like…?'

'Someone came to see me. The hostess from the opening of the blood bar. You remember her?'

With everything that's happened over the past couple of weeks – the judge, Raul, the haematopsychosis – I had forgotten her. I shouldn't have, particularly since she spent the night monopolising my girlfriend, but I did. I forgot the old-paper scent of her and the way her shadow moved around the bar just before the fire broke out. I forgot how she waved her fingers at me as she left the club that night, as though we were old friends instead of new acquaintances. And now she's visiting Drake in the middle of the night like a femme fatale.

'Can I trust you, Valentine?' he asks me. His voice is low and confidential.

'Probably not.' I cross my arms over my chest, pinning the duvet in place.

'Can you be serious for one minute? This is important.'

'Fine,' I say, because he looks so pathetic right now that it's the only reply I can give him.

Killian Drake: pathetic mess. I don't like that. It feels like a ploy.

'Her name's Yolande Leclercq,' he says. 'She was hired by Sir Percy to be the public face of the bar. She wants to make a deal.'

'What kind of a deal?' I ask.

'Something's about to happen at Crimson. She wants amnesty in return for her cooperation.'

'Amnesty for…?'

'Whatever's about to happen at Crimson,' he says, speaking slowly, as though he thinks I'm totally dense.

'Yes, I understood that. I meant: what exactly is about to happen at Crimson?'

He pushes his hair back from his face. It's so messy today that I'm left wondering if he normally uses product.

'That's the problem,' he says. 'She won't tell me until I grant amnesty, and I'm not sure I even have the power to do that.'

I shrug. 'You're the baron.'

'And what happens if the person orchestrating all this is the Primus?'

'You think that's what's going on?' I ask. 'Shit.'

'*Shit* is right.'

The Invicti might not outrank Drake, but the Primus definitely does. If he's behind whatever's about to happen at Crimson, then Drake won't have the authority to protect Leclercq from him. If he stands between her and the Primus, he'll have to do it by force. I don't think that's a fight he could win.

'I'm trying to get to the bottom of this,' he goes on, 'but it's not easy. I could use your help.'

'Why me?'

'There's no one else I trust.'

'Pff,' I snort.

'I'm serious.'

I look at him carefully, but I can't see the lie. For the first time, I wonder what life is like for Killian Drake in that huge mansion of his. He's always surrounded by goons, always dating beautiful women, and yet his girlfriend doesn't stay the night. I woke up with Tabitha in my arms this morning, but if Drake slept at all last night, he did so alone. I wonder if his life is lonely.

I hate him for that. I don't want to think of him as a person with feelings. I'd rather think of him as a bastard with an agenda.

Then I remember that he has Raul locked in a cell in his basement and my sympathy evaporates.

'Poor little rich boy,' I say. 'So lonely in your castle.'

'I don't know,' he says. 'I had so many visitors last night that I'm thinking about installing a revolving door.'

'Classy as always,' I sneer.

'Please,' he says. 'This affects every single one of us. I need you, Valentine.'

I tell myself it's the *please* that convinces me, that I care about making sure no more humans get caught in the crossfire, that this is about justice, and not about the way Drake's eyes lock with mine before his gaze flicks to my lips, to my neck, to the place where the duvet gathers over my chest.

I'm sitting in the bed I share with my girlfriend, my skin impregnated with her scent mark, so it couldn't be about anything else. Not with him.

His teeth deep in my skin.

His fingers tight around my wrists.

His knuckles hard across my face.

Never with him.

'Cam and I are talking to Windsor today,' I say grudgingly. 'I'll see what I can get out of him.'

Drake looks surprised.

'Are you actually going to cooperate with me?'

Which is the question, of course.

'Depends what Windsor says,' I hedge. 'I'm not making any promises.'

'You only have to promise me one thing: that you won't tell anyone about Leclercq. Not even Dr Ross.'

'No,' I say, because the thought of keeping more of Drake's secrets from her makes me nauseous. 'Besides, she'll know you were here. She'll smell your scent.'

He shrugs, as though it's no big deal.

'You can't ask me to keep her in the dark,' I insist.

'I can, and I will. She works for the Invicti. She's on their side. Have you forgotten about that? You can't trust her with this.'

'But I can trust *you*?' I laugh incredulously. 'Is that really the line you're taking here? After everything you've done–'

Stop fighting, Valentine.

He tries to interrupt – doubtless wanting to argue the existence of haematopsychosis – but I don't let him.

'Don't think I've forgotten about *that*,' I say. 'I will never forget it, or forgive it. But you're the baron and, even if I think the Primus was having an off day when he appointed you, we do have to work together.'

'I never–'

I hold up my hand, stopping his words before we start retreading old ground.

'I don't want to hear it,' I say. 'Nothing you can say will make me think you're less of a bastard, so let's not waste our time. I'll talk to Windsor, but that's all.'

Abruptly, I want him gone. He should never have come here in the first place, but I should never have let him stay. I don't know how I'll explain that to Tabitha. She'll never understand, even if I decide to tell her the truth.

Which I should.

'I smell blood,' Drake says. 'Dr Ross's blood.' His tone is almost offended.

'What I do with my girlfriend in the privacy of our bedroom is none of your business. We're done here. Goodbye.'

'So you did bite her?'

His indignation pushes me over the edge.

'Out,' I say, pointing at the door.

'I'm just concerned. If she's wrong about haematopsychosis–'

'She's not. She's good at what she does. Do you really think she'd risk my safety if she wasn't entirely sure? Is that how little you think of her? Just because you'd do it, doesn't mean she would.'

He gives me a long, level look, then says, 'I don't know what she'd do. You don't either, not really. You don't even know what *you'll* do half the time.'

He's not wrong, but I've had enough. I wish I were wearing clothes right now, but I'm not, so I wrap the duvet around myself like a towel and push him towards the door.

'Get out.'

'Why?' he asks with a lopsided smile. 'Are you worried about what you might do if I don't?'

'No!' I yell. 'Let's get something clear, Drake. You don't come into my rooms without an invitation, and since you're never going to get an invitation, you just don't come into my rooms. Ever. Do you understand me?'

'Well, that's just rank hypocrisy,' he says.

'Excuse me?'

'How many times have you come storming into my office while I'm in the middle of a meeting, or busy working, or having a quiet post-coital drink?'

'That's your office,' I say. 'It's different. This is my

bedroom. My door is firmly closed to you. Now get out.'

He has one last look around, taking in the view: the paint peeling from the ceiling, the damp under the window and the patch of mould by the bathroom door.

'And you criticise *my* interior design,' he murmurs.

'Get. Out!'

This time, finally, he does.

22

THE DRIVE OUT to Aston would suck less if I were with Cam. I want to talk about Tabitha, and about Drake, but I'm stuck with Boyd. All he wants to talk about is last night's date with Mildred Chen. The reason he was in no rush to leave the office was that they weren't meeting until midnight. He had something special planned: a moonlight picnic. He even let her play with his telescope. I really wish that was a euphemism, but apparently last night was perfect for its lack of cloud cover rather than for its opportunities for intimacy.

The break in the weather was short-lived; today it's nothing but rain. Boyd has the windscreen wipers doing double time.

'I wouldn't have guessed you were a stargazer,' I say. 'Or a romantic.'

'Why not?' he asks. 'Astronomy is fascinating. For example, did you know that the moon moves an inch and a half further away from the Earth every year? Or that it's actually lemon-shaped rather than perfectly round?'

'Fascinating.'

I'm not really listening. Everything I know about

225

astronomy I learned from Monty Python's Galaxy Song, and that is the extent of my interest. I'd be paying more attention if Boyd were inclined to talk about the romantic aspects of the date, but apparently they're not up for discussion. He rambles on for a while about Cassiopeia and I let myself zone out. I only zone back in again when I hear my name.

'Jacqueline?' he says.

'Huh?'

'I was saying that Mildred mentioned something that might be relevant to the case.'

'Really? What? Why didn't you say earlier?'

'I was getting to it.'

'We're already in Aston. It's taken you an hour!'

Boyd's eyes are fixed on the road – he still won't let me drive – but I can see his pout. He's usually a stickler for professionalism, and he's let himself get carried away with personal chit-chat. That can't be sitting well with him.

'It's not much,' he says, defensively, 'but Mildred spoke to the assistant librarian. She remembers seeing a man matching the description of the person who stole his library keys.'

'When? Where?'

'The weekend before the murder. She was doing some shelving and saw him hanging around out front.'

'Like he was scoping the place out?'

'Maybe,' Boyd concedes. 'She and the assistant librarian are going to work with a sketch artist. Between the two of them, we should be able to get a fair likeness.'

'Okay,' I say, but I'm not holding out much hope. Eyewitnesses are notoriously unreliable, and it's been a few weeks since they saw him. We can't expect miracles.

'It might throw something up,' Boyd says. 'You never know. In the meantime, there's Sir Percival.'

The butler already has the door open as we pull up to the house. He's been expecting us.

'Please come in,' he says as we rush in out of the rain. 'Sir Percival is waiting for you in the smoking room.'

He leads us through the house to a cosy wood-panelled space that opens out into the garden through a set of patio doors. They're firmly shut today, the rain beating hard against them. The sound alone makes me feel colder, but thankfully there's a roaring fire in the grate. I stand right next to it, hoping it might dry me out by the time we have to venture outside again. The hoody I pinched from lost property doesn't repel the rain like my trusty leather jacket once did.

I've been in this room before, on the night of Windsor's party. I sat on one of these leather wingback chairs with Drake, his hand resting on the small of my back. That feels like another me, another life. Another Windsor too, one without manners.

'Won't you have a seat?' he says, all courtesy. He's wearing smart casual clothes – chinos, button-up shirt, V-neck jumper, loafers – the kind of thing that no real person wears to lounge around the house. He's even made an attempt to tame his white-blond hair. 'And perhaps a drink?' he offers. 'Tea? Coffee? Something stronger?'

'No, thank you,' Boyd answers for both of us, though honestly I could do with a gin. He takes the chair opposite Windsor's. I stay by the fire. It's going to take a crowbar to move me.

'So, how can I help you?' Windsor asks. 'I still have no idea who sent the note with… the note. I wish I did.'

His tone is so compliant that I can't help but find it unsettling. He's sitting forward in his chair, elbows resting on his knees, eager. Either he's up to something, or the judge's death truly has changed him.

'It's not about that, Sir Percival,' Boyd says. 'There have been some further developments in the case that we hoped you might be able to shed some light on.'

'I'll do my best.'

'We found an empty lockbox in the judge's chambers. Do you have any idea what was in it?'

I'm watching Windsor's face carefully, so I see the flicker of recognition before he hides it under a rueful smile.

'Means nothing to me, I'm afraid,' he says. 'Maybe it was something to do with her work?'

'It wasn't,' Boyd says. 'I've already spoken to the court clerk. It was a personal item.'

'Well, Nora never mentioned it, so I can't help there. Did you have any other questions?'

I've got to hand it to him: Windsor lies like a pro. With the exception of that first micro-expression, he is completely composed. He gives every impression of being open and honest, his bearing relaxed and guileless, but somewhere behind it all his mind must be racing.

I wish I knew what was in those files.

'You have some interesting staff at Crimson,' I say, leaning back against the gigantic marble mantelpiece. 'Could you tell us about them?'

'I suppose this is about Matthew.' He smiles at me in a way that suggests we're friends commiserating over a loveable but incorrigible puppy. 'He needs some occupation. If he has nothing else to do, he'll only get himself into trouble. I'm trying to keep him out of it.'

'And how is that going so far?'

'Well enough. He's impunctual and socially maladjusted, but he knows how to mix a drink.'

I keep perfectly still. If I look at Boyd now, I'll give our suspicions away.

'Oh?' I say, nonchalant. 'What sort of thing?'

'All sorts,' Windsor says as he settles back in his chair. 'The old classics – manhattans, martinis, the odd sex on the beach – and then a whole menu of others he concocts himself. He has a flair for the creation of blood cocktails that rivals your own, Ms Valentine. It's a shame. Had you met under different circumstances, I believe you might have been fast friends.'

I can't suppress my snort.

'I doubt it,' I say.

Windsor shrugs.

'And all of these concoctions are safe?' Boyd asks.

'One hundred percent,' Windsor replies. 'I assure you, Deputy, we don't take safety lightly at Crimson. Everything is rigorously tested on our own people before being made available to the public.'

'I hear that includes Starblood,' I say.

'Then you have been misinformed.' His tone remains pleasant, but something in his expression has locked down, which is as good as a confession. 'It's just blood, alcohol and mixers. Nothing more complicated than that. Whatever you think is going on here, you're wrong.'

I would argue, but at that moment circumstances conspire to prove him right.

It's still chucking it down outside. Sheets of rain are breaking across the windows and the wind is blowing a gale, rattling though the foliage and drawing branches along the glass in screeches that put my teeth on edge. When the patio doors crash open, at first I think the wind has overpowered the latch. It's not until Windsor speaks that I realise we have company.

'Not now,' he says, rising quickly and hurrying to the

doors. He tries to bundle the drenched newcomer out the way she came, but she puts up a fight. She's the last person I expected to see. It's just as Windsor said: whatever I thought was going on here, I was wrong.

'Don't be ridiculous, Percy!' she says. 'I'm not going back out there. I'm already *trempée jusqu'aux os*. I did as you asked and spoke to the–'

'Carlotta,' he says loudly. 'I believe you know Ms Valentine. And this is her colleague, Deputy Boyd.'

Her head snaps around and her eyes widen as she sees me, apparently for the first time. I can understand her confusion. Boyd's wingback chair has its back to the patio doors and I'm almost hidden behind the monstrous mantelpiece. She burst in here expecting to find Windsor alone.

'Hello, Ms Arden,' I say.

'Jacquéline,' she says, smiling. 'How nice to see you.'

There's not even a hint of discomfort on her face, which proves nothing except that there's a reason she's the most highly paid Silver actor in the business. If I were dressed like she is, I'd certainly be uncomfortable. She's wearing black capris and a white shirt, with black loafers that are covered in mud. Her bra is red, which I know only because the rain has rendered her shirt entirely see-through and somewhat clingy. She has no coat, no boots, no hat. Either she wasn't expecting to be caught in the rain, or she's done it for effect. If it's the latter, I'm guessing that's bad news for Drake.

'Strange time to go for a stroll,' I say as she joins me in front of the fire. 'What were you doing out there?'

'Oh, I lost an earring yesterday. I wanted to check outside before the rain washed it away.'

'You've been here since yesterday? I didn't know you two were friends.'

'Our world is small,' she says, ignoring the insinuation in

my tone. She takes a cigarette from a box on the mantelpiece and lights it from the fire. Her hands are shaking, so she loses half of it in the process. 'You're young, *chèrie*. You'll see. You get to know everyone, sooner or later.'

'But you don't have to make friends with them,' I say.

She laughs, huffing out a lungful of smoke.

'I envy your *naïveté*.'

That hits me where it hurts. I can cope with being called practically any name under the sun, but "naive" sticks its point in my stomach and twists. Naivety is what turned me Silver in the first place, because I was stupid enough to trust my childish feelings for a woman I had only just met. Drake knows that, so coming from Carlotta's lips the jab feels calculated. I wonder if he smirked when he told her how I was turned. I wonder if they curled up together in his black satin sheets and laughed over my pathetic gullibility. The shame burns.

To these ancient Silver, I will never be more than a child.

Carlotta holds her hands out to warm by the fire for a few more seconds, then says, 'I'm going up to my room to change.'

'Did you find it?' Boyd asks.

'I'm sorry?' She smiles at him in a way that would make me blush, but apparently Boyd is immune. He only has eyes for Mildred, the disaster waiting to happen.

'The earring you lost,' he says. 'Did you find it?'

'Oh. No.' She catches her smile just before it slips. 'But I'm sure it'll turn up.'

Boyd watches her, waiting for her to rush in and fill the silence with words, but she's no amateur. She carries on as though there's nothing amiss.

'Well, it was a pleasure as always, Jacquéline. Deputy Boyd.' She nods to him then saunters out of the room. I watch her go, expecting to be overwhelmed by the view, as I have been every other time I've met her, but something has soured for me. She's staying here in Windsor's house voluntarily. She's close enough to him that they're keeping secrets together. Suddenly Carlotta Arden seems like less of a pin-up and more of a suspect.

Once she's closed the door behind her, I turn back to Windsor.

'Have you two been *friends* long?'

'You have a grubby mind, Ms Valentine.' He twists his signet ring around his finger as he speaks, fiddling. He is no longer composed, I guess because he didn't want us to see Carlotta. Her arrival must have been unexpected, because he knew we were coming and could have warned her not to interrupt. Wherever she came from, she certainly didn't just pop outside to look for an earring.

'Then you're not in a relationship?' I ask.

'I'm still mourning Nora. Carlotta and I are friends. We've known each other a long time. She stays here often when she's in the country.'

'You seem to have a lot of French friends,' I say. 'Carlotta Arden, Yolande Leclercq...'

'Two,' Windsor says. 'I wouldn't characterise that as "a lot". Anyway, Carlotta is Argentinian, not French, and Yolande isn't so much a friend as an employee, so you're technically wrong on both counts.'

He's getting prickly, but I'm not backing off yet.

'How did you meet Ms Leclercq?' I ask.

'We needed someone to be the public face of the bar. Yolande was recommended by a mutual acquaintance.'

'Who?'

'I forget.' He looks away from me and concentrates on Boyd. 'Any more questions?'

'Who did Ms Arden meet this morning?' Boyd asks.

'I have no idea.'

'She said "I did as you asked", which sounds to me as though you asked her to speak to someone on your behalf.'

He laughs. 'What I asked her to do was get out of the house for a while.'

'Because we were coming to speak to you?'

'Because I needed some time alone with my grief.' His voice is gruff as he replies, with pain or anger, or both. 'It's been less than a fortnight since Nora died and her murder is still unsolved, a fact that the Seekers seem to have forgotten. Instead, you're here asking me pointless questions about my house guest and my business interests, which are both completely irrelevant.'

'Nora Mitchell was murdered because someone wanted to get at you,' Boyd points out. His tone is dispassionate, but not cruel. 'The note made that clear. Given the circumstances, your house guest and business interests, plus every other aspect of your life, are all highly relevant. If you want us to find out who did this, you could help by answering our questions honestly.'

I'm convinced he's going to throw us out. I see his jaw clench, his jowls shaking with tension, but then he lets it go. It flows out of him on a breath, leaving nothing behind but defeat. His shoulders are hunched in a posture so slouched that he looks like he might never get out of that chair again.

Whatever part Windsor played in this, he's lost his taste for it.

'I don't know who did it,' he says. His voice is flat and toneless. 'I've gone round and round trying to figure it out, but I have no clue. There are any number of Silver who want to see me suffer, but none of them knew about Nora.' He goes still for a moment, no longer fidgeting with his ring, then says, 'Or so I thought.'

It looks like he's having a horrible epiphany. We're quiet as he plays it through in his head, then Boyd's the one who prompts him.

'Sir Percival?'

'It was a month or so ago, before the bar opened,' Windsor says, eyes fixed on the carpet. 'Nora knew I would be at Crimson – we were having a pre-opening party for a few friends – and she drove me home afterwards. I wasn't in a fit state myself. I didn't tell anyone we were seeing each other, but they could have put it together.'

This is news to us. Up until now, Windsor has been adamant that no one could possibly have known about him and Nora, that no one even knew she existed.

'Can you give us a list?' Boyd asks.

'The Silver who work at Crimson. Some friends who were smoking outside: Karl Mainwaring, Alvin Harrison, Lydia Gainsborough. Some others. A couple of the Solis Invicti who helped me to the car.'

'You're friends with the Solis Invicti?' Boyd looks my way.

'Let me guess,' I say. 'Benedict.'

'Of course.' I'm surprised Windsor admits it so freely, but he doesn't seem to care about secrecy anymore. 'And a chap called Alistair. Meyer lately, too.'

I don't know Alistair, but Thomas Meyer is a surprise. He was in Oxford earlier this year to help with the David Grant case. He helped us interview Windsor, which I suppose must have been how they met. I hadn't judged Meyer to be the kind of creep who'd voluntarily hang around with someone like Windsor, but apparently I'd been wrong.

'And you trust all these people?' Boyd asks.

'Yes,' Windsor says with conviction. 'They're my friends.

My allies.'

But then his certainty seems to disappear. He covers his mouth with his hand, rubbing one finger back and forth over his upper lip. It's an anxious gesture.

After half a minute, he looks up at me with empty eyes and says, 'But no one else knew. Whoever murdered Nora, it was someone I trust.'

We leave Windsor behind with his paranoia while we brave the rain with a list of names and a loaner brolly that I have no intention of returning. It's still impossible to get us both to the car without someone getting soaked. Typically, that someone is me.

'With friends like those…' Boyd says once we're strapped in with the heater blasting. I can feel my damp clothes steaming.

'Oh, cry me a river,' I say. 'Windsor's a creep who's friends with other creeps. It's no surprise that one of them has turned on him. He should have been expecting it. You lie down with dogs, then you get up with fleas.'

'I see,' Boyd says as he drives us away from Aston Manor House. 'Someone woke up on the wrong side of bed.'

'Yeah, well.' Can't argue with that. 'I just think it's a bit rich for him to get sanctimonious about his girlfriend's murder when he's killed who knows how many people.'

'None that we can prove, Jacqueline.'

'Hmph. Proof. Sure.'

'Now is not the time for your vigilantism. If the Silver really are on the verge of civil war–'

'I know. Anyway, I'm on probation until Drake says so.'

The reminder scratches at the back of my neck, making my skin flush hot despite my clammy clothes. The last person I want in charge of my fate right now is Killian

Drake, but – as I said to him only this morning – he is the baron, and we do have to work together.

'I should have asked him again about Leclercq,' I say. 'He was opening up to us.'

'Only about Nora's murder,' Boyd says. 'Not about anything else. He still wouldn't have told you anything about Crimson. Why are you interested in her?'

'No reason,' I reply.

I don't normally keep things from my team. Okay, that's a lie; I always keep things from my team. I don't play well with others. But I wouldn't be keeping the Leclercq connection from Boyd if Drake hadn't sworn me to secrecy. Until I have more information, I need to keep the circle small.

'You still think they're connected?' Boyd asks. 'The judge and Ortiz?'

'I don't have another theory. Do you?'

'It could be a coincidence. After all, we're in the middle of a war. There are bound to be casualties on both sides.' We don't talk much about our pasts in the Seekers, but the way he says this makes me think he's speaking from personal experience. 'How much do you know about Ortiz's affiliations?'

'Um… that he doesn't have any? He's not a soldier, Deputy. He's not the kind of person who makes alliances. He's just friendly to everyone.'

'Hmm.'

He doesn't have to speak his thoughts aloud, because I can see them on his face. Ortiz has no strategic value. Despite my well-reasoned theory, Boyd's ready to write off Rachael's death as an accident.

'Raul didn't do this,' I say. 'Didn't you notice Windsor's reaction when I started talking about Starblood?'

'He changed the subject quickly.'

'I thought so, which makes me wonder whether that's what Felton's been using to spike the drinks at Crimson.'

Boyd raises his eyebrows, though his gaze remains glued to the road.

'What?' I say.

'Nothing.'

My jaw clenches involuntarily, because I know Boyd's blasé tone means I'm not going to like what he says next.

'*What?*'

'He was a Starblood user, Jacqueline,' he says. 'People who use that stuff are unstable. Plus, if Felton really is spiking drinks with Starblood, then wouldn't it have less effect on a regular user like Ortiz? Shouldn't he have built up an immunity?'

'So you're saying he can't win either way?' I hate arguing in the car, because Boyd won't meet my eye. 'Either the drinks weren't spiked, in which case it's Raul's fault, or they were spiked with Starblood, in which case he should have been immune, so it's still Raul's fault. Is that what you're saying? What have you got against him?'

'Nothing.'

The fact that Boyd is remaining cool and apathetic makes me even angrier.

'Well, you'll see,' I say. 'The results are due back from the lab tomorrow. Then you'll see.'

'I hope so.'

Five minutes pass in silence while I stew and Boyd comes up with something else to say. He's not the world's biggest talker, but he's trying, which means I must be behaving even more grumpily than usual.

'Ms Arden has obviously made herself at home,' he says eventually.

'She has to stay somewhere while she's in town.'

'It's strange that she'd choose to be an hour's drive away from Oxford when she could stay with the baron, or in a hotel. That's strange, isn't it?'

Oh, god. He's trying to be upbeat. God save me from chatty Boyd.

'Unless there's some other reason for her to be out here,' he adds.

That gets my attention. 'Like what?'

'I don't know.'

I groan. 'Add it to the long list of things we don't know about this case. Windsor knew about the lockbox, though.'

Boyd looks surprised. 'Really?'

It's not like him to miss something like that. I guess his mind was full of Mildred and astronomy.

'There was a moment when you first mentioned it,' I say. 'He knew. If he's trying to keep it secret, I'd guess it's important.'

'Then we've confirmed the motive. Whoever killed Nora Mitchell, they wanted what was in those files.'

If only we knew what that was.

23

TABITHA COMES TO my rooms after work. I can pinpoint the exact moment when she scents Drake in the bedroom from the bloom of colour that sweeps across her face.

'It's not what you think,' I say before she can get a word out. 'He came with information about the case. I had to speak to him.'

'In your bedroom.' Tabitha's little fist is clenched around the strap of her bag. 'You let the baron into your bedroom.'

'"Let" is the wrong word. He sort of broke in.'

'How is that better?' Tabitha says, flinging her bag onto the sofa.

'He was angry about the whisky.'

'What whisky?'

'The whisky I stole from his desk.'

'Oh, sweet Jesus.' She sits down and puts her head in her hands. 'What were you thinking?'

'He stole my jacket.'

'What? Why?'

'Because he's a bastard. And I guess because I stole his fancy fountain pen first.'

She drops her hands and looks up at me.

'You know what this is, don't you?' she asks.

'War?'

'No, Jack. This is kids pulling each other's pigtails in the playground to get attention. It's a very petty and childish form of flirting.'

I gawp at her, affronted.

'I am *not* flirting with Killian Drake.'

'Yes,' she says on a sigh. 'Yes, you are.'

I want to defend myself. My first instinct is to tell her all about the coup, about Leclercq and the real reason Drake came storming in here this morning. But I remember his warning and something stops me, which is stupid, because I've already decided that I'll be standing with Tabitha, whatever side she's on.

Maybe I want her to tell me the truth about the Invicti herself. Maybe I'm waiting for an invitation. Either way, I keep my mouth shut.

'Tabs,' I say, getting down on my knees in front of her. I take her hands in mine and wait for her to look at me before carrying on. 'I'm wearing your mark. After last night, it's practically dripping off me.'

She smiles despite herself, a little lopsided twitch of her lips that says she remembers last night fondly. At least one of us does.

'I'm not going to deny that I like pissing him off,' I go on, 'but that's all it is. You're the person I'm going to bed with tonight and every night afterwards. It doesn't matter how often I have to see him, or where. Nothing he says will change the fact that I want to be with you. Okay?'

The smile spreads to her eyes as it widens and plumps her cheeks. She is so beautiful.

'Okay,' she says.

I smile back. 'Okay.'

But after we've had dinner – toasties I made with cheese melted in the microwave then spread on toast, a slapdash speciality of mine – Tabitha is in no state to go to bed. We're just settling onto the sofa to binge some Netflix when I hear her heart start to race. When I look over, there's sweat on her forehead.

'Are you all right?' I ask.

'I'm fine.'

Her eyes are fixed on my tiny TV, but she's pale as a ghost and her throat is working as though she's swallowing over and over again. Then she doubles over, clutching her stomach.

'Tabby?'

'I think I'm going to be sick,' she says, then she rushes to the bathroom just before her dinner makes its reappearance. One of the minor advantages of being Silver: when you need to sprint, you can really *sprint*.

I hurry after her, feeling useless as she retches into the toilet bowl. I know the received wisdom is that I should be holding back her hair, but she's got it neatly pinned with a fork and a glass stirring rod, so I have a feeling I'd be in the way. Instead, I crouch behind her and rub her back.

'Ugh,' she moans between bouts. 'You don't want to see me like this.'

'I don't care. I'm just worried.'

'Maybe it was the food,' she says.

'The bread and cheese were both fresh.' Admittedly, that's unusual, because I have been known to cut the mouldy bits off a block of cheese and eat the rest, but I only did the shopping this afternoon. 'I ate the same thing, and I feel fine. Were you sick like this yesterday too?'

'Not this bad,' she says. She must be feeling truly awful, because she's resting her cheek on the toilet seat. 'But I guess it's the same thing.'

'You *guess*?' I tease. 'I thought you were supposed to be a doctor.'

She flashes me a weak smile, then turns back to the toilet as she starts retching again.

I'm worried. I'm really worried. The Silver don't get sick like this. We're immune to every virus and disease out there, and what we're not immune to, we have the physical resilience to withstand. I haven't vomited since I turned, at least not from natural causes; overdosing on Massacres is a special case. But Tabitha doesn't drink like I do.

'I think we should call sick bay,' I say, but she shakes her head.

'I'm fine,' she insists, spit trailing from her lips. 'It'll be fine.'

'Tabs, you're not fine, and you know this isn't normal.'

'I'm sure it's just the lab work,' she pants. 'The chemicals I'm working with. It'll pass.'

'Maybe the nurse can give you something to–'

'No!' I'm surprised by her vehemence. 'It'll pass.'

I consider making the call anyway, but after another ten minutes she seems to be feeling better. She's still hugging the toilet, though, and she doesn't want to leave the bathroom, so I bring the duvet from the bed to tuck in around her.

'You're so stubborn,' I say, sitting behind her so I can carry on rubbing her back.

She forces out a laugh. 'And you're not, hen?'

'I just want you to be okay.'

'I am. I'm sure it's just the chemicals.'

'Then take a break from the project, will you? Please? You've got your answer. You don't need to carry on.'

'What answer?' she says, her voice little more than a

whisper.

'On haematopsychosis.'

'Oh.' She sniffs and wipes her mouth. 'Right.'

She's quiet for a moment. I think she's agreeing with me, that she'll drop this now that we know what we needed to know. Fat chance.

'I have to finish the tests so I can write the report,' she murmurs. 'It's important.'

'Then how about wearing some protective gear?'

'All right,' she says. 'I will.'

'Good. Now, do you think you're going to be sick again?'

'Not right now.'

'Do you want to lie down?'

'God, yes.'

I was expecting her to go to bed, but she lays her head in my lap instead. We spend the night on the bathroom floor like that, Tabitha flat out and exhausted while I stroke her hair and wonder how someone as smart as her could be so stupid as to make herself this sick. Still, I probably shouldn't complain; if she wasn't a little stupid sometimes then she never would have fallen in love with me.

I've made a decision. When Tabitha gets up early the next morning, fully recovered, I get up too. As soon as she's left for work, I walk straight down the Cowley Road to the tattoo parlour Naia recommended. Then I see it's all locked up and realise that tattoo artists don't work the same hours as the rest of us. Who wants a tattoo at nine in the morning?

Well, me.

I come back at noon. The guy who runs the place is covered in tattoos – arms, hands, throat, face – and he's not impressed with me. I catch him rolling his eyes when I explain what I want and where, but he's kind and gentle as he talks me through the process.

I pay my money and get my ink. It's not anywhere obvious, and it's healed in the space of minutes, so no one notices the change when I roll into the office an hour later.

'I didn't think you'd be coming in today,' Cam says, not looking up from his desk. 'Boyd's lining up interviews with the people on Windsor's list, but we've already spoken to most of them. There's nothing going on.'

'I can see that,' I say. Cam is folding sheets of the judge's phone records into origami. He's working on a crane at the moment, but there's already a jumping frog, a lotus flower and a monkey lined up along his desk. 'I thought maybe Ed would have the blood test results from the sample we took at Crimson. It feels like a good day to bust Raul out of holding and put Felton in a box.'

'I wondered why you were in such a good mood.' He finishes his crane with a flourish and lines it up with the others. 'He hasn't called, but I could give him a ring and check.'

'Let's just go down there,' I suggest. 'It's not like either of us is doing anything else.'

Cam looks at his origami troupe ruefully, then pushes away from his desk and follows me out. Perhaps he'd been planning to add more members. He probably had it in mind to make a whole menagerie.

When we get to the lab, it's empty.

'Ed?' I call.

'Oh, um. Is that you, Jack?' It's Ed's voice, but there's no Ed.

'Ye-es.'

'Just you?'

'No. Cam's here too. Why?'

'Nothing. Nothing. No reason.' I'm pretty sure that the

voice is coming from beneath the lab bench. 'It's just that, well, there was a bit of an accident. I was in the middle of cleaning up.' I go to help, but he screeches, 'Don't walk around the bench!'

'Okay, okay!' I say, stepping back to the door. 'Jeez. What exactly is the problem here?'

'If you must know, I splashed some acid on my trousers, and they, well, they, um, sort of dissolved.'

'Your trousers?'

'Yes, er… Amongst other things.'

I look at Cam, who's trying not to laugh.

'Ed,' I say, 'are you trying to tell me that you're stark bollock naked under there?'

'No, no. Not completely naked. Just, you know. From the waist down.'

I swear, I am surrounded by fiendishly intelligent, yet mind-numbingly stupid people.

Deep breath.

'Cam,' I say, 'go and find Ed some trousers.'

'And pants!' Ed squeaks from behind the bench.

'And pants,' I add. Cam leaves to do just that, covering his mouth with his hand every step of the way. He doesn't keep it in for quite long enough, though: I can hear the explosion of laughter when he releases it at the end of the hall.

'Ed, have you cleaned the acid off your… Have you cleaned off the acid?'

'Yes,' he replies miserably. 'I'd just finished when you walked in.'

An awkward silence descends as we wait for Cam.

'So,' Ed says eventually. 'How's Tabby?'

'Fine. How's Carrie?'

'Oh, fine.'

That seems to be all the small talk we can manage.

Thankfully, Cam doesn't take long to return. Ed shrieks a bit when he rounds the corner of the lab bench, but Cam's seen it all before. The two of them were together for god knows how long and Ed's naked arse is hardly a revelation.

Eventually, Ed stands up.

'Thanks,' he says to Cam, who can only nod back. He's still having trouble not laughing. 'I guess you're here about the results of the sample from Crimson?'

'Yep,' I say.

Ed grabs a sheaf of papers from a stack on the windowsill and starts leafing through them.

'Right,' he says. 'Here it is. It was just blood.'

'What?'

Cam looks just as shocked as I feel.

'It can't be,' he says.

'It is,' Ed insists.

I look at Cam and say, 'Well, shit.'

Which is an understatement. I was so sure I had the answer to this. Raul saw Felton in the alley with Benedict, talking about the missing files, so Felton poisoned him. It hangs together perfectly. How could Felton's extremely suspicious, locked-away bottle contain something as harmless as blood?

'It's a mix,' Ed says, continuing to flick through the pages. 'A few different profiles. It's difficult to tell the exact make-up, but I'd guess some human and some Silver. There's nothing special about it. If they put it in the drinks with alcohol, then the effect shouldn't be any different from your famous Massacres, Jack. I wouldn't advise that everyone goes around drinking them, but it doesn't explain what happened to Raul.'

'There's nothing?' I ask. 'Not even Starblood?'

'Nope.'

'Double shit,' I say.

Ed shuffles the papers together, looking at me tentatively over his useless glasses as though I'm a bomb about to go off.

'Not what you were hoping for?' he asks.

'No,' Cam answers for me, putting his arm around my shoulders. 'It's not.'

No chemicals in the blood means no case against Felton, and no hope for Raul. Now that Tabitha's ruled out the possibility of haematopsychosis for good, I have no way of explaining what happened with Rachael.

I feel like my stomach has dropped to the floor. If I'm honest, I want to follow it down there and settle in for a good cry, which is completely off-brand for me. I am simply crushed.

'It doesn't make sense,' I say. 'If it wasn't a drug in the blood, and it wasn't haematopsychosis, then what was it?'

'Accidents happen,' Cam says, giving my shoulders a squeeze. 'You know that better than most, Jack. We see them all the time.'

'But not with people like Raul.'

He and Ed exchange a concerned look, but they don't argue with me. Still, their silence speaks volumes. Maybe Raul really did lose control, just like Boyd thought. Maybe Ed was right all along, and my friend is losing his mind.

'I'm sorry, Jack.'

Ed looks so miserable that I reach out and pat him on the shoulder, because consoling him is better than admitting that I'm the one in need of consolation.

'It's not your fault,' I say. 'I'll see you later. I'm going to have to go up to Summertown.'

'Now?' Cam asks.

'I've dragged it out long enough already.'

'Do you want me to come with you?'

'It's fine,' I say. 'I'll go on my own.'

Ed looks between the two of us uncertainly, but in the end he just hands me the lab report and sends me on my way. I stop by our office to print out a copy of Tabitha's research report, because I'll need that too, then I trudge up to Drake's mansion with heavy feet.

I have never been so devastated at solving a case.

24

THERE'S A BED at the back of the cell that looks comfortable and clean, but Raul is lying in the middle of the concrete floor, his face turned to the ceiling as though he's counting the bricks. It's looks like he's paying penance.

'Raul,' I say softly, reaching through the bars. He doesn't stir.

'He hasn't moved all day.'

I glance over my shoulder to see Drake standing at the top of the steps.

'Kulika brought me the reports,' he says, flourishing the papers as he walks down the steps. I left them with the goon at the front door. I couldn't bring myself to take them to him, to explain their content. It seemed easier to let him work it out for himself. Evidently, he has.

'Come here to gloat?' I ask. 'Fine. I should have called it at the weekend. You were right. I was wrong. Bully for you. Now fuck off.'

'I'm not here to gloat.'

I knew that, but misery has made me spiky and lashing out at him feels good. Usually. I want him to snap back, to get stuck in a pointless sniping match, but instead he sits down on the grubby concrete floor beside me.

'You'll get dirt all over your fancy suit,' I say.

'I've got other suits.' He puts the papers down on the floor between us, then turns to Tabitha's haematopsychosis report and says, 'So this is what condemned me.'

'Don't you dare play the victim. Not now.'

He drops the subject. This conversation isn't over – we both know that neither of us is finished with it – but this isn't the time or the place.

I look at Raul. He still hasn't moved. For all the attention he's paying us, we may as well not be in the room at all. Or maybe it's Raul who's becoming invisible, gradually seeping out of the world as he shuts himself down, cell by cell.

'Dr Castell is sure about the bloods?' Drake asks.

'Yes.'

This puzzles him as much as it puzzles me. He looks down at the papers intently as though he's searching for a missing clue, his dark hair falling over his face.

'You were wrong,' I say. 'Is that such a surprise?'

'In this case, yes.'

'Well, there was nothing suspicious in the house speciality, not even Starblood, and haematopsychosis doesn't exist. Two reports, two disproved theories. The end.'

He shakes his head. 'I can't believe that. There's something else here. There must be.'

'Why do you give a shit? Why the sudden concern for Raul? You wanted to box him on the first day I brought him in.'

'This isn't just about Mr Ortiz,' he says, looking into my eyes. His are so black that all I can see is the reflection of my own face. 'It's about Crimson. This is bigger than him, than you and me. This is about the future of the Silver.'

At least I was right about something, then: the Silver are

at war, and its heart is Crimson.

'Whose side are you on?' I ask.

'It's not binary,' he says, as if that's an answer.

He's being deliberately cryptic. It irritates me, the way he's looking up at me through his lashes as though he has some dark secret he wants me to guess at, as though there's a mystery to him that I haven't yet fathomed. The truth is it's all bullshit. He wears his impenetrable smirk and his shark-black eyes like a mask, flashing them aside for moments at a time to give the impression that there's something of more substance underneath. But I've seen Drake unmasked and there's nothing beneath but more darkness, empty and cold. He is a shadow of a shadow, replicated into oblivion, fishing in the light for someone gullible enough to trust him.

I will not take his bait.

'Let's just get this over with,' I say, pushing to my feet.

When Drake follows me to the cell door, there's cement powder all over the arse of his suit. He doesn't even try to brush it off. I'm expecting him to call Kulika to do his dirty work, but instead he pulls the key to Raul's cell from his pocket and swings the door open himself. Raul still doesn't move.

'Did you have to drain him?' I ask.

It's standard practice when Silver are put in holding, because otherwise they'd have the strength to bust themselves right back out again, but surely it was overkill with a captive as zombified as Raul is.

'We haven't,' Drake says, helping Raul to his feet. 'He was already catatonic.'

Which is why the two of us have to haul him between us out of the cell and through the door that leads to the boxes. It's not that Raul is particularly heavy, but he's unwieldy enough that one of us isn't enough to guide him. He doesn't smell great, either. I try to talk him through it, to reassure him, to get any flicker of a reaction whatsoever, but he's just... gone. Given where we're putting him, maybe that's just as well.

The cellar stretches all the way under Drake's mansion, a warren of tightly-packed corridors lined with stone and steel doors and lit from above by tastefully dim bulbs. They're in archaic brass settings, because the cellars have been here as long as the house has, longer than Drake has been baron. The house comes with the title. A baron isn't just the guardian of the free Silver in their city, but the guardian of the sleeping ones too.

We take the warren to the left of the main corridor, where an open door awaits us. Raul goes quietly into his box. His feet are shuffling, his eyes glazed, and his mouth a little open as though he's on the verge of saying something, and yet no words come. I take him in my arms and whisper my goodbyes in his ear, but he doesn't whisper back. When I pull away, his eyes are focussed on the middle distance, watching something I can't see. There's no connection, no comprehension, so it doesn't feel like I've said goodbye at all.

'Raul,' I say, giving his shoulders a little shake. When he doesn't react, I shake harder, until Drake pulls me away.

'Leave him,' he says, his voice so kind that I want to hit him. I don't want his kindness, his sympathy or his pity.

'We can't just leave him like this,' I say, gesturing hopelessly towards the husk of Raul Ortiz.

'And how would you have us leave him? You can't help him now. You've done what you can. If you were going into a box, would you want to do it consciously? Or would you rather walk in like he has, in a dream, and go under without ever knowing that you have?'

'But if he wakes up–'

'Valentine,' Drake says softly, turning me to face him. 'He's not going to wake up.'

I want to scream. The silence of this cellar is so oppressive that I'm dying to break it, but I resist. I let Drake strap Raul into his new home: three feet wide and deep, seven feet tall. He closes the door softly but firmly, throwing the bolts to lock Raul into the darkness of his vertical coffin.

'How long are you keeping him here?' I ask.

'A year.' Drake says. 'Or two. Or forever. You know he's not coming back.'

The softness in his voice is what does it. I'm used to Drake as my antagonist. I want him to be cruel so I can be strong, but instead he puts his hand on my shoulder and looks at me as though he cares. Before I know it, the tears are streaking down my cheeks and I'm letting him pull my forehead against his chest. I can smell the spicy dark scent of his skin and it all comes rushing back again: the kisses, the bite, the back of his hand. So why do I keep finding myself in his arms? I'm trying to make myself pull away, trying to be stone, emotionless, but I feel powerless when we're alone like this. And thrumming underneath my other emotions like a drumbeat, the grief isn't letting me go.

Raul isn't coming back.

The rhythm of it repeats over and over in my head.

He's not coming back, and neither is Rachael.

Maybe it would be easier to bear if it wasn't so random. If this could happen to Raul, the sweetest and gentlest Silver I know, then it could happen to any one of us. We could snap and take a human life. If it happened to me, maybe I wouldn't eat my heart out the way Raul has, but I'd never be the same again.

That's why I'm crying into Drake's shirt, despite

everything. It's nothing to do with him, it's just that I'm having a breakdown in his cellar and he happens to be nearby. It's embarrassing, but he's seen worse. It wasn't too far from here that he found me as a new Silver two decades ago, passed out in a pool of my own blood. Compared with that, what's a little snot on his shirt?

'I'm sorry,' he says.

'Don't.'

I turn my back to him and pull myself together, wiping my eyes on the sleeves of my top. When I'm more or less composed, I start walking back the way we came, back towards the exit, with Drake following behind me. We pass Gabriella De Palma's box on the way, labelled unceremoniously with a piece of paper shoved into a metal frame in the centre of the door. The tag doesn't need to be any more durable than that; Gabriella will be out in eight months' time. The other doors, doors that stretch off to the right side of the main corridor along the route we didn't take, have more permanent markings on their locked faces. They're etched in metal and stone, naming Silver who have been here for decades or centuries and will stay here for more. I'm too young to know all their stories, but I've heard enough to make me glad that Raul isn't amongst them. Yet.

'We talked to Windsor,' I say as we emerge into the basement room where the holding cell now stands empty. I need to talk about something to take my mind off Raul. 'I couldn't find out anything about Leclercq. He said she was referred to him by a mutual friend, but he wouldn't tell us who. He had an interesting houseguest, though.'

'Oh?'

'Did you know Carlotta was staying in Aston?'

From the way Drake freezes with one foot on the stairs up to the kitchen, I'm guessing he didn't.

'I don't think he wanted us to see her there,' I go on. 'She interrupted our interview. She said she'd been looking for a lost earring outside, but I'm pretty sure she was coming back from an errand Windsor had sent her on.'

'What kind of errand?'

'Speaking to someone. Neither of them would admit it, or tell us who she'd been talking to. Maybe you'll have more luck getting the truth from her.'

'Huh,' he says, then he carries on up the stairs, leaving me to catch up.

'Drake?'

'What makes you think that she'd talk to me?'

'Pillow talk?'

He laughs as I follow him into the kitchen. It's a bitter sound.

'If there's one thing Carlotta and I clearly don't do well, it's communication. All this time...'

He shakes his head and leans back against the kitchen island. The room is luxe. I mean, the whole mansion is luxe, but this is the kitchen of someone who really cares about good cooking. I wouldn't have pegged Drake for a foodie, but there are implements hanging from the utensil rack that I can't identify, and they've been well-used.

'What the hell is this?' I ask, scooping one down from its hook.

'It's a jam funnel.'

'And this?'

'A pastry scraper.'

'And this?'

'Don't tell me you've never seen a garlic press before.'

'I have a fridge and a microwave, and a canteen that's open all hours. I don't cook.'

He takes the utensils from me and hangs them back where

they belong. Apparently he's fastidious in the kitchen.

'Everyone should cook,' he says. 'I cook for Carlotta.'

It should be a boast, but it sounds hollow. I don't care. I ignore his feelings – I have enough of my own to contend with – and tell him the rest of what he needs to know: that the person who killed the judge was someone Windsor trusts, that we're going through his list, and that we have no evidence that any of this is linked to the captain. After a moment's hesitation, I tell him about the lockbox too.

'Files?' he asks.

'That's all we know. And that they're a "game-changer".'

'And missing.'

'Yes.'

'Well, that's not good.'

He's more worried than he should be.

'What do you know?' I ask. 'What's this all about?'

He looks around the kitchen as though he's expecting to see eavesdroppers in every corner, then says, 'Come on,' and leads me into a small room a few doors down the corridor. There are no windows and the whole space is only about ten feet by ten feet: a surveillance room with a bank of screens and a couple of rolling chairs. He kicks out the goon who's watching the monitors and closes the door behind him, taking one seat and offering me the other. I sit only because I need to hear what he has to say, not because I have any intention of staying long.

'Well?' I ask when he remains silent. 'Are you going to tell me what this is about or not?'

'It's about secrecy,' he says. 'There are more than two sides, because aren't there always? But there are two main factions. They're arguing about whether the Silver should stay hidden or reveal themselves to the human world.'

The words hit me like a physical blow. It's a good thing

I'm already sitting down, because if I wasn't then I think I might have wobbled a bit.

'But,' I say, 'what about the secrecy pact? Keeping the existence of the Silver secret from the humans is the whole point of the Seekers.'

'Which is exactly why no one's talking to you about it. All the other Silver are being sounded out, but you, the rest of the Seekers, and me…'

'The captain?' I ask, my heart in my throat.

Drake's face darkens. 'She's chosen her side.'

'Which is…?'

'Pro-reveal.'

'Fuck.'

My head is spinning. All the time I've been Silver, I've accepted as gospel that we can't reveal ourselves to humanity. There are any number of worst-case scenarios I've heard trotted out over the years whenever people have expressed anti-Seeker sentiment: humans would fear and persecute us; they'd make blood harder to obtain in order to control or eradicate us; they'd experiment on us; it would be a war that we'd win, but at huge loss of human life; we have a duty to protect them as the weaker species. There are any number of moralistic arguments, but in the end the clincher was always that the Silver preferred to live in the shadows. It seems that, for some of us at least, that is no longer the case.

'Can I assume that you're pro-secrecy?' I ask.

Drake presses his lips together. He doesn't say a word, but the look he gives me is answer enough.

'You're *pro-reveal*? Are you kidding me?'

'I'm neither,' he says.

'What?'

'It's not a simple binary. I told you, there are more than two sides. It's not just about what's right or what's safest.

Everything's bound up in economics and politics. For some people, there's a lot of money to be made.'

'You're trying to make a *profit* by selling out our future? Even for you, that's low.'

'Sure,' he says, 'believe the worst of me. Why change the habit of a lifetime? Look, the things you've been told about the secrecy pact are just one side of the coin. It's the Primus's edict, the Primus's will, but the Primus is only one man. He might be running things at the moment, but his power could be taken away in an instant. It relies on the support of the rest of the Silver, and if he loses that then suddenly everything is fluid. There'll be a vacuum, a race to the top. If there's war between the Silver, how many people from both races will get caught in the crossfire?'

'So, what?' I say. 'You're trying to keep the Primus in power?'

'No. I'm trying to make sure that if there is a transition, it's smooth and peaceful. I'm trying to prevent a war.'

'By staying neutral.'

'More or less.'

I'm guessing "less". If you can rely on Drake to do anything, it's to look out for his own interests.

'Then what was in the missing files?' I ask.

'I'm not sure.'

'But you've got an idea.'

He's looking at me in a way I can't decipher, but it feels too intimate in this tiny, dark room. I can feel my heartbeat pick up a notch, feel the air thickening in my lungs. I make to move away, but he catches my hand in his before I can get out of the chair.

'I think you should talk to Leclercq,' he says.

'Because you think it was her who took the files?'

'No. I don't know who it was, but I think she might be

able to tell us. So will you talk to her? It might help us both. Besides, what have you got to lose?'

I'm in the process of preparing a withering retort, because I like to say "no" to him as a matter of principle, but then he ruins it all by saying, 'Please?'

Maybe it's the emotional aftermath of Raul's boxing, or maybe I'm just getting used to the idea of having him as an ally. Either way, I fold.

25

MY FIRST TASK when I get back to the college is to update the team on the captain's new affiliations. It's not a fun conversation. My second task is to persuade Cam to come back to Crimson with me to talk to Leclercq. That takes a little longer, so between one thing and another, it's late afternoon by the time we walk into the bar, late enough that the doors are open. I assume that's because they're getting ready for the night ahead, but apparently I'm wrong.

'We're closed,' says the blonde behind the bar. She looks to be in her forties with a wide smile and a figure I would have killed for at twenty, but she's Silver so who knows how old she really is?

'Not opening tonight?' Cam asks.

'Nope. Not until Friday.'

'What's going on?' I ask. Now that I'm paying attention, I can see there have been some serious changes since my last visit. A crew is building banquettes around the walls and all the tables have been removed, increasing the standing room significantly. The VIP area at the back is plusher too, with booths and curtains that give extra privacy and allure.

'You're redecorating already?' Cam asks.

'The Primus is coming,' the woman says, eyes bright. 'Can you believe it? So we're sprucing the place up a bit.'

'He's coming this Friday?' I ask.

'No, he's coming on Thursday. Private party though, sorry.' She looks smug, so I guess she'll be there. 'But we've got lots to do before then, so if you wouldn't mind…' She looks pointedly towards the door, but by this time I've spotted my target.

Leclercq is here, sitting in a booth at the back as she taps on an iPad. Even like this, dressed in jeans with her platinum hair dragged into a scruffy ponytail, I find her intimidating. Something in the way she holds herself makes me feel like a little girl in the presence of a grown up. But I'm not going to let on in front of Cam and this snooty bartender.

'We're here to see Yolande, actually,' I say to her, as though Leclercq and I are old friends, then I walk straight up to her booth with Cam following behind.

'Jacqueline Valentine,' Leclercq says, with no trace of an accent. Her name might be French, but I'm not entirely sure she is. She greets me with a smile, the kind of smile that a piranha gives a smaller fish right before it slams its jaws shut on the little guy's head.

'Hi,' I say. My voice comes out sounding more tentative than I would like. 'Have we met before?'

'Not before the opening.' She turns off her tablet before I can see what's on the screen, then puts it face down on the table. 'We have a mutual friend.'

'I hope you're not talking about Windsor, because I would definitely not describe him as a friend.'

'I wasn't, actually.'

'You mean my girlfriend, then?' I ask, trying and failing to keep the venom out of my voice. 'Tabitha? You met her at the opening night.'

And held her on the dance floor like you thought she was yours, even though she's mine.

'Not her either.'

She doesn't elaborate and I'm sick of playing her game, so I drop it. I'm not going to give her the satisfaction of making me guess all night.

'This is Cameron Sawyer,' I say. 'We're Seekers.'

'I know,' she says, again without elaborating.

It's an annoying habit, because it cuts the conversation dead and leaves me scrambling for ways to resurrect it. That feels deliberate, like she's trying to put me on the back foot. I bet she gets a perverse thrill from making people work hard to talk to her, as though the little conversational nuggets she drops are so valuable that they have to be paid for in sweat and exasperation.

See? I have valid reasons to hate her. It's not just jealousy.

'We have some questions,' I say.

'Then the baron sent you,' she replies.

'Not exactly.'

'He's a friend of yours, though.' Her intonation makes it clear that this is not a question.

'I wouldn't say that.'

She looks me over with hungry eyes for perhaps a quarter of a second, then looks away. Everything about her demeanour says she thinks we're just a minor irritation, like a buzzing fly or the hum of a fridge, and that if she ignores us then we'll go away.

It is infuriating.

I turn to Cam, because I know that if I carry on trying to talk to this woman then I am going to lose my shit. I gave him the background on our walk over from the college, so he knows what we're here to find out. Given our different temperaments, stepping back to let him take over is the best call.

Unfortunately, Leclercq has other ideas.

Cam only manages to say, 'Ms Leclercq, I believe–' before she interrupts, looking directly at me.

'Surely you don't expect me to talk to you here.'

'Then where?'

'The Castle,' she says. 'The top of the mound. Ten minutes.' Then she clicks her tablet back on and gives it her full attention, ignoring us completely. We take that as our cue to leave.

'She wasn't very friendly,' Cam says when we get outside.

He's shocked by Leclercq's abruptness; he can never understand why anyone would be less than friendly. He takes rejection hard. Me, I'm used to it. If she'd been nice, I probably would have been more suspicious. Maybe then things would have played out differently.

The Castle complex is over the road from the club and a little way back towards town, a collection of restaurants and tourist attractions clustered around a half-ruined Norman castle with an impressive tower. On a Tuesday early evening in September, it's tourist central. We make our way to the mound through gaggles of European teenagers with matching backpacks, all congregating around the small amphitheatre that's been constructed next to the gift shop. I didn't know they had outdoor performances this late in the season, but the area is roped off and the stage is set for something Shakespearean, judging by the costumes. The officious man at the gate won't let us through unless we buy tickets, so Cam reluctantly proffers his credit card. It's easier than arguing with the amateur dramatist.

We climb to the top of the mound and settle ourselves on the cold stone seats to wait for Leclercq. My backside goes numb within minutes and it feels like my pelvis is being turned to ice, but at least it's stopped raining.

After fifteen minutes, Cam says, 'She's not coming, is she?'

'Of course I am.'

The voice comes from directly behind us, where there are no more steps. Leclercq has spread her coat out on the grass and made herself comfortable without either Cam or me noticing she had joined us. I already knew she was something of a ghost – she made that clear on the opening night at Crimson – but this is on another level. I didn't think anyone was capable of eluding Silver senses like this.

But the one thing she can't hide completely is her scent. Now that I'm concentrating on it, I pick up the same perfume that unsettled me at the club opening – a musty library smell mixed with sweet chocolate – and it tickles the back of my throat. It's so familiar that I feel like I'm caught in that seesaw moment after waking from a dream, trying to catch hold of the memory before it disappears into nothingness. But it won't come.

Cam gets right to business, saying, 'Will you tell us what's going on at Crimson?'

'I'm not privy to all the details.'

Of course she isn't, because that would be too easy. This case *sucks*.

'But,' she continues, 'I know some of it. The party on Thursday for the Primus? It's less of a party and more of a summit.'

'In what sense?' Cam asks.

'In the sense that the Primus is laying out his terms and the dissenters are laying out theirs.'

'You mean about whether or not the Silver should come out of the closet?' I say.

She sniffs delicately, clearly a little put out that I know as much as I do, but she still manages to give the impression that she's in control. The wind is strong up here on the top of the mound and it's blowing my hair into my face and sticking it to my lips, but it's treating Leclercq more kindly. I'm so rumpled that I must look as though I've just come out of the tumble dryer, but she is poised, with just a few strands of bone-white hair whipping across her pale face in a manner that's almost artful. She could be modelling knitwear right now with all her elegance.

God, I hate her.

'Thursday night is the deadline,' she says. 'Everyone is coming to declare their allegiances.'

'What does that mean?' Cam asks.

'It means that by Friday morning, we'll either have a new Primus or we'll be at war. The dissenters aren't going to back down.'

Leclercq says this as though it's irrefutable, but of no consequence. For all the emotion she's betraying, you'd think this has no effect on her personally.

'What's your stake?' I ask her. 'Which side are you on?'

She turns her dark grey eyes on me and says, 'Neither.'

I am getting really sick of hearing that.

'Then what's your play?' I ask. 'Why are you telling us this? Why did you want to talk to Drake? What are you even doing at Crimson?'

She shrugs one shoulder, blasé. 'I have an interest I'm trying to protect.'

'And that interest would be…'

'Private.'

I clench my teeth and gesture for Cam to take over again, because now I really am going to lose my shit. I don't think I've ever known someone so aggravating, which is saying a lot given how much time I've been spending with Drake lately.

'What you're telling us,' Cam says, his tone diplomatic, 'is that you're watching both sides play out so you can pick the winning side at the last minute. Right?'

'Correct.' She smiles. 'Clever boy. No point throwing my lot in with the loser, is there?'

'And what about the baron?' Cam asks, ignoring her condescension. 'Why tell him anything?'

'He's a wild card.'

'So you're trying to get him on-side as well.'

'It wouldn't hurt. Let me be plain: I don't think the dissidents are going to win this scuffle. They fight amongst themselves, and none of them seem to agree who should be leading them or what they're fighting about. But I do think they're serious about annulling the secrecy pact, and they're going to make a mess. If they decide to reveal themselves, it will be difficult to stop them.' She turns to me. 'Without my help, that is.'

'So that's the deal?' I ask. 'You give Drake the information he needs to stop them in return for your safety?'

'Not quite. I'll give him the information in return for amnesty for me and one other person.'

'Who?'

She taps her lip twice with her forefinger; she's not going to say.

'Your private interest?' Cam asks.

'Just so.'

There's a screech of feedback from the stage mics. Down below, the theatricals are setting up for their performance. The amphitheatre looks as full as it's going to get, but we're still a good few metres away from any of the other spectators.

I don't like sitting up here. I feel too exposed. The

problem with meeting at the top of the Castle mound is that it's high. It feels private because you're far away from the rest of the crowd, but in reality you're the most visible thing around. It's more of a gallery than it is a hiding place.

It makes us an easy target.

There's a noise: a soft buzzing, the rustle of fabric against fabric, or the beating of a moth's wings. I recognise the sound before I see the blur of movement, which is going so fast that it challenges even my Silver sight. If I hadn't heard it before, I never would have reacted quickly enough to snatch the dart out of the air.

It sits in my palm like a felled hummingbird, turquoise liquid swirling in a glass vial etched with the logo of the Solis Invicti. Just like the dart that took Drake down earlier this year. Just like the dart I saw passed between the captain and Benedict in Drake's photos. I tuck it safely into the pocket of my hoody.

'Fuck,' Cam says, looking around for the shooter, but it's impossible to pinpoint the dart's origin. 'Who was it aimed at?'

'I'm not sure,' I say. 'It could have been any one of us.'

'Looks like we're out of time, then,' says Leclercq, getting to her feet. She doesn't hurry, not seeming the slightest bit concerned that one of us almost got shot, nor that the shooter is probably still out there, watching us down the barrel of their gun. She is leisurely.

As she stands from the ground and slings her coat over her shoulders, I get another waft of her papery, sweet scent. I can almost place it, that elusive link that will allow me to place *her*, but I can't make the final connection. For a while I think it's the book smell – after all, Nora Mitchell's body was found in a library – but the scent isn't the kind that you pick up by spending time in a place, it's the kind that is an intrinsic part of her, simply the scent of *Yolande*. Her skin smells like parchment.

'You have until Thursday,' she says, then she walks away.

She never told me the identity of our "mutual friend", or her "private interest", but I have an idea of who it might be. There's one other person who seems to be playing both sides here, someone who's running go-between: Carlotta Arden. Could they be working together? It makes me wonder how much of what Leclercq told us was genuine, and how much was constructed. One way or another, we're being manipulated.

26

CAM'S PHONE BUZZES as we leave the Castle complex. I can't make out much of the conversation, but it must be urgent because he grabs my arm and pulls me to a halt before we've got to the end of the road. Looks like we're not going back to the college after all.

'Fancy a trip to London?' he says as he hangs up. 'The deputy's tracked down all the Silver on Windsor's list without solid alibis, and one of them is a member of the Solis Invicti. We can interview him at their headquarters.'

'What?' I say. 'Now?'

It's only half past seven, twilight but not dark, but it's been a busy day. I was anticipating a cosy night at home with Tabitha. She texted me earlier to say she's still feeling fine, and that she's sure last night's sickness was just a reaction to her lab chemicals, but I won't feel comfortable until I see that for myself. It also seems a bit rash to go running off to London without going back to the college to report in about the dart first. Surely the deputy should be told, even if we can't trust the captain?

But Cam is practically bouncing with impatience.

'Yes, now,' he says. 'Come on, Jack. I'm dying to see their

place. You know how I feel about the Invicti.'

I think they're a bunch of arrogant soldier boys, but Cam idolises the Solis Invicti. He has a healthier respect for authority than I do, which is admittedly not saying much, and it's always been his ambition to join their ranks. A trip to their base of operations is at the top of his wish list. I can't say no.

I sigh and ask, 'Who's the guy?'

'Alistair Jameson,' he says. 'Recent recruit. Scottish. Knows Windsor through Meyer.'

'And Meyer?'

'He has an alibi, as does Benedict, but they'll both be there at HQ.'

I groan, because Benedict is the last person I want to see, but I let Cam turn me around and walk me to the train station. He buys tickets for us both on the Seekers' credit card, and before long we're on the express to London Paddington. It's packed with reverse commuters and a few drinkers, but there aren't many people looking to party on a Tuesday night. We have most of the carriage to ourselves.

'I'm calling Tabby,' I say.

'Then I'm going to the shop. Tea?'

'No. Bring me back a proper drink.'

'They don't serve hard liquor on the cross country service.'

'Then bring me back some chocolate instead. And call Boyd. Tell him what we found out from Leclercq, and tell him about the dart.'

It's a relief when Cam leaves because, much as I love him, he's so hyped up about seeing Solis Invicti HQ that he's not very restful company right now. If he were a puppy, I'd let him off the leash for a proper run, but since he's only a human Labrador, he can play fetch instead.

As it turns out, Tabitha does sound fine. When I tell her where we're going, she gives me a quick run-down on her colleague Alistair Jameson: hypercritical and grumpy, but apparently a genius with warfare, gadgets and machinery. The way she tells it, there's not much he can't manage in terms of strategic planning or weapon design. With the memory of the dart fresh in my mind, the latter seems suspicious. It makes me wonder whether Jameson is chummy with Matthew Felton.

'Will you be home late, hen?' she asks.

'Worried I'll harass your fellow countryman?'

'Alistair is from Inverness,' she says, in the same voice she uses when the drains at the college get backed up. 'I am from Glasgow.'

'I'm sorry,' I say, suppressing a laugh. 'I didn't realise my girlfriend was such a snob. They might be different cities, but they're still in the same country.'

'Just barely. I hoped you might be home tonight. I had… plans.'

I drop my voice to a whisper and say, 'Sexy plans?'

'Damn right, they were sexy.'

And I bet they would have become even sexier when she saw my new tattoo. I think she's going to like it. Maybe I'll suggest she gets one too. Maybe a jackdaw, or a heart. Maybe my name. I'd like to see it on her skin.

That's weird, right?

'I'll get off at the next stop and run all the way back to Oxford if you like,' I say.

She laughs. 'Not necessary. I'll stay in Nash Lee tonight.'

'I'm sorry,' I say, feeling almost angry that I can't see her. 'Tomorrow? I promise I'll be home.'

'I'll hold you to that.'

We say our goodbyes, then I'm left on this stupid train to

stupid London feeling more flushed than is warranted by the carriage's radiators. I need a distraction.

For a moment, I consider calling Drake to fill him on the Leclercq situation, but that feels like a bad idea in the circumstances. Thankfully, Cam returns then with a pile of chocolate bars, so I decide to delay the dubious pleasure of calling Drake in favour of the more immediate and reliable pleasure of gluttony.

The Solis Invicti's headquarters are in the centre of the city, so we have to catch the tube from Paddington. I hate the London Underground. It's cramped and sweaty even in mid-winter, and don't get me started on how the grime-filled tunnels smell to a Silver nose. If I had any choice in the matter, we'd be going overground, but tonight we don't have the luxury of taking our time. Even with the benefit of the tube, it's already nine o'clock when we reach their building.

It is monstrous. If ever a skyscraper was built to display the affluence and influence of its occupants, it's this one. There's so much glass and shiny chrome on display that I'm blinded by the reflection of the streetlights, so I can imagine how imposing it is in full sun. And yet the doorplate is demure: a tiny brass plaque that reads *SIHQ*. The mind that came up with this understated sign is very different from the one that designed the building itself.

Benedict meets us at the door, ushering us into a foyer in which every surface is covered with marble. I'm wearing my rubber-soled boots so I don't have to worry about my balance, but I see more than one high-heeled functionary teetering across the slippery floor.

'Mr Sawyer,' Benedict says with a nod, then he adds, 'Valentine,' with a sneer.

Nice to see that the feeling is mutual.

He's dressed more casually than I've ever seen him before, his muscular frame crammed into a tight henley and jeans. The outfit makes him look like an off-duty bouncer, which is basically what he is. All brawn and no brains. The jeans are so tight that they give him a strange kind of waddle, his thighs rubbing together as he leads us into a lift and presses the button for the very top floor.

'Who are we going to see?' Cam asks.

'The Secundus.'

'Really?'

'Really.'

Cam's eyes light up with glee – he's such a dork over these guys – but it doesn't sound like good news to me. If the Secundus is getting involved then it's because he wants to protect his men, which suggests they have something to be protected from. Someone here has done something the Secundus wants to keep from us.

He doesn't let on; when the lift door opens, the Secundus is waiting on the other side, ready to greet us like we're old friends instead of irritating underlings with whom he's been forced to cooperate in the past.

The Secundus, Andrew – no last name – is less physically imposing than Benedict, but he gives the impression of intellectual superiority. I sometimes wonder whether Benedict has two braincells to rub together, but Andrew is clearly planning five steps ahead. He's tall with shoulder-length dark hair and emerald eyes, and I guess he's attractive if you like your men strong-jawed and clean-cut, but he's a little too savoury for my tastes. Just as well, really, because he's not a fan of mine. He hides it better than Benedict does, but there's still a moment of recoil when he clocks my scruffy jeans and hoody.

Everyone's a fashion critic.

'Mr Sawyer,' he says, shaking hands with Cam and then, reluctantly, with me. 'Ms Valentine. Welcome.'

'This place is amazing,' Cam gushes. 'Are the labs in this building too?'

'Yes, plus the training, development, intel and logistics departments.'

'And where do you guys stay? I mean, where do the Invicti live?'

'We have barracks down the road for those who want to live in. You're interested in joining us?'

Cam's eyes go so big that I'm worried they're going to pop out of his head.

'It's only my lifelong dream,' he says.

'Then maybe you'd like to meet two of our most recent recruits. Come right this way.' He ushers us towards the door to the right of the lift, then turns to Benedict. 'No need for you to hang around,' he says, to my relief. 'Go and enjoy your evening.'

'If you're sure.'

Benedict gives me and Cam a look that tells us to watch ourselves, then snaps off a salute to the Secundus and walks away. I feel a palpable drop in blood pressure as the lift descends, taking Benedict down with it. We're left with the Secundus and the new recruits waiting on the other side of the door. There are just two of them, sparring in a massive room carpeted with gym mats and littered with boring fitness equipment. If this were my building, I could find a better use for the top floor than converting it into a gym – say, a rooftop bar with blood and beer on tap – but apparently the Solis Invicti and I have different priorities.

'Alistair,' Andrew says. 'Adewale. Come and meet our guests.'

The two men both look to be about forty, in bodies that

went a few times around the block before they were turned Silver. Alistair is about five feet ten with a wiry frame that hides a lot of muscle, and his pale face is craggy with a scruffy half-beard. Adewale, by contrast, is over six feet tall with muscles that look like they've been sculpted onto him. His skin is dark and shining with sweat. The two of them must have been tussling for a while.

When Alistair sees us, he glances anxiously at Adewale, but the taller man just pats him on the back and shoves him towards us.

'So,' Adewale says, shaking our hands enthusiastically. 'You have questions for my boy, here.' He rests his hand on Alistair's shoulder.

'A few,' I say.

'Then let's get started.'

He leads us to a cluster of benches at the side of the room. They're not much more comfortable than the stone steps we were sitting on earlier today, designed for exercise routines rather than relaxation. These guys don't want us to hang around. I know without bothering to ask that the Secundus won't allow a private interview, nor is he likely to sit down and stop looming over us all. He's demonstrating his authority, which is unassailable in this place.

I can't imagine why Cam would want to work with this bunch of dick-swinging testosterone junkies when he could just carry on working with me forever, but his enthusiasm is undiminished. I'd be lying if I said I wasn't a little insulted.

'How long have you been here?' Cam asks Alistair.

'Since the beginning of the year,' he replies. I worry when he doesn't elaborate, predicting that we might have another Leclercq on our hands, but Adewale jumps in.

'Technically,' he says, 'we're still on probation, but I think we've proved our worth by now. Right, Secundus?'

Andrew stifles a smile. Maybe he does have a personality under all that swagger.

'You've made some useful contributions,' he admits.

'Those blood pills you use out in the field?' Adewale says. 'Those were Alistair's idea.'

They're clever things: capsules of concentrated, dried blood that can give us a boost of energy in a tight spot.

'They are very cool,' Cam says.

'It's a simple enough idea,' Alistair grumbles. 'I cannae see what the fuss is all about.'

'Then there's the handcuffs,' Adewale goes on. 'Alistair designed a pair with blades on the inside. You can coat them with a poison that will incapacitate a Silver target like *that*.' He clicks his fingers. 'But they're not quite ready yet. Alistair's been trying to refine a poison delivery system to make then reusable. Won't be long, though. He's a bit of a genius, you know.'

Adewale smiles proudly and I swear I catch a blush from Alistair. I don't get a romance vibe from the two of them, but they are clearly joined at the hip. That's not what's caught my attention, though. I think about the poison dart in my pocket, about the mark of the Solis Invicti etched into its side, and about the strange coincidence that this new weapon turned up around the same time that these two joined the Invicti.

Alistair is their new supplier.

'And who makes the poisons?' I ask, because I want to know if it's Felton. That's what Ed thought when he analysed the contents of the first dart earlier this year. If the Invicti are working with Felton, then things are even worse than I thought.

'We're getting off topic,' the Secundus interrupts, by which he means we're getting off the topics he's prepared to let us discuss. Control freak. 'I believe you had some questions for Mr Jameson about a murder you're investigating?'

'Nora Mitchell,' Cam says. 'She was a district judge based at Oxford County Court.'

'You knew her?' I ask Alistair.

'Not at all,' he says, looking confused.

'She picked Windsor up from Crimson the night of the pre-opening party,' I prompt him. 'You helped him to the car.'

'I wasnae paying much attention, to be honest. I had a few bevvies on deck, ye ken? It was my night off.'

'Do you know Windsor well?' Cam asks.

'Sir Percy? He's a bit of a toff. Tommy asked if I wanted to go to the thing, and Adewale's always on at me not to be such a loner.'

'I think my exact words were "sad old loner",' Adewale says.

'Oh, right, because you're such a paragon of socialisation, aye?'

'So you didn't see Nora Mitchell?' I ask.

'Not so as I remember.'

'And what about the night of the fifth? Where were you?'

'The fifth of September?' he asks, then he pulls his phone from a bag beneath the bench and starts scrolling. 'Err, that would be a night off too.'

'So you were…?'

'We,' Adewale says, 'were out all night. Here. In London.' He grimaces. 'We think. We were a bit worse for wear.'

'And there's no one who can confirm that?'

'No one who wasn't also trollied,' Alistair says.

'But I swear,' says Adewale, 'he was in no fit state to go anywhere. I might not *technically* be able to vouch for his whereabouts, but he was matching me drink for drink before everything went a bit… blurry.'

'I didn't realise the Invicti were the work hard, play harder types,' I say.

'Don't worry,' the Secundus says wryly. 'We'll cure them of it. We obviously haven't been training them hard enough. Speaking of which, I think it's about time I put them back to work.'

Which is our cue to exit. I'm wondering why we came all this way for such a lacklustre interview when the answer presents itself in the form of Cam, who's beaming at all three of the Invicti like they're his heroes. Now that we've finished with our official questions, he's gone full-on fanboy.

'So good to meet you,' he says, shaking Alistair and Adewale's hands. He's buzzing like a sugared-up toddler.

I make to shepherd him out before he overexcites himself into a proper state, but when I stand from the bench the poison dart I stashed in my pocket earlier falls to the ground. There must be a hole in my stupid lost property hoody. Five sets of eyes follow the vial as it rolls across the floor then comes to a stop in a slow, spinning circle at our feet.

For a moment, we all stare at it.

'Isn't that one of yours?' Adewale asks Alistair.

The Secundus sees me fingering the hole in my hoody and asks, 'Where did you get that, Ms Valentine?'

There's no point in pretending ignorance.

'Someone shot it at us earlier today,' I say. 'Someone shot the Baron of Oxford with one of the same design in May, too. The Primus wrote me a letter about it. Said it was an accident during weapons testing. I don't suppose you know anything about that, do you?'

'No, I don't,' the Secundus says, but one of the new recruits is looking shifty. 'Alistair?'

There's a long moment in which I can see the Scot struggling with indecision. He looks at me then slides his gaze sideways to the Secundus. He obviously wants me to let this go so he doesn't have to fess up in front of his boss, but I'm not inclined to help him out. I came here for answers, and I intend to get them.

'Well?' I say.

'All right,' he says. 'Yes, we were testing the darts. With the Primus's approval,' he adds before the Secundus can object. 'But we werenae shooting them at people. It was all carefully contained. We just wanted so see how the unusual weight of the liquid affected the flight of the darts. That's all. We only took a few cases out of London. We counted the darts carefully in and out, making sure they were all accounted for, but…'

'But?' the Secundus asks.

'But one of the cases went missing.'

'Of course it did,' I say. 'When did this happen?'

Alistair grimaces. 'Back in May.'

'Jesus,' the Secundus mutters.

'How many darts are in a case?' Cam asks.

'Five,' says Alistair.

'So that means there are three still out there.'

'Just two,' I say. 'There were two shot at Drake and me. I only collected one of them. The other missed us and smashed. Then there was the one earlier today. That leaves two.'

If the Secundus looks worried, then Alistair is frantic.

'The formula isnae right,' he says. 'I had to get it changed after we had some problems with that batch.'

'What kind of problems?' I ask.

'Err, life-threatening ones. It was supposed to be a tranquilliser, and it works perfectly on most Silver, but in a few cases it's proved a wee bit more dangerous.'

'It nearly killed Drake,' I say.

'The Baron of Oxford?' Alistair asks, his face paling.

'Yup.'

His swallow is audible.

The Secundus steps in. He picks up the dart from the floor and disappears it into his pocket. I guess I won't be getting it back.

'We need to find those missing darts,' he says to me. 'I'll put my best men on it. You have my word.'

Ugh, he's so chivalrous he might as well be riding around on a white charger. I think it's tedious, but Cam's lapping it up.

'If there's anything we can do to help…' he says.

'I'll call,' the Secundus replies with a smile. 'And when this case is closed, perhaps we should talk, Mr Sawyer. Give me a call when you're next in town and I'll give you the full tour.' Cam's grin is so bright it could power half of London. 'Until then, these two need to get back to training, which I promise will be merciless, and I need to brief my people on the missing darts. So unless you have any further questions…'

We don't, so we say our goodbyes and leave the glass monstrosity behind us, Cam more reluctantly than me. His head's so full of hopes and dreams that I can't get a decent conversation out of him the whole way home. I don't want to lose him to the Invicti – particularly not now – but it doesn't look as though I have much of a say in the matter.

27

WEDNESDAYS ARE ARRIVING with painful regularity. There seem to be at least three a week. If I hadn't set a calendar reminder on my phone, I would have missed my probation appointment today. Wouldn't that have been a shame.

'I wasn't sure you'd come,' Drake says as I saunter into his office.

'I nearly didn't. I see enough of you as it is.'

'It would be a breach of the terms of your probation.'

'So you'd do what, exactly? Box me like you did Raul?'

'If I were going to box you for a breach of your probation, then what makes you think I wouldn't have done it already? After all, I don't see my whisky.'

'Oh, you still haven't found that? How strange. My jacket hasn't turned up either, in case you were wondering.'

'Neither has my pen.'

I smile as I settle into a chair, pleased that – having thieved two items to his one – I'm currently one up on him.

'You look tired,' he says. 'Late night?'

'Not that it's any of your business, but someone shot at me with one of those poison darts. That was after I spoke to

Leclercq at an outdoor Shakespeare production, but before I went to London to talk to the Invicti at their secret overground lair.'

'You got shot?'

'Oh, like you care,' I scoff. 'Don't worry, I dodged.'

'Well. You have been busy. All that in the–' He checks his watch. '–eighteen hours since I saw you last.'

'Not everyone spends their life lounging around behind their desk, you know.'

'And what did Yolande have to say for herself?' He lounges back in his chair. I'm sure it's deliberate.

'Not much,' I say. 'But do you know they're having a party at Crimson tomorrow night, for the Primus?'

'A party?'

'More like a summit, she said. Didn't you tell me that all the Silver were busy choosing their sides? Well, apparently it's time for them to declare themselves.' He looks as though this troubles him. 'You didn't know?'

'No,' he says, sitting up straight. 'I shouldn't be surprised, but I am the baron of this city. You'd think that, even if they didn't want to issue an invitation, they might at least have run it by me first.'

He's playing to the petulance of his words, trying to make light of the situation, but it's a huge breach of protocol. Whoever's throwing this party – and at this point I'm more inclined to believe it's Benedict than Windsor – they're as good as telling Drake that his rank is worthless. It's a challenge he can't ignore.

'So are you going to go?' I ask.

'Of course. Are you?'

'Obviously. But not with you.'

After what happened last time I went to a party with Drake, I'd be an idiot to risk a repeat. Things are getting back to normal with me and Tabitha, and I don't want to disrupt our delicate equilibrium by consorting with the devil incarnate. I might be working with Drake out of necessity, but I haven't forgotten who he is or what he's done.

'Leclercq said something else,' I say quickly, dragging us out of dangerous waters. 'She told me the shit's going to hit the fan tomorrow night.'

He raises an eyebrow at this unlikely turn of phrase.

'Well, she didn't use those exact words,' I say, 'but she told me we'll either have a new Primus by Friday, or we'll be at war.'

'Which would be bad news for both of us. No secrecy pact means no more Seekers, and no Primus means every baron he appointed will be replaced.'

Like Drake. He may not be on the Primus's side exactly, but their interests align. Unfortunately, so do mine and Drake's, which means that for the moment at least, we're stuck with each other.

'Leclercq says she has information that would stop it,' I say.

This doesn't seem to move Drake.

'And let me guess,' he says, 'she won't hand over the information until I grant her amnesty.'

'Right. Not just for herself, either. For someone else too.'

That surprises him.

'Who?'

'She wouldn't say.'

'But you think…?'

I weigh the wisdom of telling him my suspicions about Carlotta Arden, but in the end I don't trust him enough to risk it. After all, she is his girlfriend.

'No idea,' I say.

'Then you need to find out.'

The balls on this guy.

'I don't report to you, Drake.'

He laughs. 'Oh, don't worry. I'm in absolutely no doubt about that.'

'Then stop treating me like one of your faithful little lapdogs. Are you not even going to try to negotiate with Leclercq?'

'No. If the Primus comes out on top, I won't need to.'

'And if he doesn't?'

'Then we're fucked. But it won't come to that. The one thing you have to remember about Solomon is that he's been doing this for a long time, and he always wins.'

Maybe I should find that reassuring, but I don't. The Primus is one of the few constants in my world. Humans die, Silver are boxed and schemes are spun in a landscape of ever-changing alliances, but the one thing I thought would never change is that the Primus is the one who leads us. Even though his successor would technically take his title, I can't imagine anyone but Solomon holding it.

'So why did you go to London?' Drake asks.

'To question a suspect in the Nora Mitchell case. A guy called Alistair Jameson, a new recruit. Turns out he wasn't involved.'

This isn't exciting news, but Drake looks as though it's caught his interest, and not in a good way.

'What?'

'Did you meet the other new recruit?' he asks.

'Yeah. Adewale, right?'

'Right. You know who he is?'

I give him a frank look and say, 'He's the other new recruit.'

'That's not what I meant.' He fiddles with his blotter for a moment, prevaricating. 'He's Winta's brother.'

I feel like Drake's just punched me in the stomach. All the air rushes out of me on a suffocating breath and dark spots flash in front of my eyes, which is definitely not the kind of thing that should happen to the Silver.

Winta.

She made me the Silver I am today. We had a one-night stand that I thought would last forever, but she had other ideas. She disappeared the next day, and when I finally tracked her down she was a prisoner in Drake's basement. I didn't know about the Silver. I got too close to the bars. She bit me, escaped, and has never been seen or heard from again. But after twenty years, her name still hits me like buckshot in the gut.

'I didn't know she had a brother,' I say, feeling numb. 'Is he looking for her?'

'Yes, but that doesn't mean he'll find her. How long have we been looking? We never found a trace.'

'Maybe she just didn't want us to find her.' The truth in the words hurts. She didn't want *me* to find her, ever again. 'He's her brother. She might make an exception.'

'I doubt it. She's stayed away this long.'

'Then why did you tell me?'

'I don't know. I just thought I should.'

This admission makes him as uncomfortable as it makes me. He's being considerate of my feelings, but feelings are not something Drake and I navigate well. I generally steer clear of them altogether when in his company, and he only admits to having them if he can use them to demonstrate his superiority over me. But this is awkward. He's looking at me with those black eyes of his, and I'm looking back, and it feels as though I'm looking at someone different. It isn't normal, this easy cooperation we've cultivated. Drake and I only work when we're at each other's throats. I don't know how to treat him when we're being more than just civil.

I scramble for a change of subject.

'We did learn something at Solis Invicti HQ,' I say, then I tell him about the dart testing, the defective tranquilliser formula and the missing case of vials. That makes him antsy.

'Well,' he says, 'either the Invicti are lying and they have it in for us, or there's someone out there who's brave enough to steal from the Invicti, and *they* have it in for us. Neither is good.'

'You think I was the target of yesterday's shooting?'

'Of course you were,' he says, as though he never considered another possibility. 'You have a knack for rubbing people up the wrong way. Besides which, it sounds like Yolande set you up. She put you on top of a hill and made you easy to find.'

'So who's the shooter?'

'The same person she wanted me to give amnesty to,' Drake suggests.

I have to admit that it fits. It was a strange place for us to meet Leclercq. I can understand her not wanting to talk inside the club, but why take us to the Castle mound? Why make us pay to sit in the amphitheatre, at the very top of the hill, unless she wanted us to be seen? It doesn't make sense.

I'm pondering who her accomplice could be when Drake interrupts my thoughts by clearing his throat conspicuously.

'I don't want to rile you up and prompt any more incidents of kleptomania,' he says, 'but have you considered how Dr Ross fits into all of this?'

I can feel my defensive instincts climbing my spine to coil behind my teeth. I have to tamp them down before I can reply.

'No,' I say. 'Because she doesn't. This is the last time I'll tell you, Drake: leave my girlfriend out of this.'

'I'm sorry,' he says, looking not the least bit sorry, 'but I can't. You didn't look properly, did you?'

'What?'

He pulls open the bottom drawer of his desk and takes out the stack of surveillance photos again. The last photograph is the one he slides over the top of the desk towards me, the one from Crimson, where Benedict is leaning in to speak into Tabitha's ear.

'Here,' he says, pointing at the bottom corner.

I was in a rush the last time I looked at this picture, and honestly I was too concerned about how close Benedict's face was to Tabitha's to look much beyond it, but it's clear as day now Drake's pointed it out. Clutched in Tabitha's hand is a clear plastic canister, crammed full of vials. Amongst them are a bundle of syringe darts, just like the one that poisoned Drake.

'I wasn't surveilling your girlfriend,' he murmurs. 'I was surveilling Benedict. After taking one of those darts in the neck, did you think I was just going to let it slide? But when I saw that she was involved, then yes, we started looking into her too.'

'But, Mathew Felton…' I say, my head spinning. 'Ed said the chemical signature of the poison in those darts was his work.'

'Felton's been helping, but he's not the one behind the project. He's a drug addict. He's not good enough to assemble functional chemical agents on his own. It's Dr Ross.'

'No.'

'I'm sorry, Jack, but she's in this up to her neck.'

I drop down into the nearest chair.

'There's more,' he says. 'Do you want to hear it?'

'No,' I say, but he tells me anyway.

He starts with more surveillance photos. These are a stack that I haven't seen before, taken through the window of my rooms at Solomon College. I know they're recent because in one of them I can see my borrowed hoody, and I've only had that since Sunday.

'This is my bedroom,' I say, feeling my anger simmering up to a boil. 'You've had someone spying on me.'

'They've been spying on Dr Ross, not you. Never you. Not even the doctor when the two of you were together. I gave strict instructions.'

'So you'll draw the line at them taking photos of me, but you're fine with them looking through my *bedroom window*?'

'You can be angry with me later,' he says. 'Just look at them.'

I'm waving the photos at him, about to argue, when one of them catches my eye. I stop. I drop them onto my lap and shuffle through the stack. Tabitha is searching my room. In one picture, she glances towards the bathroom – it looks like I'm in the shower – and in the next she's holding my phone. She must know my passcode, because when she turns her back to the window a series of close-ups shows that she's trawling through my emails, my calls, my messages.

I shrug and hand the photos back.

'Some people are jealous,' I say, trying to convince myself more than I'm trying to convince him. But it's true; Tabitha *has* been jealous. She's always trying to warn me away from Drake. In the circumstances, I'm not surprised that she's broken into my phone. It's a shitty thing to do to someone you love, and we'll definitely be having words about it later, but this doesn't have to be the end of us. We can get past it.

'Then she must be very jealous,' he says. 'I know you don't want to hear this, but she's been recording you too.'

'What? Why?'

'So she can send the recordings to the Invicti.' He brings me the laptop from his desk, turning it so only I can see the screen. 'This my investigator's computer. He hacked her email. And no, the irony isn't lost on me.'

I barely hear the last few words because my head fills with fog the moment my mind translates the image on the screen. It's an email addressed to Benedict from Tabitha, one of many. There are several attachments, a mix of sound files and photos, and a list in the main body of the email that sets out every piece of my life that she's betraying.

JV talks about Nora Mitchell case; Discussion about haematopsychosis; Photo of case file; JV denies relationship with KD.

That's what breaks me beyond repair. I don't think of myself as a meek person, but that's what I am now. I sit there like a lemon while Drake describes the recordings his investigator found: me talking about my cases; about the Invicti; about random shit that seems irrelevant, but was nonetheless of interest to Benedict. Worst of all are the private things I said to Tabitha when I thought no one was listening. She's recorded every word I've said to her over the past four months and she's sent the highlights to a man I hate, a man who's dangerous in ways I don't yet understand.

After what happened with Winta, I didn't think it was possible for me to fall apart again, but I was wrong. I'm no longer Jack Valentine, the untouchable Seeker with a drinking problem and a foul mouth. In the space of seconds I'm reduced to the girl I was twenty years ago, crying in the basement because I've given my heart to a beautiful vampire vixen who, as it turns out, doesn't love me at all.

I've never felt so violated.

Until, moments later, I realise that Drake has had access to it all.

'I'm sure you hated every minute,' I say, because it's easier to turn my anger on him than it is to face Tabitha's betrayal.

I will not cry in front of him, not again. I will not.

'You think I listened to it?' he asks. 'God, you really don't know me at all. I might not be one of the good guys, but I'm not actually evil. I wouldn't do that to someone I care about.'

I laugh bitterly.

'Sure. Whatever. I bet you've listened to all of it twice by now.'

He goes down on his knees next to my chair and reaches up to push my hair back from my face.

'Not a second,' he says. 'Not a single, solitary second.'

Then he takes my hand in his and presses a kiss into my palm, so softly. But I can't handle softness right now, least of all from him.

I wrench my hand away and kick out of the chair, heading for the door.

'Thanks for the heads-up,' I yell over my shoulder as the first tears start to fall.

His voice chases me out into the hall.

'I'm sorry, Valentine.'

28

THE CAPTAIN CALLS us into her office the moment I get back from Summertown. I want to track Tabitha down right now and get the truth from her, but the summons is non-negotiable. I nearly ignore it anyway, but Cam drags me along.

'What do you think you're doing?' she asks when we're all lined up in her office, eyes downcast like recalcitrant teenagers. 'Harassing local businesses. Badgering the bereaved. Interrogating the *Invicti*. Have you entirely lost your mind, Deputy, or have you just lost control of your team?'

Boyd raises his chin and meets her eye.

'With all due respect, Captain,' he says, 'I think it's you who's lost control.'

She raises a single, neat eyebrow at him. That eyebrow is legendary. I've seen centuries-old Silver reduced to mumbling wrecks by its force, but I don't think I've ever seen it raised so high.

Naia whistles under her breath. We're for it now.

'What do you mean by that?' the captain asks Boyd.

'I mean that our job is to preserve the secrecy pact,' he

says. 'The only reason the Seekers exist is to keep the Silver hidden from the humans. If someone intends to interfere with that then it's our job to bring them to account, whomever they may be, and stop them from revealing us. Don't you agree?'

There's a long moment in which Boyd's gaze is locked with the captain's. The air is thick with subtext: Boyd is as good as telling her that he knows she's a traitor. If she admits that she disagrees with his statement, she may as well walk away from the Seekers right now.

Behind her eyes, I can see the gears churning. She's not going to roll over for him.

'It's an interesting question,' she says, 'coming from a Silver who is involved in a relationship with a human. Don't you think? I'd imagine that if anything was bound to endanger the secrecy pact, it would be an intimate relationship between a Seeker and a human. I know there's no express rule against it, but it seems a little imprudent, does it not?'

She's got him there. Boyd's eye contact wavers, then breaks.

'You will leave the Invicti, Sir Percival and Crimson out of this,' the captain orders. 'Now, if there's nothing else–'

'Oh, there's something else,' I say.

Boyd glares at me, urging me to bite my tongue, and Cam grabs my arm in an attempt to reach the same end, but I am beyond being silenced. Unlike Boyd, I'm not prepared to accept a stalemate of implied threats. I am a blunt instrument woven from heartbreak, desperation and pure, burning ire. Between the captain's deceptions and Tabitha's betrayal, I've worked too long in the dark. It's time to air all our dirty laundry and find out exactly where we stand.

'The Solis Invicti are at war,' I say. 'All of the Silver are, except us apparently. But you already knew that, didn't you, Captain?'

'Control yourself, Valentine.'

'I will not,' I say, because I'm on a roll now, fuelled by the fires of righteous indignation. It's an unfamiliar feeling for me, and I'm enjoying it. 'We're trying to solve your descendant's murder, and you've just hung us out to dry. Did you know that someone shot at me and Cam yesterday evening, in the middle of the Castle complex?' Her eyes widen a little, but she tries to hide her surprise. That's how I know it's genuine. 'Yeah,' I go on. 'With a dart. The same kind of dart that the Solis Invicti have been developing in London, that almost killed Drake, and that you were seen handing over to Benedict in University Parks in May. So I think it's about time you told us exactly what *you* think *you're* doing. Don't you?'

She sighs and takes off her jacket, letting it fall in a crumpled heap at the back of her chair. This, more than anything else, tells me that we are no longer dealing with the captain we know. She is never ruffled, never rumpled, and here she is leaning into her own disarray. Things must be bad.

'I got a call,' she says. 'Not long after Nora's murder. I didn't recognise the voice, but whoever it was had worked out the connection between me and her. They said Nora's nieces, Sydney and Melbourne, would suffer if I didn't change my stance to pro-reveal. They want to abolish the secrecy pact.'

'They called *after* the murder?' Cam asks.

'And only after. Their information came from your investigation, which means there's a leak somewhere in the Seekers. Can you blame me for not telling you about it?'

'You think it was one of us?' Boyd asks.

My mouth goes dry and my stomach drops. I know where the blackmailers got their information.

I have to sit down.

'It was Tabitha,' I say.

The chorus of surprise from my teammates just adds to the noise in my head. This is why she was sending all those random conversations to Benedict: he was searching for leverage. The better he knows us, the better he can manipulate us all.

'Your girlfriend?' the captain asks.

'She's been recording my conversations, taking photos of our case files, feeding information back to the Solis Invicti.'

The surprised noises increase to outrage, all except Cam's. He's deadly quiet now in a way that I've never seen him before. He loved Tabitha too. Seeing the look on his face, seeing how she's hurt him as well, makes me angry all over again.

'So that explains the leak,' I say, shoving my emotions away, 'but it doesn't explain this.'

I pull up a picture on my phone and turn it to show the captain.

'This is you in University Parks with Benedict,' I say. 'You're passing him the empty dart, the one that nearly killed Drake. You're handing over the evidence. Why would you do that, Captain?'

'That was nothing,' she says dismissively.

'Then why did you lie about it?'

'Because a pack of these poison dart vials had gone missing and they were trying to keep it under wraps. There's nothing sinister about that; it's just normal administrative secrecy. The Invicti operate on a need-to-know basis.' Apparently the Secundus didn't need to know. 'There's a long tradition of cooperation between the Solis Invicti and the Seekers. We help them when they need us.'

'And they do nothing for us,' the deputy says. 'Ever.'

I expect the captain to argue, but she doesn't.

'What are you getting at?' Naia asks Boyd.

'The captain has been taking orders from Benedict for a while now,' he says. The captain looks crushed. 'I might have been slow to put the pieces together, but I'm not blind, Enid. I've noticed the unexplained calls, the shut doors, and the orders sending our teams to supervise blood bar openings, or halfway across the country to investigate murders that seem to have nothing to do with the Silver. Did you intend for Ellie and Quentin's team to investigate that scab murder in Derbyshire, or was it an accident that they stumbled into a genuine case? What about Benedict? What about the humans you said didn't die at Windsor's party?'

She rolls up her sleeves and runs a hand through her hair, sending the short blond bob off in all directions. I feel like I've walked into a parallel universe.

'I lied,' she says. 'It wasn't an undercover operation. Benedict killed them for the money.'

The rest of the team sits down around me. This is their watershed moment. They're probably just as shocked by the truth as they are by the fact that my conspiracy theory turned out to be right.

'I know you don't understand this,' she goes on, speaking to all of us now, 'but sometimes we have to balance the lives of a few humans against those of hundreds, thousands. We trade one for the other, whether we make an active choice or not. No one wants to make those decisions – god knows I don't – but someone has to, otherwise we're just letting everyone else decide for us, with no view to the net cost. And the few humans whose lives we traded were creeps. You know that.'

I think about the men I met at Windsor's party and I know she's right. But it still feels wrong.

The captain leans towards me.

'I know it's not pleasant,' she says. She's rambling now, so I don't interrupt. Instead, I let her dig her own grave. 'I know we, and particularly you, Jack, like to feel that we're enforcing some kind of natural justice, even when the laws the Primus gives us aren't much to work with. But the truth is that there is such a thing as an acceptable loss. That's what we're looking at here. Collateral damage. Those few lives were the price we paid for a change that we desperately need.'

'So you believe in all of this?' Boyd asks. 'Even without the threat to the girls, you believe we should reveal ourselves to humanity?'

'I didn't at first, but now?' She bites her lip hard enough to make it bleed. 'I don't think Nora would have died if we'd lived openly. She would have known the risk of associating with Sir Percival, and she would have steered clear. I don't think Sydney and Melbourne would be in danger right now if we weren't all so invested in retaining the intrigue of our concealment. If we were out in the open, I would have been able to see my girls grow up without having to lie about who I am. I don't want to lie anymore. Do you, Deputy?'

Their eyes lock and something passes between them, something potent enough that it scares me. I can't let her change Boyd's mind.

'Who killed Nora Mitchell?' I ask.

'You think I know?' she says. 'If I did, I'd be doing something about it. But you've told me to stay out of it. It's your case. If it's connected to this summit, then someone will pay for that, but it's your job to work out who.'

I can't argue with that.

'But you agree that you've compromised your position,' Boyd says. He seems to have had an idea. 'The whole purpose of the Seekers is to conceal the existence of the Silver. If you are now a pro-revelation rebel, then you find yourself in a serious conflict of interest. Correct?'

We all know where this is going, the captain more than the rest of us. Boyd has been nipping at her heels for years. To her credit, she doesn't flinch from it.

'That is correct,' she says.

'That being the case, would you also agree that it would be inappropriate for you to attend Crimson tomorrow night?'

I can see the captain gritting her teeth, but she nods her assent.

'And would you further agree that it behoves us, as Seekers, to ensure that there is an official presence at the summit tomorrow to support the Baron of Oxford and demonstrate our ongoing commitment to our mission?'

I have to restrain myself from rolling my eyes. Seriously, Boyd, when was the last time anyone said "behoves" in real life?

'Yes, all right, we get your point, Deputy,' the captain says, standing from her chair. 'Or should I say, Acting Captain? I'm sick of the politics anyway.' She collects her jacket and briefcase and walks to the door. 'You'd better call the baron, because I sure as shit am not going to do it for you.'

Then she's gone.

I guess Boyd's moving up the ladder. He beams at us all, but to be honest, I don't feel much like smiling.

29

WE SPEND THE afternoon planning for tomorrow's event, but wrap up early enough that I'm waiting for Tabitha when she gets home that night. She kicks off her shoes and hangs her coat up on the back of the door, then smiles as she sees me standing by the bedroom, leaning in the doorway. I don't smile back. I've been standing here for a while now, letting my rage coil around me.

It's time for my own personal showdown.

'Hi,' she says, tentatively.

'Is there something you want to tell me?' I ask.

'No, hen.' She tilts her head. 'Should there be?'

'You know what I'm talking about.' I push off from the wall and take a step towards her.

'I don't.'

Her voice is small. She glances over my shoulder for a way out, but I'm moving closer all the time and now she's backed up against the door.

'You're lying to me,' I say.

I feel my hands curling into fists with a pleasant stretch of tendons. I like it. I've liked so many new and aggressive sensations over the past few days that it doesn't even feel strange.

'Jack,' she says, her eyes now bright with fear. 'Hen. I don't know what you're talking about.'

'You should. Because you know everything, don't you? All this time, you've known *everything*, whether I wanted you to or not.'

'Jack, I…'

I slam my fist into the door next to her head, hard enough to splinter the wood.

'Stop lying to me!'

She licks her lips, her gaze darting all over the place, looking for a way out, but there is none. I'm standing right in front of her. She might have more years on me, but I have more bulk. I'm strong enough to overpower her.

'Jack,' she says carefully. 'That blood vial Ed gave me. Are you sure it was yours?'

'I don't care about your stupid experiment right now, Tabitha.'

She's panicking, frantic, looking for an exit. But I am immoveable, calm and contained in my rage.

'Jack, listen to me very carefully.' Her voice is shaking. 'You need to give me some of your blood. Right now. Please.'

I can hear every word she's saying, but as if it's coming from far away. She's there, but what she's saying is irrelevant. It makes no impact on me.

I take another step towards her, so we are toe-to-toe.

She grabs my penknife from my pocket and takes my hand, still fisting at my side. I feel like I'm looking down on the scene from above, so removed from it that I don't even feel her touch. She slices my wrist open and pulls it towards her mouth. I snatch it away, but she follows it, falling to her knees on the floor. I shove her back.

'What the fuck are you doing?' I yell.

'Jack, I made a mistake.' She's on her knees, begging, pitiful. 'You need to give me some of your blood. Please. I made a mistake.'

'You don't make mistakes,' I say. 'You make choices. The wrong fucking choices. Every single time.'

'You don't understand,' she says, scooching away from me until her back is against the wall. 'It was the blood, Jack. When you bit me–'

'You asked me to bite you. And you liked it, didn't you?'

I hear my voice and I know it's mine, but it doesn't sound like me. It sounds like a twisted version of who I am, a person who's deliberately breaking everything in her path, pressing every single trigger she can find, even though she knows exactly how destructive it is. I'm hanging from a cliff, pulling my own fingers away from the edge one at a time, and I can't seem to stop myself.

'Is that what you want?' says the person who is me, and not me. 'You want me to bite you?'

'Jack…'

I know it's wrong, but I do it anyway.

I don't kiss her this time. I don't try to gentle the pain with my mark, because that's not the game I'm playing tonight. Instead, I haul her up by her shoulders and slam her into the wall. The force makes the room shake; the mirror by the door falls to the ground and smashes into a million pieces on the floorboards. I hold her against the wall with my forearm, her bare toes dancing in the shards.

'Please, hen,' she whispers. There are tears in her eyes.

I am unmoved, because she deserves this. I pin her tiny hands in one of mine so she can't fight back.

She should know better. She belongs to me. She needs to learn that, but this is more than just a lesson.

This is revenge.

When my teeth break the skin of her neck, she screams. I lose myself in it, in the blood and the noise and the kicking of her heels against the wall. Somewhere in the middle of it all, she gets one of her hands free and pulls my slit wrist up to her mouth. I feel her lips on my skin just before the world shifts.

Spins.

Stops.

I drop like a stone. For a second I'm blind – everything is black behind my eyes – then I blink and find myself sprawled on the floor. Tabitha has slid down the wall and is slumped there with her hand pressed against her neck, her chest rising with the rapid in and out of her breath. She doesn't need the extra oxygen; it's a reaction that has nothing to do with biology and everything to do with instinct.

For one long, perfect minute, I am empty. There's nothing inside me at all. Then it comes rushing in all at once: the taste of Tabitha's blood in my mouth, the scent of her fear in the air, the guilt.

What have I just done?

I can't look at her. I close my eyes, but the backs of my eyelids are printed with the image of her pleading face. My fingers can still feel her wrists struggling against my grip as I held her to my will, intent on nothing but keeping her quiet and compliant. I don't have to imagine how she felt in that moment because I know all too well: she felt exactly as impotent as I did when Drake did the same to me, exactly as hurt and exactly as helpless.

I lunge for the kitchen sink just in time to catch most of the blood I've just drunk from her on its way back up.

'Jack,' she whispers.

I wipe my mouth and slide back down to the floor.

'What the hell just happened?' I ask. 'Tabby…'

I'm crying now. I'm not sure when it started, but the tears are streaming down my cheeks.

She won't look at me.

'Haematopsychosis is real.' She swallows. 'But you can neutralise it if it's not one way, if you drink each other's blood. That vial of blood Ed took from you–'

'I thought you were using it for testing.' I can hear the emptiness in my own voice.

'I drank it before we… Before you…'

She drank it before I bit her, last time, so that it would counteract the haematopsychosis.

'But it didn't work,' I say.

'It should have done. It did, when I drank straight from your veins today. That was why you… stopped.'

'Oh god.'

I hang my head between my knees, dragging my hair back from my face and clutching it in handfuls at the base of my skull. I feel like I'm going to be sick again.

'I hurt you,' I whisper.

'It shouldn't have happened,' she wails. 'I did all the tests. I made sure!'

'You were wrong.'

I want to be furious, but every time that trickle of fire starts up in my veins, I remember all the other times I've felt irrationally angry since I bit her. I remember the possessiveness, the impulse to control and mark her with my name. I flash back to her scream, to her wide eyes as I brought my teeth down on her neck. Since I can't be angry I'm nothing at all, deflated, crumpled on the floor like a discarded sock.

'It must have been the wrong sample,' she says, hopelessly. 'It can't have been your blood.'

Which means Ed mixed up the two vials I gave him. He tested my blood, and gave the sample from Crimson to Tabitha.

Which she drank.

'That's why you were sick,' I mumble. 'You drank the blood from the club, like Raul. For fuck's sake.'

'I'm sorry,' she says, crawling over to me. 'I'm so sorry.'

'Why?' I ask, talking to the floor. 'Why would you do this?'

There's a long pause before she replies.

'You know why,' she says. 'Baron Drake.'

'What?' I look up. 'Because he told me you were spying for the Invicti?'

'Spying for…' She shakes her head, frustrated, and looks away. 'I didn't know he'd told you that.'

'He showed me the photos. He found the recordings.'

'Of course he did.'

'What's that supposed to mean?'

'It means he's always trying to come between us. So yes, I lied because I had to, because of the job. But everything comes back to Baron Drake. This is his fault.'

'Because he held a gun to your head and made you record every word I've ever said to you? You're the one who chose to… What? Go undercover and get yourself into a relationship with me so you could spy on the Seekers?' The shame on her face tells me I'm right. 'None of this was ever real, was it?'

'It is!' she insists, grabbing for my hand. I shake her off. 'It's real, hen. Maybe it wasn't the best way for us to start, but where we've ended up… Doesn't that matter? And the baron—'

I laugh, because I can't believe she's still trying to make this about him. She faked the haematopsychosis trial. She faked her interest in me. She faked our whole relationship.

'All of this just to make me think Drake was a monster?' I say, stuttering the last word because I know that if it's true of him, it's true of me now as well. 'Was it worth it?'

'He's always there!' she yells. 'Your probation, and these games you keep playing with him–'

'I told you I only do that to piss him off.'

'But if you didn't care then you wouldn't bother at all. Can't you see that? He's driving us apart, hen.'

'No,' I say, getting unsteadily to my feet. 'You've done that all on your own.'

'Jack–'

'Do you have any idea how much you've fucked up?' I ask, my voice so cold it startles me. 'This isn't just about us. You haven't just lied to me, you've lied to *everyone*. You've faked test results. Raul is stuck in a box right now, all because *you* said haematopsychosis wasn't real. You had a choice: do the right thing by me and Raul, or fuck over Drake for the Invicti and their little rebellion. You chose them, Tabitha. You *chose* this.'

Her face pales.

'You're going to rewrite your report,' I say with a calmness I don't feel. 'And you're going to write a letter to Drake detailing your reaction to the blood you drank. You're going to get me the evidence I need to get Raul free, and you're going to do it now.'

'Jack, please–'

I'm glad when we're interrupted, because I don't want to be here anymore. I don't want to listen to her explaining away the terrible things she's done. I don't want to sit here knowing what *I've* done, feeling like it's her fault, but knowing that it's mine. Psychosis or not, I've done the unforgivable. There's no coming back from this.

So for a split-second, I'm grateful when Boyd barrels into my rooms without knocking. He's pushed the lock clean through the doorframe.

'I'm sorry,' he says, seeing that Tabitha and are in the middle of something. 'But I– I'm sorry.'

At first, I'm too surprised to say anything. This version of Boyd is not someone I know. Just a few hours ago he was riding high, soon to be the new captain of the Seekers, buoyed at having got the one thing he's been chasing for as long as I've known him. He should be sitting in his new office, busily optimising the workspace and scheduling meetings. That's the Boyd I know. He's always in control. He doesn't go breaking down doors in the middle of the night, barefoot in jeans and an unbuttoned shirt. He and I also aren't the best of friends – more colleagues, really – so why he would break his way into my rooms is something of a mystery. If I didn't know any better, I'd think he was drunk, but that's not his style. He always stops after a single whisky.

Then I see the blood at the edge of his mouth. I can scent something too, heavy pheromones and pure animal terror. Pretty much the same scents that are filling my own rooms right now.

'What is it?' I ask, on instant alert.

'Mildred,' he says. 'It's Mildred.'

30

SHE'S IN HIS bedroom.

I've never been allowed past the front door of Boyd's rooms before. It turns out that they're a lot like mine, only a bit bigger and a lot more bloody.

I slap my palm over the bite on Mildred's neck and press down as hard as I can. She's bleeding heavily, her blood already soaking the sheets, but she's still breathing. I can feel the hot liquid trying to pulse between my fingers.

'Get me a towel,' I say to Boyd.

He grabs one from the bathroom then watches like a statue as I fold it into a pad and press it against the wound. He knows how to do all this. He should have done it before coming to get help. He's better at human first aid than I am, but somehow he's forgotten everything he should do. Instead, he's doing nothing at all.

Tabitha is right beside me, opening each of Mildred's eyes in turn then checking her pulse.

'Go to sick bay for help,' she says to Boyd.

He doesn't move.

'Deputy!' She tries again, yelling this time. 'Go to sick bay and get help. We need blood. Lots of it. Now.'

Boyd snaps out of it and runs from the room at supernatural speed. I have a moment's concern that he might not even have heard what Tabitha asked, but he's back inside a minute with the nurse from sick bay, carrying armfuls of blood bags and tubing.

Even in that short period of time, Mildred's pulse has slowed. I can hear it thudding more and more slowly, slurping as though her veins have filled with treacle. I get out of the way and let Tabitha and the nurse do their jobs: quick, messy surgery and transfusions of more blood than I drink in a week.

Boyd and I hover at the door.

'Is she going to be okay?' he asks me.

The deputy's a tall man, and he seems taller still because he holds himself with perfect, regal posture. On a normal day, no one could look at him and fail to understand that he is in charge. Not tonight, though. Tonight his shoulders are hunched, his body trying to curl in on itself like an overstrung bow.

'What happened?' I ask him softly.

'I don't know.'

He's crying. The tears are running down his dark cheeks, carving shining trails across his skin. Boyd doesn't cry. Boyd barely has emotions. This is one of the most disconcerting things I've ever seen.

We stand out of the way as another Silver rushes through with a stretcher, then all we can do is trail after them as they transfer Mildred down to sick bay and hook her up to a raft of beeping machines.

'Is she going to be okay?' Boyd asks.

'We don't know yet,' says the nurse. 'Stand back, please.'

Then we're both pushed out of the room into the waiting area, ragged and blood-stained. The nurse shuts the door in our faces.

It's going to be a long night.

A couple of hours later, Mildred is finally stable and the nurse sends us off to clean ourselves up. I have to drag Boyd to his rooms because, even though he could be back at sick bay in the blink of an eye if they call him, he can't seem to handle the distance. I, on the other hand, am more than happy to put some extra space between me and Tabitha.

When we get up to our corridor, Cam and Naia are examining my ruined doorframe. They stop talking when they see us coming, eyes widening at the sight of Boyd.

'Accident,' I say, and that's enough.

Cam takes Boyd into his own rooms to shower while I go into Boyd's to collect some clean clothes. We both assume that the deputy won't want to look at Mildred's blood right now. In the meantime, Naia strips the sheets and does her best to clear away the mess. When I've rushed through the shower myself, the official clean-up crew has already sealed off the corridor.

I make a quick call before joining the others. Boyd is sitting on Cam's sofa looking about as catatonic as Raul did the last time I saw him.

'You went to Crimson to celebrate?' I ask, sitting down next to him. Cam and Naia are watching us anxiously from the other side of the room.

Boyd doesn't respond.

'Mildred probably wanted to go, because it's the only bar you've ever been to together. You had one of their blood cocktails, I bet.'

There's a pause, but he nods.

I look up at Cam and Naia and say, 'Ed got the vials mixed up. I just confirmed it with him. The sample he tested didn't come from Crimson.'

Which means that Raul is only as culpable for Rachael's death as Boyd is for what just happened to Mildred. I'm betting that Felton's really to blame.

'How did you know?' Naia asks.

'I talked to Tabitha.'

I fill them in on my night, trying to leave out the bits that make me burn with shame. Unfortunately, that's not really possible. They need to know that the blood from Crimson was switched. There's no way to explain all that without telling them that Tabitha lied about haematopsychosis, and that she took what she thought was my blood in order to counteract it. I'm not explicit about the blood-drinking itself, but suffice it to say that everyone now understands why I've been grumpier than normal over the past few days.

Except Boyd. He doesn't seem to understand much of anything.

'This wasn't you,' I say to him, trying to stop his slide. 'This is something they're doing. I'm sorry I was too late to warn you.'

Maybe if I'd gone to him right away, this wouldn't have happened. Those last few minutes could have been enough to stop him, but instead I wasted time arguing with Tabitha, as though there were any way to salvage our relationship after what she's done. If only I'd known he was going to Crimson.

'But Mildred's fine,' Cam says, 'and you'll be fine. We're here for you.'

'And we'll catch the bastards who are doing this and cut them up into teeny tiny pieces,' Naia adds.

'I'll get another sample,' I promise. 'We'll get our proof.'

Boyd just nods, staring at the wall across the room, then gets up and walks back down to sick bay.

* * *

We all wait with Boyd until the early hours of the morning, by which time he's vomiting his guts up, true to form. The pattern is so familiar that I'm certain, even more than I was when we took the first sample, that this is the fault of one of Felton's concoctions.

Finally, the sickness seems to die down and the nurse comes out of Mildred's room to tell us she's awake. I don't know what Boyd's going to say to her, but I can't think of any way he can explain this without telling her the truth. I wouldn't blame him if he did. At this point, so many Silver are pro-revelation that I'm not even sure breaking the secrecy pact is wrong anymore.

He leaves us, grim-faced, just as Tabitha emerges. The welcome she receives from Cam and Naia is decidedly frosty.

'You told them, then,' she says.

'Of course I told them.'

She looks between the three of us for a moment, then says to me, 'Can we talk?'

I'm reluctant, but don't they say closure is good for you? Either way, I'm too exhausted to argue, so I don't protest when she leads me off into the corridor where we have the illusion, if not the reality, of privacy.

'Thank you for saving Mildred,' I say gruffly, because she deserves that much. She could so easily have let her die.

'It's my job, hen.'

I close my eyes.

'Please don't call me that.'

She takes a step towards me. 'Hen?'

'We're done,' I say quietly.

'No,' she says. 'Please, let me explain. Look, you're young. You haven't lived in secret for centuries, hiding what you are, and I can tell you: it's awful,' she says, with feeling.

'Every day when I wake up and slap on my smile and go to work in the hospital with humans, pretending I'm one of them, I feel like a piece of me is being sliced away. It hurts me to pretend.'

'And yet you're so good at it.'

'Because I've had to be,' she says, her cheeks pinking. 'You ask us to lie every day of our lives, the Primus, the Baron of Oxford, the Seekers. Are you really surprised that we've developed a talent for it? I don't want to live like this anymore.' Her voice is intensely quiet. 'I hate it.'

'Then you must hate me too, because it's everything I stand for. If the Silver come out of the shadows, then humans will die. Silver will die. Can't you see that?'

'You don't know that,' she says, shaking her head hopelessly. 'That's just what the baron's told you. You don't have to do this. You don't have to let him win.'

'This isn't about Drake.'

'*Everything* is about him! He's the one who bit you first. He's the one who marked you first. He's basically the one who *saw* you first and he'll never let me forget it.'

I can't believe what I'm hearing.

'Do you have any idea how petty you sound right now? Does how I feel not matter at all to you? I don't care what Drake wants. I wanted you.'

'Please don't past-tense me. Please don't give up on us. I made one stupid mistake.'

I laugh, but there's no pleasure in it.

'Is that what you call it?'

'This thing between us is real,' she insists.

'How can it be? I hurt you, Tabitha. Whatever you say about the haematopsychosis, I *hurt* you. I can't forget that or forgive myself for it and, right or wrong, I can't stop blaming you for it. You've done nothing but lie to me.'

'But I love you.'

'This isn't love. This is *nothing* like love.'

'I'm not trying to pretend that it's perfect,' she says desperately. 'I know it's not, but I love you, and that's got to mean something, hasn't it?'

I laugh again, not because this is funny, but because I once thought we had the perfect relationship. I can't believe how spectacularly wrong I was.

'Don't you dare make light of this,' she says, tears welling in her eyes. I wish I could believe they were real.

'You can't just slap three magic words on all the shit that's happened between us and expect them to make it all better,' I say.

'I messed up. Badly,' she adds before I can cut in, then she takes my hands in hers. 'I'm sorry. I'm truly sorry. But when I started this, I wasn't expecting to feel this way about you. Whatever else has happened between us, my feelings are real. You have to believe that.'

'Then show me your silver.'

'What?' She drops my hands like they're hot.

'Show me your silver. You say you love me, and yet you've manipulated me, spied on me for the Invicti, violated my privacy and lied to me in the worst way I can imagine. You turned me into a monster. You put me and people I care about through hell, and now you're asking me to believe that you love me. So show me.'

'You know that's not how it works. Hardly anyone silvers these days, even if they feel–'

'Show me!'

She looks down and closes her eyes for a moment. When she opens them again, I can see the silver threading through the whites of her eyes, but there's nothing in her irises. She hasn't silvered.

'It doesn't mean anything,' she whispers.

I know she's right, but it doesn't help. In the face of her betrayal I need some kind of proof, but she has none to offer me.

'You love me, Jack,' she says, fast and anxious. 'I know you do, even if you haven't said it. But you can't show me the evidence of it any more than I can show you. Emotions aren't simple. This isn't science. You have to trust–'

She stops herself there. My trust is the last thing I can give her right now.

'You're wrong,' I say. 'Not about me loving you. I do. I did. I may not have silvered, but I haven't been lying to you for four months either, and I have something to show for it, too.'

I pull down the waistband of my jeans to reveal the tattoo I acquired yesterday morning: a stylised cat with stripes, perched low beside my right hipbone.

'You got…' She looks up at me, her eyes shining with unshed tears. 'You got that for me?'

I nod tersely, trying not to cry. I can't go to pieces. She'll take it the wrong way and think I'm giving in, but I can't fold. Whatever me and Tabitha had, she's detonated it. It's lying in tiny pieces all around us, smouldering and beyond repair. There's no way we're putting it back together again.

So I walk away.

31

AFTER STAYING UP all night with Boyd, I'm exhausted. I'm young enough that I need almost as much sleep as a human or I start to fall apart. I can already feel the edges of myself fraying, as though everything's just a little further away than it normally is, and I'm panicking in my attempts to snatch it close. I really should sleep, like the others are right now, but I know I won't, so I go to the office instead to paw through the Nora Mitchell case in the desultory hope of finding something new.

I'm barely concentrating, but it doesn't matter. I'm only killing time until Crimson opens for the day.

When it does, I don't piss about. I walk straight in, go behind the bar – ignoring the protests of the bar staff – and smash open the cabinet that holds Felton's precious concoction. I'm in and out in sixty seconds, then on my way back to the college with my prize.

Ed works faster this time too. He doesn't have much choice, because I camp out in his lab and watch every move he makes until the test results are in. It still takes longer than I'd like, long enough for me to think through every lie Tabitha's ever told me, my gut clenching with each one, until

I've run out of bad memories and I'm neck-deep in the good ones: her pink-cheeked smile, the tousle of her hair on my pillow, the way she squeaked with pleasure when I licked her skin.

Despite every way she violated and used me, I miss her. I wonder if this is how Cam feels when he looks at Ed: empty and full at the same time, stuck between flying and falling. I am sick with it.

'Okay,' Ed says. 'Done.'

'And?'

Always the suspense with this guy. I have no patience for it today, which must be obvious because he hurries on.

'It's a kind of catalyst,' Ed says. 'A nasty one. I've seen some studies coming from the Solis Invicti about a drug like this. It's a double whammy, because not only does it make the Silver sick, which is basically impossible with normal drugs, but it makes us volatile.'

'Volatile how?'

'Hungry,' he says. 'Uninhibited.'

'So they might be more likely to mark someone?' I ask.

'Yes, but that's not the problem. There's no haematopsychosis between Silver and humans, remember? The problem is that it makes us bitey. Really, really bitey. If you mix that volatility with a nearby human… Well, it's a recipe for disaster. If you're too close to a human in the first couple of hours, they're going to get bitten eventually. Then you'll have a few days of throwing your guts up.'

'Like Boyd is at the moment?'

Like Raul did in his cell. Like Tabitha did for days after she drank the sample from Crimson.

'Exactly. He'll be okay, but sickness like that could kill a new vampire. There's a reason the Invicti kept the full formula under lock and key.'

The phrase sets off an alarm in my head.

'They what?' I ask.

'Yeah, well, it's standard practice for them. They have to be secretive. They don't want just anyone to be able to replicate the dangerous stuff, so they share the basics but none of the details. The formulae themselves are a closely guarded secret.'

And just like that, I think I know what was in the files from the judge's lockbox.

The formulae are the game-changer. That's the prize Nora Mitchell was killed to retrieve. I guess the rebels must have stolen them so Felton could brew up the poison to use on their enemies. The poisoned Silver would turn on humans and end up boxed, with no one the wiser about the cause of their sudden ferocity. It's a clever way to pick off opponents, and to force the Silver to reveal themselves, like Boyd will doubtless have to reveal himself to Mildred. It feels like the answer.

'You've got the report?' I ask Ed, trying to contain my excitement.

'Right here.' He hands it over.

'And you're sure?'

'I could not be more certain.'

It's exactly what I need to hear. I jump over the bench and kiss Ed on the forehead.

'You beautiful man,' I say. 'I am going to get you so drunk later.'

He blinks at me.

'Um, okay?'

'Got to go!' I yell, already on my way out of the door to fetch Boyd and the others. With this, I have the proof I need to put Felton away for a lifetime.

We've got him. We've finally got him.

Felton is toast.

I'm not allowed to go and question Felton myself because it would be a breach of my stupid probation, but I can eavesdrop from outside the meeting room we use for our interrogations. I watch from around the corner as Boyd and Cam haul him in, protesting every step of the way, then I take up residence in the corridor. The room is sound-proofed, but Cam leaves the door very slightly ajar. He knows I don't want to miss this.

'Mr Felton,' Boyd says. 'As you can imagine, I'm not very happy with you.' That's an understatement and a half. I can hear the vitriol in his voice. 'So let me make one thing very clear: we have the evidence we need to box you right now, so don't bother with the denials. Your only hope for leniency is if you make this quick and easy. Understand?'

Even from out here, I can hear Felton's gulp.

Cam takes over.

'Why don't you tell us what happened?'

Felton takes a deep breath, then says in a rush, 'Fine. I killed her. I broke into her place the night before, stole her camera, poisoned her breakfast, then took her to the library and waited for her to die. I planted the photos overnight. Stole the key from some pretentious fucking kid on a bike. I killed her, all right? Can you put me in a nice, safe box now, please? I killed her.'

'The judge?' Boyd is as surprised as I am. This not the direction we were expecting this to go in.

'Yeah. Nora. The human Percy was banging.' There's a heavy pause. 'Is that not what this is about?'

'No,' Cam assures him. 'It is. Go on.'

Felton killed Nora Mitchell.

It's so obvious that I can't believe I didn't put it together sooner. I should have twigged the moment we came across all those crap camera puns. If there's one Silver in Oxford who thinks he's ten times cleverer than he actually is, it's Matthew Felton. The man's such a genius that he thinks sampling his own pharmaceuticals is good business sense and not slow suicide. Of course he came up with the "cryptic" clues.

'You should be happy,' he says.

'Happy?' Boyd asks. 'That you killed a district judge?'

'Happy that I bumped one off from their side. Taking Nora out of the picture has ruined that fucker Percy for good. You guys are loyalists, right?'

'Loyalists?'

In the silence that follows, Felton seems to realise his mistake and tries to row back. I wouldn't have credited him with enough braincells to scramble like this, but apparently there are still a few lonely neurones firing in his drug-addled mind. It's futile, of course, because Boyd is on the ball. What happened with Mildred seems to have honed his edge, making him even sharper than usual.

'Loyal to the Primus?' he asks. 'So who, exactly, is not?'

'No one. It's nothing. Nothing at all. Forget I mentioned it.'

'Mr Felton—'

'I'm just trying to get by, man. I'm stuck in the middle here, being everyone's punching bag as bloody usual. I did you a favour, okay? I just wanted to give that prick a taste of his own medicine. He pushes me around, then I get set on fire by your lot and he laughs. He fucking *laughs*. My whole life went up in smoke and he thinks it's hilarious. So yeah, I killed his girl. He deserved some payback, and I'd say he got it. Did you see what that shit I concocted did to her face? Man, I was not expecting that. It took *ages* to kill her. You have no idea. But I needed her to tell me where the lockbox was, and that shit worked like a charm.'

'You're the one who took the files?' Cam asks.

'Files? What are you talking about?'

'The files in the judge's lockbox.'

'What? There were no files.' He sounds genuinely confused. 'Oh wait, I see how you could get that wrong. They were *vials*. Some genius from the Invicti came up with this cool shit and Percy got his hands on some of the test vials, then stashed them away where he thought no one would ever look. He asked me to make more, but it turns out that's fucking impossible. Good news for you guys. You woke up with a bit of the old redeye the morning after the opening, right? Well, that was the test run for my version. Useless. But if it had worked, you would have been fucked. Trust me when I say that it's in everyone's interests that Percy didn't get to keep the original vials.'

'You're talking about the stuff that's in the poison darts?' Cam asks.

'That shit?' Felton laughs dismissively. 'No, man. This is something else.'

'What?'

'Nuh-uh,' Felton says. 'I'm not saying anything else about it. Unlike you lot, I value my life.'

'Where are the vials?' Boyd presses, but Felton doesn't reply.

There's a pause while Boyd and Cam confer, their voices so low they're beneath my hearing. After a moment, Cam clears his throat.

'So it's what you put in the drinks at Crimson?' he asks. 'The vials?'

'No,' he says, and now I'm totally lost. I was sure that the poison he put in the drinks was the big secret the judge had kept locked away. 'What I put in the drinks was a little something I cooked up myself, following some helpful clues from the Invicti. They really should be more careful about what they put in their reports. I might not be the best Silver chemist, but I'm pretty good. Good enough to take down the deputy of the Seekers anyway, right?'

His laugh is cut off by the sound of choking. From the way Cam is yelling, I'd guess Boyd has just gone for his throat. I'd be cheering him on from the sidelines if I wasn't trying to remain inconspicuous. Felton deserves it. For Rachael, for Raul, and for Mildred.

Cam wins out eventually, because I can hear Felton coughing as he gulps down the air.

'Not cool,' he croaks.

'You poisoned me.' Boyd's voice is a growl.

'Whoa, man, it was nothing personal. Well, nothing personal against you, anyway. The librarian remembered me from when I was scoping things out, so I needed her out of the way. And plus, you work with that bitch Valentine, and I knew it would piss her off. It was like a two-for-one.'

'And Raul Ortiz?' Cam asks.

'Oh, right. Well, everyone knows him and Valentine are bumping uglies, right? Have been for years.'

Are you kidding me? I'm about to barge in there to defend my honour, and Raul's, when the door at the end of the corridor opens, the one that leads outside. By the time I jump guiltily to my feet, they've already seen me.

Benedict and Meyer.

They're walking with such grim purpose that it's obvious something is about to go down.

'What's up?' I ask.

They ignore me and barge straight into the meeting room, emerging two seconds later with Felton held between them.

'Hey!' Boyd yells. 'We're in the middle of interrogating him! He's just confessed to two murders and one attempted.'

'Great,' says Benedict. 'We'll add them to the list.'

Felton is twisting and squirming in their grip. He lunges at me, putting his lips against my ear.

'You have no idea what they're planning,' he says in an urgent whisper. 'Tonight–'

Benedict interrupts by pulling him back and punching him in the side of his head. He goes still, his eyes closed, and falls. Meyer catches him and slings him over his shoulder, then he and Benedict walk back down the corridor, leaving Boyd spluttering in their wake.

'You can't just–'

'We can, Deputy,' says Benedict as he swings the back door open. 'Evidently, we just have.'

'The Secundus said you might want this,' says Meyer, tossing a small black case at Boyd. He fumbles the catch, but I manage to grab it before it hits the floor. 'We found it at Crimson, hidden in Yolande Leclercq's things.'

Then they're gone, letting the wind slam the door shut behind them.

I unzip the case and open it up. Inside, there's a single dart.

Cam comes up beside me. 'There's still one missing,' he says.

'I'll put this in the locker,' Boyd says, taking the case from me and zipping it carefully closed.

'But what about Felton?' I ask.

'He's not our problem anymore.'

'But you can't just–'

'What else do you expect me to do, Jacqueline?' His voice is too loud, and aggressive like I've never heard it before. He gets wound up sometimes, usually when we're pranking him, but he's never vicious like this. 'The Solis Invicti just took our prisoner,' he goes on. 'They outrank us. That's the end of it, okay? We're all going to have to deal with it. Now, if you'll excuse me, I need to go and see Mildred.'

He strides off down the corridor, taking the dart case with him.

'Shit,' I say. 'He's in a state.'

'You're one to talk,' Cam replies. 'You look like a zombie. You need to go to bed.'

'I'm fine.'

'You're not.'

'Cam, I am *fine*.'

'Whatever you say.' He gives me a once over and does not look impressed. 'But I suppose if you're not going to sleep then you may as well make yourself useful.'

'What are you proposing?'

'First we call the baron and get him to unbox Raul. And then,' he says, smiling grimly. 'Let's go and find Leclercq.'

32

I'M NOT SURE that we should take the Invicti's word for Leclercq's guilt, but either way, we need to talk to her. Unfortunately, perhaps predictably, she is nowhere to be found. We check her usual haunts and find them empty, her flat stripped clean, her friends and coworkers oblivious. For someone who makes such an impression in person, she has left no impression on her surroundings at all.

It's a fitting end to a shitty case. Of course we can't find her. No one cares if we do or not, because the Seekers don't matter. Half of the Silver don't trust us and the other half want to abolish us entirely. It's enough to make me question the point of it all. Not only have I been thwarted in my attempts to bring Felton to justice, but I've been made to feel useless. Worse, I've been made to feel that the Seekers are useless. Our only contribution to this case was working out why Nora Mitchell was killed and, in the grand scheme of things, it's not worth anything at all. There's still a coup going on, and we still have only the vaguest idea of the players.

So why did we bother? What's the point of doing this job if the Solis Invicti will always be calling the shots, good or bad?

It's in this kind of foul mood that I find myself returning to the college at the end of the afternoon, empty-handed. It doesn't help that I'm carrying around a load of guilt for Felton's poisonings. It was his personal vendetta against me that got Rachael killed and Mildred injured. I'm not sure I'll ever be able to get out from under that.

Knowing all that we do now, I'm worried about seeing Boyd, but I have no choice. He's acting captain, and he wants to brief us before we head over to Crimson for the summit. He takes four times longer over the meeting than he needs to, but I'm not sure whether that's because he's being extra officious or because he's exhausted, like the rest of us. Tonight is not the best time for us to be attending a sensitive event like the summit, but Boyd won't put a different team on it. We do manage to convince him to stay at home, though, so he can be with Mildred.

'It was my fault,' I say to Cam as we gather our gear in our office. 'All of it was my fault. Raul, Rachael, Mildred. If I hadn't pissed Felton off so much, then this would never have happened.'

'Look,' he says, 'I'll grant you that burning Felton alive was a little rash, but if a bastard like him decides to start poisoning your friends to get back at you, I don't think you can take all the blame. Though it might be a valuable lesson in the dangers of holding a grudge?'

I cross my arms and say, 'I don't know what you're implying.'

'Just promise me you're not going to burn down his lab again.'

'What would be the point?' I ask. 'Felton couldn't replicate the formula and the other side, whoever they are, already have it.'

'If he was even telling the truth,' Cam says.

'You think he was lying?'

'I don't know, but I wouldn't be surprised. He's not exactly a reliable witness.'

'Well, even if he wasn't telling us the whole truth, I'm willing to accept that there were vials in that lockbox. It's the kind of thing that Felton would kill for.'

'But the question is: what was in the vials?' Cam says. 'Felton wants us to believe it's some mysterious new drug, but that means we also have to believe that he managed to reconstruct the formula he used in the drinks using the Solis Invicti's redacted reports. I'm not convinced. If Ed couldn't do it, I don't rate Felton's chances. I just don't think he's that clever. I think the vials in the lockbox were what he used to poison the drinks, and now they're gone. End of story.'

'Are you sure you're not just saying that out of misplaced loyalty to Ed?'

'Pff,' he says. 'Of course not. That's over and done with. Keep up, Jack.'

He throws on his coat and leads the way out of the college. I grab Naia and follow on behind.

I hope he's right about Felton, but I have my doubts. I can't stop hearing the echo of the last word he said to me.

Tonight…

Going to an Invicti-dense event with Cam is not ideal, because if he gets starstruck by a couple of newbies and the Secundus then a room full of them is going to send him positively loopy. In a situation where we're supposed to be unbiased, that's not going to be helpful. The problem is that we can't leave him at home either. I can just imagine his big brown eyes and downcast face if we did, like a spaniel who's been told off for jumping up on the sofa. But bringing Naia along too is a good deal. If Cam displays any fanboy behaviour then she'll mock him into submission, which means I won't have to.

'Do you think we should have dressed up?' Cam asks as we approach the club.

'No,' I reply. 'We're not here as guests.'

I thought the opening night was the ultimate in discreet chic, but I was wrong. Tonight is much more luxe, but also more understated. There's no pomp or glitz about Crimson tonight, none of the crowd-drawing splendour, but that's deliberate. The clientele of this party doesn't want to be seen. The front windows are so full of lights that it's impossible to make out the bar inside. Anything could be going on in there, and it would be invisible to the street.

I have my hand on the front door when it swings open. Carlotta Arden is coming out for a cigarette.

'Jacquéline!' she says with her usual enthusiasm, kissing me twice on each cheek. 'I didn't expect you to be here.'

'Well, I am.'

I don't know where she stands anymore, so I don't know how to react. Until, that is, Benedict follows her outside. He gives me what I suppose might be an attempt at a smile.

'You know Ben?' Carlotta says.

'Of course we know *Ben*,' I reply, mirroring his weird saccharine grimace, then I push past them both, leading Cam and Naia into the bar.

At least that's one mystery solved. That day in Aston, before she saw that Boyd and I were in the sitting room, she told Windsor she had spoken to "the" somebody. I'm willing to bet that, if we hadn't cut her off, she would have finished that sentence with "Tertius". They certainly seem very chummy now.

I suppose that might mean the end of Carlotta and Drake. I

try not to feel happy about that. It's not that I want Drake to suffer like I'm suffering, but it wouldn't make me *un*happy. I know things would have come to a head between me and Tabitha sooner or later, and I know it's better that I found out the truth sooner rather than later, but part of me really wants to shoot the messenger. With both barrels. In the face.

'You take the bar,' Naia says to Cam. 'I'll take the VIP area. Jack, you take the stage.'

'Got it.'

We head to our posts.

The atmosphere inside Crimson is… weird. The stage is set up at one end of the bar, but there's a large white sheet hung up behind it. It looks more like someone's got the decorators in than that we're in the middle of a fancy shindig, though none of the guests seem to think it's strange. They're lined up in front of the stage, crowding close even though, so far, there's nothing to be seen. Whatever's about to happen, the spots up front have premium value.

The lights go out, and I mean *all* the lights. Not even the LEDs behind the optics are still lit. I'm about to ask the bar staff where the fusebox is when a single spotlight comes on over the stage. Apparently, the dramatic darkness occurred by design.

A woman walks through the crowd. They part for her, stepping just far enough back that she doesn't touch them as she moves past, but still staying close enough that, if they wanted, they could reach out and touch her. When she steps up onto the stage, I sympathise with that impulse. I recognise her from the bar's opening night: she was the troublemaker sitting at the bar. She's petite, perhaps shorter even than Tabitha, and she's wearing skyscraper heels and not much else. And her skin. In the warmth of the spotlight, the brown glows gold. Her features are South Asian, her hair falls in a black sheet to her waist, and her expression says *Don't fuck with me*.

I understand why the crowd is salivating.

'It's a ritual,' Drake says.

I wish he'd stop creeping up on me like that. He's dressed to the nines tonight in his fancy suit and shiny shoes, but he appears to be flying solo and looking for company. I don't want to talk to him right now. I remember the way he looked at me as he told me the truth about Tabitha: with pity. I can't stand to be pitied by him. Worse, if he looks into my eyes right now I'm worried that he'll know what I did to her. Somehow, he'll know that for that brief slice of time last night, I felt his rage and I understood.

I can't let him see that.

'Fuck off,' I say, my gaze fixed on the stage.

'No, it's true.'

'I believe you. Just fuck off.'

'Valentine…'

Then the music starts. It's a low hum at first, but it builds steadily as the woman on stage begins to move, swaying her hips to the beat.

'You won't like this next bit,' Drake whispers in my ear, so close that I can feel the heat of his breath. I shove him away and he laughs, rebounding like a punching bag.

Then I see what he means.

The Secundus and the Tertius, Andrew and Benedict, are up on stage. They're holding a man between them. A human man. He's the only human in the room at a gathering I thought was exclusively for the Silver. Then Andrew pulls out the knife, the famed Fidelis blade that he carries on his belt. It flashes through the air so quickly that for a moment I think it was all for show, but then a line appears on the human's neck that opens wide and vomits gouts of blood.

Benedict holds him in place while Andrew collects the blood in a wide ceremonial bowl. By the time it's full, the man is dead, discarded like an empty tube of toothpaste.

Drake was right: I don't like it.

I think of the men in the room at Windsor's house, the ones who were scammed out of millions of pounds with the promise of turning Silver and were rewarded with death at the hands of Benedict and his crew. I think of the captain explaining that their deaths were necessary in order to fund this rebellion, in order to protect so many more, and I wonder what this man has died for. Not to save others, not for a rebellion, but for ritual.

I think I'm going to be sick. I've made it through the whole day without wobbling, but I'm suddenly conscious that it's been far too long since I last slept.

Then the woman starts dancing again, plunging her hands into the bowl and running them over her bare skin, covering herself with blood as the music surges. Every time she flicks her hair, droplets scatter over the white sheet behind her in sprays of red, and she does it over and over again as she writhes. By the time the crescendo hits, the sheet is thick with spatter and she's already dripping with blood, but she takes the bowl anyway and pours the dregs over her head, then dives into the crowd. It closes around her, a frantic blur of Silver movement, and seconds later she steps out spotless, licked clean.

I *really* don't like it. I know I got into the biting thing for a while there, but blood orgies are not my idea of a good time. The smell of it all – the pheromones, the fear, the heavy scent of blood – turns my stomach until I become unsteady on my feet. Drake notices. He slides one hand around my waist and puts the other on my shoulder to hold me at his side. I let him do it because if I don't, I'm pretty sure I'm going to black out.

'What was that?' I ask, unable to look away from the blood that's still pooling on the stage.

'This is what we are, Valentine,' he whispers. 'We kill. We drink. We fight. We do what we like without remorse because we can, then we hide it all away so our actions have no consequences. If we can't manage that then we're ruining it for everyone else, so we deserve to be boxed.'

It feels like he's talking about Raul. The injustice of that burns, because Raul is the sweetest, the kindest, the best of us. Doesn't that make him more worthy, not less?

I've been a vampire for twenty years and I still don't understand my world at all.

'That's what you really believe?' I ask.

'It's why the Seekers exist. You tidy away our messes for us. You maintain the status quo.'

'We administer justice.'

Drake laughs. 'Not even you believe that. There's no justice for us, no morality. There's only what is within or beyond our power. You need to accept that. You need to face it if you want to change it.'

I look at him, *really* look at him, and for the first time in years I feel like I see him clearly.

'Is that what you're trying to do?'

'I'm no angel, Valentine,' he says, 'but I'm not the monster you think I am, either.'

His voice is almost tender, but I don't want tenderness from him. This is the man who has ruined my life over and over: with Winta, with Tabitha, with soft words and hard teeth. He lies and he insinuates and he never just comes out and says what he means. Even with haematopsychosis proved, I'd be a fool to trust him, and Jack Valentine is no one's fool, despite what recent events might imply to the contrary.

I push him away.

'No,' I say.

'No what?' he asks.

'Just no.'

I turn away from him and walk straight into Tabitha, who drops her drink. Now that the music has ramped back down, the sound of her glass detonating on the floor is loud enough to silence conversation around us. Some wanker in the back starts a slow clap, but no one joins in.

Tabitha looks beautiful tonight, hair hanging to her waist in loose curls while her bias-cut gown clings like velcro to every one of her generous curves. Only yesterday morning, I thought I would be with this woman forever. Now I know that I'll never touch her again and even though it's my decision, even though I know it's the right one, it breaks my heart to be denied her.

'I didn't know you'd be here,' she says.

'Really? I was pretty sure you would be, along with your Invicti buddies.'

I push past her and make for the bar, because it's definitely time to start drinking. Cam is waiting for me there, gin bottle in hand.

'I thought you might need this,' he says, handing it over with a glass.

'You're my hero.'

While I pour, he waves Naia over. Her brown skin has gone very pale.

'What,' she says, 'the *fuck* was that performance?'

'Apparently it's totally normal,' I say, swilling back a couple of shots of gin in a single mouthful. 'Every time these crazy kids get together, they kill a human and have a weird sexy blood dance thing. It's traditional, so it's got to be okay, right?' I fill up the glass. 'Plus – get this – *plus*, it's our job to clear up after them. The murders, I mean. Did you know that? I didn't know that. I didn't know I was just some petty functionary clearing up after the important people when they've murdered a bunch of humans.'

Gin slops from my glass onto the bar.

'Jack,' Cam says. 'Calm down. You're hysterical.'

'It's *true!*' I insist.

'Don't call women hysterical,' Naia says to him. 'It's…' She grimaces.

'I'm sorry,' Cam says to me. 'It's not that I don't believe you. I saw it too. Between that and what the captain said… But I think you need more sleep.'

I drop my head down onto the bar. Some dickhead has spilled gin all over it, so now my face is wet. Great.

'Can I sleep here?' I ask.

'For a minute or two,' Naia says. 'The representatives of both sides are going to have a private discussion, then they'll talk to the crowd, then everyone will cast votes.'

'Everyone except us,' adds Cam.

We're going to be supervising the vote instead. With the Solis Invicti at each other's throats, we're the only option.

'But this can't be all the Silver in the UK,' I say, looking around the room. It's packed, but there must be hundreds missing.

'It's the important ones,' says Cam.

'This isn't democracy, it's aristocracy,' says Naia to me. 'Didn't you know?'

Yet another thing to add to the tally of my ignorance.

'Seems like I'm learning a lot tonight,' I say.

Then the Primus walks in. The moment he does, the room seems to shrink. He makes it feel small.

The Primus, Solomon – another Silver who is strictly first

name only, like Cher – is the ice king. He has blond hair and pale blue eyes that are so cold that I'm not sure he's capable of glaring, because that would require heat. He has the apathy of an angel. It's a good comparison, actually, because his hair is curled like a cherub's and his features are so perfect they could be carved from stone. He carries with him an aura of permanence, as though his reign over the Silver is endless and unchangeable. I wouldn't want to be the one to put that to the test.

There's a ripple through the crowd that tells me a lot of them are unsure about it too.

We watch as he and the main players file back into the VIP area for their parley. The Secundus and Tertius are there, obviously, but I'm surprised to see Carlotta Arden following them with a group of civilians I don't recognise. They aren't back there long, but they emerge into factions I don't expect: the Primus on one side with a couple of the civilians, and Carlotta Arden on the other with both the Secundus and the Tertius. If the reaction of the crowd is anything to go by, they weren't expecting this division either.

'Shit,' Naia mutters.

Here's the problem: the Secundus is the Primus's right-hand man. He swears loyalty to the Primus in the same way that all the Solis Invicti do, but there's a particularly close relationship between the two of them. The Secundus always has his back, so for him to oppose the Primus openly like this… It's not good. I thought this rebellion was just about Benedict being an evil bastard, but I was wrong. This isn't a rebellion at all, it's a revolution.

'Gentlemen,' the Primus says to the other faction. 'Your statement?'

Andrew is the more senior of the two, but it's Benedict who speaks.

'The secrecy pact should be annulled,' he says. 'It's time we took our proper place.'

'And I take the contrary position,' the Primus concludes. 'I believe our interests are better served by secrecy. You know our reasons. Cast your votes.'

'We're on,' Naia murmurs, leading me and Cam into the VIP area.

There's a single table set up behind a curtained-off space in the back. On its top is an ornate red pottery vase decorated with cavorting black figures. It's probably something unique and priceless and ancient, but for our purposes it's the voting urn. Everyone has two bone tokens – I don't want to know whose bones they're carved from – one of which is red, for the Primus, and one of which is blue, for the rebels. Our job is to make sure everyone casts their votes properly: one into the urn to be counted and the other to be destroyed in the brazier that's burning merrily beside it. I'm sure it's probably a fire hazard, but if I've learned anything tonight it's that tradition is unassailable amongst the Silver aristocracy. That's why someone's chanting Latin right now in the main bar while we take up our positions: Cam and Naia to either side of the curtain to manage the queue, and me inside it, behind the table, to make sure there's no funny business.

So much for secret ballots.

But monitoring them is a boring job. It goes like this: the person comes in, gives me a dirty look, puts one tile in the urn and the other in the brazier, gives me a second dirty look, then walks out with a final dirty look over their shoulder, just to make sure I've got the message. I get it; they don't like being supervised. I'm trying my best not to notice their votes, because it seems invasive to watch, but it's impossible to miss the fact that there are an awful lot of blue tiles going into the voting urn. Meanwhile, the brazier is full of red.

None of the official representatives are voting, which I suppose is only fair, so I don't see the main players or Carlotta Arden, but apparently barons are not excluded.

When Drake walks in to cast his vote, I can tell from the look on his face that he's worried. He puts his red tile in the urn, his blue one in the flames, then mouths *How's it looking?*

I smile and mouth back, *We're fucked.*

A few voters are notably absent: Windsor, Felton and, of course, Yolande Leclercq. I'm so busy looking out for her, hoping against hope that she might decide to show her face, that I forget about the one person I really wanted to avoid.

Her arrival is heralded by frantic whispering from Cam and Naia, but they can't deny her the right to vote. It's her aristocratic duty, though up until this moment I hadn't considered my girlfriend – *ex*-girlfriend – to be an aristocrat. Which is stupid, in retrospect. She's hundreds of years old, she works for the Invicti, and she has her own lab in her back garden, along with all the high-tech kit. I was so caught up in our honeymoon days, crammed together naked in a single bed that felt just the right size for the two of us, that I forgot who she is. I thought we stayed at my place because it was more convenient for both of us, but I wonder now if she just didn't want me poking around hers.

'Jack,' she says, her voice soft.

She shows me her tiles, the blue in one hand, the red in the other. She holds my gaze as she puts the blue in the urn and tosses the red into the fire, making sure I see.

'I know you don't understand why I'm doing this,' she says, 'but I believe I'm doing it for the right reasons. It was a mistake to lie about haematopsychosis, and I'm sorry, but I truly believe that everything else I've done was done for the best.'

I don't say anything. What can I say that I haven't said already? There's no point in going over it again here. There are some mistakes that can't be forgiven.

'But I can see you're trying to work,' Tabitha says, glancing down at her feet. When she looks up again, her eyes are shining. 'I'll have the full haematopsychosis report, with the correct data, on your desk tomorrow morning. I've already sent the baron a letter in support of Raul's release. I'm sorry, hen. I really do love you, you know.'

Then she's gone and I'm left second-guessing everything that's happened over the past twenty-four hours. But I've done the right thing. I know I have. It's just that I'm so tired I can't think straight.

I barely notice the rest of the voters. It seems like it's over in no time at all. When the last vote has been cast, the six main players are already waiting in the VIP bar to watch them be counted. Cam and Naia collect the voting urn and turn its contents out onto the floor, where a group of Silver crouches to sort them into colours.

In the end, there's no need to count the bones to determine the winner. It's obvious from the size of the piles. Against all odds, the Primus has won.

33

THE CELEBRATIONS ARE muted at first, but the rebels take their defeat with good grace. Benedict is chief amongst them, all smiles as he shakes the Primus's hand. I'm pleasantly surprised by that. Maybe he's not such a wanker after all. Before long, winners and losers alike seem to have forgotten their differences in favour of focussing on the opportunity to drink, dance and generally be merry. They're a wild bunch when they get going and, now that our assignment is finished, Naia and Cam aren't holding back either. They've got good reason to party: with the Primus's position secure, so is the secrecy pact and the future of the Seekers.

Maybe I should be celebrating too, despite my dark mood. The problem is that I don't want to join them on the dance floor, but I also don't want to ruin their fun by sneaking off, so I'm hovering. Unfortunately, that leaves me open to unwanted approaches from people I'm avoiding. Like Drake.

'See?' he says. 'I told you it would all work out for the best.'

Oh, good. It's I-told-you-so Drake. I could really do with another drink.

'No sign of Leclercq,' he says.

'She's long gone.'

It's pretty easy to hide from the world when you've got super powers. I doubt we'll ever see her again. That makes me feel like a failure.

'Did you ever find out who she wanted amnesty for?' Drake asks.

'No,' I snap, 'did you ever find out who organised this party behind your back?'

'That would be me,' a voice says from over my shoulder.

I know it's bad before I even turn around, because Drake is already halfway into a bow. There's only one Silver in the world he bothers to defer to, and that's the Primus, which means I am in deep shit. As I turn to face him, I feel like a rotisserie chicken spinning on a spit.

'Primus,' I say, hiding my blush in a bow.

'My apologies, Baron Drake,' he says, ignoring me entirely. Sure, it's rude, but I can't deny that it's a relief to be out of the firing line. 'I had no idea that an invitation had not been extended. I asked my Tertius to make the arrangements and assumed you would have been consulted.'

Drake smiles ruefully and says, 'We're not on the best of terms.'

I take a step backwards, hoping to fade into the shadows and make my escape, but Drake grabs my wrist and pulls me forcibly to his side.

'I'm not sure if you're aware,' he goes on, 'but there's been a series of incidents that has created some animosity between the Tertius and the Seekers.'

'Oh?'

'This is Jack Valentine.'

'Oh.'

Clearly, my infamy precedes me.

'Benedict and I don't really get on,' I say.

'So I've heard. But why should that affect how he treats you, Baron?'

Drake smirks at me. 'Because Valentine and I *do* really get on.'

'That's a serious exaggeration,' I say, trying to laugh it off.

He's deliberately trying to wind me up, and in front of the Primus too. It's bad enough that I'm standing here in my borrowed, holey hoody. I don't need Drake making things worse by implying that I might actually like him.

I can see waiters circulating in the background with trays of drinks. I try to catch the eye of one of them, because I desperately need an alcohol-flavoured sedative, but they're all ignoring me. Finally, one makes a beeline for the Primus with a tray of what looks like whisky on the rocks. I bloody hate whisky, but it's better than nothing. I'm already trying to persuade my tastebuds to ignore the wet-dirt flavour when some utter bastard waylays the waiter and swipes a glass from the tray. A couple of others follow his lead, so by the time the waiter has extricated himself, protesting all the time that these are specially for the Primus, there are only two glasses left.

The Primus takes one. Drake takes the other. I settle in for a sulk.

'What?' Drake says to me. 'You hate whisky.'

'I'm parched.'

He sighs and says to the waiter, 'Get her a gin, would you? Please?'

'He means a bottle,' I call after the waiter, but he's already disappeared into the crowd, slipping between the gaggle of booze-snatching bastards.

'So, Ms Valentine,' the Primus says. 'How long have you been a Seeker?'

I open my mouth to reply, but something stops me. It takes me a moment to work out what's wrong.

The booze snatchers behind the Primus are looking at each other in confusion. At first they're silent and bewildered, but then their voices start rising above the level of background chatter and they're staring wide-eyed into each other's faces as though their eyes are… Their eyes.

The Primus already has the glass resting against his bottom lip. I knock it out of his hand, sending it smashing down onto the floor and, not for the first time tonight, I find myself at the centre of a circle of silent onlookers.

'Jack,' Drake says. 'What are you–'

'Did you drink it?' I ask him, gripping his shoulders as I look into his eyes.

'What?' He looks at the glass in his hand. 'No, I–'

'Good.'

'But–'

'Look,' I say, pointing at the group behind the Primus. They both follow my finger. 'Look at their eyes.'

They can see it too, and now everyone sees: the silver in their eyes is no longer hidden. We're so used to keeping it concealed that for most of us it's become an instinct; whenever we're out in public, we don't show the filaments of silver that trail through the whites of our eyes and mark us as *other*. But now, for the group who drank the spiked whisky, it seems that hiding their silver is no longer an option. They're trying, straining until I can see the blood vessels pinking behind the silver, but it won't go away.

The panic is spreading, glasses smashing and drinks spilling around us. I guess that's the end of Crimson. No one will trust their cocktails again.

'Where did that waiter go?' the Primus asks, but no one seems to know.

He calls over his Secundus and his Tertius, apparently still trusting in their dubious loyalty, and sends them off to find answers. In the meantime, I take the glass from Drake's unresisting hand and pass it to Cam, my own back up.

'Take it to Ed,' I say.

'On it.'

But we both already know what he'll find in it: *this* is the game-changer. This was what was in the lockbox vials. Felton even tried to warn me.

Tonight...

A drug that unmasks every Silver who drinks it. That really would force the end of the secrecy pact. The replicated version might only have given us a bit of temporary redeye, but who knows how long the effects of this real, silvereye version will last? The Invicti are already leading the affected unfortunates away, so I'll probably never know.

'I overheard the waiter when he was on his way over,' I say. 'You were the target of this, Primus. He said that tray of drinks was specially for you.'

Silver are leaving the building in droves, but the Primus goes right up to the bar and starts sorting through it himself. There are a few empty vials in the bin under the bar: coated on the inside with the remains of a liquid so light blue it's practically iridescent. It reminds me of his eyes.

'We'll take it back to HQ,' the Secundus says, opening an evidence bag wide so the Primus can drop the vials inside. He's the kind of boy scout who always comes prepared. Swot. 'I'll get them tested to see if they match the vials we're missing from R and D.'

'Two batches of missing drugs?' I say. 'Between these vials and the missing poison darts, I'm starting to think your HQ isn't that secure.'

The Secundus gives me a vicious look then walks away,

taking the evidence with him. I'm sure he'll find that the vials match. For all I know, he might have been the one who stole them from the lab in the first place.

'I think I'm starting to understand why my Tertius dislikes you,' the Primus says, but he's smiling as he follows Andrew out through the back of the club.

'This will only be the beginning,' Drake says to me.

'I know.'

Leclercq told me the rebels wouldn't take no for an answer, and she was right. If they can't get what they want through legitimate means, they won't stop. They'll use every other method at their disposal to force our revelation. And if they can get one batch of the silvereye formula, they can get more.

The bar is almost empty now, but there are a couple of Invicti still milling around, picking over the wreckage of the night. Behind them, I see Tabitha making for the front door.

She has the evidence bag full of vials in her hand.

In that moment, I remember Cam talking about Felton, about how he's not clever enough to have put the formulae together on his own. I remember Felton saying that "some genius from the Invicti" came up with the formula for the lockbox vials. And Drake: *Felton's been helping, but he's not the one behind the project. He's a drug addict. He's not good enough to assemble functional chemical agents on his own. It's Dr Ross.*

Tabitha stops at the door. When she sees me, sees the way I'm looking at the evidence bag, she turns back as though she wants to talk.

I don't want that. I don't want her to explain. I don't want any of this.

Before I think about what I'm doing, I'm running, pushing through the stragglers to get out, I don't care where, just out.

I kick through the side door and out into the alley, desperately seeking air. I feel like I'm going to cry, but it's absolutely the last thing I want to do right now, so instead I gulp down the cold air and push my emotions away, trying to concentrate on my body instead of my heart.

I hate the feeling of being this tired – headachey and sick and sweaty even though it's bloody freezing out here – but now the thought of sleep terrifies me. How can I go back to my empty bed, the sheets still impregnated with the scent of my and Tabitha's mixed marks, and even hope to rest?

I lean against the brick and let the cold seep through my crappy borrowed hoody. I could really do with a cigarette. It would taste like shit, but I can't feel any worse than I do already, so I'm willing to give it a punt. In fact, I'm fixating on it like it's a lifeline. There must be someone I can bum a cigarette from around here. The alley seems to be empty, except…

Except down at the very end, where there's a small loading bay that serves the bar's cellar. There's a transit van back there, motor running, and I'm sure I can smell smoke. It's worth investigating.

I peek around the corner to see the Primus leaning up against the wall next to the club's back door. He has his hands in his pockets, perfectly relaxed in his victory, as a couple of other Silver carry the brazier and urn out to the van. I suppose it makes sense that he would be the owner of the ceremonial items; he's probably the one who instituted the traditions in the first place. Rumour has it that he's millennia old, so for all I know he could have bought the original urn hot from the kiln.

I'm about to slink away when a third Silver comes out of the club carrying the ceremonial urn. I'm exhausted enough that I don't recognise the problem for a couple of seconds, but then I stop dead and do a double take. There's only one urn, and it's already in the van. So where did the second one come from?

Blue tiles. Piles and piles of blue bones, mounting up in the urn. Red bones charring in the fire. And yet the vote came back for red.

The Primus sees me watching and holds his finger to his lips, then he winks at me and walks away.

Then I know for sure. There was a moment, just a second, when the urn was unattended. It must have happened in the blink of an eye between me leaving the table, and Naia and Cam collecting the urn so the votes could be counted. He switched the urns and rigged the vote.

The Primus cheated. The rebels should have won.

34

I WAKE UP with what feels like a booze hangover, but it's probably just emotional. I didn't drink nearly enough last night to be feeling this bad. It's the first time I've had any sleep since, well, everything, but I'm on the sofa because even though I've changed the sheets, I still keep catching tendrils of Tabitha's scent. I've had to cover up the full-length mirror too because if I don't, I might glimpse the tattoo. That fucking tattoo.

Ugh, feelings. I understand Naia's disdain for them.

When I drag myself out of my rooms, my leather jacket is hanging from my doorknob. There's a note in the pocket on a piece of cream card written, I can't help but notice, in blue biro. Drake must have other fountain pens, but apparently he's still hammering his point home.

The note reads: *I'm sorry about Dr Ross. I got her letter. Truce?*

I'm not sure about the truce, but at least I have my jacket back. That's the first thing about today that doesn't suck. The second is that Cam is waiting in our office with an enormous cup of coffee and a bottle of blood.

'Praise the lord,' I say, accepting both. 'I am saved.'

'Tabitha came by.' He nods to a bound set of papers that have been left on my desk. 'She said it's all there, all the correct data.'

'I'm glad I was late this morning.'

'I wish I had been.'

I fall into my chair and flick through the first few pages. I don't get into the detail, but the summary is right there up front: "Haematopsychosis exists".

'There's this, too.' He hands me a piece of paper. 'From the sketch artist who worked with Ms Chen and the assistant librarian. This is the guy they saw hanging around the library.'

It's Felton, but with a ridiculous hairstyle.

'Huh,' I say. 'Do you think it was a wig, or a chemistry accident?'

'Both? Either way, it looks like he really did murder Nora Mitchell.'

'Did we not check his alibi?' I ask.

'No. His name wasn't on either of the lists Sir Percival gave us.'

If Felton wasn't such a vile bastard, that might be a little sad. Either Windsor thought so little of him that he didn't consider him a threat, or he didn't think of him at all.

'I wonder where he ended up,' I say.

'Given how hard he was begging us to box him, it must be somewhere pretty awful. I think the Invicti are more ruthless than we are.'

'Good.' That feels like my kind of justice.

'And there's more good news,' Cam says. 'Mildred's up and about.'

'No. Already?'

'Yep. According to the deputy–'

'Acting captain,' I correct him.

'Sorry, according to the *acting captain* – Christ, that's a mouthful – she's going to be absolutely fine. Physically, at least.'

I wince and say, 'So he told her about the Silver?'

'He did.'

'That goes against the whole principle of him being acting captain of the Seekers, doesn't it?'

'Why, did you want the job?'

'Fuck, no. You?'

'Nope nope nope,' Cam says, looking absolutely horrified. 'Let's just accept that he's a hypocrite and move on, shall we?'

'Agreed.'

There's a ringing in my head. God, emotional hangovers suck.

'Are you going to get that?' Cam asks.

Oh, right. Not in my head, in my pocket.

'Hello?' I say, answering the phone.

'Ms Valentine?' The voice on the other end of the line sounds even worse than I feel. Significantly drunker, too; it takes him two attempts to spit out my name.

'Yes?'

'Percy Windsor.' That's a surprise. I wave urgently at Cam, then set the phone on the desk and put it on speaker. 'Heard you're looking for Yolande Lecurl... Lecler... Yolande.'

The man is three sheets to the wind.

'Yes,' I say patiently. 'Do you know where she is?'

'Maybe. You asked who recommended her to me.'

'And you couldn't remember.'

'Lied, actually. It was the bastard who killed my Nora.' He starts to cry. 'It was Matthew fugging Felton.'

And now we know where to find her. Today is really

looking up.

The house on Iffley Road has seen better days. Four months later, even with all the drug money behind the reconstruction, Felton's house is covered in scaffolding. It makes it easy to break in. Cam pulls back the boards covering what used to be the attic window while I slip inside, then he follows me in. The room is a shell of ash and charred wood held together with tarpaulin, staples and wishful thinking. It makes me proud to see how thoroughly I trashed the place. A job well done.

'You hear that?' Cam whispers, his voice so soft that I can barely make it out.

'No,' I whisper back.

Cam's hearing is better than mine by several orders of magnitude, so it's no surprise that he's picking up things that I'm not.

'There,' he says.

I hear it this time. It's not much, just the brush of cotton against cotton several storeys below us.

'Can you pick out a heartbeat?' I ask.

'One. Silver. Resting.'

'Asleep?'

'Here's hoping.'

'Then let's go.'

We creep out to the staircase as quietly as we can. We're probably being overly cautious, because here's the thing about enhanced Silver senses: if you want them to work, you have to stay awake. When we're two flights down and our target still hasn't moved, I'm pretty sure we're safe, but it's not easy going. The fire ate its way out of the attic and down the staircase, possibly assisted by an accelerant I may or may not have applied, so now the stairs are stripped back to the bare frame, which makes them perilously unstable. They threaten to creak with every step or, worse, collapse entirely. That would definitely announce our presence, whether Leclercq is sleeping or not.

Most of the storeys look soot-stained and uninhabited, but when we hit the first floor there are signs that someone has been living here. The walls have been washed, the carpets stripped, and there are makeshift additions littered along the corridor in an attempt to make the place more liveable: a fridge, a microwave, a kettle. Three doors stand ajar. We can see from here that the nearest one is a bathroom. The other two warrant investigation.

Cam nods me on ahead of him, so I creep into the corridor and gently push the first door open. The room's empty, but it's been used recently. There's a mattress on the floor and a row of fridges lined up along the wall. All of them have a collection of chemistry equipment littering their tops. I'd recognise that this was Felton's bedroom even if I couldn't smell the reek of his pharmaceutically-soured scent.

Which just leaves door number three. Cam holds a finger to his lips then executes a complicated series of hand movements that I don't understand. Someone's been studying Invicti signals again. I give him a bewildered look. He rolls his eyes and mouths, *She's in there. You go first.*

I know she's in there, because I can smell that elusive scent again: papery, rich, sweet. There's that tug of familiarity, the connection I can't quite place, and then it disappears. Just as well. I need to focus on what happens next. I take a deep breath and push open the door.

But Yolande Leclercq is very much not asleep. During the time that we've been creeping down the stairs, she's been rigging up explosives. When I push open the door, she nips out of the window, leaving me and Cam to take a face full of nails, wood chips, and whatever other crap she's scrounged from around this building site. I throw up an arm in time to block most of the blast, but I still get a lance of shrapnel through my cheek and, once I've blinked away the dust, I can only see out of one eye.

'Are you okay?' Cam asks. He's been thrown back against the corridor wall, but he only has a few scratches.

'I'll be fine,' I say, looking ruefully at my sleeve. 'But my jacket will never be the same again. And I only just got it back.'

'I'll buy you another one. Here,' he chucks me a handful of blood tablets. 'Catch me up!'

Then he's out of the window and after Leclercq, leaving me to follow. I swallow my medicine and give chase. By the time I join them at the end of the garden, my eye is already healing, spitting out shards of wood and metal as it repairs the flesh beneath. Cam has Leclercq pinned up against the garden fence, but it's too flimsy to take the strain. Leclercq twists and then they're both tumbling through it, wood splintering, limbs flailing. I wade into the fray.

We must have caught her hungry, because she's barely moving at Silver speed. If she'd been drinking blood recently, she would have had the strength to outrun us long before we'd even got out of the house. As it is, she's flagging physically, but she fights like a drunk. She's so unpredictable that I don't see the blows coming, one after another: Cam's jaw, my gut, Cam's groin. That last one takes him out of action for the time being, leaving me to fight on alone.

And I am spoiling for a brawl. I have so much pent-up aggression coiling in my fists that Leclercq feels as light as air when I grab her by the collar and haul her to her feet. She grapples at my wrist, slithering out of my grip like a snake as she tries to kick my feet out from under me, but I'm ready for it. I jump over her sweeping leg and kick out at her body, my foot landing solidly in the centre of her chest. The force is enough to slam her back up the garden, where she stumbles over the pots that are scattered prolifically around the house's back steps, filled only with weeds. She's still trying to right herself when Naia steps out of the back door and shoves something into Leclercq's neck.

Leclercq drops like a stone.

'Everyone all right?' Naia yells.

Cam and I go to join her on the steps, Cam still limping from the blow to his goolies. It makes me grateful to be a woman.

'You took your time,' he says to Naia.

'I was waiting for my moment.' She brandishes the poison dart, now empty. It's the one Boyd took away. She must have retrieved it from the evidence locker before we left the college.

'That could have killed her,' Cam says reproachfully.

'It didn't.'

'But it could have,' he insists.

'Technically, yes. But would anyone have actually cared?'

They carry on bickering as we haul the unconscious Leclercq back through the house. When we reach the front door, Naia takes one last look around the gutted building.

'First time I've seen it since the fire,' she says to me, then she smiles. 'I love what you've done with the place.'

<h1 style="text-align:center">35</h1>

CAM AND I drive Leclercq up to Summertown. Kulika meets us at the door alone. Usually Drake would be here with her. At first I think he must be in London, cementing the Primus's position after last night's vote – last night's *rigged* vote – but when I look up at the window to his office, I can see his silhouette. Maybe he's finally giving me some space.

I'm glad he's keeping to himself, because things are about to get emotional. We're not only here to box Leclercq, we're going to collect Raul as well.

'Ortiz is in the kitchen,' Kulika says.

'Thanks. Can you look after her for a minute?' I ask, nodding towards the car. Yolande Leclercq is still spark out in the back seat; she's not going anywhere for a while.

Kulika's lip twitches, but all she says is, 'Don't be long.'

It takes a while for the Silver to thaw out from a boxing. Raul's been back in the world for twenty-four hours, taking regular transfusions and meals of blood under the supervision of a Silver doctor, but you wouldn't know it from the state of him. He still looks like death.

'Hey, Raul,' I say as Cam and I walk into the kitchen.

'How are you feeling?'

'Pretty shit,' he laughs.

Although his laughter has a bitter edge, I'm relieved to find he isn't the catatonic husk I left in Drake's cellar. He's not his old self, but he's not a complete wreck either. He even gets up from his seat at the kitchen table to shake Cam's hand.

'Hey, man,' he says. 'Cam, right?'

'That's right. Did they tell you what happened?'

'A little.'

'You want to know the rest?' I ask.

'I think I probably should,' says Raul, so we sit down with him and run through everything that's happened since the accident with Rachael.

'It wasn't your fault,' I say, just as I have said to him before. This time, it looks like he might actually believe it. 'Your drink at Crimson *was* drugged. We didn't find out until later because something went wrong at the lab and the samples got switched.'

'Just my luck,' he says.

'But it wasn't just you,' I say, hurrying on before he asks me how we found out about the switched samples. 'It was one of ours, too. Our deputy, Boyd. He got dosed and bit his…' I'm not sure what to call her, but Cam comes to the rescue.

'Girlfriend,' he says.

'Right. Girlfriend. You might want to speak to him. I don't know. It could help to talk it over with someone who's been through the same thing?'

It strikes me then that I'm advising Raul to talk about his trauma with a fellow survivor, while I can't even bring myself to admit to Drake that I've gone haematopsychotic. I guess that makes me a hypocrite, but I've never been very good at taking my own advice.

'I'm sure we could put you up in the college,' Cam offers. 'Just while things get back to normal. We can drive you back there if you like?'

'Thanks,' Raul says. 'Yeah, I need to get my life back on track. I don't think I can do that at home, not right away.'

'I'll help,' says Cam.

'I probably won't,' I say, because I know very well that I am not a good influence, 'but I'll be around. And if you do any more Starblood then I'll set Naia on you.'

'Deal.'

Raul is all compliance and smiles now, but it's not going to be enough. He isn't going to bounce back. He'll probably never be the same again. This is just the high before the inevitable low. He's celebrating because he's out of the box, he wasn't responsible for Rachael's death, and he's grateful for that. What he's feeling right now is relief. Later, there'll be grief and guilt: even if it was Felton's drugs that made him kill Rachael, did the other substances he'd taken make him more susceptible? Was that why Boyd managed to pull back before killing Mildred, but Raul couldn't do it to save Rachael? However chipper he appears, bad things are snapping at his heels, and I don't want to help them catch up with him. But there's something he has to know.

'It was because of me,' I say. 'The drug that Felton put in your drink? He did it to get at me.'

'What?' He sounds shocked, but not angry.

'Yeah.'

'But why.'

'He thought we were, you know…'

'Lovers,' Cam finishes.

Then Raul laughs, and it's not a bitter sound at all. It's rich and warm and just like the old Raul, the one who kept me company when I was blue, even when that meant having to drink me under the table, and who always gave the best hugs. He's still in there somewhere. Despite everything that's happened to him, he isn't broken. I can't help but feel that, if I'd been in the same situation, the result would have been very different.

I am not as strong as him. I worry that, maybe, I'm not strong enough for any of this.

'You know,' Raul says, 'when I woke up with the doctor, I kind of thought you might have sent your girlfriend to look after me, but it was some old dude instead.'

'Tabitha and I are over,' I say. The words kick me in the gut on their way out.

Then, because he's Raul, he gets up from his chair, walks around the table, and folds me into his arms.

'I'm sorry,' he says, squeezing me tight.

'Don't be. A lot of this was her fault.'

'Then good riddance, right?' He pulls away so he can smile at me.

'Right,' I say.

I try to smile back, but it won't come.

I grab a couple of things from the car then send Cam back to the college with Raul. There's no point in us all waiting here for Leclercq to wake up, and we do need her to wake up. There are some questions I want answered before she goes in the box.

Kulika and I wrangle her downstairs to the cell, then Kulika drains her blood. It's grotesque to watch, Leclercq's body rigged up with needles and tubes and slow-filling bags. I've never seen this part of the process before, the part where we siphon off all the strength from a Silver and turn them into a creature too weak to beat its way out of a box. I don't like it.

'It'll make everything quicker,' Kulika says when she sees my grimace. 'The more of her blood we take, the more of the poison will go with it.'

That doesn't sound very scientific to me, but what do I know about science?

It still takes all day for Leclercq to wake up. Kulika and I sit in the basement next to the cell, passing the time first in silence, then playing cards, and finally just talking. As it turns out, she's all right.

Drake doesn't disturb us. In fact, we don't hear or see anything of him all day. It makes me jumpy.

'Did Drake say how long he was giving her?' I ask Kulika.

'The *baron*,' she says, chastising me for not using his proper title, 'said it depends on what she tells us.'

'What's he going to ask her?'

'Let me rephrase: it depends on what she tells *you*. He's not coming down.'

'Really?'

'Really. You got what you wanted. He's leaving you alone.'

'I never said—'

'You didn't have to. Though if you ask me—'

'I didn't,' I say. Best not to open that particular can of worms. 'Anyway, look. Leclercq's waking up.'

But she won't talk. I ask her every question on my list: who was the amnesty for? What information does she have about the rebels? Who is she working with? How does she know Felton? Every one is met with a wry smile and a shake of her head. She won't even open her mouth.

'Then it's ten years,' Kulika says, 'for attempting to kill the Baron of Oxford in May, and for your part in endangering the Seekers at the Castle mound.'

We have to carry her to the box. Kulika's drained her so much that she can't walk on her own. Between the two of us, we get her propped in the corner of her vertical coffin and strapped in. By then I've convinced myself that there's no point in even trying to talk to her, that she's going to go silently into her ten-year slumber.

I'm wrong.

'She's coming back for you, Jack,' she whispers as the door swings shut. 'It won't be long.'

Kulika slams the bolt home then turns to me and says, 'Who's coming back?'

'I don't know,' I lie.

Because, finally, I have it. It's not the scent of paper on Leclercq that tripped me up, it's the sweet chocolate smell. She wasn't wearing it the first time I scented her in the club, or when I noticed her as the shadow in the crowds. It only came later, when she left the club after the opening, and when I saw her there after boxing Raul. There's a reason for that: it isn't her scent. It's a scent mark, a possessive one. The mark of someone she kissed.

Cocoa butter.

I never wear the stuff. When I saw some on Tabitha's dressing table, I threw it in the bin, burying it under the rest of the rubbish so she wouldn't notice I'd chucked it. I can't abide the smell. It's not that I hate it, rather that it has associations I didn't want to explain to my girlfriend.

It was the last thing I smelled before I was turned Silver. When I woke, it was the scent mark on my skin. There's only one Silver I've ever met who carried that scent, and I thought she was gone forever. Apparently I was wrong.

Winta has come home.

<h1 style="text-align:center">36</h1>

I SUCK AT handling my emotions at the best of times, but after a week in which I've boxed and unboxed a good friend, broken up with my first proper girlfriend, then found out that the former love of my life – who is also a murderer – is back in town, it's safe to say that I'm a little unstable. Okay, I'm a lot unstable. I'm spoiling for a fight. That's the only explanation I have for what happens next.

'Here,' I say, slamming the bottle of whisky down onto Drake's desk. 'I hope you choke on it.' I put the fountain pen down beside it, surrendering all my magpie treasures. I meant to leave them downstairs, but here I am, barging into his office again.

What can I say? Shouting at him makes me feel better.

'I'm glad to see there are no hard feelings,' he says.

'Don't sit there and pretend you're not loving this. You and your smug tone and your smug face and your smug hair.'

'Smug hair?' He raises an eyebrow at me.

Fine, it didn't make much sense, but I'm not backtracking.

'Have you ever considered that it might be unhealthy to take so much joy in the destruction of other people?' I ask.

'You've not been destroyed,' he says, picking up the fountain pen. 'You've just had a bad break up. It happens to all of us, sooner or later.'

He holds the pen at each end between his forefingers and thumbs, then snaps it delicately in half and drops it onto the desk. Black ink drips from the fracture, spreading across the blotter like a dark cloud.

'Carlotta?' I ask, not even attempting to sound sympathetic.

'It wasn't working.' He sighs. 'It was never going to work.'

'Things were working perfectly with Tabs,' I say, throwing myself down into one of his armchairs. 'Until you got in the way.'

'How is this my fault?'

I tip my head back until I'm looking at the ceiling, suddenly exhausted with everything.

'Don't pretend you don't know,' I say. 'You've been getting in the way for months. You're always there, poking and prodding and insinuating yourself into my life.'

'That's unfair.'

'Is it?' I sit up and look him in the eye. 'Ever since Tabs came on the scene, you've been doing everything in your power to get between us. The party at Windsor's–'

'That was your idea.'

'–the bite–'

'You asked me to do that.'

'–this stupid probation. If you hadn't been piling on the pressure, she never would have–' I blink, and all I can see is her terrified face while I was caught up in the haematopsychosis. '–done what she did. It was you, Drake. It was all you. Are you never going to get tired of messing with me?'

Drake looks at me for a long moment then walks over to the bar. He fetches two glasses, one of which he fills with my favourite gin – Tanqueray 10, an impressive ninety-five proof – and the other with his precious Macallan 1926. He hands me the first, then settles in the armchair next to me with the second.

I take a long slug of my drink.

He drains his dry.

'You want the truth?' he asks, setting his empty glass aside. 'I'm not messing with you. On the contrary, I am deadly serious.'

'About being a pain in the arse,' I mutter.

'About you.'

The world flips upside-down for a moment. I look at the gin accusingly, but that's not the problem. The glass is still more than half full.

'That's why it went wrong with Carlotta,' he goes on. 'That's why I looked into Dr Ross. But if I hadn't, how long would it have been before you found out about her allegiances?'

'No.' I get to my feet. 'You don't get to do this. You don't get to ruin my life with your constant meddling then say you only did it to help. Just because things have turned out the way you wanted them to, it doesn't mean what you did was right.'

He stands from his chair.

'It was absolutely wrong,' he says, prowling towards me. 'I'm not pretending otherwise. I intentionally put pressure on your relationship, to see if it would break. Because I wanted it to. I'm not a good man, Valentine. I did warn you.'

It's true; he warned me from the very start, on the first night he kissed me. I'm not sure if he's deliberately trying to recall that moment, but somehow it's hanging in the air between us now like a pheromone-filled balloon, just waiting to pop.

'You don't get to do this, Drake.'

He's close now, and getting closer every moment. I put my hands against his chest to push him away, but the second my palms touch his shirt it's like an electric current is flowing between us. It's familiar and awful and I can smell his scent in the air already, before our lips have even touched.

I can't let this go any further.

I give him a shove, but he grabs hold of my waist to drag me with him as he falls back into the nearest armchair. Somehow I'm straddling him, my knees digging into the cushions.

'Give me a reason, Valentine,' he whispers. 'Give me one good reason why you're pushing me away.'

'I could give you a hundred,' I snarl.

'Give me one.'

My mind goes blank. Completely blank. All I know is the deep black of his eyes and the spicy copper smell of his skin. There's a little voice in the back of my head that says: *We are the same kind of monster.*

'I've just broken up with my girlfriend,' I blurt.

'If anything, that's a point in my favour.'

'I'm on the rebound.'

'So? I don't care.'

He doesn't care.

The words ring out in my head and just like that, this becomes the simplest equation in the world. I'm free. He's free. There's all this tension between us, and a very easy solution. After all, it's just sex.

He said it himself: he doesn't actually care.

So what's the harm?

I'm not sure who leans in first, but either way we're kissing and that's all *I* care about. His hands are in my hair, not gentle but greedy, pulling me down towards him as though every inch of air between us is an insult. His lips part mine only a moment after they touch: no hesitation, no delicacy, just instant possession. When I catch my breath I'm drinking not just the taste of his mouth, but the mingled scent of his mark and mine. Our bodies are quick to claim each other.

'Valentine,' he whispers.

'Shut up,' I say, kissing him harder to make him quiet.

'Bite me.'

'Only if you bite me first.'

I've learned my lesson on that score. From now on, it's mutual biting or no biting at all. Thankfully, Drake and I are well-matched in our tastes. Nothing about this is awkward. His mark isn't a sedative; it's caffeinated cocaine, fizzing through me in a maddening rush of uncontrollable *want*.

He pulls away to look me in the eye, to make sure I want what I'm asking for. We search each other's eyes for a second, dark brown on black, then he pulls me close and kisses my mouth, my cheek, my throat, my neck with exquisite softness. When his teeth pierce my skin, it's like a dopamine flood through my veins.

Maybe that's exactly what it is. I don't know; I don't do science. Not anymore.

I push the thought away at the same time as I push him away from my neck. His lips are stained with my blood and his eyes are dark with pleasure, but then they always are. If his pupils were dilated, I wouldn't be able to tell.

'Have you ever done this before?' I ask him.

'Only with you.'

'Then you've never been–'

'No.'

He licks his lips then takes my face in his hands and kisses me. I can taste the blood on his tongue.

'Do it,' he says, his voice so thick with desire that it surprises me. 'I've been waiting four months for this, Valentine. Don't make me wait any longer.'

'You shouldn't have told me that,' I say. 'Now I'm going to make you suffer.'

He groans and lies back in the chair.

I loosen his tie first, testing the water. He's impatient already, his hands stroking up my thighs then clutching around my hips, trying to urge me faster, closer. I realise then that he's not even manipulating me anymore. He wants this. He wants it badly.

For the first time in my life, I have Killian Drake at my mercy. I intend to make the most of it.

'How much have you been wanting it?' I ask, ripping open the top buttons of his shirt. They ping off somewhere behind me.

'Do you want me to beg, Valentine?'

I shrug. 'It wouldn't hurt.'

'Then I'll beg you. I'll do anything you want.'

'Anything?'

'Anything.' His voice is ragged now, coming in growls and breaths.

Leaning forward, I press my lips to the notch at the base of his throat. When he groans again, I can feel it reverberating through his collarbones.

'Every day,' he whispers. 'Every fucking day I see that desk.'

I kiss my way up his throat, a reward for his disclosure, then around to the side of his neck where his jugular beats beneath my lips.

'I stare at it,' he confesses, quiet as a prayer. 'I stand where I stood then and remember.'

'Remember what?'

My tongue flickers at his skin, tasting the sharp tang of our mixed marks. Whereas my mark and Tabitha's together made a balanced scent, sharp and sweet, the combination of mine and Drake's is something far more intense. Instead of balancing, we magnify each other, sharp as unripe citrus, burning like ginger and rich as the smell of the earth after rain. It's so brutal that I'm not sure I should like it, and yet I do.

'I remember this,' Drake says, standing and carrying me to the desk in one smooth motion.

I lean back to clear the top with my arm, because I remember this just as well as he does. I remember him dragging my legs around his hips, pulling my jacket from my shoulders, laying me on the desk and standing between my legs, looking down at me before he bit. He does it all again now, but this time I drag him down with me, so that as my shoulders meet the desk my teeth break the skin of his neck.

He bucks in my arms, gasping as I start to draw blood, but my legs are tight around him and he's going nowhere. I have some fairly strong clues that he's enjoying himself, one of them being the way his hands clasp my hips, another being the fact that he's groaning like he's manning a phone sex line, and the other... Well, look, my legs are wrapped around his waist. Certain body parts are adjacent. I don't have to spell it out for you.

And it's not all him, either. I'm expecting that grim sense of possession to come over me, the feeling that I need to dominate him, to make him mine, but this is nothing like it was with Tabitha. Instead, there's a feedback loop between us, enhanced when he latches on to my neck again, so we're both drinking from each other. Maybe there's something in the simultaneous exchange, but I can feel how much he's enjoying himself and it is killing me. The bite doesn't even hurt; there's just a wave of dizzying, glorious pleasure, like an entire cake that tastes as good as the first bite, a never-ending first drag of a cigarette, an endless orgasm. His blood on my tongue is like the best kind of Massacre. If I could bottle this feeling and sell it, I'd make a damn fortune.

I'm not sure how long we stay locked together like that – I guess in theory we could do it forever – but when we finally pull apart my head's spinning so much that I feel brand new. Sounds are louder, my vision is fracturing with the brightness of the ceiling lights, and the smell of the mark surrounding us is the most potent drug I've ever taken.

'Fuck,' I say, pushing him back so I can sit up. I'm unsteady. 'I understand how someone could get addicted to that.'

'That was...' He runs a hand back through his hair. His skin is pale, but his cheeks are pink, his eyes flashing in the same way I imagine mine are right now. 'Fuck.'

We both laugh.

There's an awkward pause. I'm still sitting on his desk, but he's stepped away so we're no longer touching. The bites on our necks are healing already, fuelled by each other's blood. I wonder how that works. Tabitha would know. A chill comes with the thought, and I realise with a strange sense of clarity that I'm about to walk away.

This is where we left it last time. Last time, I freaked out and ran, and I'm not seeing any indication that this time is going to end differently. I start to reach for my tattered jacket, abandoned on the floor.

But he says, 'No.'

'What?'

Drake's face has fallen, the euphoria replaced by a kind of hopeless anger.

'I see that look in your eye, Valentine. You're not running out on me, not again. We've got unfinished business, and it ends tonight.'

'Here?' I ask.

I look around the office, at its uncovered windows. All the lights are on and it's dark outside, so we might as well be putting on a show for the neighbours. That didn't bother me five minutes ago, but now I'm looking for reasons to bail.

'I shouldn't have come,' I say.

'Maybe not, but you're here now, and you want this. Tell me I'm wrong.'

I meet his eyes and see insecurity there. He's genuine. He'll stop if I say so. He'll let me walk out of here knowing that I've seen his vulnerability, giving me power over him that I didn't have to fight to win.

Maybe that's why I give him the truth in return.

'You're not wrong,' I whisper.

He exhales heavily. I realise that he's been holding his breath. I don't know what to make of that. We're both in uncharted territory here, beyond the shores of Jack and Drake and well into the dragon-filled waters of Killian and Valentine.

He draws me close, kissing me long and slow, then takes my hand and leads me upstairs.

Drake's bedroom is a palace, four times the size of mine with an enormous bed that I envy instantly, but he doesn't give me time to admire the space. He stops long enough to draw the curtains – a tasteful navy to match the decor – then his lips are on mine. He closes the door by shoving me up against it.

'No regrets, Valentine?'

He's anxious, tentative. I think before I answer.

'One night?' I ask between kisses.

'One night,' he confirms.

'No consequences?'

'I anticipate an incredible amount of pleasure for both of us,' he says, 'but otherwise, no. None at all.'

'And you're not going to be weird?'

'You're the one being weird. Now shut up and kiss me.'

It's such a simple thing, kissing. Lips to lips, tongue to tongue, the odd nip with the teeth if you're feeling adventurous. I've done it plenty of times before, so why is my head spinning, my blood rushing, my fingers grasping at his hair? He's marking me again, and I'm marking him, our scents combining in the air around us, and we're stuck in this endless cycle in which we'll never stop claiming each other, never stop kissing.

Somehow, it's even more intoxicating than the thing with the blood.

'Bastard,' I mutter, offended by how much I'm enjoying this.

'Ingrate,' he replies.

'Sicko.'

'Deviant.'

'Troll.'

He smiles against my mouth. 'Liar.'

Grabbing my hips, he turns us around and starts backing me towards the bed. His hands are under my top, sliding up my back and across my stomach. The trails his fingertips leave in their wake reverberate all the way down to my core. Seconds later, he strips the top off over my head and starts working on my fly.

He sees the tabby tattoo the moment he shoves down my

jeans. As I step out of them, he leans back to get a better look.

'You got a tattoo for your girlfriend after only four months?' he says. 'Christ, you're such a cliché.'

'Shut up.'

He runs his finger over the inked skin, then says decisively, 'I don't like it.'

'I don't care. Now shut up. It's harder to imagine you're someone else when you won't stop babbling.'

He laughs.

'Who are you trying to fool? We both know that the only person in your head right now is me. Or would you rather I stopped?'

I groan, because his hands have stilled on my hips when they should be busy divesting me of my pants, or at the very least my bra.

'Fine, Drake. You win.'

'Ah-ah-ah,' he says in a tone of voice that connotes finger-wagging. 'Say my name. Say the one you want to whisper to me.' He leans in so his lips are brushing my earlobe, his voice as quiet as a breath. 'The one you want to moan.'

I mean to deny him, but then he unclasps my bra, slipping it from my shoulders. His mouth blazes a trail down my neck, across my collarbones and down my chest until his tongue is teasing my nipple.

'Fuck, Killian,' I breathe. It's entirely involuntary, which somehow makes it worse.

'That's better.'

His mouth closes around the tip of my breast and I forget that I hate him. I forget about Tabitha, I forget how fucked up this is, and instead I let him lay me back on his bed and kiss his way down to my toes.

'Pervert,' I say as he nuzzles at my foot.

'And? Did you want me to stop?'

'Fuck, no.'

'Then be quiet, if you're capable of it.'

It turns out that I'm not. I'm loud in the sack, always have been, but as he works his way up my body, Killian is wringing noises from me that I didn't even know I could make. My legs are twitching so much that I've kneed him in the stomach twice already. By the time he joins me on the bed, I am a bundle of overstimulation. He pulls back the duvet. Contrary to expectations, his sheets are not black satin but simple white cotton. Perhaps he's not the devil incarnate after all.

I have to revise that assessment when he slips off my knickers and starts swirling his tongue up my inner thigh.

'Stop,' I gasp. 'Fuck, stop.'

'Make up your mind,' he purrs.

'Stop. You're still fully clothed.'

'And?'

'And *I* am *naked*.'

He grins up at me. 'I know.'

I can't let him get away with that.

I push him off me so he's standing next to the bed. He takes the opportunity to stare at me for a few long seconds, raking my body with his gaze from top to toe. I'm sure he's seen bodies that are objectively more attractive – he's seen Carlotta Arden, for starters – but I'm not self-conscious about my nudity. If he wants me, then this is what he gets, and Jack Valentine naked is a fucking treat.

'You're not coming back over here until you've taken your clothes off,' I say.

He raises an eyebrow. 'I don't striptease.'

'Less of the tease, more of the stripping. Clothes off. Now.'

'You're demanding when you're naked.'

'And you're annoying when you're not. I'm hoping that without your clothes you might be slightly less irritating.'

They come off, one by one, and quickly. Tie first, then shirt, then all the rest. Honestly, I get a bit distracted after he loses the shirt because it turns out that he's a fucking treat naked, too. He's not heavily muscled, but there's more definition to his stomach than I was expecting. I didn't think I was fussed about the toned look, but I was dead wrong. By the time his boxer briefs have joined his suit on the floor, revealing the most biteable backside I've ever seen, I'm about to pass out from lust.

The man is gorgeous.

'So,' he says, 'am I less irritating now?'

I open my mouth, then find myself grasping for a witty retort.

'Um, yeah.'

It's not the best repartee of my life, but in my defence, Killian naked is excessively distracting. And now that he's naked, I have the satisfaction of knowing that he's equally distracted by me. The evidence of that is *right there*.

'Enough looking,' he says, joining me on the bed. 'More touching.'

I could not agree more.

37

I WAKE UP in Killian's bed.

Last night was… cathartic. It was also memorably erotic and maddeningly sensual, but let's just go with *cathartic*. It feels like a safer word. There was a lot of sex, a lot of screaming, and I'm pretty sure we've broken at least one of the slats under the mattress, but I've got it out of my system now. I've got *him* out of my system.

Finally.

For the first time in five months, I feel almost calm.

Killian is still asleep. His body is curled around mine, which is surprising because I didn't think he'd be the cuddling type. Still, it's not unpleasant. He's warm and he smells of sex and the blend of our scent marks. I have a moment's anxiety that everyone I see today will smell his mark on me and know exactly what happened last night, but then I think, *Who cares?* If I don't care, and Killian doesn't care, then what does it matter?

We fucked. So what? It was a one-time thing. Get over it.

He stirs behind me, pulling me close against his chest. From the insistent prod of a certain part of his anatomy, I'm pretty sure we're about to fuck again.

Well, why not?

'Good morning, Valentine.'

His words are a whisper on my skin.

He leans over to kiss my shoulder, my collarbone, the back of my neck. When he reaches the place where he bit me last night, he licks the skin and gives it a playful nip; not enough to break it, but enough to remind me that he could. The memory has me clenching my thighs together.

He can tell.

He groans and runs his hand down my stomach, then lets it settle between my legs, exactly where I want it. It only takes one brush of his fingers to make me groan back at him.

'Holy shit,' I whisper. 'You're going to make me self-combust.'

I try to turn around to face him, but his other arm wraps beneath me and around my stomach, pulling me back.

'You're not going anywhere. Not yet.'

His fingers are moving, relentless and rhythmic. He makes me ache with it, his lips on my neck and his touch unerring, until I'm desperate for more. Desperate enough to lay my pride at his feet. Desperate enough to beg.

'Please…'

'Jack Valentine said *please*,' he whispers. 'It must be bad.'

He increases the pressure until I can hardly bear it, but it's still not enough. I want more.

'Tell me what you want,' he says.

When I just groan in response, he asks again.

'Tell me.'

'I want you inside me,' I moan. 'Now.'

'Holy fuck, that's hot.'

He buries his face in my neck, but his fingers are still moving and I still don't have what I want.

'Killian…'

Just as I think I'm about to plummet over the edge without him, he shifts and slides into me from behind in one long, slow stroke that has me gasping for breath.

'Valentine,' he groans.

He tightens his grip until we can't be any closer together, my back to his front, wrapping himself around me, inside me, enveloping every inch of me until I feel like I couldn't belong to him any more completely. That's the mark talking, but nonetheless I have to grab his hand to still his fingers, because I can't cope with their teasing now, not while he's surrounding me like this. I'm not ready for this last time to be over so quickly, and if his fingers don't stop then I won't have a choice.

Then he starts to move, slowly and gently at first, but it's not long before we both need it harder and deeper. We are neither of us gentle lovers.

Nor are we quiet. My throat is hoarse when his hand creeps back between my legs. I try to push him away, but he murmurs, 'It has to be now, Valentine. Please.'

I'm not inclined to argue.

When we scream our satisfaction, we do it together, the wave of pleasure washing through both of us at the same moment. He timed it perfectly, the bastard. I could resent him for it, but in the afterglow I can only berate myself for not falling into bed with him sooner. If I'd known the sex would be this good, I might have taken him and Carlotta up on their offer.

'Jesus Christ,' I murmur, all the tension rushing from my body. 'I didn't think it would be like this.'

'Good or bad?' he asks, pressing a kiss to my shoulder.

'Good,' I laugh. 'Definitely good.'

'You have so little faith. All that fighting had to be leading somewhere.'

'The fighting was genuine. You're still a dick. Don't go thinking that one night will change anything, because it doesn't.'

'Sure, whatever, lay down the law.'

'I'm serious. Just because we have surprisingly good chemistry—'

'Who's surprised? I always knew it would be like this, with you and me. And for the next twenty-four hours, the mark says you're mine.' He kisses his way up my neck, then whispers in my ear, 'Valentine.'

There's a smile in his voice, so I know the game's back on. Whatever this competition is between the two of us, it's not going to end in this bed.

I roll over to face him and he smiles lazily, his black shark eyes twinkling, too blissed out to hide his silver from me. For the first time, I think ever, I can see the outline of his pupils.

But… something's wrong.

It takes me a moment to put my finger on what it is, and when I do, I'm flying out of bed and pulling my clothes on at a speed that's fast even for a Silver. He's still blinking with shock as I run out of the door, down the stairs, out of his house and back to Solomon College.

It won't be far enough, I realise. Nowhere will be far enough.

I thought this would just be a quick fuck to get it over and done with, but I couldn't have been more wrong.

Oh shit.

I am in so much trouble.

Killian Fucking Drake has silvered.

If you enjoyed *Judgement Day*, why not read *Winta's Day*? It's the third book in the *Seekers* series, and it carries on right where *Judgement Day* left off.

***

Join my Readers' Club and receive a FREE short story

www.josiejaffrey.com/subscribe

***

Please leave a review!

If you enjoyed *Judgement Day*, I'd be so grateful if you would please review it. Book reviews can make a huge difference to the success of a novel, particularly those of self-published authors like me. If you have time to leave a review, even if it's just a sentence or two, then I'd really appreciate it.

***

Explore the rest of the Silverse…

This book is just one small part of the Silverse, a whole world of vampires that's waiting for you to explore. There are more novels, short stories, serialised story episodes, and even audio drama podcasts. They're all interrelated, although each series stands alone.

Find out more on my website at www.josiejaffrey.com

Acknowledgements

Thanks to Vicky for beta-reading, moral support and everything else she does behind the scenes as my publicist.

Thanks to Asha for proof-reading and beta-reading everything, and for all the admin she does as my author assistant, with endless positivity and cat photos.

Thanks to my Patreon supporters Caine, Careta, Dee, Justine and Oz, without whose support I might never have collected the motivation to finish this novel.

And above all, thanks to Max, as always.

CONTENT WARNINGS

General warning for violence/murder.

General warning for blood/gore, including blood drinking, description of injuries, dead bodies, forensic investigation, detailed autopsy.

General warning for sexual content (consensual).

Pressure to take part in kink during otherwise consensual sex.

Blood drinking as sexual/pleasurable behaviour.

Some swearing (up to and including 'fuck').

Use of drugs and poisons, including drugged drinks.

Mention of child neglect.